Hero

I. Allan Sealy was born in Allahabad, India. He taught for some years at universities in the United States, Australia and Canada. His first novel, *The Trotter-Nama*, was judged Best First Book (Eurasia) for the 1989 Commonwealth Writer's Prize. He is married to a New Zealander and divides his time between India and New Zealand.

I. ALLAN SEALY

HERO

A Fable

Minerva

A Minerva Paperback
HERO

First published in Great Britain 1991
by Martin Secker & Warburg Limited
This Minerva edition published 1992
by Mandarin Paperbacks
Michelin House, 81 Fulham Road, London SW3 6RB

Minerva is an imprint of the Octopus Publishing Group,
a division of Reed International Books Limited

Copyright © I. Allan Sealy 1990

A CIP catalogue record for this title
is available from the British Library

ISBN 0 7493 9150 2

Printed and bound in Great Britain
by Cox & Wyman Ltd, Reading, Berks

For my father and my wife

Contents

Yatha praja tatha raja
Such the people, thus the king

ENTRANCE

He stood six feet tall but it was his slouch that made him a hero.

But wait. Let me back up a bit.

We are sitting in the Rex Cafe and Stores in a time warp, you with your book, I with my pen. When I look across the table you are there; if you look up from your book I am here. We salute one another. There is one cup of tea on the table: yours, mine, the skin already forming on it. They use rich milk here. There is also a plate of Parsi cakes and a kind of finger-biscuit whose name I have tried to determine but which the waiter, a shabby man with a phenomenal memory and wondrous powers of calculation, assures me is just *biscuit*.

Very shortly we will pay the bill (allow me) and go next door, just up the street really, to the Byculla Talkies.

Your book is entitled *Hero*, the very word I, on the other side of the time warp, have just written with my pen. This is a necessary synchronicity, but consider a stranger coincidence. On a bus from Delhi to Dehra Dun the other day I lost my pen. When I went to the local Tibetan refugee market to replace it, I saw a pen which I bought without the slightest hesitation. It is green, with a broad gold-washed nib, made in China, and probably smuggled across the border from Nepal. It is called: *Hero*.

Other links will bind us. But you can break the spell by putting down the book, by going away. I will pay the bill.

Since you're still with me, I will tell you that the film we are about to see, or you are about to see, as I will be sitting in a different part of the theatre and not always looking (think of me as a kind of usher) is also called *Hero*.

We will meet again in the Intermission, and I promise to be there at the end by the exit door.

There are no doors, strictly speaking, at the Byculla Talkies, just heavy black curtains, and I should warn you that there is no air-conditioning either, just electric fans to stir the Byculla air. The only other possible venue in Bombay was the old Opera House, but the charming betel-chewing scented old queen there assured me that the best seats in the house were not for single patrons, and you are alone. You cannot have the box to yourself. At the Byculla Talkies you will have the best seat.

So. Let us enjoy our coffee until the movie starts. I will order another round of these cup-cakes and the finger-biscuit called *biscuit*.

And I will talk. Of actors, stars, heroes.

Excuse the formal tone: we've only just met. It will change.

When we're ready to leave, the waiter will appear, tell at a glance how many cakes, how many biscuits, calculate our bill and shout the total out to the owner's son who mans the till at the door. He does this for twelve tables: takes orders, serves, counts, calculates, shouts totals, and is never wrong.

The owner's son sits at his counter, sells shaving cream, buns, possibly elastic, takes your money, gives you

14

change, is polite, has about him the stillness of an ancient people.

Above him is a picture of Zoroaster.

The owner, who also has a long white beard, glides in with a censer, offers it to God. The room fills up with holy smoke.

So. When John Wilkes Booth, unemployed actor, shot Abraham Lincoln, president, at the theatre, he chalked up a professional debt which it took more than a hundred years for another American actor, from Hollywood, to discharge.

In this country I know of no heads of state rolled by an actor – other than the one you're about to see. Yet the acting profession has felt more than commonly bound to repay the old, the bad, debt. We have more film stars-turned-politicians than any country on earth. A reasonable man might ask why. The phenomenon is said to be on the wane, but I see no evidence of its passing – until the movies themselves pass on, giving way to TV. And then we'll have TV stars-turned-politicians. Unless of course the politicians, chill thought, turn TV stars. There are today at least four former actors in parliament at any given time and the number of chief ministers and lesser legislators with filmi backgrounds remains cheerfully constant.

Film star to politician: strange, retrograde metamorphosis. As if a butterfly should turn into a caterpillar.

Hero will tell the story of one such. It is not a true story, but it is not a lie. For example it did happen that an actor-villain shot an actor-hero in Madras not so long ago.

It is also a story of Bombay and Delhi – of filmi glamour and khadi, homespun, power. Dehra Dun contributes Zero, no mean contribution as you will see.

The South contributes Hero.

In February 1986, I was returning from London after a year of unsuccessfully peddling the manuscript of my first novel, *The Trotter-Nama*. The manuscript was already two

15

years old and the ideas were from the 1970s. I had lived by The Book for seven years, and had nothing to show for it. A novelist without a novel is like a snake-charmer without a snake. People notice. I felt tired and stale. I had some fine cheese, though, Red Stilton, in my suitcase at three degrees or whatever the temperature is in the hold at thirty thousand feet.

The plane landed at Delhi, but my discount ticket was to Bombay. It was either an unscheduled stop or my travel agent had forgotten to tell me about it, but Delhi was where I wanted to go. My final destination was Dehra Dun, two hundred kilometres north of Delhi. I explained this to the Air-India hostess and then to the chief steward. Could I get off here? But the ticket was to Bombay, they said. I explained about the travel agent. But the luggage was booked to Bombay. Was there some way of unbooking it? No, because it was in the Bombay container. I was free to get off but my suitcase would go to Bombay.

I watched Delhi drop away through the window.

Two hours and a thousand kilometres later we arrived in Bombay. I went to the railway station to book a seat on the Rajdhani Express back to Delhi, a seventeen-hour journey. There wasn't a vacancy for another three days. It was thirty-three degrees celsius, My cheese had begun to sweat an hour after landing.

Four days later, in Dehra Dun, the cheese was spoiled. But on the Rajdhani Express I shed my gloom. It happened like this.

In the chair car I fell in with two men, one from Delhi and one from Bombay, both former students, like myself, of Delhi University. When they heard I was gathering material for a filmi-political novel they filled me in on the gossip I'd missed. It had been all around me, but I was in another country: the Past. I'd had my head down, writing the Last and Final Draft for three years straight. (Among

16

other things I missed in those years was the arrival of video.) One of their stories went like this.

The Bombay man was travelling down South, Madras way, on another long-distance train when he looked up to find a new passenger seated beside him. The man, snappily dressed, with a large and complex hair-style, began to talk, asking him many questions about his career. My friend answered each one carefully and noticed a certain irritation in the man at not being asked in turn about his own career. Finally my friend obliged. 'And what is your profession?' he asked . The man looked down and flicked a speck of dust off his cuff. 'Me?' he said. 'I'm a star.'

We laughed so loudly and so long that the other passengers round about began to smile at us in a tolerant sort of way.

When the laughter subsided I found I had a title in my lap: *Star*.

I already had *Hero*, but then I found there was at least one film by that name already in existence. So I crossed out *Hero* on my file and wrote *Star* above it.

Later that year *The Trotter-Nama* found a publisher. I was to spend another two years waiting for the book to appear. I swam in the cold Pacific. I painted a miniature for the jacket. When I looked up, *Hero* was sitting there again, not *Star*. But there was room for a compromise.

Now, it has never been decreed that every Bombay movie shall have a Song, a Dance, a Fight, a Cabaret, a Rape, a Chase, a Rescue and so forth, but there are some laws – the law of profitable returns for instance – which every producer and director imbibes with his mother's milk. Or rather with his instant infant formula. The adult formula to which he graduates is his masala, his curry powder. The Bombay Mix.

So my chapters are preordained, the masala beyond my control. Blame Bombay, not Dehra Dun.

But there's more Delhi than Bombay in *Hero*.

Politics in the novel, says Stendhal, *is like a pistol-shot at a concert*. A Delhi novel *without* politics is like a Bombay movie without the masala. So I'm sorry to have to spoil the concert, but shots will be fired. And one or two questions asked, not in parliament, about leaders and followers.

For instance: do we get the leaders we deserve?

May I quote again? *A leader is only a reflection of the people he leads*. Gandhi.

When I look at newsphotos of leaders I find I'm hardly ever interested in the man at the centre of the picture. It's the men around him, the men at the edges, his lackeys, hangers on, officials, even simple onlookers, that I want to know about. Who are these flunkeys? I ask myself. What are they doing in the picture?

Someone, I think the astronomer Carl Sagan, has spoken of the awe God inspires in man as being akin to the awe man inspires in a dog. Who, then, are these dogs – and they can be readily identified: the pye, the poodle, the bulldog, the pom – and what do they want, or need? Why have they surrendered themselves – their selves – to the leader? The latest dictator in Sierra Huevon has his pack of soldier-dogs, their fingers on triggers, their eyes blank. Tomorrow they will guard the new man. The chief minister of Vindhyachal has his cabinet-dogs, their tongues moist, their eyes shifting. Now and then a plain civilian-dog will sneak in. Is it simply power that attracts them, or is there something else?

GOD-DOG is a Delhi equation. With Bombay a new element enters in: CAT. The dyad becomes a triad, useful in *Hero*:

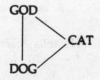

Cat is not in awe of God. Cat is indifferent to Dog. Cat and Dog don't mix. Dog secretly worships Cat. God secretly worships Cat. Does God exploit the division between Dog and Cat? What if Snake should come into the picture? Does a new triad open beside the old? And would Bird, say a parrot, further complicate the diagram, making for a pentad, even a pentarchy? A Gang of Five?

The ancients universally used beast fables to make a point. Aesop liked ours enough to steal them, the old fox.

Come. It's time. We've missed the ads, the trailers, the stills, the burning red hole of the crossed-out cigarette in the No Smoking slide which invariably has the front row lighting up. With a little luck we'll miss the censor's certificate.

Here's the Byculla Talkies.

Notice the sloping tiled roof, surely the last in India. Wide verandahs. You can hear the electric trains on the other side of the wall behind the screen. There are some murals in the verandah, fading mementos of Europe in India, but we can look at those in the interval.

Through the black curtains. The credits have started. Watch your step.

There. The best seat.

Zero's a scriptwriter. He tells the story. His script is called *STAR*.

Here's Hero.

Song

He stood six feet tall but it was his slouch that made him a hero. He had the shoulders of a bull and when he walked it was a bull slouching. It was part sway, part swagger, and part simple locomotion, bulk in motion. It was a habit that became a defining, even endearing trait, since it was clear that he meant no harm – or meant it only to villains.

He made slouching a national pastime, even after he gave it up himself. Later he went the other way, became hopelessly rigid. But by then He was a prisoner in his own house – that is, until the fateful gunshot.

I can still slip back into the habit of his capital H, that copywriter's toy, even though it belongs only to a particular phase: when he was gunning for Prime Minister himself.

What made him tick? (That word still makes me jump, *tick*.) What made him run? They'd have paid me a fortune for the inside story, lakhs, maybe crores of rupees at one time (the rupee wasn't worth much by the time he finished with it) but I had my principles. Now of course it doesn't matter (the price has come down) so I can yap.

It's his story – mine too, and hers, but mostly his – so I shall call my script *STAR*, and wait for the right director to come along.

Trust the dead – one inch, was his policy. His wife would wake up in the morning and find him asleep on any one of a dozen divans he had installed in the fortress palace they learnt to call their home.

'Doggy,' He said to me, *he* said to me, 'would you say this dish was poisoned?'

'Saab,' I said.

'Go on, try it.' And he spooned out a fat kofta – marrow kofta; he was a strict vegetarian – onto my plate.

I wolfed it down at once and we waited those awful ten minutes. But I have a good nose for poison.

I have a good ear too, even if my memory will play tricks. Once – I remember the monsoon was late and the frogs were calling *video*, *video* – there was a blood-red hibiscus on the bush in the tiny walled garden he had made under his tower (he liked it in there because he always had a wall behind him) and I went and picked it for him. He shrank back from it like a vampire from garlic and had the bush uprooted that very day. After that I offered white flowers only – except once, forgetfully – and he'd shrug and pat me. *Good boy*, he'd say. And I glowed and knew I was in the presence of God.

Now I sit here in the retirement valley, staring into the dusk and wondering what I did in my previous life to merit such serenity. I see the whole country spread out at my feet. The view leaves me unmoved. I miss nothing, I require nothing. Nothing has changed, just the masters. There are no new tricks.

Fidelity still pays. Look at Makkhan Singh. You could paint FIDO over his door. Youth leader to state party chief in ninety days; party chief to Member of the Legislative Assembly in forty days; MLA to minister in two weeks: all by sticking close to his master's heels. Now he wants

21

to go to Delhi, the Centre beckons, so he's making loyal noises whenever the PM's Secretary is in town, which is every weekend, because of Makkhan's wife. There are no limits to fidelity. Mrs Singh knows that too. After all, she would like to be a Union cabinet minister's wife (to tell the truth she would like to be First Lady), so strictly speaking she is an honourable wife, dedicated to her husband's advancement, faithful to their joint if unspoken dream. There are no limits to fidelity.

My master too had his dream (I had my dreams for that matter: once as an experiment he nudged me awake with his toe when I was snuffling, saying, *What is it, Doggy? You were yelping. What were you chasing?* and I was only confused and embarrassed.) Yes, he had his dream.

Dreams, I should say, though the plural cheapens. When he was very young, he told me, they were of mammaries, large golden floppy ones. When he grew up a little they were of food; puris, he said, bloated and golden like the ones he'd seen in some North Indian restaurant. Then they were of mammaries again, on a melamine plate, served by an epicene fisherman. And then he took his dreams to the Hind Talkies. Not in the aimless way of front-row loafers, though, that eternal cordon of wolf-whistlers and beedi-smokers.

True, he spent the shopping money on the cheap seats in the Hind Talkies, and sat in the front row with his legs stretched out, dreaming. There were others beside him with shopping money misspent and legs stretched out, but they were smoking beedis and their dreams were doggy dreams. They came out confused and embarrassed, fuddled by the sun. He never smoked, or not till later, when his worries started. He came out transfigured, made strong. On the way he took a wallet from the balcony crowd coming down stubbing out expensive cigarettes and belching soda, and he did the shopping three hours late, pointing to a pumpkin like a king.

Desire lives in the present, he corrected me, when I confessed to an eternal passion. *The object may exist in the future, but we are slaves of time. Time* ticks *on*, he said, and laughed when I jumped. Playfully he pulled my dish of kofta curry – real meatballs, I'm strictly non-vegetarian – away so I had to prove his point for him.

So he sprawled there in the front row of the Hind Talkies, flush with unspoken desire, his object coalescing in front of him in gigantic shadowy forms on a screen which even in those days, when the hall was new, had a rip in it near the middle.

Once he stood up during the show to see what sort of shadow he cast – he had to go up close to catch the light – but it was a disappointment, a small black mole upon those classic white feet (Nandita's, I like to think) and the whistles and cat-calls of the crowd drove him back. He ducked the rain of beedis and abuse and sheared off through a side-door. Afterwards he wished he'd strolled out, and in the pain and anguish of self-reproach he discovered dignity, even heroism.

Trembling in the toilet, his dry spigot in his hands, naphthalene rankling in his nose, he re-ran that departure through the black curtains under the light that said, in witching red, EXIT. It was like dying, ignominiously. And that night he passed through the exit door a thousand times, each time more slowly than the last, until he was gliding, a raja leaving court, wafted across a pink marble floor, a gold umbrella over his head, the beedis bouquets.

It gave him his slouch. That lazy, cloudlike onset that Frankie Pillai and Hunky Gaurav and Kaddoo Kumar imitate to this day. With less success, I might say, than the urchins who stroll out of *Uttar Dakshin* (North and South) re-runs.

He stood five-foot-eleven (if truth be told), so it can't have been his height. I'm five-ten-and-a-half and it hasn't helped me. When heels came in (with him; he was lucky that way) he was pleased. They gave him the wanting

23

inch, and when they went out he stuck with them for a year or two till he got so big it didn't matter any more.

His face was bovine, not canny (like mine), but alert enough, and robed with succulent flesh. The dewlap helped, I think. It suggested dissipation while speaking purity. It conjured up an age of holiness before the complications of the machine, a pastoral idyll of milk and honey. Milk, anyway. Our national obsession. *Opiate*, I was going to say, but we have another better suited to this age when even milkmen and halvais keep their accounts on a floppy disc.

After he was elected I had to stop him going out at five in the morning, can in hand, for his milk. *They'll laugh at you*, I warned him, and he looked puzzled. He was one of the people, he thought. Besides, was this not the cow-belt, the electoral heart of Hindu India? *The foreign press will say you're going into the fields to do your business*, I said. (Actually, they were not fields but a golf course.) That too mystified him. All he wanted was fresh unadulterated milk from the cow, udder-warm and frothing, before the water went in. *We pollute what we love*, he said, speaking of the nation with his new plural, *and what we love most we pollute most*. So he feared most for his milk. And there was, towards the end, the poison worry. Anybody could say a lizard fell into the milk and killed our PM.

Well, I ended up fetching his milk. Just as I fetched his slippers (might a scorpion have crept in there?), the morning paper, and (later on) the coffee, the rice, his favourite little Southy bananas, and his scented white flowers, especially the heady mahua he loved best.

But that was not the opiate I was talking about.

Understand first that I'm writing up the post-mortem not just of a man or even of an industry but of an era. The old idols lie broken, the old gods are dead.

The new god – and he is One – stands about one-foot-something high, if you don't count his pedestal. His face

24

is dull, cold, squarish, smooth and slightly convex, like that forgotten actor's in the old *Ramayana*, a sort of fluorescent grey-green when asleep and every conceivable colour when awake. His shrine is the living-room, and never was that room more aptly named. All significant life is lived there. And yet there are children today old enough to remember a time when that room was called – impossibly quaint now – the drawing-room. Like all one-and-only gods, he is jealous, his curfew strict: recall the boy who ventured out on the streets during a Sunday morning darshan and was struck down by lightning.

The god is, to come to the point and end this childish game, television.

There's our opiate, though there was a time when opium was the television of the masses. You may remember that brief flutter when filmi magazines and Bombay columnists talked bravely of a revival. This TV mania would pass; it was a phase, a craze. But they were whistling past the graveyard. Who wouldn't, with all those prowling celebrated ghouls, those nameless vamps turning in unquiet graves?

There are still actors who want to go from the box to the box-office, but the big break is the other way now. The big screen is (again, but finally) in a terminal way. There'll be a spark or two, a dying spurt perhaps, but one might as well, like the best newspapers, have its obituary ready.

You could see it coming even in the old black-and-white days. My father was among the first to buy a box when the nation started telecasting. Doordarshan, DD, we called it in those bygone days: the Distantview. He traded in his magic-light radio in about 20 BH. (*Before Hero*, though I think of it as simply Before Him.)

The odd part is, you won't believe it, I was once a star in my own right. A small one, true, a falling one, perhaps, but I had my little flare, my fling. And might have been

25

consumed by the dark – that terrible dark we all dread, but stars more than most – had it not been for him.

He had a vision all right. I remember a movie we went to together once in the early days, he, she, and I. It was at the old Opera House, where the previous week, just for fun, I tried to get a box seat. I asked for a box ticket for one and the man at the window jeered at me. This time I made sure He was with me, and UD, my love.

We made a threesome in the dark. It was an old black-and-white potboiler, *Kala Pani* (Across the Black Water), about a doctor and some mosquitoes.

When we came home UD was in high spirits so we got her to sing a song from a recent movie. She gave a little giggle and rushed coyly to the corner of the room. There she arched her back, bashful cheek to the wall, while the music – a spastic bass guitar with conga backing – came clomping out of the nightsky. She turned, twitched one, two, three, and sang Dumpy Shinde's disco hit 'Star Baby'. The chorus stays with me after all these years.

> *Saturday May, Sunday June,*
> *I'm in love with the Man in the Moon.*
> *I'm so happy I could cry,*
> *See the hours rocket by:*
> *Tick-tock tick-tock tick-tock tick!*
> *Ding-dong ding-dong ding-dong – hic!*
> *Sun and moon and spangled stars,*
> *I'm in love with the Man from Mars.*

'I want to heal,' he said to me afterwards, when my UD had gone to bed. 'I want to heal the sores of the people.' He could say *the people* without sounding stilted. 'Not the sores on their bodies. There are plenty of doctors for that. I want to soothe their cares, to brush away their fears, to heal their minds. They can't afford psychiatrists or psychoanalysts, and in any case there are not enough to go around. Ours is a poor country.' He could say *Ours is a poor country* and get away with it. 'I want to cure hundreds, thousands at a time.'

I nodded, intrigued again.

'I think I've found the cure,' he went on. He crossed purposefully to my ancient fridge. There might have been the ultimate vaccine stored in there. Outside the night was black. He made himself a Rooh Afza with lots of ice and a squeeze of lime and a capful of my gin. Then he shook it till the red swirl flooded the glass. 'Pink gin,' he said deferentially, holding it up. 'Do you mind?'

'Boss!' I said.

'You see – ' He paused to take a sip. 'You, now. You went to that window last week and asked for a box ticket and the guy laughed at you. He should have smiled, maybe, and said, *Look, it's like this*. But no, he laughs – and you cry.'

I was close to tears again, but now it was the sympathy.

'Every day, ten times a day, people like us – ' Another sip; he knew instinctively the value of the hiatus, of complicity. 'People like us are humiliated, spat upon, shamed, or just generally pushed around for no good reason.'

'Come to bed,' UD called.

'Ten times a day we push others around or sit on them. We expect punishment, they expect compensation, everyone expects what-you-call-it.'

'Atonement, boss?'

'A tonement. We know there is a universal karmic force which makes amends, a Law of Moral Checks and Balances. Our sages are agreed on that. But it's too abstract, too far away. What I want is something here-and-now, some sort of concrete expression of that abstract law, a kind of particle accelerator which speeds up the just desserts, which settles the score where it matters most – in the mind.'

He was speaking of the video, but we didn't know it at the time. At the time he meant (and I took him to mean; it wasn't the first time he'd held forth) his Karmascope.

'Come to bed,' UD called.

'Settle the score in here,' he tapped his forehead, that silky bovine slope, with a godlike tapering finger, 'and all is well, more or less. Of course there are fresh humiliations to be faced out in the world, new trials for, for the factory worker, the wife in the kitchen, the girl on the bus – '

'Come, *na*!' from UD.

'But every time they will come back to my Karmascope for nourishment, for, for satisfaction. For peace. For justice.'

I couldn't help but clap. '*Vah!* boss, *vah!*' I said.

'*Come!*' UD commanded. There was a note of finality in her voice, and something else. For the first time it occurred to me that it might not be me she was calling. I felt a rush of excitement such as I'd never felt before, but felt many times after, and from that moment on I was the slave of an image so tender and rigid, so sweet and salt, at once dominion and surrender, lord and mistress, that my mouth still goes dry at the thought of it.

For an hour or a minute (probably a minute) we looked at each other, he and I. The tears were his now. And then I made a slight snivelling motion of release with the tip of my nose, a wet tremor towards the bedroom door. He took it as leave, and it might have been. It *was*. He was, I think, shocked. And so was I, but in the static electrified way I've described. He made a very poor exit – or a very good vacillating one: *Hero Misdoubts Him* – and the bedroom door closed on me.

I went to the fridge and made myself a pink gin.

I fell asleep on the sofa just when the sky was turning red.

When I awoke his umbrella was gone. UD spent longer

on her teeth than usual. At breakfast she claimed not to have known who it was in the dark, but her eyes were glued to the parrot and she found him looking sick.

It was her parrot but it lived with me, more or less, like its mistress. *Zero! Zero!* it screeched when I came home.

I had two rooms on Madame Cama Road in a Marwari-baroque five-storey mansion (six if you counted the roof) of honey-coloured stone. There was a lift whose station downstairs was a tangle of wrought iron flames from which the cage rose like a reluctant phoenix. Floor by floor it climbed, jiggling in its cable, giving its inmates time to examine each other, as UD did me the first time we met. She got in on the second floor; by the third we were acquaintances, by the fourth old friends. At the fifth, where my flat was, it was clear she must live there too, someday. Which she did eventually, with the parrot. An ally, though I was the one who remembered to feed it.

'Poor Pedro,' she babbled. 'Cho chick. Chuch a chickly fellow.'

Zero, Pedro called.

'Cho chweet.'

Pedro looked helplessly at me. I gave him a shred of marmalade.

A week later she moved out. I came home with a couple of Alphonso mangoes of great price and saw her things were gone. But the birdcage was there and the familiar gruff choking cry came cranking up and rattled the bars of the empty flat: *Zero! Zero!*

I sat down and wept. Later I gave him one of the Alphonsos. From the look he gave me, he knew where she'd gone.

'QT's here,' Hero admitted when I went to fetch back what was my own, a volume of the *Chandogya Upanishad* from the four-volume set translated by Quentin Sweet. I have never read them, but a set is a set.

QT was his jokey variation on UD, a rebaptism designed, all unconsciously I don't doubt, to put the bloom back on soiled goods. But was it there when she came to me? I didn't care – rather the contrary. *U.D. Cologne* was simply the name I made to make her name in the trade, and it worked its public spell sure enough. It was intoxicating, sweet, seductive, but not fatal. It was expensive but within reach; it made her charm (I do not say charms) somehow affordable, if an extravagance. And it had the sort of chaste vulgarity the industry demanded, whereas Shiraz (her real name) belonged to another, simpler age. Besides, the UD was phonetically accurate, even for convent-educated ladies. No one in all of India said *eau de*, or even *oh duh*. It was *yoo dee* cologne. Of course it didn't last, gimmicks won't, but it served its purpose.

QT was no more than a private, and passing, ploy. The next time it was UD again.

Dance

I went back to my scripts. There was money in them, not a lot, but enough. Friends would taunt me about the expense of spirit, but there was nothing real to write about. Real misery was all around me, but the moment you wrote about it, it became abstract, painfully abstract. Scripts were solid objects; the streets were unreal, and scrofulous besides.

A lot happened in that year, mainly to him, with his career.

Then came a note. *Why don't you visit us?* His handwriting, her cologne.

The *us* stung for a bit, and then the sting went to work. When I finished I put down my pencil, slipped on my jeans and took a 123 from the Museum stop around the corner. I sat on the top deck at the back and hummed Dumpy Shinde's mindless 'Postman, Take a Holiday'. The conductor veered towards me, keeping a miraculous perpendicular as the bus hurtled along Marine Drive. Over to the right the grisly 1930s apartments swayed

31

recklessly. The conductor, a Southy from Andhra, took my money and issued a flimsy ticket. I folded and refolded it till it was a damp pellet between my thumb and forefinger as I stood before the door of his Malabar Hill home. *Their* home. *Us.*

'Zero!'

I embraced him, expiring momently. He pushed me away, holding me at arm's length while he looked me up and down.

'My God, he's lost weight!'

The third person singular, delivered askance, saved me. I stiffened and detached myself as the wayward *he* shot clear around my shoulders and ricocheted towards someone coming through the bedroom door.

'Good evening,' I said, or went to say. And then I saw it was her, transformed. She took the hesitation for a compliment and hugged me. A tree of perfume grew out of her neck and bent low over us. I shed a tear on her naked shoulder and knew I still loved her.

'Come,' Hero intervened.

I went in, treading gingerly on the wall-to-wall carpeting (yes, in Bombay.)

'What'll it be?'

'A girl, I hope.'

'Scriptwriter!' He bit his tongue, the star.

'Star!'

'Come *on*. What'll you have?'

'Pink gin?' I ventured.

He looked guardedly at me, then relaxed.

'OK, pink gin. UD?'

No more QT, then.

'Oh. Rum and croak.'

'OK, two pink gins and a rum and croak.'

Already they had their little jokes. A servant, in white, presented himself, his buttons gleaming, his eyes sheathed daggers. But my master waved him off and went to work himself. I was instantly appeased and said, to make amends, looking around conspicuously:

'Kafi nice.'

They were still on the fringe of the hill proper, though his fee was going up respectably. There was no sea-breeze to speak of, no view.

'So – ' he said. And taking me up: ' – yes, it's nicer than the last place.' *But not as good as the next*, I thought. ' – how have you been?'

'Oh, just, you know.'

'What have you been up to?'

'Bit of this, bit of that.'

'Where have you been?'

'Here and there.'

He abandoned that line.

'Seen any good flims?' He always said *flims*, even later, with elocution.

I said: 'I've seen all of yours.' I had.

'I said *good* ones, yaar.'

'But *Kartavya* was good.' Despite the script, by one 'Alley' Billimoria.

'It *was*,' UD underlined, joining us. She'd been in the kitchen giving orders. She sat down on the floor, not quite at his feet but near enough.

'I suppose so,' Hero conceded, and added on reflection, slipping his shoes off: 'I suppose so.'

We considered the movie in silence for a moment, then because it was too early for silence all three of us began to speak at the same time.

'Not that – '

'Of course, if – '

'Though when – '

And again:

'Sorry – '

'No, you – '

'No, please – '

And again:

'No, no.'

'After you.'

'Please.'

Then UD said: 'Oh foah, what is this? Tara Shankar's Finishing School! Zero, what's the matter with you? Why haven't you been eating? Look at you! You're staying for dinner, it's all fixed up. I've told Francis. Yes, you are. Nothing doing. That's what you think. You just taste his Mughlai lamb. Yes you will. You're staying and that's all there is to it. Bas, finished.'

'No, no,' I protested feebly: there was some dal in the fridge at home and a bun, and I could defrost a kabab or two. But it can't have been convincing. After all, I was among actors. The Mughlai lamb did it. I said: 'No, *really*.'

'Good, then it's settled,' she said and began to massage his feet. As she pressed those sleek tapering toes she sang 'Lord, Your Handmaid Waits at the Door of the Hut.' Music sprang from the bolsters, the pelmets, the chandeliers, dying at last in a tooled sandalwood-box on the coffee-table.

We said *vah! vah!* he and I, and then he wanted her to dance, so she did, with four costume changes and again the music poured out of nowhere till we drowned it with our clapping and cheering which found partisan echoes in the walls.

Looking back I see how my screenplay of their lives was already taking shape. I had already begun to see them as a camera might. Let me share these glimpses with my director.

STAR *camera may transport UD to Sikkim, to Kovalam, to Agra, and to Khajuraho for the dance sequence, tracking her as she spins from snow to sand, from polished marble to enchanted stone.*

She ended at his feet once more and then Francis announced the Mughlai lamb which, I felt afterwards, had surely fed on honeydew in that same Kashmiri vale where Hero frolicked with Preeti Juneja in *Shalimar*.

Then, since it was late – the last bus long since gone down the hill – and there was a homicidal maniac loose in the city and Hero was too tired to drive, UD said I must stay the night. I said: 'No, really,' and stroked the Bombay Dyeing sheets and pillow-case she produced from a steel cupboard. (In the next house they had a linen closet that ran the entire length of one wall with sliding mirrors for doors.)

I told myself *I* was there to protect *them*. I didn't like the look of this Francis, whatever his virtues as a cook. Only the other day I'd read of a servant (was his name also Francis?) who'd done his master and mistress in with a marble rolling-pin. I could see his side of it, but these were my friends. Us. I slipped off my moccasins.

I cannot describe to you the seismic yearnings of that night so I had better not try.

I will try.

When all the lights were out, I waited half-an-hour, forty minutes, forty-five, then very gently opened the guest room door and crept out along a sort of hallway. The carpeting helped. At the end of the hall was the master-bedroom (that *master* made me faint with excitement; I repeated it like a mantra) where he and my mistress slept.

Their door was open, no curtain drawn, and I heard above the air-conditioner the little popping sound UD's lips made when she slept on her back. The air smelt of bananas, those Southy finger-bananas which they fancied, she as much as he, and which I could not abide. That gave pause, that bond, but fleetingly, for my feet were not governed by reason. I found myself outside the door, committed to the future in the blind headstrong way a gamete belongs already to its partner.

I dropped to the floor silently, with an athleticism that would have surprised me had I been aware of it. Jackal-like I inched forward, biding my time (though time no

35

longer made sense), freezing when he turned suddenly in the sheets, then thawing when his breath settled into a rhythm. UD was a heavy sleeper, I knew (if knowing, if the past, had any meaning that night.) Pedro alone could wake her, and then only after ten, when breakfast was cold. I was not so sure about *him*. A furtive night light washed one side of the room violet. His side: I remembered (if memory meant anything) his telling me of a childhood fear of the dark.

I crept in, my back slung low, the balls of my feet alive with tingling nerves. There was no carpeting in there and my knees hurt till I unbent them and threw my weight onto my hands. My mouth was open from the strain and my neck bent back in terrible traction.

It was a small room by Malabar Hill standards, but three or four times the size of my own on Madame Cama Road. Not that I had a bedroom as such, much less a master-bedroom. *Master, master*: what did it mean? The bed was a gigantic heart-shaped frilly affair. Every star had one, with electric candles, like an altar. There were even ribbons, satin, from the feel of one I brushed past.

I muscled silently towards the popping, sweat flowing freely off my back. There must have been wet prints where my hands came down on the cool mosaic floor.

UD was splayed diagonally across the bed, her head pillowed on the left auricle of the heart. Her arm stuck out over the edge, not unlike Padmini's in *Khoon Ki Awaaz* (Blood Cried Out) or her own in the sadly forgotten *Doctor Farookh, Shaitan*, a sort of curry *Frankenstein*. Her hand was half-open in mute appeal. I sniffed it, brought the cave of my mouth up to and past the tip of the thumb. In the same way I swallowed up the forefinger which had parted company from the others. She'd cut her nails. An infinitesimal lick informed my tongue of salt, too strong to be hers.

I retreated and worked my way up the other side of the

bed. He lay there on his side, sunk in God knows what dreams, his five-foot-eleven-and-a-half stripped with the ruthlessness of sleep. The vulnerability of that body, its simple defenceless *bodyness* impressed me and I anticipated his later fear of sleeping in the same bed twice. A simple knife-thrust, I realise now, would have altered history. But a knife-thrust is not simple.

On his thumb, just below the cuticle was a wart I hadn't noticed before. Close up in the violet light it looked like a ruined ziggurat on some desert plain. I was tempted to level it with my incisors when he shifted again in his sleep and brought it to his own mouth, the nail half disappearing past those famous lips. I gagged.

My master was sucking his thumb!

There was such innocence in the gesture I felt ashamed at myself for witnessing it. But I might, I told myself, be an indulgent watchful mother. His eyelids were fluttering with the tremulous repose which betokens troubled dreams, or subterfuge.

I retreated once again until I was back at the cusp of the heart, between their feet: his long and sleek, hers short and sleek, the toes tending to curl.

STAR camera, perched where the wall meets the ceiling above the head of the bed, may look down on the sleepers and then, gently tracking down the middle of the bed, find me at the foot, clothed in violet light.

I stood up now, a guardian – or avenging? – angel from a genre painting of my grandparents' era, defying intruders, looking for my chance. It came as if in obedience to my will: the two rolled murmuring apart.

Gently, protectively, I eased myself into the space my will had made, and lay or levitated there, staring at the ceiling. I remember keenly the sensation of floating above

37

the sheets, my only contact with the world the warm flesh of my mistress and my master.

UD, moved possibly by a familiar if abandoned scent, rolled back and laid across me the arm that earlier had stuck out over the edge of the bed. She nuzzled my familiar forsaken side and mumbled some tender nonsense. I turned and kissed her forehead. Her hand, crooked in appeal, now dug Hero and he answered with a soft caress. I kissed UD more boldly and she responded in her sleep, clawing at the air behind me, or it might have been at my master, whose dreams grew feverish, as did mine and UD's doubling back on his and surging through me as if I were nothing, nothing but the empty space between two electrodes, yet capable of conveying a charge of unutterable potency.

I eased myself back onto the floor and crept out at the door. Halfway down the hall I stopped and went in search of those bananas. I had only to follow my nose. They lay in a brass bowl like a severed hand. I took them to my room where I peeled and ate the lot. Then I fell asleep and didn't wake till lunch time. When I awoke I lay very still and tried to catch the fragments of a curious dream. Finally I gave up and dismissed the thing as foolishness. I swung my feet over the edge of the bed, looking for familiar slippers. I felt instead something cold and slimy. It was a heap of banana skins, soft and gold and rank. The dream came back all at once, like shame.

'Really, no,' I said to lunch. UD didn't press me, and Hero did not appear. I surprised myself by leaving unfed. But I had two scripts promised and shooting had begun on both.

Fight

He was born, he said, in August, but he may have been exaggerating. Four months earlier, for a week in April, his parents were honeymooning down in Kanyakumari, at the cape where India ends, or, as he liked to think of it, begins.

There was a great heaving of oily seas outside the hotel window and his father, a postman and socialist, looked out and felt sick. He had married only the day before and the holiday came with the dowry. The hotel intimidated him. It was cheap and simple but he had never been in one before. The rooms, he knew, were designed for sleeping in away from home, but there was a hitch with this one: there was a stranger in his bed.

She was fat and fair (he was milletish himself, and slim) and bashful. She had in fact turned her face to the wall. His face was at the window. All in all he had done well, but the sight of the sea reminded him of his own insides. Straight ahead was the Indian Ocean, to the left the Bay of Bengal, to the right the Arabian Sea. At Kanyakumari three seas met, but they all looked much the same in the dark.

Then he had an idea. It would put off going to bed. He would write a letter to his son, post it here sc it bore the ultimate franking stamp of Kanyakumari, and then deliver it himself, at home. But of course when he stopped to think, there was no postcard and no pen, so it would have to wait till tomorrow. It could not be helped. Nor, he realized, was there any son, though there was supposed to be something he should do about that.

He turned from the sea. The letter was a good idea twice over. It would break the silence too. He approached the bed and laid a hand on his wife's shoulder. The shoulder because the head would have been disrespectful, the hip too forward, the arm irresolute. She turned her trusting and still-new face towards his. The honeymoon had been her father's notion, the whim of a Westernized man who had chosen the husband for his views, not his prospects. Hesitantly this husband outlined his little plan: the pen, the paper, the son. She saw the missing link at once and said matter-of-factly: 'Well, we can't make pen or paper tonight.'

Fat and fair *and* clever! He slipped into the bed beside his marvel.

The next day they went to the post office and then strolled by the sea. The postcard was written and posted. He would carry the postcard, she would carry the boy.

At least that was how the story went. I heard it more than once and each time the postcard was produced as evidence. The writing was all Southern curlicues but the postmark undoubtedly said KANYAKUMARI and above that 1-4- and then an illegible, or was it defaced, set of numerals. The year would always be unclear. The stamp, however, was of Free India.

So he was younger than me. I'm a Raj model myself.

When the baby was born the neighbours crowded
40

round and chorused 'How fair!' But they were just saying it. Ranga was not even milletish; he was at best a sort of chameleon grey, and with the passing years he would darken beautifully.

The postcard got to their village, Kottagode, in the landlocked Southern state of Kizhanadu, in less than five months; sometimes it helped to have a father in the post office. The young Ranga was shown it and photographed with it, his first publicity still. *My first movie*, he would correct me, pointing to a blurred foot.

The photo shows a little calf of a boy with a postcard stuck between his fingers. Occupying half the picture, broadside on, is the shoulder of his mother, fat and fair and no longer bashful. One senses the excitement of the occasion, a borrowed camera, hilarity. The boy's face, reflecting adult laughter, absorbing the drama of the moment, holds no promise of a flair for the cinema. Baby pictures seldom have anything to say. Mine were said to herald an inventor, which was a polite way of saying I was ugly. Ranga certainly was not. But a future ringmaster, I would have said, nothing more. Or a band-major. Don't get me wrong. This man, remember, would one day melt the collective marrow of Indian womanhood by simply raising an eyebrow. But I could not see even his mother (her shoulder looks sensible) swooning over that vacuous new-born calf. It might simply have been that he was premature.

But calves will grow up. They put away calvish things, become veteran traffic hazards. The bull he stands stock-still in the middle of the road and men and machines will go around him. Women bless him, old men are indulgent; the world pays homage and goes on its way.

Did I mention the hump?

It was there, between the shoulder-blades. Women saw it, and loved it; men couldn't, and wondered what the fuss was about – until he opened his mouth. UD described it as a zone of mystic bliss; at other times she denied its

41

existence. Others said it was cartilage, or fat. In certain lights, certain men were privileged, but I will confess at once that I never caught the most fleeting glimpse, not even by violet light. The still camera couldn't catch it either. Moving pictures were safe all round, he felt, but for stills he never risked any but frontal shots. The baby picture is front on, and he was not photographed again until he was seventeen.

He told me of the hump (he bore its crushing weight) though he never saw it himself. It made sitting in cinema-hall seats difficult (he sat forward, or half lay, his feet out) and he had to sleep on his side. It might have been a foetal hump which stayed because he was premature.

He was early for most things. Where other stars made mortals wait, he was on the set before the Number 2 Villain. He was early for dinners, for weddings, for mahurats, those incestuous premières. *I had an early start*, he would say, and you wondered whether he meant today or in life. He made exits, not entrances. And of course his last curtain call was premature too.

It was the classic story, his career: of the movies, for the movies, but real enough. The postman died when he was seven, of food-poisoning, along with fifteen other guests at some wedding; a lizard had fallen in the milk. A year later the mother, in white, made a pilgrimage to Kanya-kumari to wash away the sin of surviving her husband. Ranga went along as a prop. He was shown the post office, the promenade. He watched his mother bobbing in the green water near the rocks where India peters out. Then they went home to Kottagode. Their money was running out. The pension was tied up in the state capital; some clerk had not been paid his fee, and there was another clerk further in. When it came through it was a cruel joke. The rice became coarser, soupier; schoolbooks were an extravagance.

About the time I was being got ready to go to the Silver

Spoon in Dehra Dun (we turned our spoons in at the gate and got back a whole set of fish-forks when we left) he was getting ready to quit the government school in Kottagode. His mother intervened, sensing great things in store for a boy with a hump that felt like bliss. They would go to another part of town, where they were not known. She could open a shop, a schoolroom, take in tailoring – take in travellers for that matter: there was no end to the number of things you could do when you were an outsider.

They took a couple of rooms in the Tank area on the edge of town. The tailoring and the travellers came and went and my master's schooling was completed at the local government school. Languages and mathematics were his favourite subjects. The government's three-language formula (Hindi, English, and the regional language – his mother tongue, Kuzhiya) might have been tailor-made for him. I don't doubt he would have learnt Chinese, Japanese and Russian had he had the chance. The sounds, the shapes, the colours of a language delighted his budding mind – especially the sounds. Fellow students recalled how he took pleasure in being called upon to read out loud, in rolling each syllable on his tongue as if it were a sucking sweet. His low, slow, ruminative delivery – so out of keeping with his free and easy manner outside the classroom – bound them to him even then. He, more than their schoolmaster, was the high-priest of language, pouring libations at its altar.

Hero Pontifex.

Of course he learnt the local version, got the accent or the intonation wrong, but his diction never suffered.

With numbers his facility was rather less orthodox. He took shortcuts with theorems and equations which brought him sharply up against the right answer while his classmates were struggling with the approved methods. His teacher first accused him of cheating and then,

43

when an isolation test produced the same results, of inspired guesswork. Ranga agreed; he hardly understood how he got there himself. Like the hump, these gifts were a mystery, but they had their practical benefits. His tongue made him an actor; his figuring gave him another sort of independence. Later on, while other stars mortgaged their careers to creative accountants, he managed his own finances in his unorthodox way.

And so, while I was being taught to fork a pea and say film properly (and not *movie*, or worse, *the pictures*, as they said in Anglo-Indian schools), he said *flim-show* and went about his business.

He opened a garage. Not his own, his master's. One of his mother's visitors had a small cycle-repair shop and Ranga was sometimes entrusted with the key. On mornings when this man wished to sleep in and be fussed over by the fat and fair Rangamma, Ranga was sent to open up the shop. He took down the shutters and put out the sign that said: jUPITER CYCLE WORKS, LTD, and the spare wheels and tubes and multi-coloured spoke brushes. Then he brought out the air pump and filled tyres and mended punctures for the early workers at the government dairy going one way and the paper factory going the other. He made friends easily. From the deaf and dumb sign-painter who rode by each morning he took no money; from the junk collector who pushed a cart he took payment in kind, now a hub-cap, now an old tube, now a scooter tyre past mending, but mostly scrap metal.

When his master arrived he went to school. In the afternoon he was back to cut the spokes off a wheel and thread the new ones, or wash a heap of nuts and bolts in kerosene, or simply fetch tools for his master. The best part, he said, was holding a fat pink tube underwater to find the puncture. The water was cool and the stream of bubbles against the skin a sort of heaven.

Hero Afflator.

Tips came his way from grateful scooter riders and more often from their stranded wives who would have liked to stroke the boy. He saved the coins, laid bets with urchins and loafers and bought himself a used pump. Then one day he came earlier than usual to work and began to deck the mango tree across the road with his collection of spent tubes. He stood a scooter tyre against the tree trunk and hung a polished hub-cap on a nail driven in at eye-level. He strewed the ground round about with impressive quantities of scrap metal. A little later the sign-painter showed up with a red sign that said: STAR SCOOTER & AUTOMOTIVE REPAIRS. They hammered it up.

He got onto an imaginary scooter and rode past his garage to see how it looked. When he drew level with the mango tree he jammed on his brakes. It was quite convincing.

In a little while his former master turned up. When he recovered from his surprise he was indulgent, even admiring. The scent of Rangamma was still on him. He made a rude gesture across the road and grinned. Ranga returned the grin, waggled his fist and forearm back and went on pumping, jumping into the air with every stroke.

For a week it was air money, filling cycle tyres as before. The paper factory workers stopped under his tree; the dairy workers, riding the other way, stopped at the jupiter Cycle Works. Then an out-of-work mechanic came to him with a proposition.

'Do you have tools?' Ranga asked.

The mechanic produced a wrench, a spanner, a screwdriver, a cold chisel.

'Partner,' Ranga said, like an actor in an English movie, and they shook hands.

Real scooters began to stop there, real money trickled in. Half of it went at the mechanic's insistence on real tools, half on props. The mechanic tinkered, Ranga trimmed his tree. At length the mango branches groaned

45

with silencers, dented hub-caps, red plastic reflectors, yellow dusters, green jerry-cans.

His old master no longer grinned across the road. The jupiter Cycle Works didn't lose any customers, but the Star workshop gained all the new ones, a car or two among them. There appeared awnings, the beginnings of a garage, a plausible tin roof which sloped down to the ground on one side. Ranga painted it red, with a white six-pointed star. Cars spotting it from a distance would slow down, sometimes stop. Ranga wiped their windshields, looked knowingly under the bonnet, laid a screwdriver against the plugs and, touching bright metal, raised an important shower of sparks. Then he called his partner and went off to attend to bigger jobs. The money was tittuping in, but already he was restless. The big trucks seldom stopped at the Star, and he began to wonder where the road went.

And then he saw *Public Carrier*, starring Karan Talwar, every trucker's hero. Languages and mathematics and certainly bicycle tubes looked a little limp beside that.

His partner panicked when he told him. All he wanted was a steady job. 'Then go across the road,' Ranga said, 'and I'll sell him the goodwill.'

'Goodwill?' his former master said, coming over. He kicked a rusty basin; its bottom fell out. He walked in silence up and down among the scrap metal. 'Goodwill!' he repeated. But when Ranga took him along to the road for an imaginary scooter ride he had to admit there was something there.

'Do you know what work means?' the man asked all the same.

Ranga knew, a little, and thought it was not all there was. There was the Hind Talkies, for instance, where he liked to measure time.

'This is not what you build a country on,' the man said. 'On nothing.' He kicked an empty tin.

'Nor on bed tea,' Ranga thought, but said nothing. He got a quarter of his figure, payable to his mother, and the mechanic crossed the road to the jupiter Cycle Works. The Star Scooter & Automotive Repairs workshop lasted another week; then one day, just as suddenly as it had materialized, it vanished and the mango tree stood bare of ornament. But by then Ranga had disappeared down the road.

Hero Errant.

He got on the back of a truck. The truck stopped at a cashew plantation where he worked picking nuts. Halfway through the season he was sacked for eating more than he picked. The workers were required by tradition to sing as they sorted and it was no use his protesting that he couldn't sing. (He couldn't.) The foreman would have cuffed him, but Ranga was taller than most adults, so he simply sent him on his way. The women pickers shed private tears; one ventured to pat the hump and fell senseless to the ground.

He worked his way east through coffee plantations, tea gardens, cardamom slopes, delighting in every change of scenery. The sky, the scented hills, the yellow rivers, the shifting greens of the forest, the waving fans of banana leaves, were a delirious spinning tunnel from the back of a truck. The telegraph wires swooped past in hanks spun for his private pleasure; great trees leapt away, then stood their ground at a distance and watched him disappear. He could have lived his life on the back of a truck, he said. It was a screen of sorts, that bright rectangle above the tailgate, except he was always out of the picture.

'Not that I minded that, Zero,' he said, locking his eyes on me. It was still *Zero* in those days. 'In fact I was so happy I could have just got sucked into nothing.'

'No, boss,' I whined. The thought of him not there was devastating.

Of course he didn't get sucked into nothing, or our

47

history might have been radically different. Or would it? Are those hills and trees still streaming away, with my master and the truck and the South and this entire benighted country eternally disappearing down some tangential time-tunnel on an endless Möbian highway?

He didn't disappear. He joined the Astro Circus instead.

Yes, the script says *circus*. So I must roll out the tent walls, light hoops of fire. Bring on the animals, high-wire acts, pyramids of callipygian girls on bicycles, a band.

Lastly, a human cannonball.

How he got the hump down the barrel I don't know, but it was the only job going. There were clowns aplenty and, since the lion died, one lion-tamer too many, but if he was willing to defy a toothless death, the manager said, *Please to come in*. Ranga was willing.

Hero Intrepidus.

This costume of his I love more than any other, though I never saw him in it, and I saw him in a thousand others. So you must indulge my fancy. Very few of my countrymen got to see him in it, relatively speaking, and I dare say none know him in that incarnation. He never played that role on the screen.

STAR director will use a stunt man, no doubt, and it won't be the same thing, since my master always did his own stunts.

So this will be a revelation: our Leader, the Big Gun, *in* the big gun. It sounds like a betrayal of trust, this window (or breach) on his hidden past, but now it doesn't matter, and besides I'm pledged to the truth. I cannot betray my caste.

My caste. The caste of Bluffers. *Bahuroopiya*, of a thousand faces.

It is our duty to deceive. Not the thuggee way, not that sort of deceiver. No lethal scarves; we're quite harmless.

We dress up as policemen complete with wooden revolver-butt in holster and pretend to arrest you for some imagined crime. Or a postman with a silly telegram, or a godman with a mission. And when we've fooled you, raised your blood pressure, convinced you with our act, our artistry, we reveal all. And ask our payment, a few coins, a cup of tea, biscuits, what you will. A slap in the face sometimes, since people, especially smart people, don't like to be outsmarted. Read about us in any ethnographic dictionary, any survey of the castes of India, or else just come to Dehra Dun and hang around the Clock Tower looking smart. You'll be fooled by one of us, but never cheated. We're honest fakes, and in this country that's saying something. When all is said and done we tell the truth. And you cherish it more for having been hustled through a lie. But now I'm getting moral and that's bad; we're never moral.

Zero Trickster.

Besides, my father abandoned his hereditary profession and made his fortune selling car parts. Then he decided to posh (or push) me up and sent me to the Silver Spoon. But all the time I was there I had time only for the stage. It was assumed by my classmates that I would go on to the movies. So I started out an actor, which is more (or less) than you can say for Him. I just happened to stray into scriptwriting.

Which is what I had better get on with. My script, his story.

His costume, then. A helmet, naturally, red in that alert, monitory, patinated way that traffic reflectors are, to catch the spotlight from the very instant he's shot out of the cannon mouth through every stage of that heart-stopping trajectory. For the rest he wears black, from his collar down to his boots. A bomber jacket of imitation leather from Taiwan, black pants of some sort of polyurethane, pigskin army boots buffed to a high gloss, and at

49

all the contact points – elbows, knees, chest, and presumably, hump – puttees of black leather with recessed metal studs. Black leather driving gloves with punched holes at the knuckles that send a shiver up my legs, and at the wrist a spiked black band of unbridled potency.

Observe him then, while the bicyclists in taffeta are pedalling in a human pyramid about the arena, the outer ones broadcasting confetti, the inner scattering resplendent smiles.

STAR camera is off to one side. Retreating focus perhaps, from girls in brilliant light to Hero in the semi-dark. He tests his puttees, bends his knees once to relieve a chafing at the ball-guards, undoes and refastens the chinstrap on his helmet. Then he climbs the ladder while the clowns test the net for the last time. At the top he leans on the cannon sight, then deftly swings both feet up and sits on the lip to steady himself. Close-up as he mutters a prayer: the lips move against a shimmering background of white taffeta. Then he rolls over and slides down on his stomach, disappearing from view. Camera comes round to look straight down the cannon mouth which expands to fill the frame. The last shot in this sequence: a red billiard ball slips into a pocket and is gone. Cut.

But I can take you further in.

My master is now in the barrel. His feet have come to rest against the huge piston which will in just over a minute eject him into the public eye. Is this, I wonder, with the advantage of hindsight, so very different from waiting to address the nation on TV?

Well. The bicyclists have ridden off into the wings, the pyramid coming apart from the top. The band has turned a page and struck up its most fearsome fanfare, the ringmaster is announcing to the crowd the imminence of an act of superlative courage, the clowns fall about in an ecstasy of fear, and Ranga braces himself in total darkness.

Not *total* total darkness; there's no such thing on earth. But let the screen go blank for a moment, a sympathetic black. It won't be completely black; there are always those surreptitious EXIT lights, those sneaky red dots from the smokers in the front row, that residual halogen glare of the projector lamp. But let it be X-ray-negative dark for a bit.

Inside the now black helmet my master's brain, twice encased, is humming with electrical impulses. A quarter of a million or so tighten the diaphragm, an equal number loosen the large bowel, an override directive locks the sphincter, preventing accidents. Meshing with the voluntary system, the man who is my master crooks his knees an inch or two and holds them in elastic readiness to absorb the shock: rigidity in that quarter could snap any bone along the track of impact up to the hip, ram cartilage into cartilage, dislodge ball from socket, rip tendons, crumple skeins of nerves, burst the sac of fluid at the knee and fire off the kneecaps in quick succession. The top half of the body is straight but not taut, the arms outstretched above the head, fists clenched, knuckles (O Lord!) popping vulnerably through the driving gloves. My master is as close to extinction as any gallows-treader on his trapdoor or any blindfold executionee before a firing squad.

The gunpowder man is ready down below, the thunderclap man a second behind. The spotlight flicks on, the drumroll mounts, the ringmaster barks: FIRE!

Instantly there is a flash at the breach, an explosion below, and there, suspended in the arc-light:

HERO

How often have I not enacted this moment in my head! Freezing him there more sharply than any video, postponing the moment, hanging on a collective gasp from the locked jaws of the crowd, the terrified clowns, the little bicyclist from the top of the pyramid, whose eyes speak pained concern, whose heart is bound up with that hump, or with his heart, as if she herself flew there in his stead and braved death for him.

And then it's over. The cymbals crash, the spotlight flicks off and Ranga lands in his net, there to bounce a while.

Ninety-five times he submits to this rite of dispatch at the hands of the firing squad, and every time the little bicyclist is there, trembling in a way she never did when the lion-tamer had his head in the drugged lion's mouth. Can Ranga fail to see her standing there after her mates have gone back to the girls' tent? He takes a bow and staggers into the wings still giddy from his flight – and there she is, her slender legs not yet fully formed, her mouth a trembling bow.

She was his first love, he hers.

I would like to change the script and make her an india-rubber girl, but the fact is balance, not contortion, was her forte. (With scriptwriters it's the other way around.) He watched her from the semi-darkness, she leaned towards him as the pyramid swept past the gun. He bought her squares of the cashew toffee of the region, she worked a plastic amulet for his safety.

'I have never forgotten her, Doggy,' he said one day in his wife's hearing, and she narrowed her lips. I imagine she'd heard the story before.

I simply hung my head and re-ran one of those explosive emissions, stopping him in his tracks halfway so that the smoke froze and the spotlight splintered on his many studs and ricocheted off the segments of the big tent to lodge in the wide eyes of the tender bicyclist. He might have been a comet in her nightsky.

She had a narrow melancholy heart-shaped face and heavy eyebrows. I like to think of her as India, or less dramatically, Indu. She was his first and only obsession.

There was another rival for her love, a Chinese acrobat. He'd watched the bicyclist grow up while Ranga was pumping tyres back in Kottagode, and felt a prior claim. But his somersaults went unnoticed and she wove him no amulet. There were brushes between the two men, and once, a fight.

STAR fight-director has a free hand.

'Human cottonball!'

Hero spun around to face the leering acrobat. The acrobat sprang and cracked him across the jaw with a yellow fist, DISH! They fell against a stack of empty barrels on which the clowns nightly raced backwards around the arena. The barrels came tumbling down. The acrobat, up first, picked one up in both hands and hurled it at Hero, who side-stepped coolly and watched it smash against the bars of the tiger-cage. The tiger set up a hollow roaring. The yellow invader leaped through the air feet first. His heel caught Hero squarely in the stomach, DHUK! Hero fell back against the cage winded, but sat up just as the tiger sprang. The acrobat, who sprang at the same instant (he had left Hong Kong at the age of three) found himself launched on an unenviable journey. Hero's feet came up and caught him on the chest, DHAR! For a moment he hung there, the trapeze artist, then Hero rocked back, and those knees which had braced the human cannonball against ninety, no ninety-five, firings of a big gun, kicked: PHATAAK! and the acrobat flew headlong into the leaping tiger, saved only by the cage bars which stopped him in mid-air: THANNG!

As the circus moved on, the rivalry between the two men became a matter of prestige: the high trapeze versus the big gun, the little bicyclist almost lost sight of. The menfolk tended to side with the acrobat: they'd known him longer, and besides, their women tended to favour

53

Ranga. For Hero, Indu was the earth he came down to after every flight, steadying him when he swung off the net with a giddy head. For the acrobat she was a distraction, a near fatal one. His concentration gone, he mistimed a somersault and plummeted fifty feet into the net. The net saved his life, but he struck a tent pole all the same. It ended his career with the circus, but when his head was mended he would take up karate.

For Hero too it was a sign. Already most of the circus people had come to see the rivalry as unhealthy, and now here was proof. The men blamed Ranga; the women, under pressure, felt compelled to take their part. Only the little bicyclist remained constant, and Ranga took to looking for her as he flew through the air, that tiny patient white taffeta flower far below that opened for him alone.

And yet, the more intense his longing, the more he idolized her. He ached to kiss her lips but found himself stooping to touch her feet.

One night he sang to her under a filmi moon: *Your suffering eyes tug at my heartstrings. Why do those eyebeams so enchain me?*

The stars above shed a tinkling light upon the circus; night flowers spilled their fragrance at her feet. My master's voice might have poured from the horn of an antique gramophone. (STAR *will use a playback singer, sitar and strings.*) He crossed the beaten earth to the big top, which he circumambulated once, plucking the guy ropes as he went. A shower of harp notes was released thence, floating across to the girls' dormitory. Indu drew a veil across her face.

Why torment me so, dearest? Hero went on. *Your bond-slave would willingly spend ten lakh years in the dungeon of your pure castle ere the least pion of desire besmirched the precious footprints of those feet he so adores.*

Indu drew back the mosquito net and slipped out of the tent. Her companions slept a charmed sleep.

Well then, place chain on chain if you will. Here are my hands, my wrists, my ankles, my penance-withered shanks. Pierce my tongue with a trident if I lie, but my love is unsullied. I swear it by this earth.

He hung languidly from the parallel bars and took up a pinch of dust. Righting himself, he came face to face with her.

She had never felt so light and free.

Gore me, flay me, throw me from the castle wall! he sang.

Never had she looked so beautiful and innocent and open. His face brushed hers. Trembling she inclined her head and closed her eyes.

But never doubt my intentions, he ended and moved off towards the single men's tents. The air was heavy with crushed blossoms.

'It was calf-love, Zero,' he joked, and I saw he was covering up a real hurt. She was, I realize now, his virtue; she would remain his deepest source of wonder. But there was something skew-whiff about his passion, a suspect radiance, a doubtful heat. When he said he loved her, he lost sight of her for tears. I don't doubt the love; I doubt the passion. It seems to me too much like patriotism: not love of Indu but love of the love of Indu.

The next night as he flew across the arena in his black suit, he saw the taffeta flower was not there. With a heavy heart he knew the time had come to leave.

Two days later the circus train pulled in at Madras Central.

Flashback

Has Hero seen no films so far? Has his early life been all fight? Why have I withheld what every curious reader is bursting to know about, namely his first encounter with the screen? Was it a profoundly shaping event, this primal screen? Was there a hero so titanic (Karan Talwar, let us say) or a heroine so ravishing (Nandita, after *College Girl* perhaps) that their images are branded upon the boy's psyche? Lurks there an epic of Indian film-making which compelled his youthful imagination and made of cinema not only a profession but a calling?

I am sorry to disappoint the young girl in Bandra, Bombay. Her cousin in Georgetown, Madras too must brace himself against the unpalatable truth.

There *was* no stirring epic in his early life – but I should answer my questions in the order in which they were raised, or raised themselves. So, going back.

Yes. (That is, Yes, he has seen some, not Yes, he has no bananas.)

No.

Because there is to be a flashback.
No.

No. There wasn't a hero in it at all. In the first film he ever saw there were two leads, both male, neither of them of heroic stuff. The heroine was pretty, fair and fat, rather like his mother, but not ravishing. Not that he was a competent judge at six. It was a foreign film, or flim, with Bud Abbott and Lou Costello as archaeologists in the pyramids of Egypt, and a third actor, unidentifiable for the bandages, that everyone, puzzlingly, called Mummy.

Well then.

EXT. Daytime, early morning, Shot 73. The camera, which has traversed first at considerable speed, then slowing down, the nameless faces of travellers on a railway platform, draws to a halt – slight jerk – in front of a pillar bearing the sign: MADRAS CENTRAL.

Hero steps down from the circus train. He is not the first off. First is the Number 2 Villain, the acrobat, who has also decided to leave the circus but waited, like Hero, for his free ride. Head bandaged, he looks back down the train at Hero, nods slowly, villainously, and is gone.

Hero's face shows incredulity at being in a big city. His instinct is to shrink back into the bosom of his circus family. But he is in bad odour there. He stares at the metropolitan faces, wonders at their secrets, their self-possession. They show no interest in him, which only whets his interest in them as they flow past, intent on their business. One passing woman, though, is briefly separated from her family as she goes around him. She brushes his mystic hump and registers immediate shock.

STAR *camera records her double-take, her flush, her instinctive drawing over the head of the pallav of her sari. Cut to: Hero looks back at the train.*

57

Hero notices none of the little drama just past. He has remembered his love from whom he must now part. She, sensing his departure, is leaning out at the door of the last carriage.

Long shot down the train of her hanging there by the yellow handlebars, scanning the platform.

Hero sees her. She sees him. He half waves, then turns about, hot tears in his eyes. She watches, her own eyes wide and steady and sad.

Hero Lorn.

He hurries up the platform carrying his Kuwait Airways airbag crammed with spare shirt and hair-oil and amulet. (The black costume was circus property.) Platform, passengers and train are now a wet blur; *STAR camera registers this.* He slips through the exit where the Number 2 Villain slipped through earlier, and is swallowed up by the crowd in the main concourse.

High shot of him moving through the crowd. Camera zooms down on him by degrees throughout the following action.

On the far side of the hall he stops before a weighing machine with flashing coloured lights. He steps up onto the scales and reads the directions. A red-and-white disc spins, then slows to a stop. He inserts a coin; the machine sticks. He thumps the glass. The machine obliges, issuing a ticket with his weight stamped on one side and his fortune on the other. He reads the weight, then turns the ticket over and reads the two lines there. Tears give way to a brave smile.

He looks up at the wall.

STAR camera, so long weepy, dries its tears on a jolly movie poster.

RIALTO CINEMA

SUNDAY MATINÉE SHOW

Bud Abbott and Lou Costello
Meet the Mummy

Fade to flashback.

Young Ranga shifts in his seat. His face is lit with the flickering light of a movie in progress. Beside him sits his mother, the fat and fair Rangamma, in the aisle seat, and on the inside, his father, the postman. It is the Sunday matinee, at the Hind Talkies in Kottagode, showing Bud Abbott and Lou Costello and the bandaged character called, incomprehensibly, the Mummy. The postman has already explained about pyramids and mummies, but young Ranga holds his mother's hand all the same, inspecting it from time to time and comparing it with those on the screen. Will it suddenly sprout bandages? Perhaps his mother is incomplete? He prefers her as she is. He is not especially afraid – his parents are – when the Mummy appears behind the unsuspecting fat man. In fact he can't remain interested in their antics for long. It's funny when the thin man hits the fat man on the head with a spade and it makes a loud noise, DHATTOING! but in between they just talk and talk the way grown-ups do.

He slides off the strange soft seat which folds up on its own; when he first sat down on it he was afraid of slipping through the gap. Now he squats on the floor examining the big feet all around him. In the row ahead of him a man's foot and a woman's foot are entangled; helpfully he separates them. His father clouts him. His mother drags him back up and pets him; she knows about the hump. He watches the flim for a while, then turns around and kneels on the seat, facing backwards.

For the first time he notices the beam.

In the middle of the back wall, where the balcony is,

are several small windows. From one of these shines a bright white light which slants down over the balcony rail, widening as it comes, right over his head, to end at the screen. He follows the path back from the screen to the window over and over, his head tilting further and further back till he must swivel around in his seat. Shadows flit along the bright white path, shifting and changing; sometimes the beam narrows and half the screen is in darkness, sometimes the stream is full and wide, flooding the screen with blinding desert light. Its track is an endless source of fascination, but where, he wonders, does it come from?

'After the flim,' his father whispers (so that's where this flim business started) when he asks.

And afterwards they go up the balcony stair to the projection room and the postman asks the projectionist if his son can peep in.

Ranga is already in.

He is in heaven.

There before him is the source. It might be the godhead for the awe with which he approaches it. It is busy rewinding the last reel, humming and clicking away, rolling up the world.

It is a moment of such magic the mother trembles for her son. He stands transfigured, the little calf, greedy eyes feeding on the machine, grazing randomly upon its chrome and black surfaces, its lenses, runners, sprockets, wheels. Here is the ultimate toy, here is enough for a lifetime's enquiry, starting now. If his father did not hold him back he would stick a finger in that spinning wheel. Given the chance, he would fling himself at it, hurt himself, hurt it, kiss it, smash it, gobble it up.

And so he did, eventually.

Joke

He stood there a moment on the weighing machine, prolonging the delicious mobile springy feel of the plate beneath his feet. Then he turned to step off the scales, going to pocket his ticket as he did, and looked straight into the face of a tall thin man.

'The machine makes you happy?' the man said, nodding at Hero's fortune ticket. He had the morose look of the gambler-and-loser.

Hero made a noncommittal gesture.

'I think you must be new here,' the man went on. 'The machine never tells the truth.' He produced a wad of tickets and read out two or three predictions. 'Nothing happened,' he said. 'But you look lucky.'

Ranga glanced reflexively at the mirror in the machine. Framed by the flashing lights, he saw the face of a movie star. Was it his own? Was there a photo behind the glass? Was this some kind of joke?

'Maybe you can get the job I applied for,' the man said.

A job so soon! Ranga was happy to follow. They crossed

the road to another station and he paid for two tickets to Kodambakkam. They stood all the way, then walked along the busy Arcot highway till they came to a gate which said: MOHINI STUDIOS.

'They are looking for a Number 2 Villain's sidekick,' the man said. 'Go try your luck. If you get it I take half the pay.'

Ranga went in.

'Come back tomorrow,' a man with a clipboard told him. 'We are doing a crowd scene.'

The next day he came early, but the role he wanted had been filled. 'Number 2 Villain,' someone pointed. And there on the set, beside the Number 2 Villain, fly-kicking and sawing at the air as he flew, he saw the acrobat from Hong Kong.

Hero turns to go. As he does so he brushes against the heroine, who has arrived late. It is Srilata. He recognizes her at once from a dozen movies. She, for her part, registers the same stricken, even slain, expression of the woman at the railway stition. The hump has gone to work.

STAR camera may repeat the platform performance just past, double-taking the double-take.

Ranga stayed for the crowd scene. (Was the tall thin man waiting outside, wondering?) All day he and Srilata exchanged glances. By the end of the week they had exchanged a word or two.

Then one morning a gang of toughs surrounded Ranga.

'They say the air in Bombay is much cooler,' said the leader, walking slowly around Ranga while another man held him in an armlock from behind. 'Here in Madras a man could die of the heat.'

The director watched the proceedings from a window.

'Go,' said Srilata, snatching a moment afterwards. 'My

husband will kill you. Take this.' She put a silver anklet in his hand.

He bowed his head. Then he took the suburban train back to Madras Central. He hadn't been paid for the crowd scene.

The tall thin man was standing at his post beside the weighing machine. Waiting for newcomers with spare change and open lives. Hero turned away.

Was he one of us, a Bahuroopiya, that stranger? I've often wondered about him. Does our caste extend so far?

It was a long journey. Ranga slept all the way, laughing in his sleep. When he awoke – to a constable – the carriage was empty. He looked out. The sign said: BOMBAY CENTRAL..

He got off the train, handed his ticket to the ticket-collector. In the main concourse he came upon an identical weighing machine, and weighed himself. He took out his wallet to compare the weights, but the old ticket said MADRAS-BOMBAY. He'd surrendered the wrong one at the barrier.

He looked up, half expecting to see a tall thin man. Instead he saw a joker.

It was a matinée poster which showed the greatest hero of them all with the greatest heroine. Karan Talwar and Nandita. Their faces were very close, but – ah, Indian modesty! – there was a whisper of blue sky between their lips.

Kiss

'It was love at first sight, Zero,' he said after the movie. He was describing the first time he saw Nandita in that classic romance, *Joker*.

It was the nth time around for me too, that Sunday. We'd met in the foyer during the interval. I was having an ice-cream; he had his Kuwait Airways airbag slung over his shoulder. He must have come straight from the station. We stood in front of the classic poster pinned up in one of those glassed wall-cabinets, each of us dwelling privately on that near-kiss, and then he began to talk.

I don't remember what he said then; in fact I don't remember seeing the second half of the movie that Sunday, and I don't remember what he said afterwards, except for that clichéd confession. But I felt in my innards I'd made a friend. I was so pleased with his voice I invited him home to continue his story there. He had, I suppose, what is called a way.

He slept on the sofa, ate a big breakfast, a big lunch, a big dinner. And he talked.

And even afterwards, when he was drifting from one friend's sofa to the next, from coffee-house to coffee-house, from Irani to Irani, and hanging around the university campus attending classes unofficially, I looked forward to his knock, his feet on the windowsill, his hand in the bag of monkey-nuts and his voice gilding the shabby room on Madame Cama Road.

He told and retold the story of that first visit to the projection room of the Hind Talkies.

'It was then, Zero, that my Karmascope was born,' he said, drinking my beer. 'Naturally, I was too young to formulate it, as such,' (*per se*, yes; he would have been six years old) 'but the seed was sown there and then. And so often I've thought: here, in this medium, in flim, is the best, the strongest, medicine. I mean, they have barefoot doctors in China, roving acupuncturists and whatnot, but we can go one step further. We gave them Buddha, remember. We have to heal the mind, the psyche, the soul. The *soul*, Zero,' he pounded softly on the table, despairing of my comprehension. 'I mean – oh, what the hell.'

'Try, boss,' I said.

He got up and helped himself to another beer.

'Look,' he burst out. There was a plate of buns on the table between us for my dinner. They were hot-cross buns, though that meant nothing special. They looked fancy that way with those strips of pastry, so lately bakers had begun to make their buns that way all year round. You'd have been hard pressed to find a plain bun anywhere east of Back Bay. I ate three, with a kabab and some potato bhaji of an evening. He held one up.

'Here.'

It might have been a trick of light, but in his hands the bun glowed a little.

'The soul *suffers*, Zero.' He took a knife and began to hack at the bun this way and that. 'It's not hidden away

65

safely in some ivory tower like, you know, above it all. It suffers, it feels. Every day the world lays traps for it; strangers, enemies, even *friends*, jab it and cut it and stab it and chop it and do their best to grind it into nothing.'

(Remember, gentle patron, life was still a battle for him. He'd only been in Bombay a year or two, selling insurance policies or was it unit trusts to small businessmen, usually his friends' fathers.)

The bun lay in little pieces. With a delicate turn of the wrist he swept up handfuls of it which he shook into his mouth, chewing while his eyes flashed.

'They try to destroy the evidence,' he raged. 'They want to finish you off. Day after day the same thing. At night there's some respite' (he said re-*spite*, spitting it out) 'naturally. The soul takes refuge' (re-*fuge*) 'in dreams. And dreams assuage' (a-*sewage*) 'its suffering. But they can't repair it – because, you're unconscious. And when you wake up they vanish; you forget them, or forget the important part. So actually you're back where you started. Or may be even further back.'

He chewed for a bit in silence. He had picked out the candied peel, my favourite part; the bits lay strewn between his hands like precious stones.

'OK, so we live not by bread alone. We are creatures of longing, of hope, of fantasy. All of this is reflected in our dreams. But in our dreams – our night-dreams – we have no control. No. We must dream constructively.' He paused. 'This is where the Karmascope comes in. Constructive day-dreams: careful, conscious, concentrated dreaming. I mean, you look at the cinema today and you see useless, altu-faltu dreaming.'

'Doggy dreams,' I said.

'Exactly. Whereas, what I would like to see, what I would present, is useful dreams, tactical fantasy. The poor are not going to become rich all of a sudden, the weak won't become strong just like that – but they can become healthy. Inside. My Karmascope will repair their hearts, cleanse their souls. I will give them a chance to confess, to forgive themselves, to forget the score, to live ideally for a few hours. With Karmascope they can rewrite the script they are condemned to follow outside. With Karmascope you can refuse the bribe you took yesterday, unspeak that foolish remark to your boss, unwrite that letter to your brother, unbeat your wife, in short erase your karma.'

I clapped softly.

'I know,' he waved a hand, 'until I get the finance even this is a dream, altu-faltu dreaming.'

He was silent for a while, chewing a bitter cud. The bun was gone.

'But you'll see, someday, I'll make it work, I'll make them see that you can heal yourself. For the price of a flim ticket you can have a new soul.'

I placed another bun in front of him. He looked up.

'No butter?'

I would have run down five flights of steps for some.

It was the sort of coffee-house discourse he had picked up on that phoos-phaas circuit. The idea was his own, but he could just as easily have been peddling the karma-phone or the karmacooker. Or karmic unit trusts. The arts, you may recall, had just come out of a particularly vicious moral phase which was now threatening the popular sphere, with mixed success. In fact, he and the new moralism arrived in Bombay around the same time, though not on the same train.

It was about the time of Nandita's first flop. She'd been slipping for some time, and there was the usual bevy of newcomers with tighter bellies and fewer scruples. But then came (and quickly went) *Miss India*, which only went to show how long it had been since *College Girl*. It was an error of strategy, hers and her manager's, and the audience's eyes were opened. Nor did they forgive her for their hibernation of – could it be? – fifteen years. Rule One of the Bombay screen is to reassure the audience that it is awake. When the rather more substantial *Aasman Ka Pinjara* (Heaven's Cage) was released distributors were edgy and the audience gave them good cause after the Second Towering Week, going instead to *Chalta Hai* (She'll Be Right) which happened to star the up-and-coming Preeti Juneja. To cap it all, she went and spoke those fatal words in an interview with Felix Fonseca in *Talkie-Talkie*.

She said: 'I am Number 1.'

For Nandita the nonesuch to have to say so! After that the slide was swift and unstoppable. When Ranga arrived at Central Station he could hardly have known that the great Nandita, whose every flim he had seen nine times over, was privately seeded at Number 6 or 7 and falling daily. But the coffee-house crowd soon put him right on that.

Often I'd find him at Gustav's beer parlour on Shahid Bhagat Singh Marg among the rich hangers-on he seemed to attract without trying. They bought him chilled beer; he charmed them with his Southy accent and tales of his yexploits among the yelephants, but also with his talent for mimicry. He could do a female voice, a Nandita for instance, and you would swear he had a tape-recorder under the table. He would recite vast and florid filmi dialogues – *di-laags* – verbatim. And yet his preferred reading, schoolgirl comics apart, was in quantum physics.

Inevitably, he met somebody who knew Nandita. It was Rita, one of his female admirers, who had just finished saying: 'You should be in the movies, yaar!'

'I swear on God, Zero,' he said to me, 'uptil that moment I hadn't even thought about it. At least' (he was honest) 'not seriously.'

I can believe it. Di-laag reciters were pretty thick on the ground in those days, though admittedly he was the king. Making it in the movies was something that might have

68

occurred in an idle sort of way to any young man with time on his hands, but only in passing, half-consciously, while flipping through *Talkie-Talkie* or looking out of a bus-window at one of those larger-than-life canvas or plywood hoardings.

I've stumbled on it: it was the larger-than-lifeness that deterred, that scared one off. The idea, the image, the object was simply too big to be taken seriously, like distances in stellar space. I know it from my own experience: the glamour, the sheer scale of the enterprise made it unreal to an outsider. And yet once you were in – even as a lights boy – it shrank down to life-size, to what particle physicists, brought sharply down to earth, call the zone of middle dimensions. Midway between the very big and the very small. There's life in Newton yet.

Besides, he was too easygoing to have dwelt seriously on the movies as a career. The ones who did were earnest young hunks with some hidden grievance, an incurable wound tucked away, or else chubby over-achievers with pushy mothers. Given a knack with words they'd have made feckless admen. They went for it with a vengeance gruesome to behold, and they made it, to Assistant Hero, sometimes Associate Hero, even, briefly, to Full Hero. But mostly they made Number 2 Villains.

Which reminds me. I have not yet introduced the Number 1 Villain.

For that I must take you back again, this time up North. Yes, he's a Northy. (There was a time when I contemplated a novel – not a film script – to be called *North and South*, but somebody had already done one: Mrs Gaskell, in 1855; which left *North and South II*, but an American, from the South, I believe, took care of that.) Up North, then, to Bihar. *North* Bihar.

STAR camera takes a distant shot at Khichdipur, Bihar. It pans an exhausted plain of stupefying flatness broken by a single chimney. The chimney belongs to a government condom factory, the chief, and formerly sole, reason for Khichdipur's existence. It is one of those featureless industrial towns, the result of the Third or Fourth Five-Year-Plan. The idea was to bring, at one and the same time, employment and family planning to the poorest state in the union.

There is little to detain us in Khichdipur (the lone chimney is its apt totem) beyond the workers' colony where one K.K. Sinha, night-watchman, dearly wishes he had heard about the Nirodh condom before he went and fathered a son out of wedlock. Forced to acknowledge his own, he calls the child, in a fit of remorse, or it might be spleen, Anirodh.

Enter (into the world) our Number 1 Villain.

Anirodh has a hard life (*scenes of a hard life may be shown*) and turns up, like Ranga, in Bombay. He is handsome, but in the lean cantankerous way reserved for villains. The chip on his shoulder, like Ranga's hump, affects his posture, making for a slight, and villainous, tilt. In Khichdipur he tries twice to blow up the only factory, against which he holds a mistaken grudge, and spends time in one of Bihar's infamous jails. In Bombay he supplies film stars, including the ex-Number 1 Heroine, with narcotics and becomes in the process one of Nandita's chamchas, a spoon in at least two senses. Through assiduous chamcha-giri he lands himself a role in *Jo Hukum* (Your Wish, My Command) and acquits himself well. About the time Ranga goes to call on Nandita, Anirodh is chief spoon. His friends call him Niru. He calls himself, when the villain's credits come up:

NERO

It was getting to be easy to meet Nandita, so quickly did she dispose of her young men, but Ranga did it properly, by introduction and appointment. He wore his best, arrived early, was nervous when the door opened.

STAR *camera will show him on her doorstep smoothing back his hair. Closing in, it will focus on a tic where one of his downy earlobes meets the elongate jaw.*
Hero Tremulant.

The divan she sat on, like a smouldering ice-barge, rode on black marble.

It was Nandita's practice when greeting strangers to either make an entrance or be surprised, latterly in disha-bille. Today she was genuinely surprised, having forgotten the appointment; besides, he was early. Her set of spoons was late (nowadays they turned up at lunch time with excuses she had heard before, used on bygone sets herself, before she became too big for excuses) and she'd overslept, not on the heart-shaped bed but on the drawing-room divan where she'd nodded off after last night's party. On the floor, fallen from her hands, was Count Lev Tolstoy's *War and Peace*. Her body sagging, she'd begun sensibly to improve her mind. It was remarkable how once you got the long names figured out, the story was really quite straightforward. She decided to quiz the visitor, very likely a muckraker in disguise, about the Russian, knock him out on both counts.

When the phone rang, the gateman announcing the visitors, she was on a dream set, of *Shanti Aur Yudh* (Peace and War), yelling something through a megaphone at the invading Chinese general, Po-Lian, whose right hand, from the bitter Himalayan cold, kept creeping towards his vest-pocket. She groaned and rubbed the sleep from her eyes: more invaders and her face in yesterday's war-paint. Well, let it be; Tolstoy would have to do double duty.

The doorbell rang. She leaned over and took up the phone again.

71

'Oh, Rita! Come.' She dialled nine; a buzzer sounded.

A black bull stood in her doorway.

It might have been part of the dream.

Sometimes in the history of human collisions which constitutes society there occurs a chance coming together of age and youth in the persons of two individuals whose natural affinities are so utterly attuned that the relative difference in their ages appears less a social mockery than a negative charge of intense and natural rightness. This does not prevent the principals from labouring under a sense of injustice. When the older happens to be a woman and the younger a man, the obstacles to their union appear magnified and the more unjust for being arbitrary. The woman will lament that cruel fate which brought her on the stage too soon, or him too late, when in her heart she knows time to be a fiction. The man will rail against the dictates of convention when he knows instinctively the irrelevance of that court. When finally either nature has its way and society closes its ranks, or society triumphs and the individuals go their separate ways, a surplus of energy remains. Either the transgression yields a bonus for society whose store of cautionary tales increases by one, or the failure of courage haunts the individuals with that measure of rightness unfulfilled. In other words, society wants the individuals to conform but needs them to err, while nature wants them to err but needs them to conform.

By which mouthful I don't want you to think (*I would not have you believe*, I almost wrote, to please the Victorian shade of Mr Penn-Brierly, sometime English master at the Silver Spoon; *Plumbum*, we called him, and there was a leaden quality to his lightest utterance) I don't want you to think I side with either nature or society. But I would like my Hero and Nandita to get together. I suspect you would too and are wondering why I don't leave the nineteenth century to its own devices.

Zero Lev-ite.

Besides, they did get together, even though nature and society reared their several heads.

It was the stuff not of classic but of romantic novels. He stood rooted to the. She had never seen such. All his life he had. In a single moment they.

This might have gone on for some time had Rita not begun the introductions. Nandita recovered first and composed herself upon the divan. She reclined on her side, propped up at the elbow by a peppermint green bolster. She was wearing a long silk evening-gown of turquoise with a peacock's tail pattern which covered her person with what could have been either vertical eyes or yonis. Her legs, bared at a slit down the side, as once in the black-and-white *Farishta* (Angel), sloped photo-genically towards a white plaster pillar wreathed in a painted plaster grapevine.

The shock of those glabrous legs when he expected a chaste morning sari like the one in *Sati Savitri* (Diana Empyreal) ran through him, riffling the hair at the nape of his neck. She saw it at once and regretted the frivolous dinner party. He might still be a muckraker, if a moral one. She inclined her head to his pious namaste, smiled her signature smile, indicated chairs. The silver chain around his neck she read, correctly, as a concession to Bombay in an alien. The quiet, almost shy smile, the economical movements, the inwardness, more than his features, marked him instantly as a South Indian. The slouch did not deceive her; he'd remembered it halfway across the room. It covered up a mincing gait which suggested a childhood in lungis, not pants or pyjamas. It wouldn't do for the screen, of course – and why else was he here? Not a journalist, she decided, and relaxed. She would teach him how to walk, in time. And get him to shave off that ridiculous moustache.

He in turn would have liked to see her move, but so far she had not stirred from the divan. She shifted once to tuck a leg under her so there now remained but one offending limb with its chaste redemptive foot. And then she was still, an idol.

It made most newcomers squirm, eventually. She saw he remained calm; he saw she saw, and grew very still himself, the complete devotee. It was Rita who, flustered by so much stillness, felt obliged to intervene and invent and extemporize. At length, put out by her onerous irrelevance, she pleaded a lunch appointment and left.

He saw her to the door as if the house were his. It is, Nandita heard herself say to her master. Everything is yours.

I wasn't there (nor was anyone else, the sharp reader has noticed; the coast is clear) but I know how she felt.

In fact somebody else was there. As Rita stepped out at the gate a carful of spoons pulled up, Nandita's chamchas come for lunch. The car was Nero's, a white Ambassador, and the owner was in it, though not at the wheel (his dark glasses could be seen at the back), but that was not enough to gain entry today. The guard had orders to let no one in. He ignored the threats, the ten-rupee notes shoved through the window and went back to sit beside the telephone.

Now the coast is clear.

My master returns to his chair, sits in his finical precise mode (the converse of the coffee-house mode) and asks Nandita polite questions about this or that flim. Her lips move and the familiar voice pours from them, but riper, more resonant. He quotes a line of di-laag from his favourite flim *Barsaati* (The Room on the Roof) and she takes him up on the response. Imperceptibly his voice begins to mimic Karan Talwar's, hers grows softer, younger. He does not miss a cue: it is she who stumbles. He prompts her in her own voice. Stunned, she moves for the first time, sitting up in the mode: *She Sits Up*. Is she being made fun of? His clear eyes reassure her: not a trace of guile there, and she reads deception daily in the inverting eyes of her spoons. She reclines again, her legs – both of them now – sloping without show or conceal-ment, trust reviving in her heart. They complete the sequence, then sit in silence a moment. At the close of the original di-laag, Karan Talwar, lodger, takes the landlord's daughter in his arms and the violins go skittering down five flights of stairs while the tabla plods back up.

Nandita waits, suspecting a ruse, admiring his youthful effrontery. Hero, who simply meant to compliment her, sees an opening. The disjunction between the Nandita of his dreams, always in faery motion, and this teasing statue has worked a potent magic on his soul, but he is still an outsider in awe of the zone of infinite dimensions. But neither is he unaware of his effect on women. Nor is he a fool.

He rises, crosses the floor to the divan, and bending plants a reverential kiss upon Nandita's feet.

Then, his heart galumphing away, he backs on clopping hooves towards the door.

The idol springs to life, offers tea, a cold drink, lunch, talks weather, gabbles Tolstoy, extracts at last a promise that he will come again. On the contrary, he protests, he must beg permission to return. Tuesday, then? Tuesday.

Outside the gate, the white Ambassador is still there, parked across Nandita's driveway. Nero is leaning against the back door, arms folded. He hears the guard approach-ing and removes his dark glasses in a pantomime of tried patience finally rewarded. His cronies stretch and yawn with noisy jocularity, eager to see what it was that kept them from their lunch. But there is no lunch for them today. They fall silent as the latch is drawn.

STAR *camera is across the street, watching them watching the gate. The gate opens.*

75

Hero steps out.

He looks up and down the street, on unfamiliar terrain. If he sees the car and its owner on the kerb he doesn't register them.

Nero, slighted, curious and aggressive from hunger, sneers loud enough for the newcomer to hear: 'Must have been *pressing* business!' His companions snigger.

Hero casts his eyes idly over the Ambassador crew and walks off down the hill in search of a bus-stop.

As he turns away, Nero catches sight of the hump. (He was one of the few men to be so privileged.)

STAR camera, which has come over to follow Hero's back downhill, turns about and zooms in on Nero's face. There are beads of sweat on his forehead. He puts his dark glasses back on and looks steadily after the departing figure. Camera moves still closer till Hero is a pair of tiny dwindling homunculii reflected in Nero's smuggled Ray-Bans.

Dialogue

His first film was in the can six months from that Tuesday. Nandita's influence among producers had not declined with her ratings; if anything, it had increased. Her old associates were eager to make amends for neglect; they would meet her more than halfway – so long as her suit concerned somebody else. It was a demonstration of loyalty, it did her a good turn and it saved them screening scores of hopefuls. She was, after all, qualified to judge heroes. And with this newcomer she had never judged better.

   Let it be said at once of my master's spectacular success in films that it was not fortuitous. He could act. He could outact any comer, he could act the combined opposition into the ground. (Later, in politics, he did just that, but barring exceptions it was no longer an aesthetic virtue.) Look at the wooden heroes of today, the tin soldiers, the straw men, and even his first attempt, *Comrade Ravi* looks good. There's the freshness of face for a start, the rampant energy of the performance, his undoubted sympathy with

77

the hero. Shot after shot – even at this distance in time – crackles with his sheer presence. And that despite a shoddy script by one Hosi Billimoria. I gather Nandita was daily on the set, so it was a command performance, but the man was a natural.

Next, in quick succession, came *Khabardar* (Forbidden), *Kamal Aur Kichad* (The Lotus and the Mire), and *Kasam* (Oath). Three Ks in a row, don't ask me why. Then he did *Uttar Dakshin*, which made his slouch a sort of signature. Nandita went down South with him. After that came *Shalimar* on location in Kashmir with Preeti Juneja. Nandita followed them there, chauffeured to the remotest locations in her pink Bentley. She'd got rid of her chamchas, but couldn't shake off Felix Fonseca who gave chase in his matchbox. When she got back to Bombay, Kitty Dixit of *Twinkletoes* had a lot to say. Golgappa of the *Bollywood Tatler* actually followed her home one day and asked was it true about the engagement cards? He got a fat lip for his pains because Hero happened to be in the Bentley at the time, but Nandita simply smiled her sphinx-like smile and swept up the drive.

Ancient as the pyramids, silent as the sphinx, began Golgappa's next column, and went on about young camels in season, though the tone of high injury argued suspension of disbelief. He'd got the hump wrong anyway. But when Early Bird, in the more sedate *Matinée* carried the story, it was confirmation.

Now, normally, new stars have a grace period when the viscid sweetness and light fair drip from the pens of the gossip aunties, and the syrup oozes until you begin to long for a draught of clear poison.

You haven't long to wait.

Ranga's honeymoon was short by even these standards. All that milk and honey, he found, went simply to fatten the calf. The praise for *Shalimar*, the little human-interest stories, the bland interviews, the photos-of-your-choice, the amusing fillers, favourite recipes, birthday greetings,

78

horoscope, left him unprepared for the knife. The first stab was a picture – no, a pic – in the *Bollywood Tatler* showing Nandita with her arm around his waist. It was taken from behind, obviously in a hurry, but the two figures were unmistakable. The caption said: *Egyptian View: Sphinx with Young Camel.*

Nandita, accustomed to the press, wrinkled her nose, but Ranga would not leave it at that. He waved the picture at her, his hand shaking.

'How does it matter?' she sniffed. 'What is important is our love.'

'Of course,' Hero said. 'But how can they get away with this sort of thing?' He would have liked to gore that swollen Golgappa and tear down the *Tatler* offices.

'Oh ho!' Nandita answered. 'So much halla-gulla over this nonsense photo.' And she tore it into little pieces.

Ranga, still trembling, watched the scraps dance at their feet. They were standing on the front verandah under a whirling ceiling fan.

'I'll . . .' He clenched his fist so hard the knuckles showed up a pale heliotrope under the skin.

'I know,' Nandita said, and putting an arm (the same one) around him, drew him into the house.

STAR *camera may show the mesh doors swinging shut behind them as his arm goes around her shoulder. They kiss just beyond the wire netting. Then the soft-focus lens dips slowly, focus sharpening, to the floor where the scraps of their romance chase one another in a widening circle.*

He came to me for advice. It was some months since the room on Madame Cama Road that I called my flat had echoed with his voice. I raised my eyebrows in mock reproof that concealed some small dudgeon at neglect.

'I say! This is slumming!'

'Come off it, yaar.'

His Fiat stood in the dusty compound below. The last time I'd seen him look so lacklustre was on the set of *Comrade Ravi*, scripted by that altu-faltu Billimoria. As it happened Nandita was not there that day and the director, my friend Kapil Grover, was having trouble sparking him. It was the scene where Ravi, in the dock, denounces the fraudulent judicial apparatus that is about to sentence him, declaring that he cannot recognize either the law which shackles him or the state whose charade it is. It was a tricky scene and Kapil was not at all sure it would get past the censors. Ranga was finding it hard to concentrate, so I suggested over the director's head that he make the entire speech with his eyes closed. Ranga looked enquiringly at me – so did Kapil – and then went ahead and tried it. He caught the smouldering rage of the speech so perfectly that St Joan herself, haranguing the Inquisition, would have been proud of him. Though Billimoria should have been ashamed of borrowing so freely from Shaw; I know he did because we were fellow students at the Silver Spoon (we called him *Alley Billi*, Alley Cat) and *Saint Joan* was the drama text in our final year.

As it happened the movie sneaked past the censors, which a blazing, gesticulating Ravi (Billimoria's Comrade Joan) might not have done.

Afterwards we had a fruit salad – mostly watermelon, I remember – in the studio canteen He, Kapil and I, and were full of stories. On other days I believe Nandita brought him dosa and sambar in a tiffin-carrier, and home-made ice-cream in a chilly-bin.

'She taught me how to *walk*, Zero!' he burst out now.

I nodded noncommittally. He must have started this conversation while parking the Fiat, or in the lift.

'But – ' He brought his fist down on the table.

'But?'

'I mean, you just have to listen to some of the things they're saying about me, I mean, about us.'

I had heard, read.

'Look. I can act, right?'

'Right.'

'I have ,' he paused, ' – looks. I mean – '

I waved aside the apology. He did have.

'I mean, it isn't like she's done everything for me.'

It wasn't. He needed an entrée and there Nandita had helped. But that was not what Kitty Dixit and Felix Fonseca and Golgappa were saying. *Puppet* and *plaything* were among their kinder words. *Prodigy or Protégé*? Kitty Korner wanted to know.

'And all because of that Golgappa business. Saying we're engaged.'

There was a silence.

'Are you, boss?'

'It's none of their bloody business if we are.'

He said *their* tactfully enough, but his response was so violent I didn't press the issue. I wrote him a solution instead.

They kept everyone guessing – and giggling, '*twice* his age!' – for six months. And in fact they were engaged; they might as well have been married for the quarrels, reported by gleeful neighbours. He had his own house on the hill but he'd more or less moved in with her. This was about the time UD moved in with me, more or less.

And then he did it. He signed *Suryanamaskar* (Salute to the Sun) without telling her and was well into the shooting before she found out. It was a multi-starrer with lots of familiar faces and room for more. In fact I managed to get UD a part through Kapil, who knew the producer though he wasn't directing. Ranga was Associate Hero with big names like Javed Ansari and Bunty Dalal. Nero was Number 1 Villain, and the Number 2 Villain was the kung-fu artiste from Hong Kong.

The movie, for those fresh back from Mars, was a sort of political science fiction in which an India on the

81

threshold of a solar-energy revolution is beset right and left (still) by pesky Pakistan and devilish China (hook nose and slant eye.) Javed was the intrepid colonel deputed to transport mad scientist Bunty Dalal and his top-secret gypsolarnometer from his home lab in the capital (Nagpur, since Delhi was destroyed in the Third World War) to the ancient Sun Temple of Konark. They have three days to beat the solar eclipse which will neutralize the good inventor's machine, sending its needles into an irreversible back-spin and India into the Dark Ages of the nuclear winter which destroyed Europe – *unless* the gypsolarnometer is aligned with a certain stone chariot-wheel and the pre-ingress sun.

Ranga was the local cop who believes Bunty is being kidnapped by Javed and tries to take him back to Nagpur where he belongs. Nero, sinister in black and armed with silicon nose and knuckle-dusters, was (by the unwritten law which states that the Number 1 Villain shall be of the subcontinent) the Pakistani saboteur, while the Number 2 Villain (by the second part of that same law) was the distinctly foreign ex-acrobat now in movies as Captain Memo. UD was a sort of kept dancer attached to the Sun Temple.

I had better not try to describe the lush visuals which won the film two national awards and one from the Orissa State Tourist Board, or Puppy Tandon's soaring stellar synthesizer so deftly mixed by P. Devadas. Nor will I spoil the Martians' fun by telling the rest of the story. I will say only what everyone knows, that Ranga stole the show. In uniform he was even more devastating than in civvies, and cinema halls were full of melting women who had seen the hump.

His last job was to dispatch Captain Memo. There was a tense moment on the set before the camera rolled; it was their first encounter since the circus, and Ranga, sharply reminded of Indu, shook his head at the distance he had

82

travelled in Nandita's arms. The kung-fu comprador came at him with arms flailing. 'It's like wrestling with noddles,' Ranga complained, but eventually he let Captain Memo get knotted and shipped him back to China in a tea-chest, the movie's last comic moment. Shortly after, Ranga was killed – shot in the back by Nero with a bullet intended for Bunty. When he died there were rivers of tears in the aisles and the salt had to be scraped off the floor of the Hind Talkies between shows.

It was the turning point. Javed's stock fell: Ranga's rose. Javed *knew* he should have died, but the script (to say nothing of the army) would not allow it. And yes, you've guessed. It was my script.

Before we exit Javed forever into the wilderness of sticks and stones that is the lot of Falling Hero, I may be allowed to (I will allow myself to anyway) open a small window on my own career. I mean my real career, from which happenchance deflected me into scriptwriting. I think I deserve more than a footnote in the annals of Bollywood Heroism. A page will do.

You may have forgotten *Zameen, Aasman Aur Sarson Ka Beej* (Heaven and Earth and a Grain of Mustard Seed.) I have not. I was to have been Full Hero, the unhappy peasant Dharti Ram, who has to sell his moiety, an acre in paradise, because he has fallen into debt to the grasping moneylender Dhani Das. The names alone date the film, with their symbolic forthrightness; nowadays the money-lender is Garib Das and a blow has been struck for irony. The details of the plot are complex and beside the point, which is that I was to have been Full Hero. And would have been but for two contingencies.

About this time Javed Ansari, whom I knew slightly at school (he turned in his spoon a year or two after I did) arrived in Bombay with heroic designs. He didn't have far to go, with an uncle in the industry, a well-enough-known producer with grossers (the word is not too strong)

83

like *Dilli Chalo* (March on Delhi – again that innocence) to his credit. In no time at all Javed had signed six contracts (to my one) and was set on a course more or less predictable. He had connections, a modicum of talent, and (some said) looks. Muscles, more like it, a surplusage of those, but let it go. To each her own. Also about this time, the Pakistani aggressor made his move and patriotic feelings were running high. *Jai Jawan, Jai Kisan*, the slogan went: Hail Soldier, Hail Peasant, and jaunty soldiers and peasants appeared on posters everywhere, striding together in their respective uniforms, with gun and plough held high, their heads raised up towards some lofty radiance, and (more to the point) their muscles rippling.

It was felt that my peasant was not muscular enough, that the peasant I made, or might make, whatever his other virtues, would be a sad reflection on the physique of Indian manhood. Somebody more like the poster peasant was wanted, and who was that flexing his muscles in the wings? Javed stepped forward, grinning. There was, with him, the argument went, the added piquancy of having an Indian Muslim playing the Hindu peasant: what could be more secular, more telling to the other side?

But what about the audition? I cried. *Have you forgotten my Dying Peasant, my Cowdusk Vignette, my painstakingly researched Tilling Mother Earth?*

Too international, the director said, looking over his shoulder, and had Javed do a woefully hammed Tilling the Motherland. He got the part.

There was still the moneylender, the director said to me afterwards. A pot belly would go down well there.

I needed the money, and I needed a break. And once I set my mind to it I made a good (that is, a not-all-bad) moneylender, altogether more credible than Javed's clod-dish noble peasant, a fact that did not escape the critics.

But after that the only offers I got were for villains, and for greasy villains at that.

There was one more fly in my ointment. I had agreed to the switch on the condition that Javed and I would get equal billing: his name would appear beside mine, or mine beside his. He could have the left slot, first read, first forgotten, but mine must follow on and lodge in the viewer's unconscious. It must not be lower down or in smaller letters or preceded by *and* or *with* or any of those humiliating precursors. Judge of my surprise, gentle cineaste, when the credits come rolling up and

ZERO

appears a whole frame and several jarring synthesizer beats after – not only Javed but – the heroine, who shall remain nameless.

I gave up the pursuit of heroism and with it my pretentious flat and took the room on Madame Cama Road where I becalmed my spirit for a new career. I bought myself an unruled pad, some 4H pencils and a pencil sharpener from the cooperative at the Cooperage corner where they write out your docket in long hand, every item in triplicate. At home I sharpened the whole box of pencils and sat down at my kitchen table. There was a jackfruit tree outside my window whose topmost branches rattled in the breeze. The tough leathery leaves were a comfort. I did a sketch of the building opposite, framed by my window. On the balcony across from me was a bare-chested man, not especially muscular, taking the evening air. I sketched him in. Then I noticed across my own window an almost perfect spider's web. I had been looking through it all along. I decided to include it in my sketch, and very lightly, with the most silken of touches, the threads began to coalesce. When I'd finished, the man appeared trapped at the very centre, like a fly.

He wasn't, as I say, especially muscular, but as I contemplated my handiwork he began to look more and more like someone I knew.

It was Javed Ansari.

After that the plot of *Suryanamaskar* simply wrote itself. I didn't offer it to him right away. I led him through *Chhoro Yaar* (Let Bygones Be Bygones), *Priya Pahalvaan* (The Soft-Hearted Wrestler), *Behosh* (Unconscious), and *Mala* (A Garland of Flowers.) Then, the script not yet complete, I showed him my intrepid colonel. He could hardly wait.

Now it was just about then that my master needed a boost. He'd made an impressive debut and followed it up with three or four adequate performances, but he needed something special, something to lift him out of the common run of heroes. If *Suryanamaskar* could do that while at the same time sealing Javed's fate, it was two birds with the one stone. Not that I killed both: I killed off Ranga to breathe life into him; I breathed life into Javed to kill him off. The rest was fate.

Fate and my master's slouch. The slouch became his trademark in a world of smartly stepping chubby boys. Its ill-assorting with the policeman's uniform in *Suryanamaskar* was both comic and, in the end, tragic, and for some months after the movie was released drill majors on police parade grounds throughout the nation had a disciplinary problem with impressionable recruits. It was a mix of insouciance and latent power; it conveyed the disdain of a yawning tiger. Nandita, who tried to cure him of it actually helped him perfect it, until the slouch so became him that it stuck. I often thought it odd that he should find his feet just when he seemed in danger of losing his balance, but there it was.

Symbolically or not, after *Suryanamaskar* my master became his own man. He moved out of Nandita's and broke off the engagement. Félix Fonseca was first with the story, but it was Kitty Dixit who gave a motive – the wrong one, as so often with her tribe. She said Nandita turned him out because her spies reported his attentions on the set to a certain temple dancer.

To refute this calumny, which touches me as much as it does her, I must bring you up to date, that date, on the career of U.D. Cologne.

She of the wide unfocussed eyes, with pupils of different sizes, and a natural flounce to her walk which clinched the temple dancer's role. She whom fate led to the phoenix lift in the Ellora Mansions on Madame Cama Road at the precise moment when it happened to be passing the second floor with me in it. She – but rest H. Rider Haggard, who first brought pollution on Zero at the Silver Spoon. U.D. Cologne is the one I mean.

She was born in that forbidding granite Parsi enclave in Colaba which looks like a Hollywood rendering of Nebuchadnezzar's palace (or the set of that vertiginous mountain fastness in *She*.) So there is no childhood of beggary or somersaulting for small coins which overtakes so many girls on the wrong side of those hulking gates. She is convented, in red socks, at the nearby Cooperage Convent of Michaela the Carpentress, and indeed spends much of her early life within the square mile which includes the Gateway of India, the Nebuchadnezzar enclave and my own Ellora Mansions. So perhaps it is not so great a coincidence that we should meet.

When I first saw her through the double bars of the lift door, the lift was already going up past the second floor. She was a jolt to the senses. I slammed the stop button and brought the phoenix to a shuddering halt between floors. I knelt and peered down at her through the gap.

'Going up?' I called.

She smiled at the caper and nodded.

'Coming down,' I sang. 'Hold on!' But I had to go all the way up first. Still, she was waiting.

She was a prefect, with limited powers but with that air of sheltered yet already threatened authority which comes so effortlessly to the senior schoolgirl. She had no great interest in studies, had been on stage, the sheltered school stage. Once she'd played Titania, twice helped organize the annual fashion show. Her parents were modern, the mother an interior decorator who outdressed her daughter. An upper-middle-class girl with upper-middle-class ambitions; she wanted to be a model or an interpreter (there was some Spanish.)

'Why not the movies?' I asked when we were drinking a cup of instant coffee, afterwards. (I always wanted to indulge, once, in that sleazy *afterwards*; for years it tantalized the adolescent Zero.) There'd been a fumble, nothing more.

'*Movies!*'

I had broached the zone of infinite dimensions. I remembered my own timorousness and felt a sympathetic pang.

'Why not? You're at least as beautiful as Preeti Juneja.'

'Preeti Juneja!' *The moon*, I might have said.

'If not more.'

'Come on!'

'Truly.'

I put my cup down and buttered her another sliced bun. She had a schoolgirl's appetite. She dug out the candied peel and ate it first.

'But you have to know how to act,' she said practically. Already, then, the zones were shifting.

'Anybody can act,' I said.

'But you have to be good.'

'You have to be ready.'

She said nothing to that (it *was* a bit vague; I was thinking of both daring and willingness, natural adversaries in every kind of art) but considered it with an attentive tilt of the head. Then she began to talk about her classmate and said she had better go and look for her flat. She must come again, I said, anxiously, and she said she would and stroked the back of my neck. That night I clipped a couple of grey hairs in my sideburns.

Her friend's flat, it turned out, was two floors down. The lift jiggled on its cable like an elderly tea-bag before coming to rest at the third floor. I waited in it till the apartment door opened to squeals of chummy laughter from the resident red socks. Before the door shut she turned and shot an effortlessly adult look in my direction, and I felt her friend would be seeing more of her.

She went on to college, made bold friends, travelled outside the square mile, but came back one day and said: 'OK.'

'OK what?'

'I'll give it a try.' She waved briefly at my scripts. Stacked in sheaves, drained of even their sombre buff in the harsh forenoon light, cheated into black-and-white, the inert files looked cheerless enough to shake my own faith. Impossible to imagine colour and motion leaping clamorous from them. But she was wearing a hibiscus-red kamiz and red low-slung shoes.

'You have to be good,' I said, uncertain.

'You have to make a name.'

Was that all it took? Not quite, but I fear she was right, not just in the movies: you had to make a noise. I didn't like the implications, but the kamiz swept me along.

We thought up a name for her, Khushboo at first, but the fragrance was too general, and several tosses later I came up with U.D. Cologne. We got her a part in *Kirti* (Glory) and found she could act at least as well as Preeti Juneja. In *Naukarani* (Maidservant) she was already camera-wise, if a touch unmarked and overfed for a servant – but then all our stars are. As a nation we're either overfed or underfed. With *Zindagi Ki Havas* (Lust for Life) she showed signs of marking time, so that Kapil

89

had to work hard to get the director to reconsider his first choice for the temple dancer in *Suryanamaskar*.

So, it may well be that she saw a lot of Ranga during location shooting in Orissa (she could hardly have avoided seeing him) but she was still happy with Pedro and me up on Madame Cama Road. Ranga was by then a regular visitor and they were friends, not lovers, until the night of the pink gin. I have their word for it.

So I am sorry to disappoint the Dixits and Golgappas and Fonsecas of this world. Nandita knew nothing of UD till later. The fact was Nandita saw her creation, her calf, begin to slip away the moment news came to her (through Nero) of his signing *Suryanamaskar*. She raged, she wept the Nile to flood, she wheedled; but Ranga's pride had been hurt. He walked out, slouched out, in the old, pre-Nandita way, and broke off the engagement. In salving his own pride he hurt hers, and she could not forgive him. Upon the ruin of their love, twice betrayed by pride, a travesty of the old order sprang up. Nero was reinstalled as head chamcha, the free lunches were resumed, and the chowkidar who barred the gate against Nero's white Ambassador was sacked.

Consider two fresh paradoxes. In Nero, Nandita must now bring herself to love the man she despises, having come to despise the man she loves. Nero's own predicament is scarcely more tolerable. He now hates Hero not because Hero took Nandita away but because he gave her back.

None of this can have been visible to the filmi press, or if it was they sadly misread the tattered semaphore. Not that I discouraged their speculation at the time. If the break-up diverted attention from the real break, Hero's big chance, so much the better. The Golgappas did my master a service where they meant to bring him down. So busy with malice are these redundant manipulators they cannot for a moment conceive of themselves as the real puppets.

Suryanamaskar was Hero's big break. It was also Nero's – only for him it was confirmation in villainy: he was now undisputed Number 1 Villain. When Naresh T. Patel announced his Mutiny historical, to be called *Kartavya* (Duty), there was no real question who the hero and villain should be. Auditions were for Number 2 and down.

No stinting on production, I remember: it was the time when huge spills of Gulf money were being skimmed off to finance risky Bombay ventures. An entire press corps was flown to Chunar, where a fortress dating back to the third century BC overlooked a bend in the river. Ill at ease in those wide stony spaces that distilled a terrible silence, the gossip merchants pestered the director with trivial suggestions, harassed production, needled the fights manager, took compromising photos of starlets, asked UD (Associate Heroine) leading questions, and finally succeeded in sparking off a fight. Later on they said Nandita had put Nero up to it, but if you knock stones together in those flinty hills, you can start a fire.

Crossed once, Hero stood still and kept the peace; crossed twice (and Nero, whether propelled by Nandita, press or private grievance, crossed him again) he put his head down and began to bellow.

BHOOOAN! he went. *BHOOOANN!!*

He stamped the earth tentatively.

SHSS! SHSS! Nero hissed and struck at my master.

They went at it DHISH, DHISH.

Now Hero teeters on the battlements (STAR camera looks straight down the cliff face at the Ganges swirling far below), now Nero, sent flying back with a kick, lands with a crunch at the bottom of a dry well, DHUCHIK! Hero leaps down after him; STAR camera is already down there, looking up. In the circle of hot

91

blue sky, the hump – which Nero carelessly forgot – shows in
silhouette on the stuntman's back.

My master, I did point out, did his own stunts.

They flailed about in the soft mud for a bit, DHICH!
KHICH! Their clothes were covered in the yellow soil of the
region, but their hairstyles –

I must put in a word about their hair. Hero, being of
Dravidian stock, had the Southy's curls. Nero, an Aryan
of sorts (all sorts came through the Khyber Pass) had the
straight hair of the Northy. In the one a touch of the
peninsular aborigine, the negroid forest tribals; in the
other the Scythians, Huns, Turks, Carpathians, Iranians,
Mongolians, and every invader as far back as those
doubtful Aryans. You would expect Hero's hair to be
straight, the villain's curly, and so it was in the old days,
but we have come far as a nation. Behold, then, my
master's curls, combed back without a parting, one ringlet
at each sideburn and a wayward tendril at the centre of
the forehead; no sign of battle there. Observe too, Nero's
locks, blown dry from right to left, puffed at the front and
bushy-bevelled at the back, fresh and virginal all round.

They fight on in the well, hair unmussed.

'This comes with my mistress's compliments,' hisses
Nero. DIKSH.

'Guttercrawler! Durst besmirch that precious one?'
DISHU.

'Not so precious as your honour,' Nero sneers, 'or am I
mistaken?'

'The phial of truth lies incongruously in those soilèd
paws.'

'Perhaps some dirt has crept under other nails than my
own.'

'Then it had better return where it belongs.' DHIKSH.

Blood springs from Nero's lip, laid open by that last

blow from my master. He wipes the wound with the back of his hand. His eyes burn in the dark.

'That was a see-rious mistake, Miss-ter Ranga,' he says, very slowly.

'I await correction.'

Black lightning, Nero strikes. But the black bull is not there. Hero has leapt into the air. He comes down foursquare on the prostrate villain, snorting and trampling, his bellow echoing in the empty well. BHOOAN! BHOOOANN! Planes of mystic light intersect at that point between his shoulder-blades which is his life's triumph and his burden.

Nero picks himself up, spies a banyan root in the well wall and clambers to the safety of a small gate halfway up. (*Handheld camera may pursue him, the counter of blue sky spinning in hazard up above.*) He is breathing hard; not since that stampede in the curry western *Gauboy* has his back felt so raw. Hero feints a lunge at the dangling root and Nero turns and flees down the narrow passage to the chief guest's bedchamber; in the old days kings got rid of trouble-makers by this route to the well. From the far end of the passage he howls his filmi warning: 'Miss-ter Ranga! We will meet again. You will live to regret this day!'

Cabaret

Shot 134. INT. Night. STAR camera in the theatre audience, front row. Gold and green lights flash on and off, streaming in series to the edge of the stage. There the twinkling ropes cascade into an electric pool where concentric circles of blue lights bubble outwards to the shore and back. Bubbachik, bubbachik, bub-bachik, goes Dumpy Shinde's synthesizer, and with every bar more lights flick on, white in the sky, then red on the horizon, then pink on twenty canvas pillars. A giant vinyl moon comes up, live peacocks swither on the water's edge and a white imported washing machine, bathed in brilliant light, is lowered gently from above. The music, which has built to a vigorous fanfare (it may be part Zarathustra and part mariachi, but no part Indian) crests the moment the celestial machine touches down centre-stage. There is a touch of the UFO about the washing machine; the post-climax music will suggest this with high-pitched electronic wails and ulular moog-talk. A portentous hush as the lid rises, then again the bubbachik, bubbachik of the start as a tentacle of foam emerges from the tub. Next a head of foam comes up, and then an endless spill of rich lather pours

from the machine. It bubbles up and runs over grows and grows until the stage is covered in winking foam.

Front lights dim. Backlit stage makes a silhouette of pillars and machine.

A peal of forced laughter, a footfall with ankle-bells. A figure, voluptuous in outline, can be made out backstage, leaning against a pillar. She might be a stone bracket, except she breaks away and darts to another pillar. From pillar to pillar she moves, as if through an enchanted forest, working her way randomly downstage towards the clearing where the machine stands bubbling.

At the edge of the clearing she pauses, her silhouette a striking contrast with the straight lines of pillar and machine. She picks up a head-load of washing tied up in a sheet, balances it, but puts it down again. It is she who wants washing.

Tentatively, theatrically, she insinuates herself into the foam. As she moves she furrows the lather, scoops up a handful, inspects it and then gently rubs it into her skin. She circles the machine, growing bolder, freer, tittering, dancing a few steps, working herself up as the music swells until she breaks into the dance proper. Lights come up slowly as she dances a piece of modern ballet at odds with her earlier movements in the foam when she could have passed for a stylized dhobin with her load of laundry. She wears, in the skimpy tradition of washerwomen, a tight choli which accentuates her bust, and a diaphanous sari. Her movements are brisk, suggestive of a ritual but energetic bath. At the end it is clear she is drying off, her experiment a success, for she gazes in rapture at her pale new skin. By the time the spotlight finds her wrapped around the miraculous machine it is plain to the audience that this white-skinned goddess in none other than the cabaret artiste of their obscurest fantasies.

It is herself, Flora Fountain.

audience will applaud wildly and Flora will bow and simper, but already the forest is filling up with maidens who flit from tree to tree. The dance is only beginning.

Now Flora switches to the Indian mode as tablas and shehnai, tabor and shawm, emerge to dominate – but not completely – the music. The washerwomen, of whom she is queen, strike poses in the forest as they approach her. They are robed in gauzy white saris, a shock against their black skins; it is not the saris that they have come to wash. Queen Flora is now installed upon her throne, whose lid she has first taken care to shut. The foam continues to ooze from under her, but the bulk of it must now be generated (and possibly has been all along) in the wings. Refulgent, regal, white (but not as white as the machine), she summons her ladies-in-waiting who step gingerly into the foam, two at a time, one to stage left, one right. Like Flora, they discover the foam's virtue and rub it in, dancing all the while.

Consider their amazement, genteel audience, when the blackness comes away! White patches appear on their arms where they have scrubbed; the patches grow and multiply. More pairs of dhobins join the fray. The dancing grows frenzied. Flora joins in, leaping into the electric pool where she pirouettes at the centre of the blue circles. The dhobins, now off-white, surround her, the whitest up front, the less successful further back. The inner circle stand, the next kneel, the outermost lie flat: together they form the petals of a giant lotus (*pink spotlight*) which opens and closes on the water. In the centre Flora spins, first one way, then the other until the music peaks and she stands breathless, her arms and those around her flung upwards.

More wild applause as the lotus trembles, opens wide. Flora's breasts are heaving, the audience roars a hungry infant's roar.

STAR *camera closes in on her till at last among the beads of sweat that trim her cleavage it spies a glittering crucifix to reassure the pious sated audience that this fair but fallen woman is only a Christian.*

Finally buoyed up by a restored synthesizer, the lotus floats over to the washing machine, bearing Flora aloft, there to reinstall her. Slowly the washing machine begins to rise, its rinse cycle run; Flora's chariot ascends into the sky, which has begun to rain bubbles of every size, some as big as the moon. She waves as she goes, the fallen/ rising whore/goddess. A strobe light comes on, the dhob- ins are transformed into disco maidens and do a parting clothes-wash number, belting imaginary clothes against the time-honoured rock – only now their movements are agitated, mechanical, their limbs moving like pistons. One by one they slip away into the forest, darting like robotic ghosts. *Bubbachik, bubbachik, bubbachik* dies Dumpy Shinde's synthesizer.

A hard act to follow, but my master was equal to it. His costume alone rivalled anything Flora might, or might not, put on. As a kingpin smuggler he could not but wear two-tone shoes and a blinding white sharkskin suit from Kothari Suitings. The lilac shirt (from Kothari Shirtings), the tangerine cravat, the turquoise socks and handkerchief to match spawned a thousand Hiralal lookalikes that year.

Yes, this was *the* Hiralal, and the year the year of *Kohinoor*. Reformed diamond smuggler with comrade and moll penetrates the vault which holds the British crown jewels and, spurning all other treasure, brings back to India only what is hers, that Golconda mountain of unrivalled light.

It had occurred to me in passing when I first thought up the story, that the man who brought the Elgin Marbles back to Greece would be a pretty fair candidate for National Hero Number 1. What acclaim then would not wrap around the man who restored the world's best-known diamond to its rightful home!

What Ranga needed now was a celebration. If *Kartavya* established him as undisputed hero in the traditional mould – it was after all a historical – *Kohinoor* was his ceremonial investiture. It invested him with the glamour and modernity the masses require, without which (their memory is short) historical figures, howsoever heroic, quickly become intangible and unreal, even quaint: all those silly swords. The patrons in the cheap seats who are our bread and butter, lacking a present object, learn readily to patronize the past. I needed, then, to bring history up to date, to dress my master up in pants, not pantaloons, and send him out among them. As one *of* them – to the power of ten.

UD was the moll, and for a moment I confess I toyed with the notion of playing Jinda, Hiralal's bonded comrade who pays with his life for some slight delay of UD's. The original script had Hiralal delay, but it was felt that the woman should be the stooge and I submitted. (I did however smuggle in some reparation by insisting that UD and not Hiralal shoot the beefeater, a scene that went down well in the cow-belt.) The Anglo who played the queen did a Bush House accent when Palace English was called for, but One's attitude was thought sufficiently provocative to justify a break-in.

It was a sensation. The public with its customary intransigence refused to differentiate between fact and fiction: the Kohinoor, as far as they were concerned, was back for keeps. 'Thousand-carat patriot!' strangers called out when they saw him in the street. Processions were taken out, committees formed to felicitate him, posters appeared – often stuck right on the movie hoarding – calling for his decoration. *An act of transcendental valour*, one newspaper said, while Kothari Suitings (and Shirtings) placed a full-page colour ad in the leading magazines congratulating Our Hero on his success. Another newspaper ran a story claiming that the Tower of London now housed a fake jewel, the glass facsimile Ranga (not Hiralal) had left in place of the real Kohinoor. About this time the peddlers along Marine Drive began to offer cut-price Kohinoors on keychains. Encouraged, a gutter-press baron claimed that the peacock throne in Tehran was a cunning imitation; the real one, which the Irani invader Nadir Shah carried off to Persia two hundred years ago was now back safely in the vaults of the Red Fort in Delhi under army protection, thanks to a certain somebody. He then offered to finance Ranga's next film. And in fact I had begun to contemplate a sequel to *Kohinoor* when the torrent of claims forestalled me. One by one India's looted treasures came home or were found never to have left our shores: Aurangzeb's mammoth cannon which for years stood outside the Royal Military barracks in Woolwich, the entire Indian collection at the Victoria and Albert Museum in London, the San Francisco Nandi, were all clever replicas installed by my master – the last, a granite bull, proof of his personal interest.

'Publicity-shublicity,' Nero sneered to Nandita. Nandita said nothing; she was not about to share her hatred for a man she could still conceive of loving with a man she could only occasionally bring herself to touch.

'Will no one rid me of this man?' she muttered to herself, hardly aware herself of which man she meant. Nero, whose ears were serpent-sharp, had no such doubts. Instinctively he flattened himself against the moss-green cushions, and when he raised his head cold mischief glittered in his eyes.

Nero was not wrong about the publicity. I thought even then that the hand of Guppy Agarwal, publicist, was discernible in the gala, cocking the hoop of trashy hype which *I* for one would never have stooped to. He overdid it, naturally; as one columnist acidly observed, with so much treasure coming in it was odd that the country still had a balance-of-payments problem. But in Bollywood excess is the bottom line, and it worked.

It worked so well I was able to make the next film UD's and almost get away with it. It was the blockbuster *Gateway of India*, and it could have established her, much as *Suryanamaskar* established Ranga, but so besotted with their Hero was the public that the heroine came off second-best again.

You might remember the opening shot of the Gateway from the Taj Hotel with the winter sun coming up and one distraught bat rushing home. A couple of crows flap idly by; one swoops down to poke around in a rubbish-bin. (This was before the city corporation came up with that hysterical row of gaping penguins.) From the top left – we are looking down – a sweeperess wielding a broom enters the frame and works her way towards the Gateway sweeping up empty chip packets and twists of newspaper from the gram vendors of the night before. The sun, top right, is a round of lemon floating in a dead cocktail. At bottom left a yellow-top taxi pulls up. The young man who lurches drunkenly from the hotel, his elegant suit crumpled from the night's dissipation, ignores his cab and ploughs a jibbing furrow to the Gateway.

I wanted them both in at the very first frame, moving inexorably towards each other from their separate worlds, just as the last shot had – or should have had – them moving inexorably apart.

Neither of them could have been unaware of the irony of origins as they rehearsed that first meeting. The sweep-eress in rags had grown up not ten minutes by foot from the Gateway with pocket-money to spend on florentines from the patisserie at the Taj Hotel. (They showed in her cheeks still; how many full-cheeked sweeperesses do you see?) The rake in the crumpled suit who staggers from the hotel door, to a big salute from the burly Sikh doorman, and totters – at sniffing distance from the patisserie – Gatewaywards grew up a thousand kilometres away by train, pumping cycle tyres for a living. It was almost better than the script, and I sometimes felt I should be doing their story instead of a story starring them. Well, now I am, and I find one story takes you as near the truth as another.

This one was a paen to Bombay, to the energy of ten million busy persistent souls: the boatmen by the Gateway, the early morning walkers, the pavement sleepers, the bus-drivers, the waiters, the dock-workers, the young girls doing somersaults, the conscientious newspaper boys, the shirt-sellers, the industrious beggars, the sweepers, the stars.

'I used to come here, Zero,' he confessed the day we shot that opening scene. We stood in the cordoned-off hotel foyer looking out while a flunkey rumpled his coat. 'I'd come and stand over there and watch the tamasha.' He pointed to the small but persistent crowd of watchers who daily congregate opposite the hotel portico to watch the rich and foreign go in and out of those magic doors. Today they were distracted by the shooting further out, but there were a few hardened watchers who were not going to be deprived of their habitual shot of the high life.

'I used to stand there and look at them coming out, the foreigners and Arabs and businessmen and their families, girls wearing pants and no sleeves, fat little chaps carrying white boxes of pastries. It was good fun, I tell you, I never once felt, I swear on God, felt, what-you-call-it.'

'Envious.'

'Envious, not once. I would say to myself: that's you. One day *you* will walk out of there with your stomach full *and* a box of pastries. And the doorman will give you a big salaam.'

And then it was time to put on the coat and the camera

101

was rolling and he stepped out of the front door of the Taj towards the waiting taxi and the Gateway.

I must confess I wasn't terribly interested in my master's character, that is, in this rich young wastrel: it was UD, or rather the sweeperess, I wanted to develop.

I'd watched her prototype from my window with endless fascination, sweeping the dusty compound below of an early morning. There was a sort of tea-shop down there where I got my buns and where passersby stopped for a samosa or a cigarette, leaving the usual litter of leaf plates and empty cigarette packets and so on.

Every morning at 6.30 the sweeperess arrived with a little boy in tow and took up her broom. The boy was six or seven years old, dressed in a white, short-sleeved shirt and khaki shorts, and his hair, carefully combed and parted, shone in the morning sunlight; he was on his way to school. His mother would post him on the gatekeeper's stool and there he would sit with his shining face and watch her with solemn intelligent eyes.

She started at the gate and worked her way up the drive to where the drive widened into an empty yard bounded on one side by the property wall and on the other by the mansion. The tea-shop was there and beyond it more open ground where the employees of the electricity board, which rented the second floor, parked their cycles.

It was a dusty job, the ground beaten earth. To start with, she picked up the stool and swept clear the gatekeeper's beedi-butts and matchsticks. Then she swept along the gate, her strokes making regular arcs in the dust as she went. When she reached the other side she turned, changed hands, and worked the broom the other way, making a fresh row of arcs, concave to convex. Back and forth she went, changing hands and sweeping, leaving behind her a widening strip of ground, scoured of the previous day's debris and patterned with her arcs. As the rows piled up, they looked like basket-weave, precise and clean.

Looking down I wanted to cheer her on as she drove the wicked flotsam back; in certain lights it seemed to me an act heroic, of good faith with some private code, her dharma. In twenty minutes the entire compound was swept clean, the rubbish piled in the far corner where it was periodically burnt. Her duty done, the woman stood her broom in its niche against a drainpipe and walked across her patterned floor to where her son, impatient from his wait, was already on his feet. Her footprints marked the first track across the newly minted yard; in a little while early customers would criss-cross it, then bicycle tyres, car tyres, and the daily rain of litter. But when she left, walking with an erectness which was her moot striking feature, she left behind a burnished plain. Her cheeks, incidentally, were neither concave nor (like UD's) convex, and she was, still more incidentally, handsome. In fact I often felt I could have happily married her (there was never a husband in evidence) and lived in domestic harmony, she weaving her baskets and I spinning my webs, but then UD came along and I realized I didn't even know the woman's name.

Zero Romancer!

UD became a ready substitute, an engrossing one to be sure; or perhaps the sweeperess (Laxmi, in the movie) was all along a substitute for the UD to come, filling the space UD was to occupy, or swell, with her convexities. Cheeks apart, and sundries, UD did Laxmi to a T. She brought such delicate sympathy to bear on the original, whom she watched at work, studying her from our vantage on the fifth floor, that I felt they were sisters parted by the machinery of some pitiless farce. When I confessed my infatuation, she smiled and called me a sentimental idiot, but she seemed to redouble her efforts to capture Laxmi, to hollow her out and inhabit her. She

103

succeeded so well that the prototype Laxmi became – for me – a ghost, while the imitation was real enough to move audiences – and me – to tears.

Not that UD slyly jerked those tears from us: that was the director's doing. B.B. Shah, in headlong flight from a brush with art cinema out East, had found refuge in Bollywood's capacious bosom some ten years earlier, warming readily to its sighs and tears (and tears.) The glycerine that man squandered in his quest for solace would have made a sapper weep. Nor were tears enough: he must glamourize my sweeperess, paint her, twist her arm, dunk her in the Arabian Sea, till my beloved UD (or was it Laxmi?) stood dripping and unrecognizable.

'The bastards!' she fumed one day when production and picturization – Shah's favourite word – had finished with her. 'What sort of animals are they?'

'Hot-blooded,' Hero answered, making a joke of it because he saw she was upset.

'Cold-blooded,' I ventured.

'You!' she turned on me. 'You said: *You have to be* good.' She mimicked my voice. I was surprised to hear how mealy-mouthed I sounded.

'I said you have to be ready, also.'

'What ready! Ready for anything that creep wants?'

'Or the audience wants.'

'Bullshit! They want all that because creeps like him have spoilt them.'

She was right, so I said only what I'd meant to earlier.

'You were good, anyway.'

'Damn good,' Hero put in.

'What's the point,' she raged, 'if he cuts out all the good bits?'

He did, did B.B. Shah. The basket-weave scene was one of the first casualties.

'Not enough happening,' he said. 'Too flat.'

And it wasn't just the cuts – if anything he increased
104

her footage – it was what he added on. Every addition diminished her, that is, diminished Laxmi, while UD became the audience's sweetheart. The marvel was that her performance survived the distortions, though that was not what made her popular. It was like being applauded for your slips while your catches went unnoticed. Bit by bit he subdued her – to Hero, as it happened – till at the end her efforts and those of the sweepers she represented were dissolved in a dream of rescue, the lucky lottery of her social uplift by the debonair drunk – whose reform now becomes her life's mission. Unbeknownst to me – the screenwriter – an uncle turns up who proves she's not really a sweeperess at all. And so there was a marriage after all, a wedding at the end with orchestra and fireworks and a reception at the Taj and the Gateway blocked off again for a dance sequence by the sweepers and sweeperesses of Bombay.

Two hundred brooms were purchased for the scene and many metres of calico, green and saffron for the women and white for the men. Draped in the colours of the national flag, they danced in the shadow of the filmi gate another set of masters built to welcome a king-emperor. They danced with abandon, their backs to the sea. The men clacked their broomsticks like staves in mock battle, the women rode theirs like cock-horses. Now the stick end was waved in the air, now the business end; now they beat the handles on the paving stones, now they twirled the brooms in the air and ran right and left in interweaving skeins to the banter of tannery drums. They leapt into the air, lay flat upon the ground, penetrated broomstick tunnels, rode broomstick palanquins. Their brooms were flowers, javelins, guitars, but never, for the moment, brooms.

Fair enough, but why a wedding?

'A fitting farewell,' B.B. Shah beamed, sneaking into his own movie as the uncle. Her former comrades had come to say goodbye to Laxmi who though no longer one of them by blood or circumstance came down and danced (without a broom) at their head. Hero, my master, was obliged to join her and there they capered, he high-kicking in white seersucker flares, she prancing in gold hotpants, so that as the fireworks went up and the nightsky exploded with saffron-white-and-green broom-sticks, the wedding guests turned to one another and asked with sticky smiles: was not the bride a piece of gold?

They were married, without fireworks, in real life not long after. Nature and Society: deuce. She had in fact been sharing his house for some time, so the wedding could hardly warrant see-rious dhoom-dhaam. His fat and fair (and now ageing) mother came up to Bombay on her first flight ever which she described to UD's parents with such glee that the interior decorator forgot her airs and gave herself up to whinnies of toothy laughter that awoke in her husband the most sombre reflections on married life. He was only grateful that the postman was too dead by twenty years to be present. Rangamma, now comfort-ably remarried herself, to the proprietor of the jupiter Cycle Works, babbled to the press of how faithfully her son supported her – and a whole string of orphanages in Kizhanadu.

The press, in a honeymoon cycle, reported all, and more; the orphans multiplied, their tear-stained faces only half prepared to grace throwaway paper-bags, the fate of filmi magazines in every corner of the land. Ranga was their darling, their black-eyed bull again; the treacle began to ooze once more. Golgappa apart – he would never forget that fat lip, and his pen might have served a Nicobarese for a poisoned dart – the Dixits and Fonsecas sheathed their claws and set up a purring of such naus-eous persistence that *any* fate, I felt, was preferable to that of Forgiven Hero. They rubbed themselves up against the chair he sat on; they got between his legs; they rolled over for him and nosed any given flank; they padded prissily away, then turned with a coyness loathsome to behold, and smirking horribly, made vicarious little dabs at some pillar or plant. They nuzzled his two-tone shoes, covered his ankles with uncalled for love-bites and yowled till every follicle in my master's legs revolted at their gratuitous frottage. Felix Fonseca was, I think, the worst. His sudden presence, his sidling line, the ingratiating jokes he left behind him like a spoor, would irk my master out of all patience.

'God damn it, Zero,' he said one day. 'Don't these buggers have any pride?'

I could have said no – it wasn't a real question – but something made me take him up. I said: 'Yes, boss. They do.'

'Then?'

'You are their pride, boss.'

He absorbed this for a moment.

'So what do they have left?'

'Nothing, boss. *You* make them something. You're their reason for living.'

'They love me so much?'

'They don't love you, boss. They love what they've given you.'

He grew impatient. 'Don't give me this phoos-phaas, yaar. Hate I can understand. Take Nero. He hates my guts. He'd like to kill me, I know.'

This was not paranoia. I'd heard Nero had bought himself a gun – a handgun, so he wasn't after partridge.

'But these guys...' His voice trailed off in scorn as he switched back. 'What the hell do they want?'

'They want you alive, boss.'

'What, forever and ever?'

'Till they find someone else – to fatten up.'

I spoke the last bit under my breath but he picked it up.

'*I* feed *them!*'he cried, exasperated. 'They're the ones

107

who get fat, anyway.' He looked down at the figure he'd kept remarkably well in a world of chubby boys. He thumbed his chest. 'I give them something to write about. Without me they'd have nothing to say.'

'They *have* nothing to say.'

He snorted bitterly. 'Then it must be my fault.'

'Or mine,' I almost said, but I had already said too much. Besides, I may (or may not) have been responsible but that didn't mean I wasn't in his thrall as much as any Fonseca or for that matter any front-row loafer at the Hind Talkies.

The fact was he had, like Betelgeuse, presence. Massive presence, which did attract by some cosmic gravity, or maybe simple mathematics, people who were nothing. I should know. I, Zero, felt myself elevated from a cipher in his company. I became whole for that duration, took on his value, was assigned a function. We may between us have staged a coup in Bollywood, but he was its first officer, its first-magnitude star. He was Number 1. His aura was undeniable – even without the hump. People's faces, knotted by the daily struggle, opened up miraculously at a chance glimpse of him. I saw this happen again and again. He was their common weal and they would have brought him their daughters as small recompense for that gift of presence. (And perchance for pelf.) I speak of men; women, or that number struck by the hump, threw marigolds at his feet and themselves under his juggernaut wheels (he had two Mercedes now.) There were some who might have fought their daughters for the privilege.

UD, who knew him, and was now his wife, understood the fuss but didn't feel obliged to join. She put away the hot-pants and talked of joining serious cinema but I could see her settling down to a life of cards and coffee-tables, yoga and creative cookery. She might do a bit of modelling on the side – we would see her wrapped in luxury towels

– or become an interpreter to passing Latins. There might even be, to while away the long afternoons when Ranga was prancing on one set or another, or on location in the Andamans, a Latin lover. Latched onto Number 1, she felt the need for personal striving slip away. She had run that race, or was it gauntlet, and would now happily let it be run by proxy. Her movie career was just a fling; that was not the real UD, or should I say, Shiraz. There was no need now to undergo fresh humiliations in chains or ropes or wet saris. Let them strip some other woman if they must, she said, and stopped to ask herself whether by *them* she didn't mean *him*.

Who called the shots in that marriage, I still don't know. She may have seen the hump at the start (that is, before, at my place) but marriage is a long lesson in sleepwalking, and she was a good sleeper. She lost sight of the hump anyway, or turned a blind eye to it, because later on she denied its existence when a fair fraction of Indian womanhood would have sworn otherwise. At any rate she was not in awe of him like those millions of sisters who were her natural or notional rivals, those fantasists who darkly hoped to see him do what they would never pay for, or those less fastidious men who paid to see him do what they could never hope to.

She (and the shifty Francis) cooked him his favourite dishes – sambar, idli, loki kofta, polished rice and coconut chutney – bought him those potent yellow finger-bananas which she had come to like herself, and occasionally they ate out, usually at the Hankow because it was dark and expensive and you could get a decent vegetarian meal. Not that she gave up her fish patia and mutton dhansak – and he was liberal enough to pass the dish when they had guests. She accompanied him to mahurats for luck, attended the annual awards; she even turned up on the nearer sets, but there were no tiffin-carriers of alu paratha and chilly-bins of home-made ice-cream. And when he came home from a hard day's work (unlike outsiders, she knew acting was work) she might massage his back. So she was entitled to an opinion on the hump.

For his part he took her opinion seriously and also her advice on gesture and delivery. He flipped through her books, not looking for letters but because he felt he must keep up with the arts – and she had been to university the proper way. At night they might play a round of rummy on the heart-shaped bed, and in the morning he would submit to a yoga lesson delivered with the zeal of the convert. He even learnt a word or two of Spanish to please her (which, apart from Pedro's name, was more than I ever did) and found he had not lost his gift of tongues. He brought her pearls from the Andamans, Kashmiri shawls, bidri jewel-boxes, Sikkimese brocade.

And he admired her exquisite body with the eye, alas, of a connoisseur.

It was not for nothing that Golgappa had begun to speak of Ranga the colourful, as Rangila, the concupiscent. From Preeti Juneja on down, he'd covered every leading lady (who'd let him) in the business, and worked his way down through supporting actress and promising newcomer to cabaret artiste and vamp. Put that way it sounds methodical, even mechanical, but from all contemporary reports (my confidante Rati Ganguli's in particular, and she was no mean voluptuary herself) the earth moved every time and Ranga's rapture shook the skies.

BHOOAN, he went. BHOOOANNNNN!

He would confess his pleasure to me quite innocently if we chanced to pass one of his ladies, and the transparent delight of that ecstasy revisited convinced me he wasn't crowing. Certainly he never thought of them as conquests: they were rather a garland of flowers – and then several garlands – hung by destiny about his neck and if he could have reached past the dewlap he would have gobbled them up again. I have my own seigneurage theory and I feel that certain men (and women) are set apart for certain excesses, and that is that. But the world will ever look upon them with a jaundiced eye.

Will ever look! Rejoice the soul of Plumbum!

I blame the hump, though blame is too strong a word. I don't know who or what UD blamed – I hope not me. But when Golgappa printed a nursery rhyme under Hero's photograph which went:

> *Twinkle, twinkle, megastar,*
> *How I wonder what you are!*
> *Up above the world so bright,*
> *Is it wifey's turn tonight?*

She was furious. She wouldn't speak to him for days and finally left the clipping under his razor where Francis wouldn't see it. Discovered, he was upset too. He came to see me, heavily disguised.

I was still in the room on Madame Cama Road; there were family debts to pay off. When I opened the door I got a fright.

'Zero,' he said, removing, one by one, the dark gogs I once lent him, the guava pink turban, and the bushy beard.

'Baas!'

Hero! Hero! Pedro sang from his cage till I put a table-cloth over him.

'Zero, I'm in trouble.'

I looked again at the megastar's disguise.

'Police, baas?'

He stretched me a humourless smile. 'If it was only that. You got a cigarette?'

I gave him one and lit it for him. This was new. It was dinner-time and I despaired of my buns which lay exposed in the centre of the table. He took a few drags

111

and then, blowing the smoke out of his nostrils, said: 'UD.'

My blood ran cold. 'You haven't – ?' I had a sudden vision of her lying very still.

'Relax, yaar,' he said. 'Here.' He unbuttoned his shirt-pocket and took out the cutting. 'Have a look at this.' He handled it like a scorpion. I read the nursery rhyme; the sting in the tail made me gasp. It must have hurt her much more.

'So,' he said.

I said nothing. I would not have treated her so, but that was purely hypothetical now. She'd chosen him, made her bed as it were; if she had it to herself most nights, well that was how it was. I didn't blame him either. Saddled with a hump, what would I have done?

He took my silence for reproof.

'I can't help it, Zero,' he pleaded.

'I know, boss.'

'I mean – it just comes over me.'

I'd just been reading about the man in Kenya, or was it Wisconsin, who couldn't help eating his guests, and serving the leftovers to the next guest. After all, these things happen. I could never understand Plumbum's Pauline dictum about cutting off what offends you. Cut off a hump?

'Look. What would you do in my place?'

'Same thing boss, probably.'

I was suddenly overcome by a desire to be with UD, to stroke and comfort her.

'She hates me now,' he said, self-pity welling up.

I knew she didn't and wouldn't. But she would hate the position she'd been put in by him. He might be hardened to the press now in his turn, but she was still soft and vulnerable, my UD.

'Let me catch that bastard Golgappa. I'll roast his bloody kidneys on a skewer.'

This was decidedly non-veg. I grew alarmed and said: 'He's not worth your attention, boss. He's just a bloated windbag. He's nothing.'

He stood up. 'He's less than nothing, the bloody Gujju. I'll make mincemeat of him. I'll feed him to the crows.'

Hero Wroth.

'I mean,' he went on, 'let him be a man. Let him attack me. What the hell do I care? But why does he have to bring her into it?'

He was pacing from the window to the door and back. My table stood in the way so he had to make a little detour each time.

'I mean, what sort of guys are these?' He stopped at the table and picked up a bun. It disappeared past those soft dark lips. I thought irrelevantly of those tight-lipped foreign heroes and shuddered inwardly; suddenly I was glad we had him, pleased for the industry. But there was still the Golgappa business.

'Blackmail the bugger,' I said on sudden inspiration. 'He's the biggest lech in town.' Well, almost. 'His wife thinks he goes down to Kalba Devi for second-hand books.'

He looked at me with new respect, and I saw his henchmen striking out purposefully. Golgappa would be sorry he'd turned from prose to verse. He'd be so thoroughly exposed, his moneyed wife would walk out on him and leave him to survive on his tawdry brand of journalism. His love for Ranga would not increase thereby, but living in a glass house he should have known better than to rock the boat – if I may quote. His former colleagues, scenting blood, would turn on him with their pitiless jungle hatred of failure. *Reel-Life Revenge* headed Kitty Dixit's next column. *A classic case*, said Felix Fonseca, *of the sink calling the bathtub white*. But his racial ironies were lost on a readership who thought Ranga handsome in spite of, not because of, his colour. So Hero

113

would win on points, but at the cost of adding another to his list of mortal enemies.

And Golgappa was certainly present on my master's last night.

When we ended our confabulation Ranga looked as if a burden had been lifted from his shoulders. I'd got off lightly too – there were still two buns left – but the relief was plainly his. It wasn't the blackmail idea, though that was pretty much a *fait accompli*; it was the last few words of advice that made the difference.

'What am I going to do, Zero?' he said, remembering UD. He'd been so busy plotting Golgappa's comeuppance he'd forgotten about her until he started to put his disguise back on. 'I mean, what if it comes over me again? I'm like those full-moon guys.'

I glanced nervously at my square of nightsky. 'Lycanthropes?' I said.

'Like anthropes,' he agreed, swinging the beard gently. 'What to do?'

The sky was a reassuring black, peppered with bright stars.

'Work, boss,' I said. ' Work.'

He heard me all right, because the beard stopped swinging, but he didn't say anything. I knew him well enough to understand that silence meant a point taken. He sat on for a few moments, then stood up suddenly and looped the beard round his head. Then he put on the turban and picked up the dark glasses – my dark gogs – and his car keys.

'Zero – ' he said, 'your – '

For a moment I thought he'd remembered about the glasses, but he put them back on and said: 'You're OK, you know,' and turned to go.

I felt like Miss d'Mello's pet, standing there before the class (at St Aloysius's, before the Silver Spoon) my face on fire. Some return, I felt, was due for the glow in my heart.

'You're not hungry or anything?' I called after him, and added lamely: 'I mean, it's late.'

'That's true,' he said, stopping. 'There won't be any dinner waiting for me tonight, that's for sure.' His eyes found the plate of buns. 'I'll take one of these to chew in the car.'

'Take both, boss.'

He hesitated. 'You *sure*?'

'Baas!'

Then we went down in the tea-bag and I waved him off. He'd come in the old Fiat, just in case.

Penance

He took me seriously about the work. True, they were ready for him with scripts and contracts, white money and black (*Number 1* and *Number 2* in the old days), open datings and flexible schedules, but these were simply grist to the awesome mill that had begun to turn in him. He signed anything that spelt work, anything to distract him from the hump. Yoked to that private mill, he seemed indifferent to the weight of those gigantic quern-stones. Round and round I watched him go, grinding his desire, pulling with a fury, producers and publicists applauded but never understood.

In some lights he seemed to me a sage of old, practising the fiercest of austerities in the forest, intent on wresting from the gods a potent boon. Quite what the boon was he wasn't sure himself, but for the moment the penance was enough.

Austerity and boon: that immemorial dream of misfits under a harsh sun! Unbridled licence, then the anxious lacing up, then the fit reward, and so on from age to age:

urgent self-denial paying dividends of limitless self-fulfilment. Well, there are pathologies of comfort too, look abroad. And who am I to cavil, spinning my webs in patient solitude? Have I not dreamed of slaying the wicked Asuras, of conquering the gods in heaven? Ah, Zero! low and cunning pariah, to sell your master short!

He stood six-foot-one (if you recall) so the gauboy roles were his by right. Then there were the mythologicals (for which he nipped back down to Madras) recalling a time when men were strapping men, if not hulking gods, roles tailor-made for him. Romances, historicals, musicals, Tarzan: there wasn't a genre where that head-and-shoulders advantage didn't pay. The cop, the corporal, the villager, the king, all gained a cubit by his casting. And there was, associated with his height and bulk and looks, that presence I spoke of. But he might have been bereft of all these qualities and still had his pick of roles because he could act – the virtue, you would think, that becomes the actor most.

Alas for theory! So many actors of that sorry era were either lookers or dancers or gesticulators or (recall a certain peasant) simply musclemen that the word *actor* fell into neglect. Quite reasonably, they preferred *star*. Shine they could, these little lights, but acting was beyond them, and here was my master, willing and able – and all those other things besides. Not surprisingly then (except to the occluded stars) the scripts came to him first; what he left they took.

Was there a mythological he couldn't fit in? K.G. Iyer grabbed it and was grateful. This eastern stetson on Kaddoo Kumar's head? There by the grace of Ranga's schedule. Cyrus Amrohliwala's briefly famous don? My master let it go because the stars, his stars, were wrong. Did I mention his superstitiousness? I did. White flowers, never red, later on. Curious in an amateur astronomer (did I mention that?) but, yes, the seeds of superstition

117

were there. And I'm damned if Cyrus didn't break his back on the set of *Kane Ka Kalank* (The Mark of Cain), scripted by the notorious Dippy Kainthola.

He worked three shifts a day, six days a week. Thursdays he took off, and there was a bloodstone he wore that had something to do with it, but apart from that day, which was UD's, he was married to his job. At any given time he might have forty films on hand; there was a stage when he touched fifty and Guppy Agarwal staunch celebrant of quantity, approached the *Guinness Book of Records*. How he kept the lines apart from set to set I don't know. Not that it really mattered if they crossed over: he was taking on scripts from any hack who wandered by. I will say that he gave my own scripts, *Khoj* (Quest) for instance, in which he carried a lamp through Delhi in search of an honest man, the special care they deserved, but for the rest it was a matter of cramming in the back seat of either the white or the black Mercedes as he was driven from studio to studio across town. He must have sounded to his driver, and I daresay felt himself, like a radio station flicked from station to station by some idle twiddler.

STAR director may intercut the shuttling Mercedes with UD stationary in her living-room, her face lit by the blue dial light of a Japanese receiver. She sits expressionless and still, her only movement a finger which comes up like slow clockwork to spin the heavy chrome tuning knob. Once, by a freak chance, or synchronicity, the needle conjures up a di-laag: it is his voice, from Khabardar, *and her eyes light up momentarily as if they recognized some familiar strain, but the finger, moving independently, comes up and falls again.*

My master's voice deserves a line or two. There was prime bull in it, black velvet bull, as if the dewlap, which trembled when he spoke, contributed its share. It came out effortlessly; the deep dark cords might have been
118

perpetually vibrating in his throat, so gently did they release their silken freight of sound. That voice comforted the sick, gave succour to the dying, caressed his leading ladies, wrapped villains in a mist of fear. He could pitch it, place it with uncanny skill. He'd even taught himself ventriloquism, and once volunteered to teach Pedro after scaring the pants off me. ('How's UD?' I asked, and Pedro answered: *Oh, a bit down today*, while Ranga looked blandly at him.) He seldom raised his voice. When he did shout, at cattle for instance, as in the curry western *Gauboy*, it came out as a bellow: BHOOAN! which at the top – BHOOANNKR! – threatened to break, endangering his dignity. So he rarely shouted, or did so by proxy.

There was something else he did in this way, that is, had done for him, and I hope I will not be misunderstood when I say that here I outshone my master. It is of singing I speak. (*I speak of singing*, Plumbum.) It's a gift, to be sure; I claim no credit. Some have it, some don't. My master didn't. So when the time came, as it did five or six times in the course of a movie, to gird up his loins and sing, he girded up his loins and Akhtar Ali sang. Or Nishikant Bannerji sang. Or, once, I did. Recall 'Tukda Tukda Mera Dil' (My Broken Heart.) He simply mouthed the words; my voice flooded hall and screen with sweetness, and in that rare union my master's voice was mine.

He did his stunts himself, though. Mostly, the chubby boys got stunt men and stand-ins, oddly lean, to do the dirty work, the jumping off horses, the rolling downhill, the leap into the moat from some kerosene inferno. Not my master. He had, after all, been blasted ninety times from a circus cannon. Was there a branch to hang from, just clear of the snapping crocodiles? My master, not a hired hand, hung there. Was there a rope to swing from, sword in hand? Behold Hero fencing. In *Rocky VI* neither he nor the Number 2 Villain pulled punches. (It was Captain Memo, still slogging for Number 1 and now with

119

further cause for grievance, for while Hero had a second Mercedes, he, Memo, still rode on two wheels, a model whose name no longer beckoned but rather chafed unbearably every time he kicked to life his Hero Honda.)

The knockout in *Rocky VI* was saved for Number 1 Villain Nero. Here again my master's pursuit of authenticity was evident in every punch, but it got him into trouble. He took his part so seriously he knocked out Nero cold at every take – and the director, faithful to his own pursuit, required six. Each time Hero was the first with water, towel, apologies of such profusion that Nero, sensing a ridicule that wasn't there, found his cup of hatred full. 'Next time,' he spluttered, 'next time.' And although the director finally declared himself satisfied, there *was* another time, on another set.

Meantime Hero took on still more work to douse the hump. It was his busiest period but not his best. To tell the truth, his best films were behind him. I won't say he overreached himself; had the scripts been right who knows what heights he might have scaled? But I simply could not keep up, and there were scores of lesser talents purveying tripe. Already he was in danger of repeating himself. But – no: *and* – he couldn't put a foot wrong. For repetition was precisely what his audience wanted. So it was also the period of his greatest popularity. *Rocky VII*! the front-row loafers howled – and they meant it.

I will say that even at the height of his popularity he never fancied himself. Perhaps he didn't need to. So much adulation carries a man past pride, or will turn a certain sort of head and not another. Ranga's was that other, bowed by nature, the eyes sleepy and introspective, the jaw, whatever its other merits, designed principally for rumination. The films he starred in might owe their success entirely to him – the ones he passed up flopped as often as not – but he never behaved as if they did, or as if he knew they did. There were no star-turn tantrums

120

on the set, no delays or interference; there was instead a humility which struck most people as odd and some as insincere. I feel qualified to deny the latter charge. Insincerity was not one of his failings: insecurity was.

It may have had to do with the pace he set himself; also a consciousness that not all his work was worthy of him. He was certainly aware of how his schedule fragmented the man called Ranga, and he often remarked how incidental his contribution to a movie seemed.

'I just turn up on the sets, spout my lines, swing from that rope and – *sataak!* – I'm on the next set.'

'You're going too fast, boss.'

He didn't hear me.

'It's like I keep finding smaller and smaller pieces of Ranga.'

'Rushes, boss. Too much rushing.'

'I mean, sometimes I look out of the window of the car and I see myself – hundred feet high – looking back at me.'

He may have been thinking of that huge plywood cut-out for *Khoj* which stood for 50 Golden Weeks over Marine Drive at Chowpatty Beach. (*Cowpatty Beach*, UD called it, but it was horse – and human – dung.)

'And it's damn strange, because when I see it I don't feel big. I feel – not small – I don't know how to say – empty – like *nothing*.'

'Nothing wrong with that, boss.'

'You know, you feel like, I mean, light—and lighter and lighter, and emptier and emptier – and – oh, hell – '

The big black eyes glistened as he spoke and a lucid drop, not glycerine, threatened to run over.

'What the hell, Zero, what the *hell* – '

His voice trailed off.

'Baas, baas.'

Next I heard they'd moved into their new Carlton Correa mansion at Juhu. It was rumoured to have solid gold fittings in the bathroom and a bath hollowed out of a block of Italian marble. Not true, I discovered on my first visit, expecting *nero antico*, but there was a jade jacuzzi. There were air-conditioners in every room, including the huge toilets. A bar half as long as Marine Drive, with Maserati and Rolls-Royce model ashtrays jockeying on rosewood, and all the Scotch that Scotland could distil. The paintings, not his cup of tea, spoke interior decor – Veenu 'Six Lakhs' Nautiyal's, I believe – here rhyming with a Persian rug, there capping wittily a vase. One or two signatures of note in UD's boudoir, tucked away from instrusive eyes, brought home to me the gulf between us, though she invited me to make myself at home, take off my shoes. Her own were already off, fallen under the bed with – I noticed – a hundred others. Joy did heady battle with Poison on her duchesse and in my head; not a trace of eau-de-cologne.

UD, I said, *I'm sorry, Shiraz, O my God, please, no, I can't, I mustn't, I have two scripts overdue, for him.*

'Him!' she hissed, retracting her civet claws, and then the danger passed and we stood together trembling before a hellish red-and-black Hassan called 'Boredom II'.

'It was almost better when he was sleeping around,' she said, weeping softly.

'He's tired.'

'Tired! He's worn out. And over *what*! The shit they load on him, and he just puts his head down and takes it. That's what makes me want to scream.'

On the way out I peeped into their bedroom. No steel almirahs now. And they'd disposed of the heart, I noticed. In its place stood a mammoth four-poster with net curtains and scalloped bunches of little gathered frills. The general impression was one of gauzy heaven anchored to a solid foundation below, whether on earth or further down I couldn't tell.

I pictured (*star may picturize*) them lying there at night, his wanderings done, her waitings over. Side by side they lie, the stars, or the megastar and the ex-star, two heavenly bodies, the dark by some paradox of relativity outshining the bright, he expanding, growing ever lighter and more rarefied, she growing heavier and contracting to a point of unimaginable density. A wall of unknowing has grown up between them so each is compelled to explore in the long cold air-conditioned hours those infinite spaces of solitude and unbeing which the night discloses. Then the first ray of sunlight comes up over Back Bay and the park with its dewy hedges clipped into peacocks, and my master yawns and stretches and my mistress freezes, dissembling sleep.

Off he rides to the sets of *Kabootarbaaz Ka Khwaab* (The Pigeon Fancier's Reverie), *Khatra-e-Kashmir* (North By Northwest), or *Khichdi Khoon Ki* (Black Pudding), contributing incidentally his share to higher learning. (There was I understand a mass-culture thesis underway at Bombay University which examined the incidence of Ks in his titles. Was it a return to the Origin, a para-foetal nostalgia for the cape of capes, Kanyakumari, cape of his conception? Or was there some deeper meaning?)

And as if the work they made for him were not enough, Hero commissioned two scripts himself: *Postman*, an act of homage to his father, and *Kanyakumari* (Cape Comorin) for his mother. The first he saw through in ten weeks; the second was to be more ambitious. He got Guppy Agarwal to arrange the finance for it, and every day the project grew. By the end of the month it was to be nothing short of a summing up of Mother India viewed from her sacred tip; all motherhood, all womanhood, all sanctity would come within its purview. Here was a glimpse of the dharmavision of the future captured for the moment by the Karmascope of his coffee-house fantasies.

Close on a crore of rupees was mobilized for the epic, and not one of those ten million was his own. He took

123

out a copyright on the word *Karmavision* which he proposed to append to every poster and publicity still, announcing the birth of a new celluloid genre. True, it was akin to the old this-scopes and that-visions already in existence, but here was something qualitatively different: the very projection at the finish would be in three tiers, not necessarily congruent, to signify the transmuting of all that was base (at Mother India's feet) into a roseate aura around her head. Mother India was, of course, to be Rangamma, the fat and fair and grey and now slightly bent mother who brought him into this wanting world, the instrument of its cleansing.

It wasn't my script so I must leash my jaded ironies. Sets of Babylonian proportions were erected on an empty lot in Kanyakumari (for some months guests in Kerala House lost their famous sea-view); the mock city did much to revive a flagging industry in plaster of Paris. The fortunes of local artisans and labourers, merchants, truckers and procurers spurted. Japanese know-how was imported for the triple-decker effect, and Vatican collaboration sought on the manufacture of haloes which though alien were not unassimilable to Indian hagiography.

And then, the sets in place, Rangamma rehearsed and ready with her one but crucial line (*Om*), UD put her foot down.

'Movies or me,' she served her placid ultimatum.

It was succinctly put. And to my master's everlasting credit, he chose her.

Fact, reliable standby, proved juicier than fiction. Here was a man who would give up a kingdom for his wife. The emotion generated by that single resolve – indeed by the choice before him – shook the country to its foundations. Mother – Mother India, no less – or wife? Mata or Sita?

Letters poured in, urging the one course or the other. By and large the split was generational: older women took

Rangamma's side, younger ones UD's. But gender played a part too. Taken together, women tended to favour UD, while men as a whole ran to Rangamma. And there were other splits too: between politicians (pro-Rangamma) and the masses (pro-UD); between industrialists (Rangamma) and workers (UD); between postmen (Rangamma) and deliverees (UD); and even between coffee-drinkers (UD) and tea-drinkers (Rangamma). Sanskrit scholars quoted ancient texts; illiterate pundits quoted precedent; newspaper editors banged the national-interest drum; sociologists droned on of cross-cutting cleavages; the thesis writer got his lectureship.

But Ranga had made up his mind.

Hero Standfast.

When he announced his decision to the press, tears sprang from scribal eyes long turned to glass. When the press announced it to the world, the flood-waters passed the *Suryanamaskar* mark. One young man in Hyderabad hanged himself, and hospitals across the country were busy sewing up slashed wrists. Yet strangely, when it came to the written word, UD's hate mail ran two to one with sympathy letters (one full of Ks) for Hero. More than one marriage came to grief on those filmi shoals. But it was the children of Kanyakumari who shamed their parents and defused the issue. They turned the would-be set into a fairground where they romped and played their tender murderous games. And then, one by one, the plaster pillars, cornices and fountains were pilfered by passersby till all the homes roundabout filled up with works of genial monstrosity. And gradually the management of Kerala House got back their sea.

If there was one of Mother India's sons especially aggrieved in the whole affair, it was Guppy Agarwal. Two lakhs out of pocket, he stormed and pleaded, threatened action, threatened tax blackmail, and finally, in badly camouflaged handwriting, threatened Hero's life.

Hero would not be moved. By some miracle he had not signed a contract.

'Tax-shax,' he grunted. The tax inspector liked Scotch and five-star meals, preferably with Flora Fountain on the floor, and toys for the children afterwards, a family man.

'But this is serious, boss,' I said, nodding at the letter.

He folded it up and put it in my pocket.

'Keep it,' he said. 'As evidence when I'm gone.'

Did he sense an early death all along? Was the brave talk standard filmi swagger? Or was it simply the levity with which each of us conventionally defies an extinction we cannot comprehend?

Rangamma retired peeved to her home behind the jupiter Cycle Works, a graceful enough exit for someone who hadn't quite made an entrance. She didn't, couldn't blame her son, really; it was that, that creature's doing. But secretly she felt a twinge of admiration for – and was it fear of? – the one woman to tame her son's hump.

So what can have been her confusion when, less than a year into their joint retirement, her daughter-in-law made of Ranga a curious request: UD wanted Hero to make, with her, one last movie!

It was my *Neta Harishchandra*.

Yes, Neta, leader, not *Raja* Harishchandra.

You may have heard (you probably haven't) of *Raja Harishchandra*. 1910, I think, I'm not sure. 1914? Our first feature movie, anyway. There can't be many alive today who saw it on its first release. 1912?

Good King Harishchandra cannot tell a lie. With Queen Taramati he runs a just kingdom, true to himself and to the old laws. Now, Sage Vishwamitra, whose penances have made him a power, is not convinced by the king's untried goodness. *This man's truth – everyman's truth –* he tells his forest colleague, Sage Vashishta, *will buckle under pressure. Truth*, counters Sage Vashishta, *is made of sterner metal; do your worst and see*. Vishwamitra does, and Hero

126

Harishchandra's ordeal begins. He loses his throne, his son, his caste, is reduced to a grave-digger. Finally he steels himself to execute his cherished queen falsely accused of murder – when, lo: the heavens open and Shiva intervenes. All is made good, and Truth stands vindicated.

1908?

Notice Truth, overarching Truth, in fact nowhere in serious jeopardy. It is small-t truth, the hero's truth, which is tested in the name of Truth. Notice too, Vishwamitra is not proved wrong – even when the hero is proved right. As exemplar, Harishchandra is faultless; but so is Vishwamitra. No *either/or* here. The invisible hand of *both/and*, that nice quibble of lax civics and quantum physics, is at work softening the blow for mortals like you and me. Truth is all very well for heroes, but in real life, ordinary life, you and I need a little extra. We still need Vishwamitra to give us that edge, that added whiteness which no other powder, not even Vashishta's, can give. At best we need *both* Vishwamitra *and* Vashishta. In the face of Necessity, Man needs that supernatural rescue or his small truth will be overwhelmed. Best meet hateful necessity halfway – in penance: then behold the reward! Suffering does not ennoble; it builds not character but expectation. Truth in suffering, your idealist cake, is fine; but pragmatism says ritualize your suffering and you can eat it too. Do not underestimate rites. Hero might have saved himself much pain if he had rited his wrongs. In the empty abstract universe of Truth, Harishchandra still needed divine intervention. How much more, I hear Vishwamitra chuckling, do you (and I) in this foetid pit under the sky!

Thus the universal swallows up the local.

Thus the people, such the king.

My *Neta Harishchandra* didn't try to meddle too much with the original story beyond bringing it up to date, like

127

those *Julius Caesars* in Nazi uniforms or *Shilappadikaram* in drag. But as usual it was transformed along the way.

In the script two Bombay rag-and-bone men, Kabadiwala Vishwamitra and Kabadiwala Vashishta, sage avatars, come cycling down a suburban road one behind the other, calling *Raddi! Raddi!* to right and left. *Trash!* they call, *Junk! Your tins, bottles, old newspapers!* They dismount in the shade of a hoarding and rest a while, discussing their new leader, Neta Harishchandra. Leader Harishchandra, thug-turned-politician, represents Andheri, the dark constituency. Can he be made to tell the truth? *I can blackmail him into telling the truth*, Vishwamitra says. *Here is an incriminating document I found among his old newspapers. Fat chance*, scoffs Kabadiwala Vashishta. *He is a congenital liar, this Harishchandra, committed to lies. The truth will not pass his lips.* Off goes Vishwamitra, but is foiled at every turn. Harishchandra lies to save his son's skin and his own, to save his job, his caste. Finally, after his wife has slept with a judge to get him off a murder charge, he lies to implicate her in his own stead. Stupefied by her husband's duplicity, she commits suicide, thus convicting herself and doubly acquitting her husband. But Neta Harishchandra, horrified by what he has done, confesses all, shocked into truth by his wife's death. *Is his truth less valuable than Raja Harishchandra's?* Vishwamitra asks Vashishta. *No, but then, what good is this Truth business?* Vashishta wants to know as they cycle away, their sacks, full to bursting, spilling tins, bottles, newspapers.

That was my script. The actual film turned out a little different. Producer and director, lensman, mock-up, gaffer, lights, the very clapper-boy, chipped away at the original until its resemblance to the finished product would have challenged a Prague structuralist.

Actor Harishchandra cannot tell a lie. With his beloved wife Taramati, sometime Number 1 Heroine, he lives the good life on the Bombay cocktail circuit: discotheques, night-clubs, charity shows, premières. One night they return to find their only son has been kidnapped – by a gang of thugs whose leader, Captain Memo, is in jail. It is not Actor Harishchandra's first brush with these hoodlums: a year ago (STAR *may flashback*) he was instrumental in Captain Memo's jailing. Retract that testimony, comes Memo's message from jail, and my men will release your son. But Actor Harishchandra cannot tell a lie, and his son is killed. He bows to his fate.

A year later the tax inspector knocks at his door. Again Actor Harishchandra cannot tell a lie: yes, there is thirty lakhs in black money in that brass telephone over there with the three monkeys that see no evil, hear no evil, speak no evil. In the biggest scandal to shake Bollywood in years, he goes to prison.

While he is in there, his wife Taramati resists the advances of the wicked Chief Minister, who offers to get her husband out. Rebuffed, the frustrated Number 1 Villain (Nero) frames Taramati in an illicit affair with a spy in the shape of the Pakistani consul (Nero, with a moustache.)

Meanwhile Hero is released on good behaviour, but finds the nation at war with Pakistan, again. Forced to choose between his wife's apparent lie and his country's manifest truth, he prepares to divorce Taramati even though he knows she will commit suicide. But just before he signs the fateful document an ascetic with a trident wanders in and reveals the truth – his wife is faithful the son didn't die, the tax business was a bad dream; in fact, Harry, there is now *sixty* lakhs in the brass telephone. To defeat this arch-villain's lie, says Shiva (for it is he, down from Mount Kailash), you must enter politics yourself. Actor Harishchandra does so and is elected. The party high command appoint him Chief Minister in Nero's stead and in the last scene he takes the oath of office.

You *see*? says Cadre Vashishta to Cadre Vishwamitra in

the audience for the swearing-in. What do you mean do *I* see! hisses Vishwamitra in a stage whisper.

What neither of them sees, till it is too late, is that the ex-Chief Minister rushes in, whips out a pistol, and shoots Actor-turned-Neta Harishchandra at point-blank range.

A humdrum potboiler, you say, yawning, and I, my hands pretty much washed of it, hasten to agree. But then the fate of the film and the fate of the real-life hero quite overshadowed that of Actor Harishchandra.

After the horrible accident the film went into hibernation. A richly deserved obscurity, no doubt (I think sometimes of the millions of potent ghostly frames suspended for years in the black limbo of those cans), and yet when finally released, it did Hero more good than my own original script might have done, as you will see.

I said *accident*, but of course nothing could be further from the truth. It was just our way of talking of it because to call it by its real name was intolerable. What happened was this.

And by the way, I had a grandstand view of it. In the final scene, which by sheer coincidence was also the last we shot, I was positioned on stage at a slight elevation above the two Chief Ministers, the outgoing and the incoming, Nero and Hero – although *inrushing* would better describe the former. I had nothing to do except smile benignly and shake my dreadlocks or my trident from time to time. Yes, I wangled the part of Shiva, my last filmi role too.

It wasn't Nero's first attempt – nor was his the only attempt. Captain Memo tried too.

Once early in the shooting I saw – and no one else did – Captain Memo sprinkle a little powder on Ranga's fruit salad just before the lunch break. It was done in a flash, very deftly. Everybody knew Ranga's plate, a platter, rather, made of brushed silver, generously heaped by one of his minions. Memo's choice of substance was good because there was usually some sort of spicy brown powder sprinkled on our fruit salads by the contract caterer to perk up the limp pineapple or melon. At lunch that day I made sure I sat beside Ranga. Reaching for the water jug I clumsily knocked over the platter before my master could begin. He clouted me one good-humouredly, and I surrendered my own salad at once while the entire cast hooted in derision. I kept my head down through the meal not because the hooting con-tinued intermittently (which it did, conducted by my master) or because Captain Memo was looking daggers at me (which he was) but because I was appalled at what was happening to the grass where the salad had fallen. Under my very eyes it shrivelled and died leaving a smoking blue crater.

That was Memo's attempt. Nero's first try was as covert, and once again I believe I was the only witness.

My master had a steel folding chair which, like the platter, travelled with him from set to set. It was a heavy old-fashioned thing, the metal seat worn smooth from endless risings and sittings between takes, the rubber cups long since fallen off the feet. He clung to it as a souvenir of sets past when everyone else, even gaffers, had switched to those light wood and canvas director's chairs.

We had just finished shooting the *deus ex machina* sequence one day when I noticed Nero for no reason at all pick up this chair of my master's and move it back a short way till it was up against my trident. Now I was in the habit of sticking my trident into the ground any old where and that day it happened to be by the canvas wall of our fake assembly building. With a show of careless-ness, Nero moved one or two of the other chairs to cover up his action and then disappeared towards the generator van. I followed him, leaping softly in my deerskin clout, just in time to see something long and black snaking up the steps of the van. When I looked again it was not a snake but an electric cable. At that moment I heard him

131

throw a heavy switch inside the van. I flew back along the cable which ran around the canvas wall to feed a Tota light kit and a couple of Hedler lights on the far side of the set. At one point it disappeared under the wall and reappeared hardly more than a foot along. I lifted the canvas where it met the grass and peeped underneath. The cable, I saw, was looped around my trident.

I didn't need to check to know that there would be a nick in the insulation at that point. In that instant I saw it all happen in my head: my master sits down, forty kilowatts of diesel-generated power shoots through him, his body shudders, threshes about, arcs like a bow, then falls back hump first (the *coup de grace*) upon – my trident! Artful Nero!

There was no time to lose. I shouted '*Snake!*' at the top of my voice and rushed to the nearest canvas window. I saw Hero, who had been on the point of sitting down, leap away at the cry so close behind him. He shouted back, his voice breaking: 'Where? Where!'

'Where!' came the anxious voices of the cast.

Nero ducked out of the generator van (or at least I saw a black snake flash down the steps) and joined the rest. 'Where?' I heard him hiss, but I didn't wait. I darted into the generator van and yanked the plug out of its socket by the cable. Then I slipped back to where the cast was milling about.

'Here he is,' someone called.

So Hero had recognized my voice behind the canvas.

'Where's this bloody snake, Zero?' he demanded.

'There!' I pointed at the black coil of cable looped around my trident, then made as if I saw my mistake, striking my forehead and generally falling about with astonishment.

There was no end to the ribbing after that. For days afterwards Hero would call out: 'Snake!' whenever I appeared and the cast would scatter in mock terror, the very extras joining in. It didn't bother me excessively. I could even bring myself to smile. I had the secret satisfaction of knowing I'd saved my master from the electric chair.

Frustrated there, Nero resorted to direct action. I imagined him reporting the failure to Nandita; I saw the famous lips curl in cruel scorn. Poor Nero! He had no choice.

And so, on that fateful day – the final day of shooting – he shaves with extra care. STAR *camera follows him from bathroom to bedroom mirror. When he turns to go there are a few flecks of talcum powder in the black V of his neck. And under his vest he has buttoned into his holster a real revolver with real bullets. He leaves the stage toy at home.*

I remember it was Divali and director Gopi wanted to reshoot the swearing-in where Nero rushes in with his gun. I remember that because everyone cursed him for picking a holiday. With great difficulty he managed to get the cameraman to agree to come, and the stars turned up grumbling; there were also the bit-part Governor and myself. UD came along to watch and sat in the audience, or where the audience would be; the actual audience scenes would be spliced on later.

'Lights!' the director called, forgetting. He had to go and turn them on himself. The Hedlers and the Flectalux snapped on.

I sat cross-legged halfway up the sky behind the incoming Chief Minister and the Governor, swaying a little, a rubber cobra around my neck.

'Action!'

The camera moved in. The director-cum-clapper boy whacked his clappers.

133

Hero lifted his right hand to take the oath. The Governor began to read from a book.

Nero came rushing in, his eyes flaring. He drew out the revolver, aimed at Hero's chest, and pulled the trigger.

THAAIN!

INTERMISSION

So. How is it?

Have a Campa Cola or something. Chips? Ice-cream?

Pretty warm in there. Let's go and have a look at the murals. I forgot it was going to be dark. Actually if you show an interest the attendant will turn on the verandah light.

There. Forty-watt bulb, but you can make out one or two details. There's a woman, sort of off-pink – kneeling, it looks like – her arms raised up. Some trees, a lot of green, bit of gold, gold in her hair, bit of white. Well, never mind. She's finished, they're all gone, even the cherubs. The green has gone mouldy.

Come. We'll get some fresh air. The heroine's very light, UD. They got a Parsi to play a Parsi, fair enough. But why so dimly? A bit more ethereal would have been right. And a *little* plainer might have been more credible. I suppose they're not in the credibility business. Now you take foreign movies: low-key plot, ordinary light, ordinary setting, ordinary dialogue, then: wham! – beauty queen up front. Handsome hero. Villain OK too, black hair maybe.

137

Hero's fine, our hero. Just the right mix of ugliness and beauty, bit repulsive, bit of a charmer. Southy, naturally. He's more or less a chubby boy; that's all right. The admen are busy selling us the lean European look (with understated bathroom tiles) and that's more worrying than a bit of flab.

Nero's skinny, and skinny is Bad. Or not Good. Well, no wonder. I used to think the difference between a middle-class Indian and the average man was language or clothes or style. But it's weight, kilograms.

Language counts, of course. We're talking English-Medium, and that sets us apart. We have a limited dialogue, shutting the rest out. English in this country is the elite talking to itself – ready English anyway. We can't pretend to serve – much less save – the masses. Inside there, sweating away, is the other India taking its pleasure.

So, what's wrong with Song-and-Dance? Music from fountains, six costume changes in the middle of a song, Kashmir to Kanyakumari in the middle of a dance, choreographed fisherwomen? I've never understood the objection to those sudden shifts. My mind – every mind in the theatre – works that way all the time, not just at night in dreams. Escape is what I want in entertainment. Maybe a little instant justice too. The other kind must be bought outside, and how many can afford it? Fantasy is cheaper, satisfies a need. Reality on the screen is just another luxury the sophisticate would like to add to his store.

But then there are your Popular Culture vultures. Over there. Hungry for kitsch, khichdi, a hash. Low is beautiful. Soon the front row will be reserved for the new critics.

Let's walk a bit – not far – just here. Maybe a hash is inevitable. It could even be useful, a kind of bricolage, cobbling together the modern and the traditional. The kitsch is less useful, that heap of fool's gold that three hundred years' scratching about has left us with. The loss of measure, of a sense of rightness, shows here on the

138

screen as much as anywhere. With the loss comes moral fraud: fake resolutions, shifty answers, soft focus.

Movies pick up the flaws because they're the closest semblance we have to real life. We can compare the two. The fraud shows in the hairline cracks, at the corners, at the edges of the picture: a sort of Doppler effect between the stars in the middle and the emptiness around them, between those who are going somewhere and those who aren't.

However wide the hero's chest it can't hide the skinny wretches on the fringes. The fact is they're both there. The fraud is pretending one or the other is God.

The task is surely to make a cinema that fits the facts – the stubborn Indian facts – without throwing out fantasy. To discover forms that belong here. The glitter, the clamour, are part of an Indian style. The style exists, not just in the movies; the forms want finding. Or we're stuck with formulas. Masala. Or else foreign imitations, high-brow or low. Dover chalk for the asli cheese. The forms are there. History, literature, the folk arts, dance, theatre: they make good raiding. (So does cinema.) They're all there, waiting.

So's Hero. We better go back. No more movies for him, would you say?

One of the first Hindi movies I saw was *Bees Saal Baad* (Twenty Years On.) A woman in the forest, at night, alone. Alone? No: walking backwards into IT. The song was as haunting as the film, but I must have looked away when the hand with claws sprang up behind her. Because I don't remember what happened next.

Melodrama is a national talent. Use it, said film-maker Ritwik Ghatak, and now I see why. We're good at nostalgia too. Use it. Use them or they use you. We break into song. We dance in the streets. Song-and-Dance.

We shoot one another on the set.

Here we are. I'll be waiting here by the door.

Go on in. You don't want to miss this shot.

Shot

The bullet hit him at an angle and smashed his left eye. He lay where he fell on the podium, the socket a bloody mess, real blood pouring down his cheek.

Bull's-eye, though Nero aimed for the chest.

There was something fitting to a death on stage for him, I remember thinking even as it happened. The reactions of those present varied from the instantaneous to the glacial, my own nearer the glacial.

Nero, quickest of the lot, leapt off the podium and dashed into the wings. He fell once, his foot caught in a cable (the Hedler, I like to think) but was up in a moment and away through a side door. No doubt his white Ambassador was parked there in readiness.

Next to respond was the Governor, who quite instinctively threw the book at him. But Nero was well gone. The rest of us moved with the slow-motion uncertainty of wakened dreamers. UD, in the front row, had her mouth open for some seconds before she screamed. Then she flung herself at the stage, scrambling up the steps to where her husband, real and fictive, lay.

My own response was slowest, though I'd had the clearest view of all. (The Governor had had his eyes on the book; the cameraman was busy and director Gopi was nursing a cold.) Maybe the reason I froze was because I saw it happen with such painful clarity. The view from the gods needed no opera glasses: it happened right under my nose.

STAR camera may look down from my perch on the wall, a god's-eye-view.

The part, my part, called for no histrionics. In fact, since I was visible in the background of the swearing-in, any hamming would have been a distraction. The lotus position was hard on my untrained legs but I bore it manfully and managed to smile the requisite purplish calendar smile. The point was mainly to look down in a heavy-lidded magisterial sort of way upon the main actors, their god from the machine. I managed this by looking smugly now at Hero and now at the Governor, and now back again at Hero, and now back again at the Governor, and so on. You get the drift. A pendulum clock on the wall might have done as well.

STAR camera may find an oscillating fan high up in the stage machinery, or perhaps after all a clock on the wall.

Possibly the rhythmic swaying to and fro induced in me that heightened awareness that yogis are supposed to attain upon first overcoming all bodily distractions in profound meditation. I don't mean the ultimate stage of dissolution of the self and the other in a supersensory apprehension of reality. No: the senses are still wide awake, so much so that every detail of the world and its

141

processes is imprinted on the consciousness with supreme clarity. Not a leaf falls but is registered there with due gravity, and all that occurs is of equal weight and value. The individual occurrence is linked with the eternal, and thus mimics recurrence. Events appear to repeat themselves – if you have eaten a plate of farm-fresh cannabis fritters you will know what I mean.

I mean that I saw Hero fall before he fell and after he fell and many times in between. I saw the bullet enter his eye a thousand times. I saw Nero take aim and fire over and over and over again. I saw the red hibiscus of my master's blood blossom and blossom again with fresh vigour through all the eternally recurring seasons of this cruel and beautiful world.

Of course we all assumed he was dead, or dying.

He lay there on his back, perfectly still, while UD crouched over him bawling. When finally she remembered me she looked up. It was a look of such complete desolation, it released me.

My legs, which might have been knotted by some cunning boy scout, came undone. The bubble of eternity burst.

I dropped the trident and jumped off my concealed platform without waiting for the ladder.

'Oh my god,' I whimpered. 'Oh my god.'

UD was blubbing hysterically.

'A doctor!' Gopi called, to nobody in particular.

'A doctor, a doctor,' the cameraman repeated the mantra. Then he broke down and flung himself at Hero.

'Give him some air, please, please – give him breathing space!' said Gopi, remembering a first-aid rule from somewhere.

'Zero!' UD pleaded.

I picked up my fallen trident and brandished it. 'Get back!' I shouted at the clinging lensman. 'Give him some air.' I felt as if I were defending not Ranga but Harishchandra, Raja Harishchandra of old. The man drew back obediently.

Then Hero moved.

'Baas!'

'Randy!' (That was new to me.)

The head moved again. His hand came up and clutched at the eye, turning red as it did. The pain must have just hit him. Then he fainted again and the arm dropped as in filmi death.

UD gave a fresh howl and threw her arms about him. She was dry-retching and rolling her head. His blood stained her cheeks, her hands, her blouse.

I laid my head on his chest and heard to my joy the heart beating there. I signalled life with a fluttering hand.

'Never mind the doctor,' Gopi said. 'We must take him to the hospital.'

So we carried him on a stretcher of locked arms to the Mercedes (the white one that day) and the driver drove at top speed to Dr Norbu's Clinic, the posh private hospital on the hill. They had every machine known to medical man. There were four of us in the car besides him: UD, Gopi, the driver and myself. Before we left we swore the other two to secrecy. I don't believe we spoke a word all the way to the hospital. UD was in the back seat with him, and the rest of us sat busy with our thoughts. I must confess mine more than once returned to the soft white upholstery sadly spattered with my master's blood.

The eye was patched up – there was no question of operating – once it was discovered the bullet had not lodged there. All we could do was wait, our own eyes ransomed to that bright erratic tadpole which marked his heartbeat on a screen.

The nation knows only too well the agony of that week; what it does not know is the simple epochal truth I am about to tell. So I will not tire my countrymen with a

143

rehearsal of their public vigil, the million blood-soaked handkerchiefs, the stock-market collapse. My task is to provide the inside view, to go beyond the cameras and bear witness to a private and hitherto unknown truth.

UD slept in a spare bed beside his; I came in at odd hours. We took turns at keeping watch, supported each other, got in the nurses' way.

As I watched I recalled the many deaths I'd seen him die: the death ecstatic in *Anand Parbat* (The Hill of Delight), the death dutiful in *Doctor Saheb*, the death dandified in *Sultana Daku* (Bandit Queen), the death tuberculotic in *Kavi Kupadh* (The Unlettered Poet, more Ks), the death audacious in several curry westerns, the death defiant in *Comrade Ravi*. And of course that death patriotic in *Surya-namaskar* which first catapulted him to fame. Death should have come easily to him by now.

On screen he'd bled at the heart, at the sleeve, at the stomach, in the back, in the neck, in the side. He'd coughed blood, spat blood, spouted blood with reckless prodigality; he'd even (in *Doctor Saheb*) donated blood at the cost of his own life.

And here he was dying the death dastardly for want of the stuff.

Until *I* opened my veins for my master.

This is the simple truth.

The best hospitals will run out of our rarest of rare blood groups, and here was something else my master and I shared. UD would have bled herself white (well, high yellow) for him, but there too they were mismatched.

He lay there on that tubular steel bed, at a slight cant to accommodate the hump. The nurses understood; Dr Norbu, a male, didn't but let him be. Drips of various kinds percolated through him, chasing my rare corpuscles, infusing this organ or that with vital nourishment.

For three days he hovered between life and death. Doctor and nurse respected our request for secrecy, but
144

someone must have blabbed because unwanted visitors tried to sneak in, some in disguise. Felix Fonseca, brain surgeon, was nabbed at the very door, and his pocket camera confiscated; the next day we ejected Felix Fonseca, trainee nurse. Outside the hospital perfect strangers greeted one another with: *How is He*? or *Will He live*?

He did live. But he couldn't go back to the movies. And that gave new life to the old adage that you don't quit the movies; the movies quit you. Big he might be, but the movies were bigger. Not even Ranga could remain Number 1 Hero with one eye gone.

Eye-patches were for rogues and villains. At best he might be offered the lead in another gauboy rehash, say *Kane Ka Badla* (Revenge of the One-Eye), and there would be the standard *Kana Phir Chala* (Kana Rides Again) and *Kana Ka Launda* (Son of Kana). But he was past such foolery: he was the boss. One might as well have asked him to fill Nero's bill – for there was another slot left vacant on that fateful evening.

A single bullet and the industry lost its two top men: the Good and the Bad. It lost me too (oh yes, Felix Fonseca and half a dozen others pounced on the Ugly), and the word *exodus* was played with.

Nero was still missing. He must have had more than his Ray-Bans to hide behind. All the facts pointed to careful planning: the chain of getaway cars, the switched tyres, the planted keys, the closure of three accounts, a paid-off chowkidar, the carelessly dropped tickets to opposite destinations, Nandita's unasked-for alibi, fake calls from the four corners of the land, random sightings in Lucknow, Asansol, Surat and Madurai. The CBI huffed and puffed and leaked contradictory stories to the press; they held prime suspects – including Nandita – incommunicado for varying periods; they took out warrants for any number of arrests, including, briefly, Gopi's; they said there was light at the end of the tunnel, the dragnet was closing in, the fox

145

was run to earth, the crook was cornered. Oh yes – and the villain was doomed. But they couldn't produce Nero. He might just as well have walked through the silver screen and vanished.

Nero, reigning villain, was a credible, even popular figure. Absconding he became a demon overnight, responsible in the nation's psyche for every pother and calamity. Did the hens stop laying in X's coop? Nero must have hidden there, surely. Were there floods in Y, an earthquake in Z? Nero had passed that way. Might the monsoon fail again this year? Not if Nero stayed away. Behave, the naughty child was warned, or Nero will come for you.

Let him go, we felt, the inner circle. Ranga was still with us, and that was the main thing.

The tadpole perked up, the hump (the nurses said) looked better already, his right eye opened.

'Baas!'

'Randy baby!'

He shifted his head.

'Indu?' he said.

I suppose he thought he was back in the big gun or had missed the net in the Big Top.

Whatever the reason, the effect on UD was palpable. She blenched, turned that high yellow and stood up. I thought she was going to rip out his life-support system; then I thought she was going to faint. She did totter, and that – the awareness of a certain histrionic residue (or was it scum?) to her suffering – saved her. She sat down again and took his hand.

I left them to it. He no longer needed my blood, and I got UD and the hospital staff to swear donor secrecy. I mention it now because it no longer matters, and the truth has its time and place.

He told me later he saw red with his left eye. Like the itch in a phantom limb, I suppose. Or maybe the red that

146

erupted in his eye at the moment of impact left its message indelibly coded on the retina, staining with its monochrome for all time (all his time) the rods and cones, staunch witnesses to that last millisecond of sight.

Or maybe the red he saw was *my* blood. His own was captured forever on film. Not ketchup, not Red Dye Number 1; the real thing. Not that that red saw the light of day straight away, much as the producer and director would have liked. Ranga refused to let the thing be screened.

Can it be that like the hump which he had learnt, bullwise, camelwise, to hoard, Ranga decided to store this last film, to hold it by some animal instinct in reserve?

At any rate *Neta Harishchandra* was not released. He saw to it it didn't get the censor's certificate right away, and procured a stay-order to make sure. The lakhs of rupees lost, and, more galling, the crores of rupees that might have been made, caused producer Chaman Lal to see red too, with both eyes, but there was nothing to be done. He moved a counter case which got bogged down, and finally he settled out of court and sold the cans to Ranga. Afterwards he turned to real estate and made a killing there, but he had a long memory.

When, much later, *Neta Harishchandra* was finally released, it was a hit all the same, but that story must wait a little.

Meanwhile my master took his first hesitant steps to where the black Mercedes stood in the hospital portico while the cops warded off the ecstatic crowd. He was on his way home with his wife at his side (I had the other arm) and he put on a brave face as he stopped to wave.

Brave new face!

The face was not the same as the one that smiled down in greeting from a lurid cut-out figure opposite the hospital. For one thing the bridge of the nose was gone. This was not the inconvenience one might have imagined, however curious it looked side-on. The fact was he'd covered up the defect, and the missing eye as well, with a pair of dark glasses which fitted far better than they had done before. Before, they'd sat astride that ridgy chump of cartilage looking extraneous and insecure. Now they fitted into the shot-away niche and seemed to belong.

Seemed, I say. For they belonged rightfully to me.

They were the dark glasses he'd worn the night he came to Madame Cama Road in disguise. I cherished those dark gogs. They'd seen me through adolescence, turning Zero into Zorro for want of a suitable mask. I was Bond, I was Brando, I was kingpin Kanhaiyalal. I dealt dark death with a slow turn of the head.

And now they were his. If rightness of the total look meant anything, they were his by right. On me they were an accessory; on him they were integral and would become inseparable. They became in fact the emblem of the new Ranga, as iconic in their way as the bicorne and hand-in-vest were, or have become, of Napoleon. There would be other items in the new Ranga's uniform, but they were accessories on him. The dark glasses summed him up. They symbolized both his striking down and his rising up. In later years when you saw his face simplified on ten thousand political posters, you registered the glasses first and got that compressed message. Only then did your eye pick up the brow magnanimous, the smile compassionate, the jaw resolute and all those shortcuts of the poster-maker's art. The glasses were not his: they were him.

So the gentle cineaste will forgive me if I have laboured my humble contribution to my master's second image.

May I, while on the subject of dark glasses, very swiftly distinguish between Hero's and Nero's?

Nero's foreign Ray-Bans, gold-rimmed and streamlined, with a shady sort of X-ray view of the little eyes behind, spelt Western sleaze and skulduggery. They were, in short, smuggled, possibly through Nepal, not far from his hometown, but probably right there on the docks in Bombay.

Hero's countrymade gogs were tacky enough, made of a brittle black plastic that quickly lost its sheen, and almost totally opaque. That is, from the outside. On the inside they said, on the frame, MADE IN USA, meaning the Ulhasnagar Sindhi Association, near Bombay, and it was clear they were from *here*, not there. (I'd picked them up in Paltan Bazaar in Dehra Dun, just a few shops down from the Clock Tower.) Down to the crude hinges, they were indigenous. *India*, they squeaked.

On Nero dark glasses meant business, dirty business; on Hero they meant, or would come to mean, politics.

Zero Hair-Splitter.

So in a sense he did do a *Kana Rides Again*. Or was it a *Revenge of Kana?*

Imagine my surprise then, when one Sunday morning the sarangiwala came by playing his one-string clay-pot violin and singing the refrain of what must have been a hit song, because the urchins round about took it up at once. My head whipped around – like the HMV Stereo dog's, I fancy – when I caught the words. A cartoonist could have inked in the flap lines around my ears.

> *Villain incarnadi-*
> *Ne-ro nefarious,*
> *He-ro knows where he is,*
> *Winks at him, Old Boss-Eye.*

Dream

In his dream he is floating down a yellow river on a banana leaf past herds of sleek cattle that lift their heads as he goes by. On another leaf is his heroine, her face turned towards the farther bank where tigers groan in caves. There shrill parrots throng the banyan trees whose aerial roots are beards for monkeys to swing on. Ahead is a waterfall where the spray booms and the long grass sings *Ki-zhanadu, Ki-zhanadu,* and the rock pythons spit blue lightning. Very shortly he must do something or they will both be swept over the falls, but he is happy where he is with his warm milk and his toy scooter. A python rears up over the falls and gapes at him: it has the postman's face and its mouth is a dark slot for postcards that can never come back. *Mother,* he cries, *turn this boat around!* The banana leaf is spattered with cold rice; underneath it is white, like Bombay City where the water grew turbulent. Anthills sprout in the dark jungle whose tree trunks are smooth as bicycle pumps. On the near bank is a young girl in a jasmine skirt; on the other bank is a woman on a tiger. He waves to them but they stare back with wide sad eyes. One of them – which one? – weeps beads of glass which trickle down into the river. There is a fisherman up to his knees in the water, casting his net. Each time he brings up a shiny black fish with six eyes and tosses it back in. The fish lands with a splash, butt-first, beside the banana leaf boat. It is not a fish but a revolver. The fisherman has a familiar beaked nose and golden breasts with black nipples. He casts his net again at the edge of the waterfall and draws in the two leaf boats. He picks up the heroine by her fish-tail, examines her and throws her back in. The hero he drops into his bag to carry home. It's hot in the bag, hot and close. Hero can hardly breathe. It's like being in the barrel of a big gun with just one eye above for light and air. There is an explosion. A patch of cloud covers the sun. He turns and twists and tries to flap his arms, but they are held fast, and there's a weight on his back that's growing heavier all the time. He must break loose or suffocate. He must fly through the air, shine like a star.

Party

Bombay is visible, Delhi is not. It isn't the skylines, high or low, that make the difference: mock Manhattan is no better than Edwardian-Mughal. Delhi is simply about invisibility. It may have to do with circles and the architect Lutyens and a vanishing horizon, but it has mainly to do with power.

Not that I, Zero, wish to slight the circle, or that flat city's physique. True, I grew up with a backdrop of hills in the Doon valley, and came of age in a port city crowned with a hill, so I have caught the hillman's contempt for cities of the plain. But even its residents will admit that in Delhi you are always getting there; you are always so many miles from somewhere else. Like its political masters, our capital does go on and on.

Nor does the climate help. In the heart of summer the city simply vanishes. May in Bombay is bearable; the sea breezes bring relief. May in Delhi is a contradiction in terms: the city simply isn't there. Has it, as it did under the moping British, got up and gone to Simla, to the hills?

Or has the heat reduced city and citizens to clear glass? The glare, even with Ray-Bans and both eyes intact, makes verification impossible. Criminals flock there for that reason, though not all of them make straight for the MP (Members of Parliament) Canteen. (There are Lutyens's roundabouts to be negotiated first.) In winter, for perhaps two months the city shimmers into some kind of focus, but by the end of February, and sometimes right after the rose show, it's gone again. And even in winter there is a point on Rajpath, the grand avenue leading up to the Presidential palace, where thanks to Lutyens's associate, Baker, who overlooked a rise, the palace, Rashtrapati Bhavan, disappears from view. On the Road of State we lose sight of the Head of State.

Two more airy nothings. The main shopping centre is a stucco circle, Connaught Circus, and parliament house, though not a circus, is also circular, both significant forms enclosing nothing. So perhaps circles do have something to do with power. Zero is a potent force, our chief contribution to the world.

In Delhi, then, what matters happens invisibly, behind the scenes, surely a problem for actors from Bombay where the scenes are all there is. Which explains why a particular white Mercedes with a Bombay number-plate is having trouble getting from A to B.

STAR camera may show it going round and round the roundabouts and passing and repassing certain landmarks, say, that new Red Fort – the Air-India building, or India Gate, making forays up radial roads which from the air look like spider-webs, stopping to ask directions, once doing a U-turn.

Point B is a dacha on the edge of Greater Delhi, well past the Qutab Minar. (*STAR camera glances at the medieval tower out of a car window, as a tourist might: it flicks past and is gone.*) A party is in progress at the dacha – he calls it his

153

farm – of Kamal Ahuja, and for the past hour cars of foreign make and line have been passing through the gate which alone costs more than some of the cars it admits.

Finally the white Mercedes draws up, a late arrival, and from it step a geisha and a scarecrow. Both are masked, for it is a masked evening in addition to being fancy dress. Kamal will provide a prize for the best costume (a weekend's shopping in Hong Kong – at his hotel) but that is hardly an attraction for guests who agree privately that Honkers is not what it used to be.

Already the neurotic driver is vacuuming up the bits of straw from the soft back seat of the Mercedes with a small battery-powered vacuum-cleaner; the indelible brown stains there can still give him bad dreams. The Scarecrow and the Geisha have made their way to Kamal's front door, he scattering straw, she perfume. She twirls the paper umbrella on her shoulder, he pulls down his battered slouch hat as they vanish into the dimmed interior. By party custom Kamal does not greet his guests by name, pretending not to recognize them – but he is there to take their hands and draw them in.

'Please,' he says, and nudges them in opposite directions to circulate.

The Geisha looks over her shoulder at the Scarecrow, then eddies away to mingle with the masked guests. The Scarecrow fails to return that look, perhaps because he has on the back of his head a second, papier mâché, face. He walks stiffly through the company, his laceless boots, their tongues sticking out, clomping loutishly among the Italian labels, his drainpipe trousers expecting floods, his battered coat – which he delighted in ripping himself – flapping as he goes, his red neckerchief alarmingly tight, the two-day growth on his cheek cultivated with the same care that went into the crops he surveys, the bared teeth painted on a surgical mask, the cheap plastic dark glasses, rammed into place just where the bridge of the nose was

154

shot away, making a dark room darker for the one
remaining eye.

*STAR camera finds much colour here nevertheless, blundering
after him among the grotesque demon masks and fantastic
costumes lit by vertical shafts of light from bulbs recessed into
the ceiling. There is something of the restaurant about this
interior, but since the patrons are circulating the effect is one of
moving through a dappled aquarium filled with tropical fish; a
wave of a fantail and the surreal shapes slip from darkness into
brilliant light. A headpiece will suddenly blossom vermilion
against the liquid dark, a lemon yellow sash flare up as the
revellers move: the lights appear to rake the people but it is the
people who are shifting, whisking from gloom to spotlight to
gloom again. Like Hero's head, the camera must swivel right
and left so its one eye catches the action. Now it is behind him,
now it is him (it is he, Plumbum, be not afraid), now it
overtakes him and shows us his stubble front. From the front it
catches the 180-degree turns of the head-which may go up and
down as well when he examines what he sees.* The message is:
looking for someone. *From behind it catches the reverse swing
of the leering papier maché mask so the effect is of a 360-degree
scanning, four eyes instead of one.*

The other guests, not all in fancy dress, respond to his
passage with the good humour of the occasion, with the
laughs and admiring glances the costume deserves, but
without the attention he would get if his identity were
known. The fact is the hump which in the old days would
have given Hero away has been so starved during his
long penance that it is sadly shrunken. It might be a lump
in the Scarecrow's stuffing for all the women guests know.
And the stiffness of the walk disguises the old giveaway
slouch; he could have bamboo poles down his trouserlegs.
One hand is deep in the tattered coat-pocket playing with

155

a naphthalene worry-bead. And he is worried, or nervous. He is here on a tip-off.

Hero knows where he is. I couldn't credit that line from the song. And yet he appeared to be steadily and wittingly tracking someone down.

Well then, who was that following the Scarecrow at a safe distance? He had a brown paper-bag over his head with holes – small holes – cut out at the eyes and a collection of bags – plastic bags, string bags, khadi bags, leather bags, satchels, air-bags, a camera-bag, even a pythonskin alms-bag – slung from his shoulders. His message, his costume, was plainly: *Bagman*, but he moved slyly and might have passed muster for Smuggler. He appeared to invite and deny scrutiny, slithering away just when you got interested in his wares.

I decided to track him in his turn. I had come to the party with Dicky Deshpande, an old schoolmate from the Silver Spoon, now a senior bureaucrat and golfing buddy of the Prime Minister's. Ever since Hero's departure from Bombay, Pedro and I had made Delhi our home too, and though our flat was a long way from his Golf Links mansion (I was in Kamla Nagar, in North Delhi) I'd wangled membership and taken up a bit of putting on the green myself. You were always running into Old Spoonies there.

So I followed the Bagman and the Bagman followed the Scarecrow and we drifted around Kamal Ahuja's stadium-sized drawing room from group to group catching snatches of conversation.

'Would you say there was poverty in this country?' a dramaturge was saying with a wicked smile.

Challenged, the World Bank poverty specialist felt obliged to justify the two million dollars being spent on his inquiry. He wore a dazzling white Nehru jacket with a pink rose in the lapel.

'Yes,' he smiled ruefully. 'Two kinds: a) b) and c).'

'Go on!' grinned a foreign correspondent, poking his nose in. He was dressed as a CIA agent with glasses like Nero's.

'Show me,' said the dramaturge. He stopped a waiter with a tray and swept three kinds of canapes onto his plate.

'Why not come to our seminar tomorrow? There's a field trip afterwards.'

'Done,' said the dramaturge, instantly making other plans. He looked disappointed.

But then the Bagman turned a corner and I had to go after him. He passed through an archway into another room where there was much hilarity. I'd seen the Scarecrow go in there earlier, walking like the Mummy that Abbot and Costello met in the pyramids. When I heard the plaudits I knew Hero would pause there with the actor's instinctive need, and sure enough the Bagman waited by the pillar while my master took his stiff bow. Then he advanced cautiously, and cautiously I followed. Screams of laughter greeted me.

'*Chhuri tej, chaku tej, kainchi tej, akal tej!*' I called. 'Your knives, your scissors, your wits sharpened!' I was got up as a knifegrinder and had a variety of sharp tools decorating my person. Not quite prize-winning material, though I had a shopping list for Hong Kong just in case. Besides (disqualification) I didn't have my grindstone on me; I'd come in a hurry when Kamal (another Old Spoonie) told me he was expecting a *special* guest. I was among the first to arrive. Knives tinkling, I made my little bow but quickly realized the convulsive laughter was not for me. A story was in progress.

'This one kept falling in the water,' a leggy model in a pink body stocking shrieked. She had on some woolly anklets that gave her the high Andean look of a llama. There wasn't a sari in sight.

'We were *supposed* to be in the water.'

'You got water on my lens, you horror!' said a floppy man in a silk chemise.

'*All the better to quench your thirst with*!' sang a second model. Both girls looked Georgian or pale Greek but spoke demotic Convent. I thought I recognized the jingle of a new carbonated soft drink commercial: it was Schlepsi, now in India, in the red-white-and-blue can.

'Let them drink cola,' said the foreign correspondent looking in.

I shuffled away in confusion, almost losing sight of the Bagman. He'd ducked into a room full of Puppies and Pappans. Relatives for the most part, they'd chosen Kamal's family lounge where a big-screen stereo TV was playing some new video release with the volume turned up high. Neither Scarecrow nor Bagman got any attention there, but a wizened Pappan with heavy gold ear-rings dived into her handbag and produced a pair of cloth shears for me to sharpen. At exactly the same time the man on the screen (not Nero) produced a knife and stabbed the good guy and ran off leaving a large pool of blood. I fled too as a posse of voices, raised above the TV, gave chase.

'Pizza.'

'Marble Arch.'

'Selfridges.'

'Omni Deluxe.'

'Pineapple pastries.'

'VCR.'

'Foreign.'

'VCP.'

'Schlepsi.'

'French fries.'

'Black Forest.'

'Disneyland.'

'Disney WORLD.'

I might have lost the Bagman had a Non-Resident Indian not buttonholed him in a hallway.

'I have ten crores to invest,' the NRI said. He was drunk. 'What do you recommend?'

The Bagman detached himself with exaggerated care.

'I recommend,' he said, stopping a waiter, 'one of these mutton kababs.'

'They're fish kababs,' the waiter said. 'But they're not real. I'm not really a waiter.'

The Bagman looked him up and down. 'That's all right,' he said. 'I'm not really hungry.' And he pushed past the NRI.

The drunk turned to me. 'I'm not really an NRI,' he confessed. 'I'm just married to a Green Card.'

I dodged his questing hand and propelled him into a bedroom where he could fall asleep and come to no harm. But there was already an adman in there with a puffy model. I recognized her from the soyabean oil commercial.

'With your neck,' the adman was saying, 'I could sell pearls to the Mikimotos.'

I glanced at the neck. There were three neat rolls of fat there, but it could have been the way she was holding her head; they looked like ropes of pearls already and I felt the adman had his work cut out. He had begun to examine them with his short hairy fingers. I left the NRI to make his own way – his millions might equally have gone into pearls or soyabeans – and dashed out into the hallway after the Bagman.

But he was gone. At the end of the passage he could have turned either left towards the kitchen or right down another hallway with doors along its length that gave it the look of a hotel. I found the kitchen empty and ran back along the second hallway testing each of the doors. I opened the first.

'Seriously!' a young woman was saying. Her friends looked briefly at me and went back to the story. 'He actually married his computer – there was a ceremony, with invitations.'

'No dowry?'

'You think I'm joking, ask Ritu, she was there.'

'Ya, he divorced his wife, ya.

'No, she divorced *him*. She said she was not IBM-compatible.'

The Bagman wasn't there. I looked in the next room.

'His father left him six villages. So he became an artist.'
The room was full of beards that bristled at my intrusion.

In the third room was a black-and-white TV with zig-zag lines like lightning ripping across its face. When I turned to go a frizzled voice told me I needed the new Jiffy disposable razor. But I already had an old-style cut-throat with me, *on* me as Knifegrinder, and felt comforted.

I shut the door behind me and ran down some steps to the basement from where loud rock music burst every time the swing doors opened. There was strenuous danc-ing underway down there. Near the door a girl on a high stool was gravely inflating multicoloured condoms and releasing them into the air above the dancers; the air was full of darting serpents. Nero would approve, I thought, and just then I spotted the Bagman. He was jerking his way across the crowded floor, dancing with nobody in particular. And then on the far side I saw the Scarecrow, his head still swivelling as he scrutinized the dancers to right and left. Once he turned around and looked the way he had come, and the Bagman at once turned around and looked my way so I had to turn around myself and examine the door. When I looked back again the Scare-crow was gone, and the Bagman was making his way towards the door on the other side. I set out in pursuit once more, with those bird-like wobblings of the head which with me pass for dancing – when I must. The floor was so crowded I made only the slowest headway. On the way I encountered at least two Spidermen, or the same Spiderman at least twice.

Finally I broke loose and swung through the door on

the other side. There was the same short flight of steps up to another door. I stepped out into the cold night, the air a shock against the skin after the warm boozy fug of the basement.

Kamal's house rambled on over to the left, but this was its backward extremity. There was a row of papaya trees along the inner wall (that wasn't the property boundary) and where the row ended was a pumphouse and some changing rooms for the swimming-pool.

Both Bagman and Scarecrow had vanished into the night. There was a fragment of early-setting moon half-way up the sky, and though it shed a little light, the shadows were forbidding.

I cocked my ears left and right, then straight ahead. I couldn't catch a sound, or not the sounds I wanted. There was a jackal howling somewhere in the distance and the clink of plates from the marquee on the other side of the house where the caterers were busy.

I stepped tentatively off the concrete shelf of the house onto the grass and found my brown canvas shoes instantly covered in dew. If that was the case my master's feet would be soaked; his Scarecrow shoes were gaping horribly, if I remembered. Then I remembered he'd been shedding straw: there was a tell-tale line of the stuff all through Kamal's house and across his expensive carpets. I looked more closely at the lawn and sure enough there was a fine sprinkling of straw, still dry, striking out across the grass towards the row of papaya trees and the swimming-pool beyond. It lay lightly upon the dark prints of a large pair of boots. Beside the Scarecrow's track was another, the prints smaller, neater. The Bagman's. I took a deep draught of cold air and set out after them.

When I reached the papaya trees something counselled caution. I paused by the first tree, seeking the shadow of its all too slender trunk. Then I gathered courage and, clasping my arms about me to silence my knives and

161

scissors, darted to the next tree. In this way, using the meagre shade allowed me, I passed from tree to tree, to the last in the row. After that there was a short moonlit stretch before the shadow of the pumphouse. I took another deep breath and leapt the gap.

Immediately I felt the reassuring presence of the rough wall against my shoulder. It still held a little heat from the day's sun. I flattened myself against it and rested my heart. It was thudding away madly under my cut-throat. When it had quieted down a bit, I decided to make my way towards the corner which hid the changing rooms from me. The changing rooms were an extension of the pumphouse, and from what I could tell ran along the side of the pool. I began to inch along the pumphouse wall.

When I reached the corner I steadied myself to whip around it as my master himself had done often enough, for example by the Residency wall in *Kartavya*, just before cutting Captain Fortram's throat – except he had his hands pressed against the wall (and the cut-throat in his mouth) and I was hugging myself, not from fear, but to muffle my tools.

I took a short hopeful breath and slid around the corner.

As I did, an arm snaked out of the dark and coiled itself around my chest. At the same time a hand clamped itself on my mouth and pinched my nose between thumb and forefinger.

The shock of it almost burst my heart. If I hadn't taken a breath before moving I might have choked immediately from fright and want of air. As it was I struggled furiously, making a long – *mmm* – noise, but my arms, already folded, were pinned down and I could feel the razor pressing into my flesh. All I could do was kick feebly backwards like a dog scattering dirt.

Then all of a sudden, just when I was preparing to meet my maker, the arm released me and the hand let go of my mouth and nose.

'Shit! *Zero!*'

I was gasping, bent double, my tools clinking madly, so I couldn't see who it was. But I recognized the voice.

'Baas!'

'What the hell do you think you're doing?'

'I could ask you, baas,' I gasped. I was still lapping up the cold night air.

'What the hell are you following me for?'

I made a pushing sign with my hands to say, give me a chance, but just then we heard something that made us spin around towards the changing rooms.

It was a deep dark chuckle, a filmi villain's chuckle, and it seemed to echo in the empty pool and wind itself around the pumphouse. Once again I recognized it immediately; Hero of course knew it intimately of old.

We ran as one for the nearest changing room. There was a frantic hunt for the light switch, but when it snapped on we saw at once that the room was empty. We rushed to the next room, presumably the ladies', but there was a padlock on the door. Only then did we realize he must have gone the other way behind the changing rooms and the pumphouse and run off along the side of the house.

'The gate!' Hero cried and was off in a cloud of straw. No stiffness from the Scarecrow now. The only other time I saw my master move so fast was in *Kohinoor*, when he had to cover the distance from the Tower of London to Tower Bridge before the bridge went up; there'd been a great leap then. Only now he was boss-eyed and it was night and he was wearing dark glasses.

Left alone I began to feel nervous and vulnerable once more. It was extraordinary how bereft you felt the moment he was gone. When I'd heard his voice a moment ago, the relief flooded my craven heart and enveloped my entire being. I could have leapt fearlessly into the chasm with – or without – him at that moment. I recalled the Englishman, Chamberlain's account of a pre-War meeting

163

with another notable charismatic in an office twelve floors above a Berlin street. 'This man,' the Führer said, prodding a motionless bodyguard, 'will unhesitatingly jump out of the window at my command. Do you wish to see?'

And here I was alone again in the shadow of the changing room verandah. When that metaphysical forlornness had shrunk to simple fear, I began to feel I would be safer in the sparse light of the moon. I stepped out of the black shadows into its pale ambergris and found myself on the edge of Kamal Ahuja's swimming-pool.

It was large for a private pool and deep at one end – just how deep it wasn't hard to see because it had been drained for the winter. Not completely drained: there was a narrow neck of water, rainwater perhaps, at the deep end where the floor sloped steeply. A pale rind of moon floated there, trembling occasionally from a breath of wind or some light-footed waterspider.

I don't know how long I stood there, held by that moon. I do believe I saw a flying-fox flap calmly across its face; and there were other minutiae, sticks and floating leaves that troubled its repose. I was half expecting someone to steal out of the changing rooms – either the empty one or the locked one – and push me in, but I stood rooted at the edge defying, even inviting, my assailant. Someone, guests at another party or perhaps the Ahuja children, had thrown coins into the water and now and then as I leaned over the edge one would catch the moonlight and glow. My mind grew calm and still – I must admit I'd forgotten my master's urgent mission – and I thought of other winter nights at home in the Doon valley when the stars seemed the blind handiwork of some prodigal jeweller.

STAR *camera, handheld, may creep up on me and teeter on the edge, dipping finally into the pool to focus on the diamonds scattered there.*

I must have been there longer than I knew, for when I stirred I found the moon had shifted just out of sight – its halo was still visible at the edge of the water on the far side – and in its place had coalesced another, more sinister, reflection.

It was the figure of a man I hadn't seen before. I must have been looking at him outlined against the halo for some time before I realized he was there. When I did it was not the image that startled me but a belch.

Bri-ibe! he belched. It was a rich ripe belch.

I looked up at him for the first time and he seemed to laugh at my discomfiture. Then, as if to rub it in, he belched again more expansively – *gra-aft*! – and said, kneading his stomach:

'Ahujaji's dinners are always worth leaving home for.'

The bulk of the voice sounded hollow across the empty pool, with a screechy edge lent it by the ceramic tiles.

'Dinner?' I said. Was it that late? But then the man's waistline told me he was usually early for dinner.

He ignored my foolish response and stood in silence for a while, scrutinizing me. I had the last of the setting moon in my face now so he might have made out something, but whether he could see me or not I felt increasingly uncomfortable under his gaze. I began to stir myself to go in search of Ranga. I felt ashamed at having forgotten him so easily; was this forgetfulness bound up with the leap of faith too, with that unhesitating jump into the chasm? As I turned to go the man spoke again.

'Your master will be wondering where you are.'

He had read my mind effortlessly, but what struck me was not his divination of my intent or even my connection with Hero, but the word *master*. I had not thought of Ranga in that light, or at any rate by that term, before. I may have thought and written so of him *since* (as in this narrative for instance), but at that point it was a revelation.

Was he my master? Was I *his*, as the word suggested?

165

Certainly the urge to protect and to obey was there, but would I heel or sit or beg? Was the bond fixed and irrevocable? Had the price been paid? I wasn't sure it had, and yet I decided, I think there and then, that I would behave as if it had been. I would *act* – duplicitous verb, which he above all would understand – as if the seal were on me, the collar, if you like, buckled on and the brass name-tag clinking like the tools of my fancy dress trade. *To act*. Consider the cleavage: both action and the imitation of action, both *I kill* and *I pretend to kill*, as if in the moment of truth (action) there is already immanent make-believe (acting).

So the stranger's words crystallized something in me that had been floating freely. By defining my status he had opened my eyes: he showed me what I was and how I must faithfully play my role. At the same time, the first prick of doubt in what had been faith entire and unspoken alerted me. It was as if in the instant of doubt knowledge was born. Thus he both chained me up and set me free.

I mumbled something about having been dreaming.

He said: 'I wonder where he is.'

There was amusement in the voice now. He had turned and begun to stroll along the other side of the pool. He wore, I noticed, a Gandhi cap, handspun clothes and an air of limitless authority.

'I must go and see,' I said, and followed suit on my side of the pool. But Hero (my master) spared us the journey by appearing out of the shadows from the marquee side of the mansion.

'The bastard's disappeared, Zero,' he called. 'I've looked high and low. But he must be here somewhere. Nobody went through that gate. Anyway I warned the gatekeeper to look out for him.'

Then he saw the stranger and looked interrogatingly at me. I spread my hands and shook my head.

'I think I can help you, Rangaji,' the stranger said.

166

My master looked at him and then back at me. I shrugged again.

'But,' the man went on, 'I must talk to you alone.' He looked pointedly at me.

Ranga said: 'Zero.'

I moved a short way off and stopped, looking back, my hand on the cut-throat.

The man dusted himself all over ostentatiously. 'I have no knife, nothing!' he called, amused again.

I pushed off, my humiliation complete. If my master wished to entrust himself without protection to a complete stranger who appeared to have some link with his enemy – well, so be it. I ran down the few steps to the basement and pushed through the swing doors. The dancing was rather more relaxed than before; it was in fact clinging, the music slower, the lights lower. Maybe dinner was over after all. I stood there for a few moments quelling the shudder that came over me as the frowst went to work on my chill pores.

Then I saw something that made me shiver in earnest.

There, on the far side of the room, dancing a rather mechanical fox-trot, without the faintest interest in geta-way cars, was the Bagman. Every now and then he would add a Bihari flourish to the ballroom steps, or a Bombay twist, to the amusement of his incognito partner. But it was not the brazenness of his reappearance that shook me so much as the innocence and vulnerability of his partner.

The Bagman was dancing with the Geisha.

I gave an involuntary cry and made for them. But the floor was still densely packed with dancers. The people nearest me turned inquiring heads in my direction but were in no hurry to make way. The Bagman looked directly at me for the first time – I could feel those evil little eyes drilling through me – and made a gesture with his right arm at once obscene, malevolent and derisive.

167

I realized immediately that he'd known I was tracking him all along. And then another thought struck me: I hadn't been the last in the series. All the time I was busy tracking the Bagman, the stranger by the pool had been busy tracking me! And then the connection became a little clearer. Just as I was the self-appointed protector of the man in front of my quarry, the stranger was the protector of the man in front of me. And if he was as powerful as his demeanour suggested, his protection was rather more valuable than mine. No wonder Nero was dancing so blithely.

My hackles rose – not with the fear such a chain of reasoning might be expected to instill, but with a sudden and animal aggression. How *dare* he! I began to push my way through the dancers, most of whom had long abandoned the tempo for a swaying embrace. When suddenly I felt my arm taken by a soft hand.

'Zero! I didn't see you at dinner!'

It was Kiran Ahuja, Kamal's wife. She was sporting a new and spiky hair-style but I knew her of old. I'd known her off and on since our schooldays in the Doon valley, longer than Kamal had, in fact. She was at our sister school, Fotheringham's, where they wore red candy-striped kamizes to match, we said, our blazers.

'Kiran – just one sec – '

'What! Don't give me this just one sec business, yaar. I see him after n years and he serves me these vague lobs. OK, months. But look at you! You on some kind of diet or something? Come on, I'll get you a plate and we can talk in my studio. Kamal's busy with some young gipsy.'

Why is it that women no sooner spot me than they want to ply me with food? Why not liquor, at least?

'Kiran, really this is life and death.'

I looked across the floor at the Bagman who leered at me through the little peepholes in his paper helmet, and leaned over the Geisha. He whispered something in her

168

ear and she nodded. Then he steered her, his hand on the small of her back, towards the double doors. They passed through, she with her hand on his shoulder, and the slaughterhouse doors swung shut.

'UD!' I tried to scream. I began to babble, my eyes fixed on the still-rocking doors. Kiran, who had followed my gaze, patted me on the arm.

'Nero?' she asked. 'He's perfectly safe. And UD can look after herself.'

I stared at her, amazed that she should know, and more, that she should speak so casually of the man. Unless I'd missed a newspaper, he was still wanted for attempted murder. I looked about us to see if anybody had heard; suddenly every masked head in the vicinity seemed to have sprouted ear-trumpets.

'Aren't you being a bit, you know, open?' I said guardedly.

'It's public knowledge, Zero. Where have you been living?'

I started to give her my Kamla Nagar address but she cut me off.

'Nero is strictly off limits, Zero. *Noli him tangere*, OK? Avoid like plague. Friends in high places – or rather, a friend in the highest place.'

'The PM?' I said, scandalized.

'Zero, Zero!' She looked pityingly at me. 'Not the puppet, the puppet*eer*. Look, how many Mr Cleans have we had?'

'I don't know. I've lost count. How many?'

'Well,' she said. She didn't sound too sure herself. 'There was the Original Mr Clean. Then the New Improved Mr Clean.' She paused looking for a new slogan perhaps.

'That makes two Mr Cleans,' I said, helping things along.

'Hold your horses, yaar,' she complained, and I realized

169

we had in that single exchange exhausted the reading habits of us English-Medium types. Wodehouse and Westerns; plus maybe Camus in translation at the Delhi University coffee-house. 'There's the present one, too,' she persevered. 'But anyway, that's not the point.'

'Then what is?'

'I was thinking of the kingmaker. This guy is the Original Mr Dirty. There's one behind every Mr Clean – the same one in his case. Somebody's got to dip their hands in the muck.'

'So who is he?'

'Gangajal Trivedi.'

I'd heard the name of course, but couldn't put a face to it. It was not a face you saw in newsphotos anyway. And even now that I'd met him I'd come away without any impression of the man beyond his voice and his waistline.

I said: 'But surely not even he would conceal a notorious criminal. I mean, there are law courts, newspapers, in this country.'

'If it gets out of hand he'll fake Nero's death and Nero'll become Sutli Singh or Rassi Ram or something. Simple.'

'But how come Nero's so important to him? I mean, if this guy is as big as you say, what does he want with a Nero?'

'That's the thousand-carat question. I don't know everything, Zero.'

'No?'

'You slime! Come on, I'll show you my darkroom.'

'I thought you were going to get me some dinner.' UD could look after herself, I decided. I'd been overreacting probably.

'Oh yes. Do you like fish kababs?'

'Real ones?'

'What do you mean real ones? Come on, there might be one left somewhere.'

And she took me by the hand and led me through the

dancers who parted miraculously like the Ganges for Sage Vishwamitra. Or was it Sage Vashishta?

We went upstairs and down the hotel corridor to the kitchen. She went to the fridge and began hauling out the contents at random, talking all the while. Cold meats and foreign cheeses, a giant plastic lettuce bin, tomatoes, a loaf of bread, several jars of American spreads and Polish relishes and (I noticed) the Duchess of Devonshire's plum chutney with fennel. She put four slices into the toaster and when they were done, four more. Then she laid them out in two rows, took up a fearsome spatula and began to smear them with butter, mayonnaise, creamy spreads, and lo-cholesterol margarine. After that she began slapping on a slice of this or that filling with right and left hand. I knew there were mountains of catered food outside – in fact I'd been rather looking forward to that rich Punjabi fare, especially since Gangajal Trivedi's pool-side recommendation. But this was for an old friend, so I sat Spartan-like on a high stool and watched a colossal club sandwich taking shape. To divert me as she worked, she slid back the hatch door so that we had a view as if on a TV screen of her guests in the huge sitting-room beyond the dining alcove. They clashed like infantry under a blue-and-white triptych of Mother Teresa.

'I see Malcolm's here,' she said of the foreign correspondent. 'That's not fancy dress, incidentally. He actually wears that CIA outfit to convince people he's not one of them. As Indophile as they come, but thinks a samosa is a Latin American dictator. Mustard? He's quite sweet, really. I suppose he can't help those ears. Going bald on top of it. You're not! Show me! Where? My God, poor Zero! Horseradish? That godman he's talking to used to be in advertising. He did an ad that said: *Come to the grandeur of a lovely Chinese meal*. Yes. Now he advises at least two governments on foreign affairs. Good friend of Our Friend, incidentally. Is that Bhaskar Chatterjee? I hope he hasn't spotted us. Just slide that door in a little

171

bit. OK. His magazine once called me a socialist when they meant socialite. Now they've gone all post-modern, or else their graphic artist has got measles. That's him next to Bhaskar in those speckled pyjamas. Anchovies? His brother does wordy cartoons for the *Mail* – or is it *Passenger*? Those are the flying Bedi sisters, Veenu and Priya, Wing and Prayer, Kamal calls them. They buzzed Safdarjang control tower last week and their Daddy had to pull hajar strings to get them off. Come on upstairs – toothpick? – before someone catches us. Schlepsi?'

The club sandwich stood on my plate like the Sears tower in – is it? – Chicago. Its engineering was sorely tried as we climbed the stairs to Kiran's studio. Framed black-and-white specimens of her work accompanied us all the way up. I noticed a portrait of Hero among them. She was a good photographer.

The studio was bigger than my flat. We sprawled on her Tibetan carpet – the carpet was bigger than my flat – under a rubber plant. She talked as she ate, growing more and more morose. Now and then I sneaked a potato chip from the wrack around the tower.

'Look at this house,' she ended, licking her black polished nails. '*Look* at the bloody muted colours, the ridiculous furniture. Tacky, my God. Look at me.' Her face had a fetching goatish jut that I'd always admired. 'Borrowed hair. Japanese camera. Using a language – abusing a language – I don't understand and calling my mistakes Indian English. Sometimes I think our English is like St Petersburg French. Fey, finished, washed up. *Look* at this newspaper! With us everything has to be spelt out, explained – like this guy's cartoons. But culture is what is not spoken. So why am I talking so much? I have a theory about names and personality. Those that end in a vowel are oral: *Mao, Castro. Zero.* Consonant ends are anal. But even that doesn't work. *Kiran.* Nothing works. Shall I shut up? I'll shut up.'

I said: 'What to say?'

'Don't say anything.' She pushed the plate aside, leaned over and kissed me.

I felt the night go humid with longing. She was wearing a gamboge kamiz with a green shalwar; together they gave her the look of a ripe mango. All over the house couples were disappearing into the tacky woodwork. Behind the house my master was undergoing his own temptation.

I said: 'How about a plate for Ranga?'

'Nosebag more like it,' she snorted, annoyed.

But we went down to forage for the Scarecrow.

Rape

Shot 265. EXT. Day. The midday meal in progress in a tribal hut in the Dhol village of Karwapani in the central state of Vindhyachal. It is a large single-roomed hut of felled trees and thatching but there is a screen at the back behind which the women of the family stand waiting for the men to finish eating. Outside the hut, in the yard of beaten earth marked out by pales, squat the other men of the village: beyond the paling crouch their women. The guests are seated on the best mat in the village. Before them are earthen bowls from which they eat: millet bread, a portion of dal cooked with gathered greens, an onion and a handful of chillies, red and green. The portions are small; no one will rise satisfied from his meal.

The women will have even less to eat than the men, but that is not what troubles them. They have a deeper hurt to bear: every woman in this village has been raped. And twelve have lost their men.

A month ago they and their men refused to go to work at the mica mine belonging to one Prem Nath, demanding payment due them. *But what about your debts?* the contractor asked. He routinely kept back a quarter of every wage. *And your parents' debts?* demanded Prem Nath. *And their parents' debts outstanding to my father?* True enough, the deputation agreed, but we must eat. *Then you need a loan*, said Prem Nath, and reached for the instruments. Between mine-owner and contractor they kept the tribals in perpetual bondage.

No more debts, the leaders said, instructed by a friend from outside. *Our wages, or we will not work. Then the mine will work without you*, said Prem Nath, and he sent his contractor to the next village to hire labour. But the next village, a farming village, refused and so did the next. The miners' friend had got there sooner; in any case the villagers there were bound to other landlords and contractors, besides owing money to moneylenders, crop-buyers and shopkeepers. In lean months they bought back their own produce at twice the price paid them, so even the credit was not their own.

The mine idle, a tender deadline passed, Prem Nath found his business threatened. He accepted penalty rates for late delivery; when his stock ran out he lost the contract. He and his sons called a meeting of the district's landed families. They exchanged stories of resistance and refusal. The Black Age had come and they agreed to fight it. The Dhol tribesmen did too. Tempers ran high; a Dhol was beaten unconscious; Prem Nath's gateman was waylaid and thrashed; a Dhol was beaten to death. The wealthy clubbed together: their private bodyguards would from now on be available to any landowner in need. Prem Nath was in need.

'Our lives are in danger!' he harangued his army. 'Our way of life is in danger, our caste is in danger, our faith is in danger!' The men waved axes, iron bars and lathis and shouted: 'Kill!' They drank a fiery round of country liquor and set out under the full moon for the village of Karwapani. Prem Nath went off to entertain the local sub-inspector and his constables. At Karwapani the goondas went from hut to hut striking down the wakened men and boys. Then they raped the women and girls. When they had finished, twelve men and an old woman lay dead, and not one woman had escaped assault.

The story made headlines in the national press. Journalists descended on the hamlet. A civil liberties group made a report in which Prem Nath's name figured.

The government sent a senior minister to calm the frightened villagers. When the minister arrived he went from his dak bungalow to the house of Prem Nath. Together they toured the block, Prem Nath pointing out where the miners had vandalized his mine, the local shops, a tubewell.

'But weren't the *tribals* attacked?' the minister asked, rubbing his eyes.

'Naturally we must protect ourselves,' Prem Nath answered, stung.

'Naturally,' the minister conceded, raising a hand.

'My son almost lost an eye.'

The son stepped forward to show a cut on the cheek where he'd been bitten during the rape of Karwapani.

'This was a peaceful place before these agitators came here.'

Voices spoke up in support.

'The fields were green, the mine was humming.'

'Every man had enough to eat.'

'The master gave us credit when we needed it.'

'He married off my daughter.'

'He saved my life.'

The minister, moved, postponed his visit to Karwapani. 'Please,' he said. 'What can I do to help?'

'We need protection,' Prem Nath said. 'Had you not come now we might have been overrun.'

'I will double the police force.'

'There are so few of them the force could be tripled.'

'It will be tripled.'

176

'That would be good. We can sleep safely in our beds now.'

When the minister returned to Delhi he briefed journalists. 'It is a law-and-order problem, basically,' he said. 'Subversives have been active in the region. We propose to upgrade the local police chowki to a thana. Severe understaffing brought on this calamity. With additional manpower and enhanced funding the situation will correct itself. Already life in Karwapani is returning to normalcy.'

The press and civil libertarians were not satisfied. Under public pressure another, lesser, minister was sent out to Karwapani on a fact-finding mission. This time he did visit the stricken village and took notes.

'We will see that the villains are brought to book,' he promised. Charges were brought against the more notorious of the goondas but they were not for murder. The men went smiling to jail on light sentences to be made lighter in time. There was money in it for them and Prem Nath would send them fruit, look after their loved ones. The one name missing from the chargesheet was Prem Nath's own. It turned out he and the lesser minister were related by marriage. Moreover, at election time he could swing three hundred votes.

STAR *camera will show Prem Nath and the minister walking up and down in the shade of a mango grove. Prem Nath 's eyes are on the ground, where he usually collects his thoughts; the minister's are in the trees, where luscious mangoes hang. After lunch there is a cordial leave-taking on the mine-owner's verandah. When the minister arrives at the nearest airfield, several crates of mangoes are among his luggage. They are loaded onto the plane by tribal women whose breasts have hung like mangoes since Kalidas wrote poetry in these parts fifteen hundred years ago.* STAR *camera, like every camera from clothed India, will find devious ways of creeping up on them for the delectation of*

177

its audience. These women are tribals: try one, *is its message. Camera may turn on its own grinning crew. Landing in Delhi, the minister finds a group of journalists waiting. They have been tipped off about the mangoes. The minister clutches his briefcase and walks stiffly through the group. The mangoes stand in the sun, unclaimed. In a few days they are rotten.*

There were no mangoes after the midday meal in the Dhol hut. We rose to wash our hands – the headman poured water – and my master belched onion.

For once I found his appetite in abeyance. He seemed occupied with some private meditation on the enormity of the crime that had stained that soil. And where I was tempted to reflect on the eternal categories called Oppressor and Victim, I sensed he was flirting out of old habit with the filmi bawd Revenge, and thus we both missed the elementary concreteness of the tragedy. He would have liked, I think, to make of justice a weapon, to take on that army of hirelings single-handed. I saw him seeing himself go through them like a knife through butter, fall on them like a ton of bricks, tear them limb from limb, crack their skulls like birds' eggs, break their bones like twigs and drive them before his rage like chaff. He would reenact the Rape of Karwapani, but this time he was waiting for them under the full moon. His mouth was set in quiet readiness; he towered there, his grim silence intercut with hurrying yabbering goondas.

STAR *camera picks up the revenge in one dreaming slow-motion sequence. Hero fells the first goonda, picks up the fallen iron bar, wades into the mob swatting right and left, fences with six men at a time, sends each one spinning into the night, breaks backs, heads, shins, loses his bar, is ducking, weaving, feinting, fly-kicking, chopping, butting, chasing, till finally he goes for the leader, to applause from* STAR *audience, whistles, cheers, cries as he slams into the man, tosses away his bright-edged axe,*
178

punches stomach, chest, ribs, nose, eye, neck, till the man falls
backward onto his own axe.

The tally now: twenty-four dead. Twelve-all. But the
first twelve, of his own chosen flock – was their death not
to have been cancelled by his presence, the protector?
And yet, if their death is rubbed out he is cheated of a
motive. Well, he must sacrifice one or two before he
swoops. Or three?

He starts, shakes his head, looks around him, and
presses his dark glasses into the shotaway bridge – a
gesture of embarrassment.

He need not worry. The fact is there is hardly a soul
among the Dhols of Karwapani who has seen a Ranga
film. They know him only as a dignitary from outside,
bigger somehow than the mineowner and the landlords
and the sub-inspector (who had accompanied him to their
village) but somehow interested in and moved by their
suffering. How moved, they cannot guess, but they sense
his confusion.

He recovers, speaks a few grave words and, stooping,
passes through the door. Some of the women outside
begin to wail, but others chide them. He and his party
walk through the village and down the path that leads to
the dusty road.

We'd been on the road, on foot, for a year.

It was his idea, his response to Gangajal Trivedi's offer.
He would, he said, have no truck with protectors of his
enemy, not even for a seat in parliament with a guaran-
teed portfolio. He would do it in his own way, he told the
khadi stranger as they went round and round the empty
swimming-pool. And he would get Nero too.

Quite what he would do in his own way, and what that
way would be he wasn't sure, he told me later, but as they
179

walked – the walking may have had something to do with it – ideas began to jostle one another in his head. I don't believe he determined to enter politics there and then, but some awareness must have dawned on him that fate having cut short one career, he must hit upon another, and here perhaps was the role, the new role, for him. It would be a greater challenge than any to come his way in the high noon of his life (my *Neta Harishchandra* excepted.)

So Gangajal Trivedi, arch catalyst, impinged on two lives that fateful evening. A fact which, had he known it (could he not?) would have caused him no heartburn since he was simply performing *his* role in life.

But whatever the prompting, the result was the pada-yatra, our cross-country march. Pilgrimage for him, foot-slog for me – but it was the journey of my life. His too, and theirs who joined us, walked with us, and fell by the way.

From Kashmir to Kanyakumari (just short, actually: Kashmir to Kizhanadu) it was our discovery of India.

We kept a straight line from north to south for the most part but had to walk around the bigger obstacles, and sometimes made a small detour to a place of particular interest. Or notoriety, as with Karwapani. Once or twice – four times – we cheated and took a train across stretches of hilly or inhospitable terrain – and then we travelled unreserved Second, the old Thud Class, with the masses. I went through five pairs of shoes, not counting full-sole repairs by roadside cobblers, once in the very heart of Connaught Place.

We started for old time's sake in the Vale of Kashmir by the fountain in the Shalimar gardens where he had danced with Kuku Kohli in *Anand Parbat* (The Peak of Bliss) and Preeti Juneja in *Shalimar*.

It was a fine September morning with just a hint of winter chill on our backs. Already the chinar trees were turning red. As we set out Ranga cupped a hand under the cascade which the emperor Jehangir's artisans turned
180

to lace by pitting the stone face underneath. He offered it to the sky, and watched the diamonds trickle through his fingers with his boss-eye. There was a cheer from the locals and the press who'd joined us, prepared to walk as far as the outskirts of the city.

I'd worried at first about the crowds. Wouldn't he be mobbed at every turn? And so we got his bodyguards to come along and a group of well-wishers. But we needn't have worried. As word spread of the padayatra, volunteers appeared out of nowhere to form a protective ring around us. Or rather, it was a horseshoe formation, with Hero and myself and one or two friends leading (UD, sensibly, stayed home) and the rest gathered around to the sides and behind. The volunteers were more jealously protective than the bodyguards: a few miles were enough to bind them to him with hoops the stronger for having been forged in the white heat of a chance encounter. They were content to rub shoulders with him (or rather with his paid bodyguards who rubbed shoulders with us who rubbed shoulders with him) but not always willing to share him with newcomers, whom they tended to discourage. Of course newcomers did join us, if only because in time even the stoutest of volunteers dropped back and out.

And what a piebald crew, our fellow travellers! Vagabonds, adventurers, hangers-on, escapees, cast-offs, runaways, elopers, untouchables, beggars, sadhus, students, thieves. There was even a food-faddist, though he dropped out with an ethnic stomach after one binge on *legumes à la Gosi Gulley*.

We walked along highways and lesser roads, using an old Survey of India map of my uncle's. Sometimes, to my delight, we found a new road where none was indicated. I took special note of the little squares where board and lodging might be had, the triangles where it was only lodging, the List of Important Places, the Places where

Delays May Occur, and marshalled our group accordingly. But as often as not Hero brushed aside my map and asked directions at crossroads or stopped to eat where no square was marked but a roadside dhaba happened to present itself. Unscientific, unmilitary! I wanted to shout, but they were already beginning to mock at me and I carefully refolded the map and packed it away. I divide the world into those who can and those who can't refold a map; Hero couldn't. The point was to keep to a straight line, due south as far as possible (I had my scouting compass – and, truth be told, a fat Swiss pocket-knife with many excellent functions.)

There were sacrifices to make to our straight line. I should have liked to revisit Dehra Dun, to go around the Clock Tower with him at my side, to show him my old haunts, the South Indian eateries – but it was out of plumb. So we stuck to the Grand Trunk Road and paused at the ancient battlefield of Kurukshetra and the medieval battlefield of Panipat while the modern battle raged around us: lorries ramming bullock carts, tempos chasing motorcyclists, mopeds on collision course with mules, a phalanx of bicyclists strung out against a speeding truck, and always the State Roadways bus with ninety captive souls bound for hell in a dust-storm.

It was an education for me too. To begin to read the characters of those patient village faces! To this day I recall the clamorous morning birds, the rich sweet smell of cowdung fires at evening, the tablas gabbling far into the night, the eternal chorus of pye-dogs. The small towns I knew better: their uneasy conceit, their prickly watchfulness. And then the smaller cities, with scruffy streets full of worried people, mostly thin, and a sprinkling of smug gentry.

Delhi was the only metropolis we entered. No conscious symbolism there – just the straight line south – but like much else on that journey, the entry had another meaning assigned it by the press.

I stood in the shade on a square of cardboard and got my shoes repaired on a pavement in Connaught Place. Across the road in D Block the Playfair cinema was showing the Keralite sexy, *Thundering Thighs*.

'Zero?' my master said tentatively, and lifted his eye to the billboard.

I must admit the thought of three hours' air-conditioning was tempting, for it was now summer again, but the poster promised a torrid afternoon: *the hotness of her body will rub itself around you by the screen*. I was not sure I could take that. Besides it would not have done his image any good, for there were photographers on every side.

So we walked on, my new shoe-leather squeaking, round the inner circle of CP rather than straight across, since not even he could stop the traffic that hurtles round the island green. Then we went up Parliament Street: again no symbolism – it was simply the shortest route to the MP Canteen on South Avenue where the food is good and cheap. Ranga would rather not have eaten there, partly because he wanted to try the Power and the Glory Punjabi restaurant on the outer circle (hardly the place for a vegetarian, I would have thought) but mostly because the canteen crawled with the very people he was out to rebuff, Members of Parliament. After all, the padayatra was his reply to Gangajal Trivedi's backscratching offer, his way of showing them.

'It's not just for MPs,' I assured him, an old hand myself. It beat a bun and scrambled eggs anyway. 'In fact it's full of foreign girls in singlets. And you can eat as much as you want. They keep bringing the rice.'

One of those inducements, I think the rice, swung him, and we marched past Rashtrapati Bhavan (without a second glance at Parliament House) and arrived at the canteen *en masse* for lunch.

It was not one of our more memorable meals. Several times during lunch MPs came over and wanted to shake his hand but he got around that by plunging it into the rice up to the wrist the way he'd grown up doing but had abandoned once he got to Bombay. I could sense the liberation in that act: he was free of past and present. But who can escape his future? Afterwards he washed his hands and ducked out, and all the way down Shanti Path I noticed him walking very straight as if to shake off the memory of those strangely cringing men of power. The old slouch – the one that made him – was gone and it would never come back. There was as it were a bone in his walk now, and it would never leave him. If anything it would petrify and in a way bring about his death.

And so we walked out of Delhi and came at length, as the old travellers say, to Karwapani. That was our half-way mark and its tragedy darkened the rest of our journey. Not that there weren't lighter moments, but it was hard to recapture the euphoria of the first half. From now on it was downhill. There were still green fields to lift our spirits and avenues of trees whose dark tunnels took us back a thousand years and more. You could imagine yourself an ancient pilgrim or a foreign traveller, Hsuan Tsang, for instance, whose account so vividly illuminates those distant times. The very Ashoka trees were descendants of those planted at the Emperor Ashoka's behest. But just when you fell in step with old Hsuan a Tata-Mercedes-Benz truck roared past, blaring its horn, its only link with the past that universal tailgate scrawl: OK-TATA.

We pressed on: Nagpur, Hyderabad, Bangalore, the change from north to south palpable once Nagpur was behind us. Such quiet refinement in the people once one was past that hairline rift! I felt ashamed of my northern-ness and at the same time felt Ranga expand and open up, as if he sniffed the cardamoms of Kizhanadu on the air. We were heading of course for the tip, for Kanyakumari, where India ends.

'Begins,' he corrected me, patiently.

We still came across peasants who didn't know him, a source of unfeigned pleasure to him. But then they turned petitioners and the stories they told would plunge him back into gloom, sordid tales of rape and skulduggery, of ceaseless litigation, of land records changed, of debt and disease and hunger. We had missed the most backward, the poorest states, and yet our latest fellow travellers told of crime after crime against the weak: the lawyer who inherited deed paper from his lawyer father – with sheets of old British India revenue stamps – and could take away your land; the judge who would rule against you unless you paid in cash or Scotch or women; the witch-doctor who cast out demons with your gold. We saw for ourselves racketeers with freaks dressed up as gods, a widow rescued from her husband's pyre, a walking skeleton, a horse flogged to death. And then we saw a whole village watching the soyabean oil woman sell potato chips on TV. So her adman was one step ahead of us, peddling his costly illusions, his cloven foot in the door. Not one handpump in that village; cola would get there sooner.

The towns were better off. You noticed with a start of pleasure glasses on a man pushing a cart, sometimes even on a woman. But the stories were familiar, the buck-passing, the percentages, the tips, the protection money, the capturing of shops, of flats, of public toilets, the vexations and indignities I remembered from my own small town. So there were limits to Southern refinement. Here too you could lose your land, your house, your savings, and the law would laugh at you.

The transition from village to town – and there were those with us undergoing that trauma, their lives' bundles on their heads – might be no more than an exchange of fatalism for cynicism. And yet one night as we looked

185

down a wretched stinking lane I saw a Chinese lantern hanging from an unfinished hovel, bathing the entire unplastered wall a deep rose-red.

In this way we came, Hsuan, to Kottagode, my master's birthplace.

It was the end of our padayatra but we didn't know it. We'd expected to pass through the town and go on down, a week's haul, to Kanyakumari, where he would walk symbolically into the sea. I saw him (and I know he saw himself) go down those last few granite steps to the little beach and scoop up a handful of water and offer it to the sun and the sea and the sky and watch the diamonds trickle through his fingers with his boss-eye. But it was not to be, thanks to a last and decisive outrage.

We were met at the town limits by a welcoming committee of the kind we had at first scorned and then learnt to welcome. His mother the fat and fair and grey Rangamma and the local notables stood in the middle of the road, surrounded by his orphans, their smiles stretched like banners, their outstretched arms supporting us even as we closed the gap with those last faltering quickened steps. Many of his boyhood friends were there, cheering wildly or simply standing in quiet admiration at the distance he had travelled from them – far greater I realized than that he had traversed on foot coming home.

It was late afternoon and after the first light refreshments – his favourite buttermilk and salted banana chips and finger-bananas – and the speeches there was some entertainment laid on for the evening. We walked (he was carried) past the Gandhi Park, the Nehru Hospital, the Shastri College, the IG Railway Station and a string of video parlours to the town maidan where rallies and Sunday wrestling were held or exhibition and circus tents were pitched.

And there before our eyes, before his boss-eye, was indeed a circus tent. It was the big top of the Astro Circus!

186

Hero Untongued.

We had an early dinner, for the show started at 8.30. There was a red carpet and special seats (a sofa) for him and for Rangamma who sat on his left, and myself who sat on his right. It must have been passing strange for him sitting there between us as the lights went down and the band struck up a jingly sort of number preparatory to the first fanfare. I could sense the muscles tightening in his thighs, as if in spite of the thousands of kilometres he had covered an old command stored these twenty years in his brain said: *On your marks!* and overrode his fatigue. One foot began ever so slightly to jiggle, and the knee with it, limbering up for some phantom performance. But tonight there was someone else in the big gun, in that sequinned black suit. The same suit? I wondered.

I realize now it was not pre-performance jitters, or even a nostalgia worked loose by that jumpy tune coming from the bandbox. No, it was simple terror, and the reason was quite simple.

Ranga was afraid of coming face to face with Indu.

Hero Unmanned.

What changes would the years have wrought in that frail girl he once sang to in the moonlight? If Hero had lost an eye to time, what forfeits might not fate have exacted from her? I watched him twitch and fidget and knew he wasn't taking in the jugglers and the ringmistress and the dreary clowns. He knew their tricks of old, he knew the very order, could have called the cues, so little had changed except the faces. He knew exactly when the bear came on, could pinpoint almost as if he were wholly blind, its fretful collar-bells behind the curtain. The acts came and went like shadows on the silver screen and left Hero unmoved. Of course he clapped with us, if anything more noisily, knowing the value circus folk set on applause, and knowing how grudgingly his countrymen

187

respond at circuses, but I could see he was disturbed, and I think Rangamma too saw through the charade.

When he could bear it no longer he got up, stooping the stoop that says: I Absolutely Must Nip Out For a Moment But Far Be It From Me To Spoil Your Entertainment So I Will Double Up Like This To Make Myself Inconspicuous. The big bang was due – the incumbent human cannonball would be limbering up in the shadows – but just before that came, he knew, the human pyramid on wheels.

What he proposed to do can't have been clear even to him; to us it was a mystery. Was he going to knock out the present man and take his place? Did he mean to spy on the smooth-legged girls as they rocked nervously back and forth on their fixed-wheel bicycles? Was it fresh air he wanted? Or was he simply going to take a leak?

I waited a few moments – half a minute – after he'd gone, and then went after him. I might have lost him had I waited to reassure Rangamma, who glanced maternally after him and then askance at me.

There was some small delay in the show, I could tell. The band was playing the same gliding waltz over and over and nothing was happening in the ring. Then a couple of clowns were drafted from the wings to do double duty, but their tricks were already stale, even to the simple audience. I veered instinctively towards the blur of white taffeta in the semi-darkness and found the pyramid in disarray. The apex was there, a tender little girl of twelve or thirteen. So Indu had clearly moved down the pyramid with the years as her shoulders widened; very likely she was the lynchpin of the base line.

And she was missing.

As I came up I saw one of the bicycles lying on its side without a rider; the other riders were mounted up, rocking to and fro on their bicycles and looking around desperately for their colleague. The manager and the ringmaster were in an anxious huddle. Just then I caught a glimpse of Hero disappearing through a canvas doorway beyond the big gun. I ran after him at once, realizing he must know the layout of the tents intimately: they were always pitched to pattern.

It was a moonless night and I could barely keep up with him as he ran between the tents, once nimbly leaping over a guy rope that brought me crashing to the ground. As I picked myself up out of the dust I saw where he was heading. There was only one tent ahead that had a light on inside, from what I could tell a dangling naked bulb which cast shadows on the striped canvas walls all round so the tent looked like some old-fashioned magic lantern. He was still a good way from the tent when I saw a shadow which curdled my blood.

It was the shadow of a hand with claws, its fingers horribly splayed. The hand came up on its shadowy arm and fell repeatedly upon the shadow of another figure in the tent.

There was a scream – cut short – and then the sound of a scuffle as Hero found the entrance to the tent. I hung back for a second, no more, then rushed forward shouting: *Bachao, bachao! Help!*

'Shut up! Zero!' my master hissed from inside the tent. The struggle continued in there and I realized he wanted to take his revenge in his own way, without interference. But already there was the sound of running feet as the circus folk responded to my call. And then suddenly the tent flap flung open and a figure, not Hero, burst out and struck me down and ran off.

I have the marks of those claws on my face to this day. But I didn't cave in right away. I heard a throaty chuckle from the departing figure and barged bleeding into the tent to see if Hero was all right. I needn't have worried about him; he'd been in fights before. But there was a

189

dead man on the ground under the naked bulb. And on the bed, alive but savagely raped, was Indu.

After that I fainted.

STAR camera would like to penetrate this zone, to inflict its own variety of rape, but I forbid it. Nor shall still cameras stick their beaks in. Black-out.

Chase

The dead man was Indu's husband. She'd married the
stilt man in the end. Big guns and high-wire men let you
down, she'd found. A small unassuming man, good with
his hands, he took giant strides around the ring three
times a day and then came down to her safe and whole.
But he'd gone drinking one night and been framed in an
assault on a Freedom Party man. The party worker had
died; this was the revenge.

Indu fainted and woke and wept and fainted again.
Rangamma sat beside her bed; the circus girls brought
coffee, then retired to their dormitory to whisper and lie
awake. The show had been called off as soon as the
murder became known. A doctor was called and he
dressed my wounds, but Indu would not let him near her
– nor would Ranga allow it. At length she fell asleep on a
sedative, mumbling snatches of her tattered dreams: she
was falling, she was afraid, was she safe? was he? UD
was so beautiful, she must be a happy woman.

Listening to her I wanted to weep. The police had come,

made their notes, taken the body for a post-mortem; a report had been lodged. The man was a corpse; it was Indu who moved me. And by a strange reversal it was I who now burned for revenge while Hero sat chastened and still. It was as if by that rape *he* had lost his innocence, his illusions.

I looked at him and recalled the time somewhere in Andhra when he stood filmi fashion in front of the bulldozer that was razing a city slum and almost got his legs chopped off because the blade was real and the dozer-driver called his bluff.

'The bloody thing kept coming, yaar,' he complained afterwards, a touch of petulance creeping in.

'You could have got killed, boss.'

Now he sat there emptied of filmi bombast at last. And here I was, falling on Nero – for it was he, I was sure; that chuckle was his – like a ton of bricks, cracking his skull like a bird's egg, snapping his bones like twigs. No doubt the cat-lash on my face had something to do with it. It burned like stripes of fire.

Not that he intended to let Nero get away with it. But this time he would do it without so large a gesture as a padayatra. He would give chase all right, filmi chase even, but when he caught up with the villain he would turn him – not inside out, but simply *in*.

This new respect for the law was a sign of a cooling in him. I was the hothead now. I wanted to crucify Nero; he simply wanted to catch him. It was also, this newfound or newly manifest level-headedness, the mark of a grow-ing craft in the man. Or was it simply a new mode of proceeding? Was this the maturing of my master? The opening of a third eye? Or just tactics?

Whatever the truth, it meant that in the chase that followed he was the ballast while I swung the wheel. He still gave directions, called the shots (more than one came our way too), but it was my foot on the pedal. Sometimes I obeyed, sometimes I pretended not to hear.

We left Indu in Rangamma's care till she was fit to go back to her only family, the circus. She had a little daughter, an india-rubber girl.

'Yes-yes-yes,' Rangamma said. 'You just go and look after your own wife.' She looked hard at her son but was baffled by the dark glasses.

I do believe he did a tiny double-take in their shade – which I had learnt, better than his mother, to read.

It said: 'Wife?'

But he shook his head sideways in pious agreement and bent to touch her feet. Her face softened and her love oozed at a thousand points like melting coconut oil.

'Come on, Zero,' he muttered, climbing in.

And I patted my bandages like the Mummy and stepped on it so our Gypsy hardtop went from 0 to 110 in sixty seconds, spraying the soil of his hometown back on Kottagode and the committee which only two days before had been strung out across the road to welcome us. We were heading back north now because that was the way Nero had gone.

We caught up with him before very long, but he always managed to keep the gap. He was driving a two-tone Ambassador – perhaps the old one with fake number-plates and the roof left white – so he wasn't hard to follow but there was always that bend in the road just when we were on him, or that bent old woman or shining schoolgirl in the way just when I changed down to overtake.

'Watch out for her, Zero, watch out, WATCH out!'

Or: 'Easy, boy, EA-sy!'

Or simply: 'ZERO!'

I don't know why he took a four-wheel drive when we spent much of that journey on two wheels. I suppose he was thinking of the terrain, but then the Ambassador grew up on Indian roads. As it happened the Gypsy was the only vehicle on hand, though Rangamma's jupiter Motor Works (Sales and Service) was doing very well. And it served our purpose eventually – better than his Mercedes might have done anyway.

Sometimes we got too close and there were bullets to duck. Nero would turn in his seat and, steering with his left hand, blaze away backwards THAAIN! THUIIN! TTHUSS! with his handgun, the very one he'd used at closer quarters on Hero. We were safe enough in the circumstances, but when (at I think it was Hyderabad) we looked up to find another figure beside him in the front, we hung back a bit because now one could aim while the other steered.

STAR *camera knows what to do throughout this sequence.*

It was of course Captain Memo, in a Startrek cabin suit and, on his slightly pointed ears, mobile perspex earrings. I'd often wondered what the two villains, Number 1 and Number 2, would do when brought together; the answer from what I could tell was: *laugh*. I should have known. There was manic laughter in that car. It floated back to us on the jasmine-scented air, spiked with heavy metal.

We might have been extraterrestrial visitors, all of us, not just Captain Memo, for any rapport we had with the countryside we flashed through. A private car, I realized as we flew just above the wretched roads, is a spaceship in this country. About the only contact we made with the lives around us was when we threshed with our tyres the harvest the farmers had laid out on the roads for that purpose. We ate that grain, but the route it travelled to our snatched vege-burgers was so obscure and convoluted we might just as well have been munching on slabs of space food.

194

And flying low we saw what we'd missed or romanticized on foot. We saw forests destroyed, rivers poisoned, huge valleys dammed and land made desert from repeated rape. We saw diseases flourishing like weeds, bright signboards that only every fifth man could read – and only every twentieth woman. We saw cracks appearing in the earth around us as if the entire country were drying up and withering away. The gaps between the states were widening – we flew across them like stuntmen – but most alarming, when we got to the Vindhyachal border, where once there had been a hairline fracture there now yawned a considerable canyon. There'd been language riots on that border, and the South, by virtue of some obscure plate tectonics – the reverse of that geologic thrust which created the Himalayas and my own Doon valley – was drifting away from India. *Dravidistan*, the posters said, as once they'd said *Pakistan*. In the North we had our own secessionists, demanding *Thistan* and *Thatland*.

Fortunately we had southern numberplates or we might have lost a windscreen to their wrath south of the border. Once we were stopped and Ranga produced his southern credentials in his Dravidian tongue; had it been daytime his face would have been enough. I remembered how as schoolboys we dismissed all those southern languages as pebbles rattled in a clay pot; that night his rattling was music to my quaking ears. Nero was less fortunate: his Ambassador was mobbed (*STAR camera is jostled*.) But he got away with a smashed rear window – which only made it easier for them to take pot-shots at us.

Released, we drove at high speed to the border. Nero was already there, pulled up at the edge of the canyon, peering in. When he saw us coming he reversed, took a short high-revving run and sailed across like Evel Knievel.

195

I didn't stop at all: we simply leaned back and thought of India. That willed the front wheels up.

We landed with a crash in the North, and there was a tyre to change. Up the road it was our turn: we were stopped by anti-southern agitationists while Nero was waved on. But Hero spoke so beautifully in Hindi he'd learnt from scripts (I felt ashamed at being bettered in my own tongue) we charmed our way through. I saw then how Bollywood could do more for national integration – he was a classic case himself – than the Indian Railways.

Afterwards he took the wheel and we lost still more time. But my face was stinging from that cat's paw swipe and I needed a rest. The roads got worse. We slowed to a crawl.

'What a country!' I complained.

'A country is not a Roadways bus, Zero,' he said, as a Roadways bus hurtled past us on the wrong side of the road.

I looked at him. Was this my master talking? This was not his way. It was hardly his voice. He kept his boss-eye on the road and slowed down still further. I watched with anguish the Ambassador dwindle to a speck.

'What do you mean, boss?' I said when it was gone. Maybe he was giving them rope. But I would rather string Nero up myself.

'There's such a thing as procedures.'

'Procedures?'

'Everything in its place and time.'

'I see.' I did not see.

'Navigating procedures, for example,' he said, reading my confusion. 'Or legal procedures. Or farming procedures.'

'Or kite-flying procedures,' I said, cuffing on.

'Exactly,' he said. 'Or parliamentary procedures.'

'But that's for Members of Parliament!' I spluttered. *Mad Dogs*, I might have said.

'Yes.' He smiled an unctuous smile.

'You're not thinking of becoming one?' I said aghast.

'Well, the canteen is not too bad.'

'Stop the car!'

He pulled over to the side of the road obediently. It was the first time I had used that tone on him.

I climbed out and was sick. He climbed out too and rubbed my back as I vomited. Then he gave me his handkerchief.

'That's it,' I said, 'This is where I get off. Don't worry, I'll get a ride.'

'But we're in the middle of nowhere.'

'Not to worry.'

My map told me we were at the very centre of our central state. My eyes told me we were in the middle of a forest. We'd reached, by any reckoning, the very heart of India. I pictured my compass needles spinning crazily round and round. I sat down on one of those white-washed tar barrels which keep night drivers on the straight and narrow. It would be dark soon.

'Come off it, Zero,' he said. 'I mean, look, what the hell do you think you are? Some kind of saint or something? I mean, I used to think like you too. Riding some kind of bloody high horse.'

'So what happened?'

'What happened? The bloody padayatra, that's what happened. Where were you at the time?'

'I heard about it.'

'But where were your *eyes*, yaar?' he huffed.

'Same place as – ' *Yours*, I was going to say, but I swallowed the rest. He brushed aside my embarrassment.

'As mine, I know. OK, maybe. But you must be completely blind if you didn't see what I saw with just one eye. You should have seen twice as much. But it looks like you need these.'

He took off his dark glasses, my dark gogs, and held

them out to me. For the first time I saw the hollow where his left eye had been. It was darker – I would have thought it should be lighter – than the skin around it and the flaps of the lids had been sewn together along the line of the lashes. It was like looking down the barrel of a gun – not Nero's tiddler, or even a circus gun, but the first gun, the Starting Gun, the gun of the Big Bang. I blinked and looked away.

'Go on. Put them on,' he said, staring at me.

A boss-eyed stare is a stare-and-a-half. I obeyed.

'Now what do you see?'

'Not much.'

'It takes a little while. Try closing your eyes.'

I'd had enough of this game. I snatched the gogs off my nose and thrust them back into his hands. Evidently he saw other things with them than I'd seen as an adolescent. He put them back on and covered the black hole, that pregnant crater that made darkness visible.

'I mean, never mind the sights,' he went on. 'Weren't you listening? Didn't you hear any of the stories? This poor guy can't get water for his crops because the thakur has bribed the civil engineer to divert the canal to his fields. That shopkeeper's shop was taken over the day before he opened and he wasn't allowed in until he paid fifty thousand. This guy's phone hasn't worked for six months because he refuses to tip the lineman; that guy's letters are not delivered because he forgot to tip the postman.' (He winced at the word *postman*.) 'This woman goes from office to office because her file has been lost. Two hundred rupees will find it for her instantly, but she can't afford to pay. Everybody has his percentage fixed. The municipal sweeper wants his tip or he won't clean your drain. The educated housewife has her sweeperess throw the rubbish into the street. The nurse in the hospital won't touch a floor swab because it's not her job – and the

198

entire bloody stinking mosquito-infested ward dies of encephalitis.'

He would have gone on but I held my hands up.

'OK, boss.'

'OK, but who's responsible for the mess? You really think it's just the leaders? I mean, these are crimes of the people, by the people, against the people. The whole show is rotten from top to bottom.'

'You mean bottom to top.'

'Maybe. I mean, the other day a block development officer told me he organized a seminar on corruption in public life for the governor but nobody came so the poor guy had to run around bribing people to attend – and he got caught.'

As he was talking a video coach came up from behind and slowed down till it drew level with us. The bus was empty but the video was going full blast so the driver and the conductor could hear the di-laag up in front. The automatic door opened and a stench of overripe fruit spilled out. Both men had a familiar look.

'Having trouble?' the driver called, turning his head only slightly towards us when he spoke.

'No, we're all right,' I said.

The conductor twisted around in his seat but kept his face from us. *'Sure?'* he said.

'Hey!' Hero shouted.

I jumped up.

The bus roared off and left us in a cloud of dust. Only when the dust settled did we recognize the mocking laughter. It was a deep Neroic chuckle.

We looked at each other. It might have been the video. Nero movies had become popular since he disappeared.

'Bugger gets around,' he said.

We sat in silence for a while. A buffalo cart went by loaded with cement sacks. The driver must have been late because every few feet he brought a stick down on the buffalo's back with all his might. There were several suppurating patches along the creature's spine where the yoke had gone in; the stink caught in my nose. A crow which was following the cart swooped down from time to time and pecked at the pink flesh. The driver took a swing at it too.

'Come on,' I said, and got back into the passenger seat.

He slammed the other door and we moved on sedately. The orange skin of the Gypsy was mantled in dust.

I took a swig of tepid water and said: 'Which party?'

He reflected for a moment. 'Independent.'

'What party is that?'

'It's not a party. You stand as an independent candidate.'

'Oh.' Politics to me meant parties.

'You're not a political animal, Zero.'

'Are you?'

'Let's see.'

And he fixed his eye on the row of tar barrels which had begun to glow blue-white in the failing light.

STAR *camera is mesmerized by the stream of barrels.*

I wondered whether he was up to night driving but didn't know how to ask.

'It doesn't affect the peripheral vision?' I said at length.

He didn't answer. I babbled on in confusion.

'I mean, they say it affects depth-of-field. You can't judge depth, distances, you know. It's like when I close one eye it all looks sort of flat.'

There was no reply. I began to worry. Had I offended him? Were we on automatic pilot? Was he asleep? Was he driving with the third eye? I got ready to grab the steering wheel if he strayed towards oncoming traffic.

'Baas?'

No reply.

'baas!'

We missed a cyclist by a whisker. A Jat, so we were back on my territory.

'Yes, Zero?'

It was the voice of Almighty God. It came down from on high and filled the car with its assurance. I sank back in my seat and laughed weakly.

'I thought you were asleep, baas.'

Silence.

'How did it feel, baas? At first. How did you feel when you woke up with – '

'One eye? I felt split in half. I felt as if half of me had gone to sleep and wouldn't wake up and I was in a moving car and the steering wheel was on the wrong side.'

It occurred to me that this was how God felt, in the beginning.

'And look at what He did.' I found I'd spoken out loud.

'Sorry?'

So he wasn't divine.

I said: 'It's all very well to blame the people, to itemize their crimes. If they're everybody's crimes they're nobody's crimes. If you spread the guilt thinly enough it disappears. No villains, no victims.'

'That's right. It's all an illusion.' He spoke lightly, humouring me. 'All leela, nothing but play.'

'Indu was real.'

I felt the Gypsy leap forward under his reflexed foot. My point had gone home, but all the same I saw his point.

Night had fallen, and the windscreen suddenly looked like a giant pair of dark glasses through which I saw more clearly than by day. A random rain of moths drawn by our headlights spattered the glass. I saw the stupendous exorbitance of the living world, the waste of it all. And in that teeming glimpse of nature's recklessness I thought I saw the villain's face. It was excess that was the villain. For every successful – every fit – survival thousands, millions, perished, were sacrificed, squandered. And history mimicked that excess: no heroism, no villainy, just the fall of the dice.

'So is Nero,' he said grimly.

'Then,' I backtracked, 'there might just be room for responsibility. After all, the dice aren't loaded.'

'What dice?'

'And as a leader your share would be greater. It's fair enough: more loot, bigger load.'

'Maybe.'

We drove (he drove) all night, while I dozed and every now and then woke up and made bright conversation to cover up my dozing.

'Go to sleep, Zero,' he said evenly, and I obeyed.

I awoke at a roadblock in the early morning. Some cops had flagged us down. I rubbed my eyes of sleep-sand and looked around. We were outside a police thana which stood hard by a dak bungalow, possibly a canal inspection-house. The cops had rifles, World War I .303s, greatcoats and toothache mufflers topped with khaki caps, and they stood like dolmens in the mist around our Gypsy. Apart from the thana jeep there was a foreign car parked in the rest-house drive, and a large blue bus. We recognized it at the same moment. It was the video coach.

Hero got out and stretched his legs. He was immediately recognized by the constables, who were reduced to star-struck schoolboys. A deputy superintendent came up to him and spoke a few whispered words with an exquisite gesture towards the canal bungalow.

I realized they'd nabbed Nero. My reaction was curiously bland for one who'd spent days fantasizing – picturizing – that final reckoning, the gun battle, the slow-motion death dance as my bullets, not my master's, found their mark. Now I simply got out of the Gypsy and tied a

202

shoe-lace that had come undone. The pleasure had clearly been in the chase; in capture the essence slipped away. The sadness, almost post-coital, may have touched Hero too.

'Breakfast, Zero,' he announced. And we went past the thana with its straggly pink oleander bushes to the white-washed rest-house. The captive villains could wait.

There was indeed a hot breakfast laid out on the table, as if our arrival had been anticipated to the minute. There were hard-boiled eggs cut in half lengthwise, a single saucer with salt and pepper mixed for dipping, fresh samosas, mint chutney, a large pot of tea and three heavy white china cups, conscientiously begrimed. Our host stepped out of the VIP suite as we entered the dining-room. He had the brisk dumpy movements and basilisk breath that for me instantly constituted, ever since that night by the empty swimming-pool, Gangajal Trivedi.

'Aaiye, aaiye, Hero Sahib!' he said. 'Well-come, well-come! You are just in time for break-fast.'

He pulled a chair back for my master and then one for himself and sat down. Then he noticed me.

'And of course the faithful Mr Zero. Please be seated. Help yourself. These are pure vegetarian eggs. I hope you do not mind my simple vegetarian offerings. Afterwards I have some non-vegetarian offerings, but first please enjoy.'

I was enjoying already, the first food I'd eaten since throwing up the day before. Ranga too began to engulf eggs and samosas but I noticed he held back, sipping tea (though he would have preferred coffee) until both Gangajal and I had eaten a few mouthfuls. It was the first time I think he saw in me a food-taster. Our host ate steadily and fresh platters appeared before us as the meal progressed. Finally we sat sucking at the grubby cups of hot sweet stewed tea. One samosa remained.

'Hero Sahib!' our host exclaimed, waving at it.

'Zero!' my master said, deflecting the offer.

I still had room for another, but something in me rebelled. I pushed the plate a short way towards our host and said expansively: 'Gangajal Sahib!'

The little eyes hooded instinctively and spat cold fire. Patronage from a nonentity! But it was over in a moment and he smiled once more at Hero. I wondered if I would have barked without my master at my back.

'Come, Ranga Sahib. Here is a lonely lady.'

And my master obliged.

'*Lots* of thanks, Ranga Sahib!' our host said. 'Now for the non-. You can have it howsoever you like.'

Hero was quiet for a while. Then he said: 'I thought he was your man.'

'Mr Nero?'

'Yes. I thought you were protecting him.'

Gangajal's eyes bulged as he mimed cordial astonishment for his guest.

'But I *was*!' he protested. 'I was keeping him for this very moment. For you. I simply wished to whet your appetite. I myself would like to watch a true-life drama. Now Mr Ranga will have the real bullets. You can finish him at your leisure, and we will say it was a police encounter. Simple.' He smiled an academic smile.

Hero looked at him, returning the smile.

'And when I have – finished,' he said, 'I will eat forever out of your hand, with twenty police witnesses. You take me for a poodle, Gangajalji.'

I bristled for my master. Gangajal looked scandalized.

'Ranga Sahib. What would I gain by that, pray tell? This way I have your gratitude; other way I become your enemy. Understand, please, it is not your obedience I require but your support – voluntary support. If I want your collaboration, your goodwill, which way will I choose? Tell!' He shook his head diagonally. 'Anyway, it looks to me like you have lost your appetite for shikar.

And your friend here also has lost, although only yesterday he was your hunting dog. Even I think he was himself the hunter, yes?'

He pushed his chair back and rose, leaning on the table. Then he stopped halfway before straightening up.

'Oh. There is one other thing my men have discovered. I think you will like to see.'

He stepped out into the verandah where a servant brought him a stainless steel tumbler of water. He threw his head back, poured a little water into the open mouth, ran it around, gargled and spat at the oleanders. Then he poured the rest in, without once letting the rim touch his mouth, and drank it down.

'Come,' he said, and led us out the way we'd come. We walked past his long green car and the tourist bus Nero had hijacked on abandoning the two-tone Ambassador. I thought of the fifty irate tourists wandering in a forest whose numerous signs proclaimed: SOCIAL FORESTRY.

At the thana a fawning sub-inspector led us to the clink. There were two cells in fact. One had a couple of ragged unfortunates – and Captain Memo in his Startrek cabin suit. The other cell, separated from the first by a passageway, held only one prisoner: Nero. He stood there defiant in his Ray-Bans, gripping the bars of his cell and staring coldly at us.

I felt again the stripes on my face and controlled a desire to lunge at him.

'I don't think you need to keep them apart,' Hero joked. 'They couldn't get their lines straight if they worked all day.'

The sub-inspector looked at the DySP. The DySP looked at Gangajal who coughed delicately and wagged a finger at the sub-inspector. The sub-inspector looked at his shoes and cleared his throat.

'You see, sir,' he said. 'It's like this. Last night we had to . . . strip the prisoners and we found that . . . Mr Nero . . .

205

that . . . he was . . . he is actually . . . You see, sir. This is the women's cell.'

You could have knocked me over with a boa. As for Hero, he didn't know where to look.

Nero a *woman*!

The Number 1 Villain he'd fought a hundred fist-fights with, two hundred gunfights with, whose deep throaty chuckle sometimes gave him real nightmares, who'd come close to finishing him off, who'd led him a wild chase across the country – to end up in the women's cell!

And then a more sombre thought struck him. If Nero was a woman, who had raped Indu?

He turned on his heel and walked out. The chase was over. His race had just begun.

Cliffhanger

The point of running was to change things. Where had I heard that before?

But I didn't doubt that he was sincere. He wanted a return to values in politics, to principles, to justice, to the rule of law rather than the rule of goondas. Nero might be a woman, but there were a million Nero understudies who were not. Everyone of them had, in a sense, had his way with Indu, and one could not tackle them in the old way, with a crowbar. One had to change the regime that protected them.

He started by changing his head. Or rather, he changed his image. He shaved his head clean, sweeping those famous curls into the dustbin of history. The head that emerged was still black and glossy, but now it was smooth and polished, like a granite lingam. It had me worried for a while: was he too black for the Indian voter? After all, up North we advertised for pale wives. True down South they cooed over every newborn babe regardless (they'd done it over *him*) 'How *fair*!' but would it work with an adult?

In the event it didn't hurt him. Or there were other things that helped him. Perhaps the head took the place of the shrivelled hump. If it did it must have sent conflicting signals to the populace. On the one hand it gave him an ascetic look, repudiating his sensual past; on the other it made of him a walking phallus, albeit a phallus in dark glasses.

However that was, he grew back his little Southy moustache to compensate for the lost hair and took to wearing white khadi, that compulsory hand-spun uniform of our politicos. He stopped shaking hands, pressing his own together in greeting in the open-fingered namaste which struck me as slack, however apt. The immediate result was that people no longer touched him, nor he them. But like his political colleagues he quickly developed a listening stoop, a dip of the head; in his case his height justified it. Thus he both withdrew from and inclined towards his new and less finicky audience.

We left Nero pacing like a lioness in her cage, and Captain Memo gibbering and fly-kicking his cell bars. Gangajal Trivedi accompanied us to Delhi, just over the Ridge it turned out. Or we accompanied him – we chased his Toyota now – and there in South Delhi, in the Ahuja's cavernous den, plans were laid for the coming election.

It seemed Gangajal – GJ, we began to call him, and in shape and colour he did rather resemble a syrupy gulab jamun – had suffered another change of heart. In the old dynastic days of Indian Heirlines, he'd been a staunch Freedom Party man. Then an unfortunate snub made him see things the Opposition way, and he backed the winning Justice and Progress Party under a new Mr Clean. Four years later he'd thrown his weight behind a Justice and Progress Party splinter, the Justice and Peace and Progress Party, the JPPP, with a new (and improved) Mr Clean, the present PM. Now that the incumbent was discredited, GJ needed a new face. He found it on my master.

He talked him out of the Independent gambit, but agreed that he should steer clear of the existing parties for the moment. Why not foster a movement instead, a movement for social hygiene (MSH) or a movement for the restoration of value-based politics (MRVBP)? In this way one could win friends and political allies among the Opposition parties right across the board, since no one in his right mind could object to the movement's high ideals. At the same time you kept aloof from each of them so that when it came to alliances they were equidistant from you (but not from each other.) Thus none of them need yield more ground than any other to reach you, while your own hovering – like a conscience – near each of them ensured that your distance from any of them was always smaller than that which separated them from each other.

Of course, if the stratagem was to work you must capture the public's imagination in greater measure than any one of them individually, and if possible – as it could very well be in Hero's case – all of them together. Then, as the election drew nearer you emerged as the only credible alternative: your movement became a party and by sheer force of gravity the others were trapped in orbit around you. They were your government, your cabinet; you tossed portfolios among them like bones.

'And you, GJ? What is your reward? Not a portfolio, I think.'

'Hero Sahib, I am past such foolishness.'

'I know you are, Trivedi Sahib. That's why I am asking. There must be something.'

'Something there must be, Hero Sahib. But it is so small I am ashamed to name it.'

'Name, GJ, name. Let us pretend I am already in power.'

'Let us go for a little walk. Around Ahujaji's swimming-pool.'

Ahuja and I took the hint and stayed where we were,

two weathered Old Spoonies facing middle life with more than a hint of tarnish. We chatted about golf clubs.

Afterwards I asked my master what happened. He looked at me coolly and said: 'The pool was full.'

'Oh.'

I must have sounded disappointed because he took me up. He was tossing bones already.

'He said he'd always wondered what it was like to live at the top of Rajpath, in Rashtrapati Bhavan.'

'He wants to be President!'

'I think his wife would like to be Mrs President.'

'Pedro would like to be Top Parrot – Pakshipati.'

'He says he's tired of power. Now he'd like a taste of glory.'

'He'd be happy as a figurehead?' I had my doubts.

'Head of State, I think so.'

'Couldn't he dismiss you once he got there?'

He frowned. 'Theoretically maybe. I don't know. What would he gain?'

'President for Life. I can think of a few.'

'This is not a banana republic, Zero. We're too big to go that way I mean, here a PM is assassinated and we carry on – no coups nothing. How many Third World countries can you say that about? We have a constitution, institutions, traditions . . .'

'Procedures.'

'Procedures. A loyal army, a free press, an ancient culture.'

'Red tape.'

'Hah! That alone would do the trick. But I mean we have three thousand years of civilization.'

He was starting to sound like Prime Minister already.

'I mean,' and his voice said he meant it, 'look what we've given the world.'

'Zero,' I suggested.

He flared up. 'What!'

'*Zero*. The decimal system – the foundation of modern mathematics, science, technology.'

'Oh yes. And philosophy.'

'The philosophy of Zero.'

'OK, OK, but poetry. Grammar. Weaving.'

'Yoga.'

'Music.'

'Calico.'

'Transcendental Meditation.'

'Curry powder.'

'Bad movies.' It was UD. She'd come in as we began to drift off among the violins. She looked fatter than I remembered, as if the Punjabi cooking up North had finally got to her. They still had Francis, their hatchet-faced Goan chef, but I saw she must be eating out on the sly. Double helpings of carrot halva from the look of it. A padayatra would have done her good, but neither she nor he would have it.

'Bad movies,' he agreed, slipping an arm around her.

I noticed she flinched minutely – or else it was a tic developed, like the overeating, while we were away walking. Long separation had made strangers of them and they would have to practise to come together naturally.

'So you're going into politics,' she said.

He'd meant to surprise her; now she caught him on the wrong foot.

'Yes.' It was a confession. He actually hung his head.

'From which seat?'

'Seat?'

I do believe he hadn't thought of that. And he was already appointing the President. Maybe that is the way to go about it.

'Ya. Which constituency?' She wasn't going to let him off.

'Oh, we'll cross that bridge when we come to it.'

It was a politic reply anyway.

The seat we picked for him turned out to be Nandi, up for by-election in the state of Vindhyachal. I almost said *border* state, so parlous a turn had North-South relations taken. There were language riots almost every day somewhere along that rift that separated us from them, the alleged Aryan North from the putative Dravidian South. Bridges were daily tumbling down along that line of discontent as the crack widened, though it wasn't equally wide everywhere. At Nandi, which was perched on the northern edge, the fault was wide enough for alarm, an alarm which underlay the bluster on both sides. It had been a safe Freedom Party seat in the old days under Indian Heirlines, but then it swung to the Justice and Progress Party under the new Mr Clean. Then it swung to the Justice and Peace and Progress Party under the new and *improved* Mr Clean, and now, given its propensity to swing, it was up for grabs.

GJ's advice was sound when it came to distancing ourselves from the Opposition. As an exercise in politicization, and to bone up on their tactics, I was sent to scout around at the Freedom plenary session. The idea appealed to the sleuth in me.

'Incognito?' I asked.

'Would you be recognized if you went cognito?'

He wasn't being cruel. All the same I got myself a homespun kurta that took me back to college days. Then, deciding that was not enough, I got the khadi pyjama trousers to match, exchanged my shoes for chappals, and turned up at the Mahalanobis Auditorium lawns where they'd been haranguing the faithful all day.

I recognized with a pleased surmise two or three of the faces you saw regularly in the papers. So they were real. Each one made sense when he spoke, even when he contradicted the previous speaker, and I found myself holding several variant positions in succession, regarding one man as the arbiter of truth until the next one had started. Then I would be tempted to applaud that man rather than the one before. I checked myself of course – suppose another of our agents should see through my disguise and observe me clapping? – but it occurred to me that if I, a professional rhetorician, were so easily swayed, how much simpler it must be with a rustic listener! These men (and one or two women) on the sheeted dais were not the buffoons one habitually took them for. And yet they were no sages. They were simply an agile, wriggly version of the species, a kind of mutant hominid.

What then was that volatile stuff in me, sapient me, that threatened to, nay longed to, boil over in enthusiastic agreement with a position I had hardly tested? Was there that in me which wanted, which needed, which cried out to be led, even misled? What was that hot momentary contract that bound me to one speaker after another? What was this perennial blind indenture to which nonentities – or for that matter entities – willingly entailed themselves in matters of governance? Was it simply that we were too busy with other things? But we showed no such enthusiasm with the other jobbers and specialists we employed: the dhobi who washed our clothes or the lawyer who fought our case. Why this perfervid and spontaneous slavishness with politicians? Even when a part of us – of every imperfect one of us, however simple – stood in unerring judgement over them and knew them to be false? Was it simply that they had what we instinctively craved but from lack of energy had ceased to covet, namely power? Or was there some other part that wanted to believe?

I realized I'd spent so much time considering the nature of leadership I hadn't worried myself over a question much nearer me: the nature of followership. Until that evening I hadn't seen for myself, or I hadn't been shown, quite how biddable my impulses could be.

The speakers came and went. I noticed even the cow-belt ones spoke a curious duoglot Hindi in which the English *rank and file*, *programme*, *policy*, even *politics* kept popping up, presumably accessible to an urban audience. Was this forked tongue symbolic, or just symptomatic of the problem? The others – not just the Southies; Eastern-ers too – used English, or Indish, a choice which immedi-ately emptied the tent. No more eloquent omen for us English-Medium types.

A Hindi speaker came on and the tent filled up again, when suddenly a Southy group began shouting slogans. The speaker strove to ignore them; then he tried to drown them. They drowned him instead. People began to move towards the source of disturbance; others, their view blocked, stood up and protested, blocking the view of those behind. Scuffles broke out, peacekeepers waded in to twist arms, the speaker battled on. To save the meeting the president stood up and took the microphone.

'Those who are crying slogans,' he called in English, 'will please refrain.'

I was reminded of the sign, in English, still evident on certain railway platforms: COMMIT NO NUISANCE.

The slogans grew louder. Opponents of the dissenters began to chant counter slogans. The peacekeepers grew impatient.

'So, I was saying – ' the speaker said. He had the microphone again.

The president took it back. 'Friends,' he called, still in English, 'I request you. This is not the way.'

Fists began to fly.

'Order! You *shall* maintain order! We will *not* allow this to happen. The decorum and decency of this forum will not be marred. Those who are creating disturbance will please desist.'

I couldn't see the rank and file taking that in. But then

214

he was addressing Southies, and they wouldn't make much sense of Hindi either. English, thou shaky bridge!

The speaker retrieved his microphone and began again.

'I was saying,' he said in Hindi. *'To mera kahna tha –'*

'I request speakers to be brief,' the chair called in English.

'I *will* be brief,' the speaker retorted. 'I will give the shortest speech in history. JODO!' he cried at the top of his voice, 'UNITE!' And he sat down trembling, vindicated.

The peacekeepers surrounded the Southy sloganeers and heaved them out of the tent. Some of the protesters were bleeding; there were several torn shirts. Ejected, they raised their slogans outside. I went out to have a look. They were licking their wounds now, crying a new slogan.

'Down with goondaism!'

'Let him come to Bangalore!' one man spat. He meant the president.

'Let him come to Bangalore,' his comrades agreed.

It was the voice of the South, speaking to Northies. I felt sure in those minutes the crack had widened.

I left with the slogans and unity calls clashing in my head. If this was the state of the Opposition we had a way to go. And over the months that followed our People's Service Movement (PSM) had to tread a fine line between unity noises and regional assurances.

When Hero's candidacy was finally announced there was a nationwide wave of euphoria. Filmi nostalgia, mainly: there were Ranga retrospectives at hundreds of Hind Talkies throughout the Union. People came out of the theatre talking as if he were already in parliament. But as the by-election drew near it was clear that nostalgia alone would not win it. The ruling party candidate was Hansraj Gupta, no pushover. He had twice been an MP and before that had spent a quarter of a century in state politics. He was a Vindhyachal man and moreover the caste equations favoured him, though of late he had antagonized his own followers by his autocratic style and abrasive manner.

Hero's followers in the newly vaunted Praja Seva Maksad (our PSM) had under GJ's guidance become a sort of disciplined task force mobilizing public opinion through his existing fan clubs, a network Hansraj Gupta publicly mocked but privately envied. In addition Ranga had the loan of hundreds, and later thousands, of campaigners from the entire gamut of the Opposition parties. For most it was a paid holiday, and their enthusiasm was almost greater than the PSM's. Naturally, the established Opposition leaders lent their troopers with an eye to attacking the ruling party rather than supporting a newcomer, but they wanted to see what he could do. If he carried Nandi they had a new ally – who would return the favour; if he lost they lost nothing individually and learnt some collective lessons for the coming general election. Meanwhile Nandi would be a test case.

In the last weeks before the by-election the ruling party launched its Clean Tricks campaign. Out of nowhere trucks appeared to carry away the mountains of rubbish that choked the by-lanes of Nandi. Drains appeared where stinking pools had been before, and they were cleaned. Shining manhole covers covered black holes that the citizenry of Nandi had long ago learnt to step around. The stench of disinfectant hung in the air. Roads were widened, straightened, and repaired; the kerbstones were painted a brilliant white. At night there appeared uncanny fluorescent yellow patches of light at regular intervals along those roads, the cause of much wonderment and awe until someone visiting from the capital revealed that these were sodium street lamps on freshly painted poles.

Nor did the improvements end with the town. Special pipes brought drinking water to the surrounding villages. New tubewells dotted the countryside, canals bisected it, and metalled roads joined bewildered hamlets. A bridge sanctioned forty years ago – at Independence – and left at pylons that the local fishermen had come to worship, was finished at high speed and inaugurated by Hansraj Gupta.

'Honour me with your vote,' he said to the assembled citizens. He patted the marble plaque and broke a coconut. 'I'm one of you,' he droned, and touched their feet. He had indeed started out a sharecropper, but a lifetime's public service had left him a millionaire. Full-length posters showed him in the obligatory poor man's garb.

Ranga refused to have his old photos used in the campaign. GJ had rustled up a stack of signed glossies which Hero had burnt in his presence. Instead he commissioned a new series of posters which showed him as he was: a shaven-headed suppliant in dark glasses. One journalist described the result as a black Gandhi, and there was some resemblance there. His ears, I noticed with a start, stuck out. Under a stack of curls they'd been for the most part invisible, and when I looked over his publicity stills from the old days I realized that, those pendulous lobes apart, not one showed his ears. Once again – I saw how luck had smiled on him; in an earlier crew-cut age he would have stood exposed, but the fashion of his heyday decreed a canopy of blow-dried waves (curls, in his case) all around the well-dressed head.

And so in those last weeks there fluttered from housetop and telephone pole strings of festive bunting which advertised the new Hero: a black Gandhi in dark gogs. It gave me a heady jolt to think those gogs were mine.

Looking back at press photos of the campaign, I find another change in Hero. In the early filmi poster days his eyes, even when they followed you as you walked under

217

a hoarding, didn't answer your look. If you stopped in your tracks and stared back they flicked away – even when they were fixed on the camera in the original shot. On the screen it was the same. How many eyeball-to-lens shots can you recall? For that matter even when you talked to him he almost never looked you in the eye. So constantly did his gaze shift you wondered whether he saw anything at all.

Now, when his eyes were shaded from the world, it seemed he could afford to look. There is a picture of him sitting cross-legged on a dais above the admiring throng. He has his arms spread in benediction or greeting and the faces down below are rapturous. One father has lifted his child up for a closer look. You can actually see a star-struck point of light in every eye, the laughing teeth, the melting reservations, despite the poor dot-matrix radio-photo reproduction. *Poor fellow-followers!* I think whenever I see this photograph. *My poor benighted god-famished fellow-followers!* But I notice also that for the first time my master appears to be looking back at them. The tilt of the head, the line of the mouth, the fall of the dewlap, the flap (there is no other word) of the ear, project attention, looking.

Now I will leave to the increasing tribe of Lacanian cinegrammarians the awful twaddle of *the gaze* and *the look*, which I notice Felix Fonseca's bearded cousin Luis (Faluda) Fonseca has begun to deal in in that shrapno-graphic journal *Frame*. May I say only that the old slippage in Hero's gaze (or look) slipped no more, or snagged on the rough edges of ordinary people. Not *the People*, for that is as slippery an entity as *the Object*. He actually simply looked at them, and for many, especially the humbler among them, it was a unique experience. At a time when the lower classes (*orders* was at the tip of my pen, Plumbum: how language shapes perception!) grow daily
218

more invisible, this recognition is less paternal than it seems.

I have always felt uncomfortable when confronted with dark glasses on a sighted stranger. It seems a breach of faith or of some even more basic animal code by which I present to another an open face. My own gogs were a juvenile toy, put away with childish things – and lent him one day for an impromptu skit which made UD laugh and laugh. Now they were part of him, and I felt his new sincerity made the opaque transparent; the dark glass was face to face.

Or perhaps there was a third eye.

Or perhaps Zero is a pettifogger.

He spoke too. I have written of his voice before, but now I must say a word or two about his speeches, for not by gaze alone did he win them but by every word of – of God I was going to say by rote, but *Dog* is nearer the truth.

The fact is I was his speechwriter.

Hardly surprising, since I was his scriptwriter once. Script and speech, reverse and obverse of the Word; I spun that lucent ringing coin for him. Heads he won, tails I lost – or yielded up, like the gogs. Gave freely, I should say, of my brightest and most sonorous for his greater glory and (latterly, I like to think) the common good. Has Zero gone moral on you? Never fear: I simply wished to set the record straight, to put the case for my voiceless colleagues everywhere. When the summiteers of the hour open their mouths, *we* fill them with honey. When my master opened his mouth I saw to it he did not put his foot in it. The keeper of the harem in days of old was a tongueless eunuch. I have never fully fathomed the true length of that missing tongue.

STAR *camera shows a public meeting about to begin. The dais is strung with marigolds. That eternal seducer, the electrician,*

219

bends low over the Chicago microphone to lisp his faithless litany: TESTING, TESTING 1,2,3,4, TESTING. *The amplifier protests, its squeals pitched to hurt. Hero comes on stage, acknowledges the applause, and the sound-system submits to his caress.* My friends, *he says, and pauses (speechwriter's pause),* as you know it is not my mother tongue, but I will try to speak in Hindi. Be so good as to bear with a novice. *Wild cheering. And he begins to speak in faultless if slightly fruity Hindi, the Hindi of the film-script-turned-campaign-speech and the audience is bewitched by his mastery.*

I kept the speeches short too. I didn't want him losing that voice or getting hoarse. Short and telling: every word must count in the general cacophony.

No, but I once trod in some, said one conductor when asked if he'd ever conducted Mahler. Unfair to Mahler, but I trod in some Billimoria in that campaign. Remember him? Like me, he quit the movies for politics – at one remove. Alley Billi, scriptor of the Bombay version of *Cats*, adaptor par excellence, cat-burglar, alley catechist. Did I mention that at the Silver Spoon he walked off with the Hindi prize under the nose – the celebrated nose – of Aditya Shrivastava, son of the cow-belt's pre-eminent playwright? Under my nose too – I make no complaint about that – but small wonder he went on to write vile speeches for Hansraj Gupta in Nandi.

'Brothers and sisters,' cried Hansraj/Billi, 'can you seriously consider voting for a spineless acrobat who slammed into the spotlight thanks to a superannuated actress whom he then heartlessly abandoned?'

Oh yes, mud was slung in that campaign, buckets of it. When you have wiped away the tears sprung from laughing at that *slammed* (I swear I quote) recall that my master was not an acrobat; he was a cannonball. It was Captain Memo who was the acrobat. Inaccuracy of this sort is the
220

bane of politics in our country. (It's the bane of engineering in our country too; for that matter it's the bane, quite simply, of the country.)

Ranga/Zero's reply? 'If there is an india-rubber man in the arena today it is that arch-contortionist Hansraj Gupta whose ageing whore, Miss Popularity, has long since deserted *him*.'

Hero Agonistes.

And so our ding-dong battle raged, speaker versus speaker, hack versus hack. Not that we avoided issues: it was just simpler and more fun to speak of evil forces and malign cancers than of anything so drab as land ceilings. A dozen didactic videos were in circulation, spitting venom at the other side; we hired some current stars from Bombay and Madras to perk up the stodgy propaganda, but only when he came on at the end – outside the tale – did the turgid humbug stir. Gupta's instant bridge, those shining manhole lids, and the like provided us with ready ammunition, but of course we were firing from dubious high ground. Once we were in power would we not resort to such lavish use of state funds for electoral ends? Naturally I didn't let him say so.

He might have done, left to himself. The tenor of his campaign could sometimes smack of righteousness. Where Hansraj Gupta used government helicopters, Ranga went everywhere on the back of a tractor. And where the tractor couldn't go he borrowed a villager's bicycle.

The cycle idea was quite unpremeditated, I can testify. It came naturally to him one day and, pleased with its implications, he let it stay. It endeared him to the whole village, not just the owner, and it won him votes, but for the rest of us it meant we had to have our own bicycles ready. My calves, sorely tried by the padayatra, were now subjected to new torture. Leaders have a way of spreading their discomfort along with their ideals. Of course the press chivvied him about the Mercedes back home, and cartoonists had a jolly time, but he – and more important, the voters – took it seriously.

STAR camera follows us along a canal bank, resting in lyric mood upon the streamers of green sedge in the water, the snowy egrets, the yellow mustard flowers in the fields, the tiny purple sunbirds. Ranga leads the pack, his shining head like a speedster's racing helmet from behind, his wraparound dark glasses like blinkers from the side. I may be shown bringing up the rear, some distance from the rest, my eyebrows trimmed with beads of sweat, courage firming the set of my jaw.

Then, out of the blue, the sightings started.

Invariably it was a woman, but they got the men worked up too. One belle after another came running from the fields to say she'd seen it: a huge blue bull moving like a monsoon cloud among the millet sheaves. Others said it was a black bull, but whatever it was it left them in a state of witless ecstasy. And all were agreed on the planes of light that intersected at its hump. In the town of Nandi it was the same story, only there it was a bull proper, wandering in the market, taking its tithe of radishes from the vendors, or standing stock-still in the middle of the road. To the uninitiate (males mostly) it was an ordinary bull, but the women of Nandi knew better.

After that Hansraj Gupta didn't really stand a chance. Instant bridges were as chaff before that bull, and Ranga's insistence on issues and programmes counted for nothing. To seal Gupta's fate, one journalist linked him with the Karwapani incident, if only by the circumstantial evidence of a certain crate of rotten mangoes at Delhi airport; it turned out he had been the lesser minister sent to investigate the mass rape. When he lost his seat the ruling party blamed it on those revelations and harassed the newspaper concerned (the *Mail*) with summonses and notices.

Gross misprision! The battle of Nandi was not won on

the playing fields of politics, nor on any fourth estate, but among those stooks of millet not far from where, the afternoon before the poll, I made a crackling plywood bonfire of my Trojan bull. Yes, I parked the tractor and burnt the cut-out bull.

Zero Joker.

TRACTOR-POWERED BULL! the headlines sang, congratulating him. His symbol was indeed the tractor, but little did they know how close they came to the mark.

There is another version of the victory which I must in fairness record for history.

In the last few days before the poll, the crack along the North-South fault seemed headed for an irrevocable split. On Nandi's southern border, where the North ended and the South began, it grew so wide people could no longer cross it even with a running jump. One or two who tried vanished into the gulf. Not that they would have been welcome on the other side had they landed safely. Where once upon a time the villagers had lived fraternally along the invisible line, ploughing identical flelds, raising identical crops, now they faced one another down, daring would-be trespassers from the enemy state.

Hansraj Gupta's Justice and Peace and Progress Party, with its northern bias, was content to concentrate on local issues. It lit up Nandi's new bridge and polished the manhole covers and buttered up the caste godfathers. I wrote a resounding speech against the *casteing* of votes, making some ingenious play on the word and picturing to myself its devastating effect on that foul Billi, but Ranga decided that a practical demonstration was called for, and the speech was filed, to rank high – who knows, someday? – among the finest undelivered speeches of our nation.

Instead he did his National Integration stunt.

He took an ordinary bucket, fastened it to a strong rope and tied the other end of the rope to the tractor which he anchored at the edge of the chasm. Then, with press photographers and the entire population of Nandi on hand, he climbed into the bucket and let himself down into the North-South rift.

And there, in semi-darkness, he hung.

Recall that he was a stunt man, had once regularly let himself down into the barrel of a circus gun. But where that trick won him gasps of shivering admiration in the big top and a circumscribed round of applause, this stunt had a national and even international audience. A touring Dutch documentary film crew got wind of it and came haring over; the ABC sent a TV news team from Sydney and with mounting interest from abroad the state-run national network could no longer afford to ignore it, to the PM's signal displeasure. The Daily Dose director lost his job as a result, but the DD crew turned up with their second-best cameraman.

STAR camera will need to do some tricks of its own here. The green jelly of Cecil B. de Mille's Red Sea, parting for Charlton Heston, will not do; this was dry land. Perhaps a cleft chocolate cake will convey the dark igneous soil of the Deccan plateau. The cliffhanger content may be played up or down as desired, but some parallels need be created with the descent into the gun. The closing shot of the sequence is perpendicular, looking down on his shaven head suspended there, darkly visible in the enclosing gloom. At a pinch it could be his cannonball helmet, steadying itself in silent readiness. Does power grow from the barrel of a gun?

He hung there for six hours altogether, spread over three days, the last three of the campaign. And then he came back up and walked away with the seat of Nandi.

This was the media version; the ruling party's, remember, was that Hansraj Gupta was smeared by the *Mail*. And some said the people voted sensibly to cement a fragmenting India. I prefer my own bull factor, but take your pick. History, as every Indian examinee knows, Is Never Monocausal.

At any rate, the front row at the Hind Talkies will be happy to learn that history can repeat itself as farce. There is a sequel to this cliffhanger: *Cliffhanger II*.

Cliffhanger II

After Nandi my master was a hero once again. In the Opposition combine his stock shot up, and any illusions of premiership the various party leaders might have entertained evaporated overnight.

The day he entered parliament he was horribly nervous. He might have been a frightened schoolboy in the annual play, and yet he was only as it were in the audience. He took his seat to applause (there'd been ovations outside, from the public, when we arrived) and he sat looking prim and attentive. I could see (I was up in the then visitors' gallery) he wasn't listening; I could tell from the way he chewed on nothing he was ill-at-ease. Once he actually sat on his hands.

Over the next few weeks his colleagues in khadi waited for that moment when the Member for Nandi would speak, when that famous voice would flood that famous chamber with its riches. But his lips were sealed. With terror, not discretion, he assured me.

'What the hell do I say, Zero?' he demanded.

226

The pressure on him was greater than on other new-comers. Something special was expected of him.

'And that makes me shit green.'

'Why not maro a one-liner, boss?'

We dug one up that night to ease his way in. The next day he rose to speak. Every eye was on him. Or, as four separate journalists put it, he was the cynosure of all eyes. Well, a dog's tail is not far off.

'Mr Speaker,' he said, 'Honourable Members. There is a bridge in Nandi. . .'

And believe it or not, his mouth went dry. He looked up at me. I looked away, then down between my feet. The house, deprived so soon of that voice, took it for a laugh pause and began to chuckle. It *was* quite funny; after all everyone in the country had heard of that bridge. Two weeks after its inauguration it had developed cracks. It lay roughly athwart the North-South divide, but those cracks had to do with its hurried construction – and they had been even more widely publicized than the instant bridge.

'There is a bridge in Nandi,' he repeated, and now the laughter from the Opposition benches was unrestrained. Even one or two of the ruling party members allowed themselves a smile.

'. . . in need of repair,' he croaked, and sat down.

It was a masterpiece of delivery. To this day I don't know whether the pause was intended or not (I didn't write it in), but it made his name as a house wit. From then on he had no trouble speaking; there was even an occasion when the Speaker had trouble stopping him.

He might have slipped into the role of entertainer but for two constraints. One was his commitment to cleaning up things and the other was the need to organize and maybe unite the Opposition. GJ met him regularly at the Ahujas' with unity proposals and advice and bits of tittle-tattle. There were the expected leadership challenges from men who felt (no doubt rightly) that they'd been in the

227

business longer than this upstart crow. But GJ saw to it by whisper campaigns and anonymous slurs on morals that Hero became the only viable choice. My master helped him by protesting that he did not wish to lead; thus he appeared (and perhaps was) the only truly disinterested party. Issues, issues, he harped, and GJ let him, but of course it was mystique that did the trick. I don't know that he didn't suspect so himself.

As everyone expected, the stumbling-block to Opposition unity was not ideological but concrete: it boiled down to the question of getting office. There was hectic jockeying among the leaders and deputies and even the state-level functionaries wanted to be sure they weren't left out. Let there be a merger, every man said, but what will my post be? The Number 1 position was Ranga's by all but universal consent (there were one or two regional leaders who continued to grumble) but from Number 2 on down it was tooth and claw all the way.

'You will have to make it 2a, 2b, 2c,' GJ advised.

'Even then there will be trouble,' Hero replied. '2c will want to know why he is not 2b.'

'That is the question,' Ahuja put in. 'Better make it 1a, 1b, 1c.'

'Upto 1z,' I suggested.

'There would not be enough alphabets,' GJ warned, 'for this *primus inter pares* business.'

'Primus *what*?' Hero said.

'First among equals,' Ahuja explained.

'OK, so I'm Number 1. Who is 2a?'

'Chandan Dubey.'

'Alok Singh.'

'Jagdish Prasad.'

We all spoke at once, naming our logical first among seconds. 'You see?' Hero pounced.

'Well then, give them equal billing, like in Bombay,' I thought out loud.

Zero Solomon.

'Equal billing?' GJ said.

'Film-style,' Ahuja explained.

And so we did: Hero on top, then the second string, equal spacing, equal lettering, extending to the end of the page. From the third level on down it didn't matter as much. Not that they were more understanding; they were simply more tractable. And there was more competition. Any post was better than none, and today's sulker was tomorrow's suppliant – on his knees if need be. Even so, our list of office bearers was so lengthy it became unwieldy, even comical. And still there were those who had to be left out. The bigger parties in the coalition wanted to hog the best posts while certain small parties threatened not to join on grounds of under-representation. But a line had to be drawn and GJ drew it.

The haggling continued to the very end – and beyond. Later we found that the most eloquent pro-merger leader, Alok Singh, was actually egging on the anti-merger voices in order to embarrass – and possibly unseat – Hero. Again, Chandan Dubey wrote Hero a civil letter swearing loyalty if he were made 2a and given the Home Ministry. The next day GJ intercepted a parallel letter to the PM which reminded him of past loyalty and hinted that the Opposition might easily be sabotaged if the PM wished. The letter was signed: *Fraternally, Chandan Dubey*. And Jagdish Prasad blew hot and cold with every passing hour. So hamfisted was their dealing that we came to think of them as the Three Stooges.

Finally, when the new PSM signboard (with a syncretic symbol dreamed up by a sharp Madras logo designer) was hammered into place above the PSM office on Porus Avenue, a group of dissidents crying *hai, hai!* tore it down. To appease them we replaced the word *Maksad*, masterplan, with *Mahapath*, highway, fiddled with the logo and repainted the board. And there was an uneasy truce.

Even as he flayed the ruling party for this or that inconsistency, Hero had to play the conciliator with his own side. In the heat of the battle he tended to forget who his allies were. Not that you could blame him: the situation was pretty fluid. I had to pass him notes in the thick of it saying *Praise Asli Ram* or *Lambaste Nakhli Ram*, and he would launch into encomia or diatribes as instructed. But it was confusing even for those on the sidelines. It might have gone to pieces after all had the PM not decided the time was ripe (or we were too raw) for a general election.

The snap election was his unmaking. Or rather it was our making: our leaders saw that if they didn't put their act together there would be nothing left of it by the time the next election came round. And each was too hungry for power, even as 2c, to wait that long. So they dug a shallow grave for their hatchets and began to talk about value-based politics again.

The other side got into its stride too. Never in my entire life have I heard so much cant about conscience and principles and self-criticism and the common man and the poorest of the poor as in those days leading up to the general election. And much of it was traceable to the pen – the felt-tipped pen – of Alley Billi. I might have begun to believe it too – for I caught a conscience chill myself – had the true face of party politics not revealed itself to me.

Party politics! That word was forever soiled for me. Nothing could have been further from the Spoonie frolic of hats and streamers and guns with pop-out flags that said BANG – the toys our alma mater equipped us with as we set out to face life. The guns were real now, if often homemade, and they went off in earnest, if not always when intended. The blood, the broken heads, the broken bodies of that campaign made the Nandi by-election look like a college prank. (Yes, more pranks. Not that Zero Bahuroopiya can scoff.)

Just how determined the rulers were to stay in power

showed from how far behind they left their Clean Tricks bag. From now on it was jungle warfare all the way – at the time I toyed with the notion of writing *The Last Jungle Book* – with every fearsome beast prowling unchecked. I saw some unclassified species too: a khadi-plated armadillo, a ten-tentacled treasurer baboon, a portfolio crawler that could live for weeks on its own excrement, a winged atrocity crocodile, a pack of particoloured jackasses, a mantis which bit off voters' heads the moment their ballots were cast. And every day there appeared new breeds of vampires, vultures, scorpions, and hyaenas, while the eternal jackal lurked on the fringes scrounging for what the others left. The chorus was deafening, the yaps and yowls, the *cucurucu*, the *chee-pawn, chee-pawn*.

But what right had I to smear the animals? It was they who stood tarred with man's brush. Nature's exorbitance was all very well, but we'd come out of that jungle – on four wheels. Man, not Nature, was the villain here, and what was democracy but a containment of villainy?

The rights of man! In this country we hadn't yet plumbed the depths of his wrongs.

The moment the election was called it was every man for himself. The by-election had been a spectacle, a sort of one-day cricket match where the nation watched from the pavilion. Now the match was everywhere, and in that action-stations mood anything went. The Election Commission, that genteel cricket board, watched helplessly as government vehicles were used for campaigning, vats of election hooch were brewed, and rival goonda gangs fought pitched battles. In this electoral match it was the sponsors who won, whatever the scoreboard might read at the end of the day. The winners strode the field, but afterwards they championed their paymasters. We who queued at the ticket booths simply went home to our lives. In the end I found that politics *was* a game – a party game – but business was in earnest. Who paid the piper called the tune. The general election was a mass forgetting of this simple law, a willing suspension of healthy disbelief.

The scramble might have been general, but particular interest focussed on Nandi, which Hero once again contested. He knew the PSM could swing the South and so he returned symbolically to this marginally northern seat.

The rift had since closed up but there were new pitfalls for the unwary, for every shining manhole cover had disappeared to be sold by weight in the scrap-iron market. More than one inconvenient cadre from either side disappeared down the manholes never to return, so I was careful. My master was addressing twenty public meetings a week across the nation; as leader of the Opposition he could hardly confine himself to Nandi. That task was left to me. True, there were one or two others, and GJ looked in from time to time, but the logistical heights were mine. I like to think I acquitted myself with grace and, as we shall see, aplomb. Afterwards it was whispered that I deserted my post when the going got rough, but why should I fear a simple manhole? Is not Zero a walking manhole? Does Zero Bahuroopiya, eternal trickster, fear the black circle of death, its shining lid of life removed and sold as scrap metal? Believe me, no.

It is time the whole truth were told.

The campaign was going well enough for us but as polling day drew near we saw that massive preparations were being made for booth-capturing, vote-buying and general intimidation of PSM supporters. Innumerable front men had registered as independents in the first place to confuse the public but also because each candidate was entitled to two umpires and these men would crowd the booths, to interfere, disrupt proceedings, and finally stuff the ballot boxes. Criminals had been released from jail to help them. The pattern was repeated all across the country – wherever votes could not be bought outright.

232

At this juncture a statistician among us computed that if all the crooked variables of the campaign were allowed free play, as they now appeared to be, we stood a good chance of losing in spite of our huge popular support. We would lose in spite of the capital H, and our very popularity would have been our downfall. What we needed was something that would render our votes so numerous that the most massive rigging in Indian electoral history would still be powerless to stop us. We needed a secret weapon.

It was then that I had my brainwave.

For some weeks I had been wandering among the manholes of Nandi, stepping with care and looking over my shoulder. Perhaps these natural cautions fuelled the desertion theory. The fact was my brain had been lately teased by a niggling memory. It was the sort of gritty itch that torments the oyster, or, to get the species right, a sort of puzzle-peg that baffles the dog.

I knew it had something to do with Bombay and I knew it was important enough to warrant leaving my post for. It was more instinct than memory since strictly speaking I didn't know what it was I was after and set out in the blind faith that I would find whatever it was when I got there.

Does the Arctic tern know what it is that sends him journeying around the globe? Can he be said to remember the Antarctic?

'An *actor* as your Prime Minister?' sneered one wall slogan. A hoopoe on the wall fanned its crest and eyed me steadily.

I got into my master's cast-off Fiat (He'd sold it to me, actually) and turned the ignition key. There was no explosion; all my pieces were intact and I thanked God. The times were like that. I drove off, nosing the car towards Bombay without quite knowing why and steering by the invisible stars or the earth's magnetic field or some sixth sense.

I was dropping down the Western Ghats, the coastal plain spread out below me, when I remembered. I turned around and drove back up to Lonavla where Hero had a country house. It was here, on the edge of the plateau and looking out towards distant Bombay, that he stored his memorabilia. The house was a kind of museum where his early publicity stills, his first movie poster, old première invitations and the like were framed. They kept company with all manner of cine curios: a magic lanthorn from eighteenth century Paris via Lucknow, another from the last century which showed a woman dancing in dishabille, old movie cameras and projectors, including the Lumière brothers' demonstration model and a rusty projector from the original Hind Talkies in Kottagode. And so on.

The gatekeeper grinned when he saw me and flung open the gates. I tipped him and roared up the drive, pulling up in the portico. The servants knew me and ran for the keys. They must have sensed the urgency of the mission for they didn't offer tea.

'Now mind you vote,' I warned them. 'Every man and woman of age.'

'Zero Sahib, how can you even . . .?'

'And no getting drunk.'

'Not till afterwards, Zero Sahib. Then we must celebrate.'

'Very good, very good,' I said feudally. 'Ranga Sahib has sent me on an urgent mission.'

I made my way briskly to the museum end of the house through clumps of draped furniture and found what my instinct had told me I wanted. The safe combination was stored in my memory proper (I'd fetched things for him before) and that didn't err either. Then I tipped the chowkidar, placed my prize on the seat beside me and roared back down the drive, intent on Bombay.

Once again I began the descent down the steep ghats.

234

It was evening now and there was a tinsel twist of river glittering in the pink haze far below. The sky was the colour of a new lemony washing powder Guppy Agarwal had launched that summer. Every now and again a hill would blot it out, and then as I took the next hairpin bend it was all around me and the Fiat would strain to plunge headlong into that all-cleansing solution.

I was just past Monkey Hill when I realized I was being followed. When I speeded up, the Ambassador behind me speeded up too; when I slowed down it slowed down. If we had company it hung back, but when we were alone it came up close as if looking for a chance to nudge me over the edge.

STAR *camera will know what to do here.*

Was that Captain Memo in the rear-view mirror? Could he have skipped jail? I couldn't be sure, but just when I was wondering if it was time for a spot of fancy jinking, the Ambassador struck.

It rammed the Fiat from the right as we were taking a tricky bend. I felt the car lift like a plane. My senses told me I was flying, like the tern, but instinct rolled me sideways against the passenger door. With a single sweep – rather more deftly than Javed in *Suryanamaskar* – I scooped up my precious freight, threw open the door and bundled out. The Fiat went tumbling over the edge, pitching through the twilight like a doomed pterodactyl. It struck a rock a thousand feet below, burst into flames and turned over a few times.

STAR *camera needs no directions.*

I lay stunned on the edge of the cliff and watched the slo-mo reruns a couple of times. Then it was back to normal speed and I heard the Ambassador's tyres squealing as my assailant and would be assassin reversed to make his getaway. My prize had fetched up against a useful culvert but my legs were dangling in the chasm.

A couple of riffs later a little pipal tree, like the one in *The Near and the Far*, presented itself, and I heaved myself up.

Down below, the Fiat was an orange torch. It was not insured, but I was safe, and so was our secret weapon.

Rescue

It was *Neta Harishchandra*. Remember it?

I left the Fiat glowing like a single coal far below and hitched a ride into Bombay. That very night we began making copies (and copies from copies) for national distribution, and five days before the election Hero was playing to packed houses in every corner of the land.

After that it was a walkover, or as the four correspondents separately put it, a cakewalk. When the audience saw my master's eye spouting blood – real blood – they tore their hair and rent their garments and, more to the point, cast their votes in the ballot-box that mattered most: their hearts.

The PM and his cronies stomped from one end of the country to the other flogging dead issues and pointing to new roads and dams (but never bridges.) But they couldn't be everywhere at once. My master could. And every time that crimson efflorescence burst from his eye people saw him not as a candidate but as the *king*. The king cut down in filmi and in real life, dead but not dead, wanting but their votive offering to live again. The king was dead; long live the king!

India a republic? Only in fusty, cloistered minds.

The crowning – the swearing-in, if you insist – found him if anything more nervous than on his first day in parliament. He had dressed with the sort of agonizing care taken only by monarchs and shorthand typists, twiddling the Nehruvian rosebud in his lapel this way and that for a good half hour until its sepals were so disarrayed it had to be replaced. UD, her own hand trembling, destroyed the replacement and I had to go out and nip a third bud from the damp garden. It was a white one and he wanted a red.

'Ze-ro!' he shucked impatiently, but submitted.

I had to hold him steady to get it in the buttonhole, he was trembling so.

UD was wearing a paisley print sari, First Lady red but PSM khadi, khadi silk all the same. Her ornaments were simple, deliberately unfilmi as if in repudiation of the past – her past. His repudiation was already behind him, sartorially at any rate, though there was always an ambiguity about his image, as if a transparent lamination of celluloid must inevitably adhere to it. But he chose on that first day to make a gesture solemnizing the repudiation. For, waiting at the door of their Golf Links residence, on a street where the least of cars was a BMW, there stood in readiness to ferry them to Rashtrapati Bhavan, in place of his Mercedes, gifted the day before to a blind school, a plain black Ambassador.

I followed later, cadging a lift in a fawn press car (the Fiat was no more, and I'd almost, but not quite, got my second-hand Maruti.) At the chandeliered Ashoka Hall I was denied entry so I had to rely on media reports. When I got home – I had his *More Democracy* speech to write – Pedro was exultant. *Hero, Hero, Hero!* he sang until I was obliged to drape him in punitive night while I worked. At mealtimes I fed him safflower kernels for his overwrought heart.

To show himself to the people, Hero graced victory celebrations at major centres across the country. How the people loved him! Subjects now, not fans, they danced in the streets, stormed bamboo barricades, held out their loyal hands for hours. He was their pride, their hope, their innocence. He shone like a newly minted coin.

Hero Imperator.

And where he could not go, the DD satellite did. We were producing sixty TV sets per second by then (but only one handpump per hour.) The new god was everywhere; the remotest hamlet had one, with a Japanese generator. In Kamla Nagar a family of five renting a single garage below me had a colour set. So why didn't I have even a black-and-white? Pedro would have liked one and looked accusingly at me every time the hit songs from *Chitrahaar* floated up to us through the garage vent. Instead I would put him to bed and drive my new/old Maruti to the Golf Links residence and we'd watch the royal progress *en famille* on the Daily Dose.

'DD,' he corrected me, reprovingly. His appetite for acronyms had been growing lately.

'OK, Doordarshan,' I said, using the original word from the old Indian Heirlines days when we called our national network, romantically, the Faroffview.

'DD,' he repeated severely, hardly a fortnight in the chair.

'All right, all right, *Didi*.'

And from that night on we called the network Didi, Big Sister.

'It's a bit like a Western,' UD giggled as we watched the Didi news. She seemed to have absorbed the levity he'd lost, or she may have been making amends for his humourlessness. 'I mean,' she persevered, with a filmi

American accent, 'You're the new sheriff, and you're gonna clean up this here town.'

He looked blankly at her, overworked already.

'And I'm the hooer with the heart of gold,' she ended, looking at me.

'Yawl drink up now,' I said rolling up my bartender's sleeves.

Then deputy sheriff Chandan Dubey flashed on the screen, his teeth twinkling like a belt of bullets. 'Our leader knows best,' he was saying. 'I have complete faith in his judgement.'

What was this? A crisis already? Then it was a curry western after all. But why was Chandan Dubey grinning? A tall morose man with quills for eyebrows and a narrow deeply scored forehead, he moved with thrifty precision and gave nothing away. I'd never known him to smile and here he was grinning sheepishly for the camera like any filmi hopeful.

I sat forward in my chair and noticed with approval that Hero did too. So he was getting canny. I had never trusted Dubey and I don't believe my master did either, so when he protested loyalty there was cause for concern. He'd got the Number 2 position – Deputy PM, 2a – but had had to settle for the Defence portfolio. The Home Ministry had gone as a sop to Jagdish Prasad, while Alok Singh lapped up Finance. All three, we knew, were content to bide their time until Hero's popularity should begin to ebb; then each would make his leadership bid. But this was surely a bit premature. Why should Dubey of all people go off at half-cock?

We got on the phone to GJ who assured us everything was under control.

'What's everything?' Hero said.

'Not to worry, Ranga Sahib. Just now I'm coming.'

He came at half-past-twelve. By then PM's Secretary, Mishra, a deadpan little man, had briefed my master on the latest developments. It seemed a crucial navy purchase file was missing from the Ministry of Defence and someone had leaked the news to the press. We were looking for a second-hand aircraft carrier at the time.

'Carelessness,' GJ said, coming in. 'Our friend took the file home to prepare for next-week's debate and it disappeared.'

'My god!'

GJ held up a hand. 'We got it back. Two pages missing, so whoever took it did not have time to take photos. I think the CIA are getting little-bit careless. Or cocksure. The press think Dubeyji did it to embarrass you, but why would he put his own job in danger, tell? He would have himself to resign.'

'So now what?' Hero said.

GJ looked around at us. Here was what the press had already begun to call my master's kitchen cabinet. Hero nodded at Mishra who pulled in his tortoise head and went out.

'Call up our Home Minister,' GJ said;

'What does he know?'

'See if his CBI have something juicy on any navy man.'

And the next day an admiral who'd been hobnobbing with the CIA was charged with espionage. The press, appeased, (a little blood will soothe the most savage pressman) said no more about ministerial carelessness. Dubey was given a dressing down but allowed to keep his portfolio in spite of the Opposition's cries.

It took me a little while to get used to the idea of the Opposition as being someone else now.

Traitor, traitor, the frogs in the garden, Hero's garden, sang the day the admiral went to jail. The golf course was wet and green from an early monsoon. We needed a good crop on our side that year and we got it.

Then Jagdish Prasad had *his* little crisis, something to do with a police firing, and no sooner had GJ sorted that out than it was Alok Singh's turn. It seemed they were indeed bent on embarrassing Hero.

'Even at the cost of bringing down the government?' UD said.

'Maybe not,' Ranga mused, 'but it looks like they want blood. What else could bring them together? They hate each other's guts.'

'Leave it to GJ.' I said. 'He can handle them.' It was comforting to think of his bulky presence ever vigilant behind the scenes.

The night of Alok Singh's famous budgetary *faux pas* in parliament (it was a point of honour with me never to miss zero hour in the house, and the Opposition halla-gulla that day was deafening) I thought I'd call on our Finance Minister to sound him out in the guise of convey-ing my master's apologies for having publicly lost his temper with the man. I was just approaching his gate when a long cream Nissan drove out with Alok Singh in it. He was driving, and he was alone.

I made a U-turn and followed him. He drove up Teen Murti Marg, turned right onto South Avenue, then swept around to Rajpath via Dalhousie. He turned right onto Rajpath and went all the way down to India Gate, did the roundabout and took Akbar Road back to Teen Murti. This was odd. Either he'd forgotten something or he was killing time. I kept my distance, my lights dipped (an optional extra in my Maruti), my eyes peeled. He glided along for a bit, then, just short of his own gate he turned sharp left down a lane and drove at some speed to Megasthenes Marg (or Ho Chi Minh Avenue; I couldn't be sure) to Jagdish Prasad's residence.

Prasad, who didn't drive, was waiting at the gate. He climbed in and together they did another aimless tour of New Delhi's splendid avenues. It was most intriguing. I was running low on petrol but I couldn't afford to lose them now. At last they swung purposefully around the

30th January roundabout and made straight for the Lodi Gardens. They parked across the road from the gardens and entered by the small gate on Amrita Shergill Marg. I parked around the corner on South End Road and slipped in after them.

They crossed the stone bridge and walked along the path towards the main tomb. I kept to the shadows, darting from tree to tree.

STAR *camera may shadow them, but must not neglect my lightfooted advance. A twig may be allowed to snap.*
Zero Vulpes.

They stopped and looked around, then continued on their way. Then I saw two men coming from the opposite side of the park towards them; they would have entered from the Lodi Road gate. One of them was tall and thin and now recognizable since he had abandoned that implausible grin. It was of course Chandan Dubey. The other man was short and squat and froglike and I might have recognized him at once but for his unlikely choice of companions.

It was Gangajal Trivedi.

I didn't wait to see any more. It was straight back to my master's house for me. They'd just moved to Chanakya Road for security reasons, so I made my way to the new address. I had to walk the last three kilometres because the petrol finally ran out, but it gave me time to think. It had begun to rain but it pleased me to think that they must have got wet too.

GJ! Who only wanted to be head of state, not PM! Who wanted glory, not power! Now gunning – I was sure – for PM-ship!

Suddenly it all made sense. He'd blackmailed Dubey over the navy file; the theft, the tip-off to the press had been his. Knowing his man, he'd very likely bribed Prasad and won over Alok Singh, poor 2c, with the promise of 2a – in a Gangajal Trivedi government. All that remained was for him to arrange for a vacancy in some unfortunate constituency by the kind of accident his men knew how to engineer (or, less drastically, by a forced resignation in any one of half a dozen pocket boroughs) and he would be GJ, MP. After that, with the Three Stooges in his other pocket, it was a short step to inverting those last two letters. GJ, PM.

And he would have ridden piggy-back to power, or, to get the species right, come in leap-frog over my master. He could not have won the election himself: he had the head, but not the face. No wonder he'd cultivated Hero so long and sedulously!

Fanciful? Maybe. But perhaps when revisionist historians come to write the definitive history of the period I will perhaps be granted a second page as one who saved the country from Bonapartist tyranny.

The next day we struck. Hero announced a cabinet reshuffle and made three new appointments, promoting 3a, 3b, and 3c from the PSM's factions to replace their erstwhile leaders – which they did with uncommon readiness and zest. The Stooges were given lesser portfolios: Chandan Dubey got the Media, Jagdish Prasad Fertilisers, and Alok Singh, poor hungry 2c, with nice irony, Power. It was not politic to throw them right out; they were given Minister of State rank (not quite full minister) and before you could say jackal they'd gulped it down and slunk off to plot again.

And that night Hero hoped out loud to the nation over Didi that all serving MPs, whether government or Opposition, would have a long and prosperous life – not one cut short by unlucky accidents such as might bring to power some longtime puppeteer.

Outmanoeuvred, GJ sued for peace. He would take Presidentship after all, he hinted, if it were offered him.

But he would never get to bob in Lutyens's art deco bath, for when the serving president's term was up, Hero had another notion. Flouting every law of minority, he appointed as President of the Republic of India, over several venerable heads, and well over GJ's, an outcaste – Vindhya, a Harijan girl.

Don't join the hoots of derision that sounded from many a respectable quarter around the nation. Oh yes, jurists and scholars and ratiocinating editors joined the baying fundamentalists. It was not my master's idea (or mine; I wish it had been) but that of a long forgotten sophist, Mohandas Karamchand Gandhi, Mahatma.

Like much else that was utopian in that visionary's skull, it worked. Once the niceties of protocol were worked out, a civil representative found for the girl, and cooks hired to replace the high-caste ones who resigned from the kitchens of Rashtrapati Bhavan, there was nothing to it. Visiting heads of state found they could converse quite readily with Vindhya, and when they had an adult question to ask they turned to her guardian, a well-known Harijan lady doctor now in retirement. Vindhya could cut a ribbon as well as any president who had preceded her, and smile rather more easily. Her expenses were exemplarily modest and the dividends in morale for a fifth of the country's population were immeasurable by standard planning econometrics.

Appointing Vindhya was Hero's first decisive action as PM. Earlier he'd let the kitchen cabinet take the decisions; now he ran on ahead of us.

'You've got to warm up,' he confessed in a moment of now rare expansiveness. 'Look at Alec Guiness. When he was a boy he was only a *messenger* in his school play, but he ran twice around the football field so he could come on stage all breathless. Same thing with big roles. Remember Abhimanyu in *Desh Seva*? How his first line is a whisper?'

'That was Dharamvir in *Golmaal*,' I said.

'And at the end his voice is ringing from the battlements.'

'From the gallows.'

'That reminds me.' And he made a note to introduce the Abolition of Capital Punishment Bill in parliament. It got bogged down along the way, but he got Vindhya (on Indu's request) to pardon Nero.

No sooner was Nero released than she set up in Delhi as a society lady. She was a sensation, the most sought-after woman in town. Men everywhere desired her depilated incarnation, while ladies gave Nero kitty parties where they showed old Nero videos and fainted when the villain appeared. Pedro too was bowled over: *Nero, Nero, Nero!* he screamed when the villainous laughter floated up to us through the garage vent. He sulked hammily, and when I stroked his beak, nipped me. It was not enough that we had no TV. Now we had no video.

Nero was not the only one dolling up. UD was too. There was a new sari coming in every day, of khadi silk, true, but her collection of shoes would have made any ousted Filipina First Lady sit up.

'I can't have him ashamed of me,' she said. She did have a lot of official walking to do, and she hadn't lost her flounce. She accompanied him on his local walkabouts, his visits to disaster areas, his five-nation tours. 'And they're made here – so no foreign exchange gets wasted. The designs come from Milan and we just copy them. We have to encourage our industries, our artisans.'

So while she encouraged local industry he tackled the foreign debt. 'Do we really need long cream-colour Nissans?' he asked in parliament, looking significantly at Alok Singh. 'Or green-colour Toyotas? Or blue-colour video coaches? No! We need red-colour buses.'

Alok Singh turned a sort of white-colour and shifted in his seat.

There was no stopping Hero after that. He ended up

cutting the import bill in half. That meant halving our defence budget, to the annoyance of the top brass, the Swedish chamber of commerce, and certain people in between.

'Madness!' the Opposition chorused.

'Ploughshares!' the Chief of Army Staff scoffed. (He lost his job and wrote a book about it.)

'Pakistan!' cried the former PM, but he'd used that card before.

And as peace broke out on the subcontinent it was found that there was money for schools in every village, for rural fair-price shops (which in the old days had been confined to towns, where people were better off), for cooperatives and tubewells and canals and vegetable gardens. Moneylenders were banished by common consent to the Sunderbans where they were gobbled up by tigers, absentee landlords had their titles annulled while landless labourers kept the land they worked, grain-hoarders were put to cleaning drains, untouchables got to drink out of upper-caste wells, unseeables got their photographs taken, mafia dons were put to work in the coal mines while the miners played kabaddi, temples had their loudspeakers confiscated, muezzins put away their microphones, five-star hotels became youth hostels, private schools became monuments, hospitals became cowsheds, servants ate with their former masters, child-labourers flew kites, politicians went into the movies, judges danced for no reason, magistrates refused bribes, movie stars read *War and Peace*, pensioners wore pashmina shawls, widows sang love songs, beggars rode horses, telephones worked, televisions didn't, the rivers were pure, the streets smooth, the air as sweet as a kiss, two ears of wheat waved where one grew before, and the PM hung a giant bell at his gate which any citizen could ring at any time (between nine and five in summer and ten and four in winter.)

It was two in the morning and we were sitting in front of Didi staring at a blank screen. We must have dozed off (UD was in her chair asleep) during that last strange video. I looked at Hero; he looked back at me.

'Did you hear a bell,' he said, 'or am I dreaming?'

I had heard a giant bell toll outside, at the gate.

'Run it back.'

I pressed the rewind button for a couple of seconds.

'OK. Play.'

I pressed *Play*. It was *Laurel and Hardy at Oxford*. No giant bell, no waving wheatfields and all the rest.

'Go and see who it is.'

I froze. 'The guard must be there. They'll see to it.'

'Go and see who it is.'

'But-'

'*Doggy . . .*'

He'd never said it out loud like that before.

I said: 'Saab.'

STAR camera must shoot this scene with minimum lighting, as far as possible in silhouette. A sodium street lamp will do for backlighting outside, beyond the gate; inside there is a dimmed brass table-lamp, plus the astral gloaming of the TV.

I went to the front door and opened it a crack. The cold night air crept in like a benediction. I prepared to meet my end. There was an assassin out there who was going to spray me full of lead. I opened the door and slipped out.

The guard was missing. The gate lights were out, but by the street light I could see that the gate stood open.

There was a bell standing there, in high heels.

We faced each other in silence for a few moments. Then the outrageous cloak parted and a hand appeared, its long nails polished with some high-gloss varnish. It held a small gun. The gun was pointing at me.

248

I closed my eyes.

But then the bell spoke, not the gun.

'*Bang*!' it said, and went off into a peal of filmi laughter.

I was so relieved I felt dizzy. The bell put its gun away into a flashy-looking gold lamé handbag. There was the clink of jewellery.

'Hull-o darr-ling,' came the familiar husky voice, and there was some more laughter.

I got a whiff of rotting fruit. I went back in.

'It's Nero,' I announced. 'She's drunk.'

We dragged her in (the stripes on my face burning again) and leaned her up against the banisters. I went back to the door. When I looked out again the place was crawling with Black Cat commandos. They seemed to be looking for somebody. I watched them for a while, coming and going like caged jaguars. Then I shut the door and went back in.

I stopped in my tracks.

UD was still asleep in her armchair, Laurel and Hardy were in the dean's double bed, and there on the staircase were two familiar shadows, Hero and Nero, in a passionate clinch.

Song

At breakfast (when it was late I stayed overnight) I found UD smiling broadly and I realized, for the first time in months, that she was no longer the suicidal depressive of the pre-First Lady days. Power, or proximity to power certainly did her no harm. I supposed I'd been too busy to notice that sort of thing in the press of affairs, what with the speechwriting and kitchen-cabineting and spying on GJ and the Three Stooges, and being general dogsbody and watchdog.

There were dosas on the table, the edges golden and crisp and frilly. She must have woken up from last night's armchair nap, switched off Didi and gone first to the kitchen to grind the various lentils for fermenting overnight. She was particular in that way, and conscientious, and caring. Because she cares. We return you to the main programme.

'What's so funny?' I asked.

My master wasn't there. He slept in on Sundays.

'Nothing. I was just thinking of that video.'

I jumped. 'Which video?' My hair stood on end. So she had seen it too! Then all those cooperatives and wheat-fields *were* logged on tape somewhere.

'That Laurel and Hardy one.'

'Oh, *that*.'

I spooned fresh coconut chutney. She cares.

'But I saw the other one too,' she said archly, and I couldn't tell whether she suspected me of procuring X-rated videos for him or whether she'd actually seen the same dreaming one as us.

'Anyway, Laurel and Hardy got into my bed. No, actually I was sandwiched between them in the dean's bed. And the dean came in and whacked us on the head with a pillow – *phataak!* – and there were feathers flying all over the place.'

'I love you, UD.'

Her smile vanished.

'What?'

'I said: *I love you, UD*.'

'Are you crazy?' She looked around nervously.

'Yes.'

'Oh my God. Here. Have another dosa.'

'I don't want another dosa. I want you.'

'Shut up, Zero. ' She looked anxiously at the kitchen to make sure Francis wasn't there.

'It's Sunday. It's his day off,' I said, not so much to reassure her as to show her I could read her mind.

'I'll take a tray up to Ranga,' she said, getting busy.

'No, *don't* – !' I said, then realized Nero would be in the guest room.

'What do you mean?' She looked at me curiously. 'He likes breakfast in bed, ya.'

'Ya.'

I stayed away for quite a while after that. I still did the speeches but I handed them to Mishra in his office and he gave me his precise bureaucratic smile which could have meant: *I know what's happened*, or simply, *Thank you*.

The next time I saw Hero was on TV. Sorry, Didi. I was passing a newsagent's – it was Sunday morning again – and there was one of those marathon holy epic series running, only this was pre-epic, a dramatization of the Vedas in nine hundred parts. Every Sunday the newsagent religiously set up his Didi where anybody off the street could come and watch; and they did come. The pattern was repeated in various shops with a Sunday licence all down the street. The agent sold no newspapers during that period and sat like a good boy at the head of the class while stray passersby crowded in behind. Not that there were many newspapers to buy; their numbers had been dwindling lately, their place taken by endlessly multiplying magazines.

Anyway, there they were watching Didi, and I was on my way to the local baker to see if he had any buns. Out of the corner of my eye I saw several chubby boys on chariots scoot across the screen when suddenly the programme was interrupted by a bulletin. It was the soyabean woman turned newscaster.

'The Prime Minister would like to wish all citizens a happy, holy day.'

And there he was, in living colour, wishing us a happy, holy day.

I stood rooted to the ground – I might well have put down roots; there was more pothole than road under me – as I digested this message. I was still there long after he'd gone, and I'll give him this: he didn't piss around. He just wished us and then we were back with the bows and arrows in Vedic times. Past PMs had promised to take us into the twenty-first century; only now, when we were there, did it come home to me that they meant BC. I blinked several times to make sure his appearance was not a delusion. The effect on the assembled watchers told

252

me it was not. They were smiling uneasily as if God had suddenly appeared to them. Then one man decided to clap and the others joined in and shortly the whole street was crackling with applause while the chubby boys mouthed their silent di-laag. From the early hesitation I gathered this was something new. Next Sunday they would be ready for Him.

I watched the programme to the end. Just before the commercial break a historian and a cultural anthropologist and a man of God came on and I watched them as well. I remember there was a cake of new yellow Chariot (or was it Bow?) detergent from Guppy Agarwal's company. Then I stepped out of my pothole and went on my way. Arrow detergent cake?

At the circle across from my bakery I saw against the sky a poster I hadn't seen before. It was not for detergent. It was black-and-white and it didn't mince words. It showed two symbols, one above the other. Above was a pair of dark gogs; I recognized them at once as mine, or formerly mine, blown up a hundred times. Below was a TV set, or a simplified sketch of one, and in between, running the length of the hoarding, was the question: HAVE YOU WATCHED DIDI TODAY?

I went home and gave Pedro the bits of red peel from my breakfast bun. He gulped them down but continued to look suspiciously at me.

'But I *have*,' I said. 'I've watched half an *hour* of it.'

He pecked me viciously.

'Of her,' I apologized. 'Of Big Sister.'

Didi, Didi, Didi! he cried and went on that way for ten minutes.

I didn't mind the racket. It gave me the cover I needed to think. I didn't want Pedro reading my mind. There was something odd about that image I'd seen of Hero on the screen, something that jarred like a sixth finger on a hand

253

just shaken. And then I had it – Hero was wearing a khadi cap! I was stunned. Had his hair grown back too?

Then I thought of something else and felt it needed immediate verification. I left Pedro to his litany, jumped into the Maruti and drove south over the Ridge, through Kashmiri Gate, past the battlements of the Red Fort, past Shah Jehan's magnificent Friday Mosque, past Delhi Gate, past the few remaining newspaper offices, under Tilak Bridge, around India Gate, up Rajpath (Vindhya's stone palace floating on the heat haze straight ahead) then off onto Janpath and finally up Chanakya Marg to their residence. There was a new set of guards so I had trouble persuading them that I was an old friend, but then Mishra happened to be coming out with a file and he said I was OK. The guard frisked me all the same and made me leave the Maruti on the other side of the street.

They were home. I knew they liked to spend a quiet Sunday, he reading one of his old quantum physics texts once Mishra's special file was taken care of, she working on a friend's horoscope.

Francis let me in, old hatchet-face.

'Doggy!' my master cried, and I knew I'd been forgiven. I felt hot and sweet and wet inside. He grabbed me; I put my arms around him. He smelt of talcum powder and soft bananas. 'Where the hell have you been?' He turned to UD and said: 'We're going to have to build him a little house at the back.'

He didn't *say* a kennel, but I saw the missing word spark anger in UD's solicitous eyes. Not that I had the stomach to chop logic, for at that very moment my hands were burning with a discovery more jarring than a sixth finger. In that welcoming embrace I learnt what I had come hoping to verify. I felt – I'm sure of it – what I had never felt before and what I still could not see: my master's hump. It was growing back.

254

Didi was on, so I was glad for an excuse to sit down. We sat around her as if she made a fourth in our midst.

'What'll it be?' Hero said, sitting back. 'Pink gin?'

'Isn't it a bit early for that?' UD said looking at me, daring me to make up my own mind.

'Shandy would go down easily,' I said.

'Good,' she smiled. 'And you're staying for lunch. Francis is here today. He takes Mondays off now.'

I wanted to say: *of* course *I'm staying for lunch*. And: *watch out for that man*.

'Francis!' she called. 'Three shandies, please.'

There was a Mahabharat rerun on the tube and our eyes kept straying from each other to the epic action. Two fluorescent chariots were tearing up a golf course.

'You know, Doggy,' he said. 'I didn't know it at the time, but this is what I really dreamt of in the old days. You remember we used to talk till late at night about my Karmascope?' He used to talk; I listened. 'In fact it was Dharmavision – Didi I was looking for. It was all there, all ready and waiting, only all along I kept thinking of a big screen!'

I said: 'What's the afternoon movie?'

'Ask the new Media Minister,' UD said in a loaded voice.

Francis brought the shandy.

Hero squirmed in silence for a bit. When Francis had gone he said: 'Look, UD, you've got to admit she's qualified.'

I said: 'What's this?'

He said: 'After Dubey and his friends left I had to fill their vacancies.'

'Dubey's gone?'

He frowned at me, happy for a diversion. 'Haven't you been following the news?'

'I don't get a newspaper delivered.' My debts were mounting.

'Who said anything about newspapers?' he flared up. 'They're so full of lies and scandals lately I'm thinking seriously of doing something about it. Didn't you watch the evening news?'

I made a wide open gesture.

'Then you should know. Dubey and four others. But I had a very cordial letter from him this morning. He must have spent the whole night writing it. He's keeping his options open. Do you want to see it?' He made to get up.

'The new Media Minister,' UD murmured, reminding him.

'Nero has potential, Baby' he pleaded.

I choked on my shandy, then with a heroic effort, reran it and swallowed it down. They were too busy fencing to notice.

'And she has more experience with at least one medium than the last guy had.'

'Movies are not the same thing as TV.'

'As *Didi*, Baby. The principles are the same, more or less.'

'Movies you go to. TV comes to you.'

'*Didi* comes. That's only one of the advantages. Besides, we have flims on Didi.'

'Ya. Movies for violence, commercials for sex, and dharmadramas for absolution.'

'UD!'

'What's the afternoon movie?' I put in to keep the peace.

'*Anandmayee Sati*,' UD scoffed.

So after lunch we watched The Joyous Suttee. Rumour had it that the actress had come close to being burnt alive on the pyre by enthusiastic extras. It was the first movie I'd seen since that strange video the night of Nero's coming, and what struck me forcibly was that once again we were back with off-white heroes and (in this case) heroines. In the video there was no disjunction, no slippage between the sham up front and the embarrassing background. Here the heroine spoke Hindi but looked Greek or Iranian; she might have been pasted on in a sort of montage, there was that cutout line around her all the time: then there was a bit of fuzz, and *then* – there we were, the Indians, at the back, at the edges. We made more movies than anyone else in the world but we were only good enough for the crowd scenes. Our front had been colonized again, but not by any outsider: we'd done it ourselves. Joyous slavery, joyous sati.

After the movie there was a panel discussion. Had the practice of sati perhaps been misunderstood? It had been misrepresented, said the man of God; the concept of self-sacrifice must be examined in its historical context, said the historian; it must not be judged from the standpoint of Western individualism, said the cultural anthropologist. There followed a commercial break, and for fifteen minutes our Iranians sold us shower nozzles and our Greeks sold us bedsheets and tribes of painted teenagers frolicked on the beach selling whatever was put into their hands. Next came an hour of sporting news from around the world (a local coach popped in at the end to say we were going to win a medal at the next Olympics), an American comedy serial, and then it was time for the evening movie, *Aag, Aansoo, Aur Sughandit Sten Gun* (The Fragrance of Revenge).

Recall, gentle cinephile, that I am history's amanuensis: I record the passing of an era. Movies *qua* movies were clumsy dinosaurs; the new films were made for television. In his enthusiasm for the new mode Hero (and his Media Minister) freely sanctioned funds for the small screen. And as the sun came up over the Delhi Ridge actors and actresses were daily to be seen on the Indian Airlines breakfast flight from Bombay with wads of black money on their persons to be paid to fixers for interviews with Didi bureaucrats.

'They must adapt to changing circumstances,' said Hero, who had done his share of adapting, 'or fall by the wayside. Didi wants only the best.'

257

'The fittest,' I agreed, and thought of the chubby boys who made it to the dharmadramas. The eye slid gently off their podgy cheeks to settle briefly on those round shoulders off which the epic bow might slip only in righteous war.

I took to watching them on Sunday mornings on my way to the bun-factor. And then I started bringing Pedro out too. He was well behaved, creating no disturbance if the power failed (as it failed poor Alok Singh) because the genset manufacturers were bribing the electricity workers. But he gripped my finger tightly with his trembling claws when the arrows began to fly. Only when my master appeared to wish everyone a happy and holy day did restraint abandon him – but then it left the other watchers too. And while the masses clapped and cheered, he climbed all over me, head and shoulders, and did an agitated dance, rotating like a weather-vane and crying all the while as if his crop should burst, *Hero, Hero, Hero!*

Had he known how closely death stalked our hero the hallelujahs would have stuck in his craw. For the time was drawing near for the shot heard around the world.

The following month, on Independence Day, I took him to the grounds of the Red Fort, from whose ramparts the PM traditionally addressed the nation.

It was an overcast day, rain threatening from a tent of clouds, a kind of big top which must have given Hero a wrench.

STAR camera will pan the fortress wall from north to south from a point in Chandni Chowk, the medieval market opposite. The colours glow in the soft grey light; red sandstone, monsoon green grass, milky sky, in bands which approximate the colours of the national flag. Under a harsh sun they would appear bleached, drained of their natural vitality; today every hue, in nature and

on man, leaps out at the spectator. At the end of its 180-degree
sweep, STAR *camera may wish to continue panning, like a head*
twisting off, to show the curious Shah Jehan's monumental
Friday Mosque, also in red sandstone, and finally Chandni
Chowk itself.

I had a pass to the VIP enclosure up on top but Pedro
would not have gone down well there, so we kept to the
fringes with the *hoi polloi* of Chandni Chowk. Because he
liked musical instruments I took him up to the elevated
row of red sandstone shops facing the fort, rented for the
most part by brass bands that did weddings, and we sat
among the bandsmen to hear Hero's speech from the
ramparts. About where we were sitting twenty thousand
of Delhi's citizens had been killed in a single day by the
Persian invader Nadir Shah.

Up on the ramparts opposite us, on a little patch of
green around the flagpole I saw a dab of red which must
be UD in a new sari with shoes to match. A bandsman
with a curly horn noticed her too.

'She's the power behind the throne,' he said to me, idly
punching his silver pistons.

I looked coldly at him and drew away along the red
stone ledge. My UD a schemer! As if she cared two hoots
for the whole charade!

Two hoots, two hoots! said Pedro, reading my mind. He
flapped his wings and leapt onto the wide rim of the
horn. The bandsman gave a contemptuous blat on the
horn and sent him flying back to me.

On the parapet Hero – a white dab – had begun his
Independence Day address to the nation. *My* Independence Day address to the nation. From my Kamla Nagar
garret. I caught a glint off his glasses; my glasses. I
listened with some little pride. It occurred to me as I sat
there among the low-caste bandsmen in the general
throng, that I alone of all these thousands, of all the

259

millions watching on Didi, knew what was coming next. I mouthed the words before he uttered them. I knew the topography of that speech like the back of my hand: its salients and dips, its maundering expanses, its gaps, its furrows, its little witty wrinkles, its hairy thickets, the tender quicks, the tough-as-nails ending.

And then I noticed something wrong. He should have said *facing the future, with our backs to the past.* Instead he said *marching forward together and never looking back.*

I sat there thunderstruck. It was the first time he had ever altered the text of a speech. I'd known him to extemporize, to lift his eye from the page and embroider for a bit, working his silken visions on the azure hoop of sky, but those were departures from the text, not alterations of it.

I listened again after that hiccup, picking up the thread, and once again my master's voice poured out of the five hundred Chicago loudspeakers and becalmed the flutter in my heart. There once more were the familiar words, bodied forth in plangent majesty precisely as I would have them, every shade of intonation exact and meet.

And then it happened again. *Heroic dawn* for *the break of day* (Pedro gave me that), and on its heels *the slaver of flattery* for *the purring of sycophants.*

From there on the changes were so frequent, emendation chasing emendation, that I could scarcely recognize my Independence Day address. My choicest squibs, my homiletic excursions, my privatization tirade bowdlerized, and behind it all, visible here and there between the shreds of my discourse, I made out, piecemeal at first, but then with growing certitude, the vulgar stripes of one Hosi Billimoria.

Alley Billi! Alley Billi! Pedro called, and I could with a single turn of the wrist have wrung his neck. *Why, O Master, why?* my soul cried out. And there might have been more lamentation but for what happened next.

260

Hero finished his speech and gave his pages a tidying shake. It was a gesture of release, the ordering of those perfidious sheets, and I still recall the clack on the lectern, amplified and carried by five hundred loudspeakers as he made the edges even. A band on the ramparts struck up the national anthem even as the crenellations sprouted buglers all along the fortress wall. A few big drops of rain came down. The VIPs stood up, and so did we. On the green surrounding the fort the masses were already standing – had been standing all through that hour-and-a-half-long speech. They had cheered him along as in the old days, taking it for a di-laag, or mono-laag, and now they fell silent. Around us the bandsmen decided informally to answer the military band and started the national anthem a whole line behind. Down the row of bandshops other private bands followed suit. There would have been a dozen national anthems in various degrees of progress.

I sang the words, not quite sure what the Sanskrit meant though I'd sung it through a hundred times before. Around me other singers were singing other lines with other words.

On the grassy slope below me, the last to start, was the Nav Bharat band. Their name was on the bass drum and their gimcrack navy-and-scarlet uniforms were embroidered, among the fantastical Bolivian Navy festoons, with gold NBs. I don't know why my eye should have singled him out, but I saw a bandsman shoulder his slide-trombone – an extended edition which didn't seem to belong – and take aim. Suppose there were, I mused, in place of music in the mouth of that egregious instrument, a set of telescopic sights? As if in answer the man squeezed a tappet. There was a sharp crack followed by the ping and whine of a ricocheting bullet.

I saw pandemonium break out on the Red Fort parapet. The bullet had struck the invisible glass shield and gone its way, finding its mark perhaps in the crowd below. Not

261

the shot that was heard around the world after all. But the VIPs behind Hero fell flat on their faces, the top brass dived under their chairs, and one or two drumsticks clattered from the hands of the otherwise impassive military band. Even UD seemed to panic until she saw her husband was safe.

He was standing there unmoved, though the bullet had left an instant spider's web in the glass six inches from his face.

'Keep playing!' he bellowed at the band. The band picked up the last line of the anthem, and my master bawled out in his execrable singing voice that victory shout: *Jaya he, jaya he, jaya he! Jaya, jaya, jaya, jaya he!*

Hail, hail, hail to thee! Hail, hail, hail, hail!

He waved to the crowd and a cheer went up. There were many who did not know what the commotion was about, but word was spreading through the crowd. Hero's security men finally got near him; earlier he'd ordered them back. They formed a ring around him and hustled him back to cover.

Below me the Nav Bharat band marched off in formation, the slide-trombonist lugging his cumbersome instrument away. For all I knew they might have been Bolivians. The police sprang into action on every side, cordoning off blocks of the crowd and screaming into walkie-talkies. Their task was hopeless. There were a hundred lanes in the old city down which an assassin might run. The crowd began to push towards Chandni Chowk; no one wanted to remain and be picked up for questioning. They saw that Hero was alive and that was enough. There were those who would have liked to run amok but a line of armoured cars poured out of the Lahore Gate and threw a ring around the fort, looking like they meant business. A tank or two hove up for good measure from the Delhi Gate end.

'Go home!' came the command over the speakers. 'Go home quietly! All is well.'

Then the rain came down in earnest. I stood as if in a dream, my clothes soaked, the people flowing silently past me.

'You!' a cop barked at me from below. 'Are you deaf? Who do you think you are? Haven't you heard the order?'

I came to with a start. The curly-hornist and his band were gone, the red stone corridor deserted. The rain had stopped. I made an ingratiating namaste to the cop and started for Kashmiri Gate. Opposite the GPO I caught a Kamla Nagar bus and sat in silence though my neighbour wished to talk about the assassination attempt. When I refused to respond he looked at me suspiciously as if I might be the guilty man making a cool getaway.

Then I heard myself singing: *Jaya he, jaya he, jaya he!* I was just as startled as the man beside me until I remembered Pedro in my pocket. The informer left his seat and had a word with the conductor. I didn't wait for developments. A jumpy populace fed on bread and circuses is not one for nice discriminations. I sprang out of the back door before the next stop and disappeared into the crowd at the inter-state bus terminal. They hadn't heard the news there, I hoped. Of course they had, so I slipped out on the far side of the ISBT and took a scooter rickshaw along Ring Road to the IP College corner. Then I skipped up Underhill Road and crossed the Ridge on foot, sucking in the cool damp air and rejoicing in the fresh green scrub around me. I lingered a while in the university rose garden, picked a white John F. Kennedy, then nipped down to the Miranda House gates and took another scooter home.

It was the first signal of discontent among the people, that shot. Not widespread discontent clearly – after all it took just one crank to press a trigger – but it was a watershed of sorts. For here was no routine Opposition salvo fired across their narrow deck in parliament. This

263

was a shot from the crowd: *a* shot, certainly, but its origin was symbolic.

Hard for him to take, naturally, accustomed as he was to fans and adulation. A pistol-shot at a concert indeed! Somebody down there did not love him. He began to cast around for motives, the more devious the better. Someone close to him must be involved, some quisling, some wolf in sheep's clothing, some asp in the bosom, some cur who bit the hand that fed him – in short, some villain. Filmi lore dies hard.

'Doggy.'

'Saab?'

'You must have heard about that shot yesterday.'

How to tell him I saw it fired?

'I heard it, baas.'

'On Didi.'

'Saab, I was there.'

'Really? I didn't notice you in the VIP tent.'

'Me, saab? You're joking!'

'But you had an invitation.'

'I was – I was late, saab.'

How to explain about Pedro?

'Where did you sit, Doggy?'

'Straight across the road from you, saab. Up in the verandah of those bandshops.'

'Those bandshops.'

'Yes.'

'Brass bands?'

'Yes, baas. You know those weddingwalas.'

'Weddingwalas. Trumpets and horns and whatnot.'

'That sort of thing, saab.'

'Straight across from me?'

'I had the best view, baas.'

'The best view.' He stroked his dewlap.

I didn't like the tone of this cross-examination. I said: 'Where's UD, saab?'

'Oh, dressing. She's a bit tired. You better not wait.'

264

I turned to go.

'Oh, Doggy.'

'Saab?'

'You know, they found the weapon.'

'*Really?*'

'Really. You know what it was made up as? One of those long horns you play like this.' He bent his elbow a couple of times. 'What's it called?'

'A slide-trombone.'

'A *sli*-de trombone.' He let the *i* glide out. 'Like those bandwalas use, no? Those weddingwalas.'

'Actually they don't – '

He cut me off, speaking rapidly. 'They found it in the verandah in front of the bandshops. Straight across from me. Someone must have left it there. I wonder who. Anyway, I'll tell UD you came.'

I bought a paper on the way home. It said the weapon had been recovered from the bottom of a well in Chandni Chowk. So he was just trying me on. And in fact the next time he welcomed me with an embrace.

But I did notice a change, or changes. The eyes – the eye – began to shift again; it no longer held you, returning its old habits, its knack of sneaking off no matter what. In this respect the dark glasses, my dark gogs, were a useful blind. And there was another thing. He now had trouble listening to you too. Not hearing trouble, no. Just listening. When you talked to him he might, by accident it seemed, absorb a vowel here and there along the way. But when you talked to someone else he picked up every word. In this he was not unlike a certain sort of busybody, the organizer, the administrator, common enough incarnations – Mishra, for example. But the fact was he was not like that temperamentally – he was getting to be that way. And as if half-conscious of this unchecked drift, he grew sly in the defensive way of the half-mad. So the eye

265

connived in the not-listening just as the ears connived in the not-looking.

It was about that time, not long after Independence Day, that GJ let fall, in an interview with the *Mail*, his unfortunate remark about the cult of personality. The cult had hardly begun, in fact, so GJ's animadversions were long-sighted enough in their own way, but they were unfortunate because they brought down Hero's wrath not just on the *Mail* but on all newspapers: they had their editions cut back, the number of pages reduced and censors-in-residence appointed. And they landed GJ himself in jail. The charge was conspiracy compounded with something else, treason perhaps, but the case simply didn't come to court and GJ languished – the word is too strong; he had his contacts – in prison the whilst.

The whilst, Plumbum!

The mistake was Hero's too. He should have known better: after all, the British raj was not so far behind us, a mere half-century ago, with its jailers and jailees, those villains and heroes of a black-and-white era. The merest whiff of a jail sentence made an ordinary man a freedom fighter, and GJ was no ordinary man to start with. There he was, discredited, defeated, fading – and here was Hero throwing him in jail! And not in an ordinary jail with run-of-the-mill criminals, but in a special cell in the Red Fort!

Tactically unsound, he realized no sooner had he done it, but to go back would be worse. So to save face he began another sort of drama. And one Sunday on Didi the nation was astonished to find, during the course of the morning dharmadrama, that God, the God whose visitation they now longed – and even dressed – for, wore a turban. A winding Rajasthani affair in pistachio green. And the next week it was saffron, tied in the Bihari way, and the next a guava pink Sikh turban (I thought I recognized that from an earlier disguise), and the next a Garhwali knitted hat, and the next a furry Kashmiri flapper, and the next an Anglo sola-topee, and the next a Gandhi cap.

For those with short memories it was a source of endless, even erotic, fascination. What lay underneath? Might head and hump have come together?

It might have been a fashion show it was so popular, only the grave academics on the panel which followed the dharmadrama gave it a solemn twist and canonized it along with his first national integration stunt, that bucket job. A museum was created (on Bahadur Shah Zafar Marg, next to the *Mail* building) for displaying each week's ceremonial headdress, once-used, and the masses flocked there on the way back from a football match at the Feroz Shah Kotla stadium, or an exhibition at the Pragati Maidan, or shopping at Pintoo Vihar, or simply on their way from South Delhi to North Delhi or vice versa.

'The people need colour in their lives, Doggy,' he said, smiling a rare smile.

He was wearing a Bhil tribal chief's headdress – it was not drab, certainly – which he'd worn to an awards ceremony for creative design in headwear. (The prize had gone to a girl who designed a Kohinoor crown.)

And to make sure the colour was not confined to the capital, he subsidized the production of colour Didis so that they should be within reach of the lower-middle-class by the following year and the broad masses by the turn of the century. In the meantime colour supplements for Monday, Tuesday, Wednesday and Thursday were required of all functioning newspapers (in addition to the existing supplements on other days.) Indeed, by a given deadline colour must supplant black-and-white newsprint altogether, just as the picture must ultimately supplant the word.

If the shot from the crowd marked a distinct phase, the turbans marked the beginning of what GJ foresaw as the cult of personality. Earlier Hero had like any other star –

like any politician – striven to build up an image for himself; now, as the image detached itself from the man, it seemed he strove to fashion an image of himself.

'I had warned the people before I had gone to jail,' said GJ in a message from prison. 'But the people had not heeded my pleas and the press had laughed. We must fight this menace by every democratic means, or I had worked in vain, had I not?' Clearly, GJ had had it. But there was one thing he wanted to make perfectly clear. 'I had told the PM on the day I was arrested itself: I cannot bring myself to conspire dishonourably.'

In parliament there was muted dissent. The noisier members of the Opposition, threatened with jail, were already underground. Some of the seats on Hero's side were empty too, though the majority of coalition MPs attended out of fear that their absence might be taken as a sign of disloyalty, a punishable offence.

'If there's one thing that makes me see red, Doggy,' he said, looking hard at me, 'it's disloyalty. It's the *crime de la crime*, don't you think so?'

'It depends, saab . . .' I said, and went on to spell out the differing shades of disloyalty. Disloyalty 1a) for example. But he wasn't listening; his eye had danced away and his ears switched off.

It was around about this time that Delhi's manhole covers began to disappear. There was always a problem with manholes in the capital – in every city and town for that matter – but now he officially requisitioned all scrap iron for the state, and that meant all inessential metal. One Sunday he put on a tank-commander's black beret for a special announcement. The enemy was massing on our borders again and we needed every iron gate and every second cooking pot and every rusty cobbler's tack for the nation's defence. And every manhole cover. (I thought I recognized the hand – cat's paw – behind that militant speech.) Which enemy? we wondered: the hook

268

nose or the slant eye? That evening and for the rest of the month we had our answer on Didi, as swarms of hook-nosed extras crossed our desert border to rape our women and murder our children. Nor was it just a matter of invaders, Didi warned the nation. The foreign hand lurked already in every nook and cranny of our mother-land – and every hole, every black circle underfoot, every treacherous zero . . . The enemy without had a potent ally in the enemy within.

One morning I was summoned to the Red Fort. An army dispatch rider in olive green on an olive green Bullet with that deep rich olive green growl brought the message to the door: there was an urgent meeting which concerned national security.

I dressed at once and, thinking I might show Pedro around the fort (he'd never been inside), dressed him too. It pleased me to think that I was still a member of the kitchen cabinet.

As the Maruti topped the rise alongside the fort I noticed something different. All along the ramparts where on Independence Day the buglers stood was a continuous hoarding which asked, in all the national languages, and no longer in black-and-white, the Didi question. Had we watched her today? And there was a new and shorter slogan: DIDI IS THE NATION. It occurred to me as I read that that it was quite true: she had become a part of every household and she was what we all, serfs apart, had in common. Unbeknownst to us that truism had become an article of faith, if an inchoate one. Now it was spelt out it became scripture.

STAR camera will move at Maruti level from north to south along Netaji Subhash Marg reading the writing on the wall. Trees, bus-shelters, pedestrians, may obstruct the view, giving the impression of life going on oblivious of the exhortations.

At the Delhi Gate I waved my letter of authority at the officer (army, not police) and we drove across the moat, Pedro in the passenger seat. There was a tarmacked zone beyond the gate where we had to park the Maruti and walk. We went around towards the Lahore Gate to do the sightseeing in the right order. I noticed all the postcard-and-knick-knackwalas in the covered bazaar were gone. I'd been hoping to buy Pedro a new mirror for his cage and one of those paper accordions with Delhi views to cover up a crack in the loo.

At the Drum House I was frisked (not very thoroughly, since they missed the bulge in my pocket that was Pedro) and permitted to proceed.

Now I don't know how well you know the Red Fort. I lived in Delhi for years before I ventured in, so don't apologize. The emperor Shah Jehan who had the palace built had his levee there in the Diwan-i-Aam, the public audience hall (there was a private audience hall, the Diwan-i-Khas, further in) from 1648 to 1656 (they say). Where he sat – everyone else stood – was called the Seat of the Shadow of God. To get there you had to cross a wide courtyard, preferably on your hands and knees, and then you got justice, or at least a glimpse of the sovereign.

Well, we crossed the courtyard (now a lawn) upright under the already hot sun, and on the other side, in the marble cavern of the Diwan-i-Aam, where all the shadows are white and where the walls and pillars are inlaid with semi-precious stones, we found the rest of kitchen cabinet standing around a billiard table at whose top right-hand corner, nearest the Seat of the Shadow of God, wearing the Kohinoor crown and rolling a billiard ball across the green baize so it struck three sides of the table and came back to him, sat Hero.

STAR camera is positioned directly above the billiard table looking down, as in a televised tournament: at times the baize rectangle
270

fills the screen – when a ball travels across the surface – at others the six figures around the table are visible, one at each pocket.

He looked at his watch as we came in. It was five-past-eight by my HMT. I recalled reading somewhere that Shah Jehan had his public audience from eight to ten in the morning.

'Sorry, saab!' I said, dripping unction. I felt a mortal trembling in my pocket.

At the corner nearest Hero stood a peacock fan. On closer inspection it turned out to be Nero, in a peacock blue-and-green georgette sari tied provocatively low. There may have been high heels underneath. She was making up her face from a flapjack. So UD must be at home, on Chanakya Road. Little Mishra stood at the side pocket nearest Hero, then there was the present Chief of Army Staff, Haq. I knew nothing of Haq except that he had two wives and kept them covered from head to foot in burqas. At the pocket diagonally across from Hero, with his back to me, was a figure I should have recognized at once had his presence there not been so unexpected. It was GJ, evidently pardoned and let out of his special cell. And finally, opposite Mishra, there stood a figure so revolting I moved instinctively, out of a desire to protect Pedro, to the other side of the billiard table. It was that deceitful feline, sometime scriptwriter and fellow Old Spoonie, Alley Billi.

Since there was no pocket for me, I leaned casually on the table between Mishra and my master.

'I didn't know you played, saab!' I said, trying a light tone.

He gave me a long slow smile, the smile Capone gave his trussed-up ex-deputy in a Chicago basement.

'It must have been a gripping newspaper this morning, Doggy,' he said, going back to rolling his chosen ball, the black. 'Unless you were watching the morning news. But

271

I'm told – ' he glanced across at his new speechwriter – 'you don't *have* a Didi.'

'Why would I need my own Didi, saab?' I said.

There was an exchange of glances all round the table – except for GJ, who looked stolidly ahead of him. I admired him for that: he had no time for the petty cash of domestic intrigue. I suddenly saw the assemblage as an Inquisition and myself as the heretic who has condemned himself out of his own mouth. What I'd meant was that I watched *their* TV, his and UD's, so why would I need to get one for myself? But I must confess when I found myself misunderstood I felt the heretic's cussed pride. If I was to be condemned, if this was to be my trial, my sainted mockery of a trial, let me go out in style. I was sure everyone there knew how I felt – except GJ, who would have no time for such childishness, and again I felt myself in awe of him.

'Never mind,' said Hero abruptly, in his getting-down-to-business voice, and my little cameo of martyrdom dissolved harmlessly. 'As you all know we have unmasked the enemy without. We are at this very moment – ' and he looked at his army chief – 'teaching them an undeclared lesson. As General Haq well knows, matters of defence are too serious to be left to politicians. The Defence Minister will therefore report to him in future. We must now deal with the enemy within. Our new Home Minister needs no introduction.' He sent a ball zig-zagging off two sides to roll obediently into GJ's pocket. 'Much less does he need any advice from us on his new and crucial task. We have had a little misunderstanding in the past but that has only served to advance our understanding of one another and to strengthen the bonds that now unite us.'

GJ stared impassively at each of us around the table with his heavy-lidded eyes.

'I have every confidence in his powers,' Hero went on, 'and he has every power in my confidence.'

I saw a feline touch there, and sure enough, the next ball rolled straight into Billi's pocket.

'After much thought,' Hero continued, 'I have decided to create a Ministry of Truth, which will concern itself with public announcements of every kind, including speeches. Statistics will also enter into Mr Billimoria's province.'

His eye flicked away from the simpering Billimoria.

'Mishra' – a single rebound into PM's Secretary Mishra's pocket – 'is, as always, Mishra. Per-manent Secretary.' He stretched out the *per*-manent with devastating effect, Billi's purr no doubt, and it gave me a jolt to remember he had been an actor.

Mishra gave his concise filing smile.

'And it has occurred to me that there is – ' Hero looked directly at Mishra for the first time – 'too much seriousness, too much gloom among us, as a nation, that is. Therefore I have decided to create a Ministry of Laughter.'

There was a low filmi chuckle, like an old-fashioned gramophone being wound up with the needle on the record. Nero's teeth looked charcoal-scrubbed as her chuckle became a laugh which developed into a hyaena call: *Hyaah! Hyaah! Hyaaannh!* which loped and frisked about the lofty marble vault. At length peace returned to the Diwan-i-Aam and Hero turned to me. There were no balls left on the table.

'Doggy,' he said, and there was a long filmi pause during which he paced a wide circle around the assembled cabinet, his hands clasped behind his back to signify: *thinking*. I noticed he was wearing knee-high leather boots, the kind he would have worn with that cannonball get-up. They gave me a little frisson as I watched them strut past us and around the billiard table. I hung my head and followed the play of light on the glossy toecaps

273

as they did that slow, clicking, winking lap and then came up the straight, to me.

STAR camera may come down from the ceiling for that lap to follow their progress from under the table.

Cock of the walk, I thought, to cheer myself up, but of course he was the bull in the story.

'Doggy,' he repeated, and for a moment I thought he was going to set off on another tour of the table. But he was good that way; another actor would have. Instead he stood up very straight in front of me. He may even have arched his springy back like a bow, and had he carried a cane I felt sure he would have flicked his boots viz it down ze side of ze leg.

'I've been thinking,' he said, looking straight at me, 'Doggy.'

'Excellent, saab,' I ventured, the comma hardly there.

'You,' he said, his eye dropping by degrees down my front, 'would, make, a, fine . . .' The eye shot back up and reamed me: 'Director of Didi.'

There are no manholes in the Diwan-i-Aam, but I felt the ground open up below me. Perhaps Shah Jehan did have his own little trapdoor there, complete with snapping crocodiles, for difficult ministers.

'In fact,' he went on, 'now that you will have a rest from speechwriting – and given your expertise with *script-writing* – I would like to put you in charge of the big screen as well as the small screen, in charge, in fact, of every kind of screen, moving and not. I think – yes – I will create a new portfolio for you. You will be Minister – Minister of State, naturally, since we have enough full ministers – Minister of Screens.'

And with that he dismissed us and disappeared through a door I hadn't seen before. A stage curtain could not have been more effective.

The cabinet dispersed, going off in ones and twos. It was our first meeting; later on we'd use the Diwan-i-Khas or hall of private audience. Alley Billi I noticed hung around for a bit, casting sidelong glances at me as if it were high time we made our peace, but I ignored him and he caught up with Nero who was making her scented way towards the Rang Mahal or Coloured Palace, behind the Diwan-i-Aam.

It was only then that I saw I'd been given Nero's Media portfolio. Or rather, portmanteau. I – Zero! – would sanction those vulgar dharmadramas. I – imagine! – would issue the ban on newspapers. And I, when the time came – O my master was a clever man! – would be responsible for banning the big screen!

I was it seemed the chosen hangman of the past. But I was also, I realized, the midwife of a monstrous future. For as things got worse out there I would have to see that they got better on the screen.

Minister of Screens! What was it that made men covet a cabinet post? I felt I was drowning in stone, Shah Jehan's red sandstone, the portfolio an iron collar around my neck. Where was that comforting leather strap, the familiar clinking brass name-tag?

Just then I heard a voice singing that plaintive song from the 1940s *Mumtaz Mahal*, where Kamini Gadhok as the stricken queen wanders in the garden taking leave of her beloved fountains:

> *O heav'n-aspiring droplets leaping,*
> *   Falling back nathless – I too,*
> *Reaching upwards, gently weeping,*
> *   Must mingle in the wave – like you!*
> *   Like you, I too,*
> *   Must kiss oblivion anew!*

I looked up and in the middle distance, in the exquisite Life-Giving Garden – which the British overhung with a row of grisly barracks – I caught a glimpse of UD. What on earth was she doing here? I waved frantically but she turned a corner and was gone, slipping behind the Pearl Mosque. Her passage was so ethereal – she was wearing a gauzy white chikan sari – that for a moment I thought I must be seeing things. She'd vanished like some phantom princess in a sound-and-light show from the old days when tourists flocked here after dark. But this was a particularly blinding forenoon.

And then I understood what she was doing here. I'd thought Hero had shifted his office to the Red Fort and summoned his cabinet here. Was this not after all Shah Jehan's office? Had the emperor not used the octagonal north tower as his private study? Certainly, but then the royal palace was here too. I'd thought Hero was simply at work in the Red Fort; in fact he was at home too. UD lived here now.

I turned away with a sinking heart. She'd cast off the vivid red saris I loved, given them up for him. So mine was not the only transfusion after all. He'd bled her white too. I shook my head. Were all heroes a kind of vampire, then?

STAR camera, perched on the Drum House roof, may follow my listless steps. From up there it can spy on the other actors too.

I made my way back to the Delhi Gate, slouching the way he used to in the old days, feeling in my pocket for the car keys. I found instead a bundle of warm feathers. *Zero, Zero, Zero*, it crooned for me. At the bottom of the drive I found my car gone.

And then I realized I lived here too.

Dance

The old order changeth and giveth place to the old order.

His troubles began almost immediately after that change of address. Or should I say our troubles.

To start with, the monsoon failed. Crops died in the fields, villagers starved, merchants hoarded foodgrains, prices shot up, goods began to disappear off shelves, a hoarder was lynched. Processions were taken out, converging on Chandni Chowk so he might look down from his fortress battlements upon the people's discontent. Posters began to appear on walls demanding action, and the few remaining newspapers called on the government to resign. In parliament, which he attended faithfully (his helicopter flying out over Chandni Chowk and then straight across to Connaught Place and up Parliament Street), his own PSM MPs began to show signs of restlessness. The people were already restless.

He responded with an unscheduled appearance on Didi; that is, not one of his regular Sunday appearances: we did announce it. His head, I saw as he walked into the

277

studio, was shaven smooth again and oiled. Behind him we projected the synoptic meteorological photo beamed down from INSAT IV. It showed the subcontinent with all its familiar dents and bumps, the wrinkled Himalayas, the strong primitive thrust of the peninsula ending at his cherished Kanyakumari, the cape of his conception. The coastline, the borders, were helpfully outlined in white, but the artist needn't have bothered, for all the features were starkly visible: there was not a cloud in the sky.

He folded his hands in greeting and spoke feelingly, paternally, about the state of the nation. We were an agricultural society, he said. All through our history we had had to contend with monsoon failures, to endure droughts. But we were a proud people; we had a rich and durable heritage. We were the oldest continuous civilization in the world. Together we must see this dark year through, succouring one another as our ancient scriptures taught us, and surely the next year would bring healing rains and a bountiful harvest.

It was like God apologizing for the weather. Later that evening on the news we saw a foreign correspondent I recognized ask him what the world could do for India in her hour of crisis.

'We need your love,' he said, 'we need your prayers.' And he smiled such a gentle soulful smile I saw he meant it.

Then when the camera turned to other things, he turned to me, his Minister of Screens.

'What's on after the news?'

'A documentary, saab.'

'What sort of documentary?'

'On the ecology of afforestation, saab.'

'Change it.'

'What shall we run, saab?'

'How am I to know? You're the specialist.'

'Movie or dharmadrama, saab?'

278

'Movie. You choose.'

So we saw an oldie, one of his (and mine), *Suryanamas-kar*, the one that sealed old Javed's fate – and set my master on course for stardom. And as the reels unrolled I once again had occasion to reflect on the nature of cause and consequence and how a man's or a nation's fate might hinge on the slenderest of chances. And after the movie, in place of the day's parliamentary report, we carried an animated cartoon from Japan introduced by the Minister of Laughter.

It worked for a while – there were women fainting again, though not as many as before, and some said it was from hunger because our men ate three quarters of the country's food – but then the processions returned, now marching to a slow drumbeat. There were strikes and jailbreaks, a housewives' petition hammered out on cooking pots. Two PSM MPs were killed and others had their cars stoned. There were mass resignations and goings underground. And then someone from the warren of lanes and dwellings around Chandni Chowk took a potshot at the PM's helicopter.

Or so the Ministry of Truth said – and it was entirely possible. As a result, the soyabean newsreader said, the PM had decided to change the venue of parliament. In accordance with old, pre-British traditions, the represen-tatives of the people would now meet in the Red Fort, where security arrangements were adequate to their needs.

The next day I watched the security arrangements being, as the newsreader put it, enhanced. Bunkers were being dug below the walls and what remained of the green roundabout was ploughed up by the wheels and chains of tanks and armoured vehicles. A line of big guns ringed the perimeter of the fort, their long barrels lifted in a kind of benign salute and pointed outwards at the city Shah Jehan built. (Convenient – heroic – shorthand! The

279

city Shah Jehan's *workers* built.) Neutral Swedish guns: whatever their magazines might hold I felt sure it wasn't human cannonballs. On the other side, Ring Road was closed off and the land running down to the river requisitioned for more gun-sites. By the end of the week it looked as if the entire stock of the Grendel Systems company was on our doorstep. And amid the alien harvest, so his subjects should not find the crop unseemly, and to set an example, Hero caused to be planted, where the soil had been ploughed up by the wheels of war, a thin gold line of Indian corn.

To appease the people, Hero sacked both the Defence and the Finance ministers and took over their portfolios himself. I recalled that he had always fought his own battles, done his own stunts, so our defence caused me no sleepless nights. Nor did the finance: in Bombay he had done his own accounts, and as a boy, mathematics, quirky but sound, had been his forte. So I had greater faith than most when I heard him pronounce that he would balance the budget in his head.

Next he promoted Chief of Army Staff General Haq to Field Marshal and put him on a short leash. And he let GJ, Home Minister, off his.

After that people began to disappear in earnest. The manholes of Delhi became more notorious than the missing fishplates on the Howrah Bridge in Calcutta. Not that Calcutta, and every other city and town, didn't have its share of disappearances. The enemy within, Didi said – and I now watched her morning and night; her broadcasting house had moved with me into the fort – was more insidious than the enemy without, who at least looked honourably different and fought like a man. Democracy, Hero said, from under a white scroll wig, was in peril; we must be vigilant if we valued our freedom, for there were those who sought to pervert it in the name of justice. (He sounded a little like the judge in *Comrade Ravi*.) The country would be best served if every man did his appointed job, his dharmic duty.

I did mine by Didi. We ran a daily report on parliament to show the people that it had not only survived the transplanting from the old Lok Sabha premises but throve in its new setting on the banks of the Yamuna. There was no question of a suspension of liberty, no suspect emergency declaration: all was proceeding to order, the regulations – his beloved procedures – would be preserved at any cost. It had to be admitted he lived by the book: if he had to use ventriloquism to achieve a quorum he did, but he respected the rules. On Fridays we had an expert on parliamentary lore come on, as tedious a stickler as ever dotted *i*, and there was a nightly *Today in the New Parliament* quiz show for toddlers. The news was shortened and the weather report extended by ten minutes. I doubled the quota of historicals and patrioticals and commissioned serials from promising young chauvinists until swashbuckling di-laags became the rage once more. Politicians, once villains, became heroes again, khadi-clad dotards sang love songs to village maidens. I wrote some scripts myself, to keep my hand in. *Indian chests were made for smashing British bullets*, I wrote late one night (very late) and it went to air as written.

But I didn't write any more speeches. And I should like to go on record as disclaiming the *Father And Mother Of The Nation* speech. Nor did I write the louring *Hung Parliament* speech with its sullen gallows humour, and certainly not the *Visited By God In A Dream* speech. All of these emanated from the Ministry of Truth whose offices adjoined the Royal Tower. My own adjoined the little museum at the other end of the royal row, where one day I discovered a corpulent Anglo painter, one Eugene Trotter, engaged to paint, and indeed painting, on velvet, a portrait of Hero and UD as celestial visitants.

It was an atrocity, that painting, but at the time I

281

couldn't stop. A foreign head of state was due and I was to learn the full extent of my responsibilities as Minister of Screens. Every slum, every public defecator, every pullulating stew on the road from the airport into town and from guest house to guest house across the country had to be screened from the King of Spain's eyes. What I chose to put on the screens – whether advertisements or Didi slogans or *trompe l'oeil* paintings of tranquil villages – was up to me. Hero, recalling a former exploit at the Star Scooter & Automotive Repairs workshop, offered advice: why didn't I try mockups of ideal village huts? And wherever the royal cavalcade stopped to mingle with the people I was on hand with my battery of chefs to fill the local pots with gourmet lentils and set the people dancing afterwards.

But the decision which pained me most was still to come. In a final repudiation of his past, or affirmation of our future, Hero turned his back on Bombay, a city he had come to distrust as decadent and western. It may have been Bombay that first turned its back on him – Didi's ratings were lowest there – but the back that mattered was his, or rather the one with the knife in it was Bombay's. He had me ban the big screen.

Not just like that: it was phased out – helped on its way, he said – but by a certain date it was to go. Hind Talkies everywhere, he said, could become cold-storage barns for storing potatoes. He offered his former colleagues jobs with Didi; he didn't want anybody out of work, and there was plenty making serials and dharma-dramas in Delhi.

Hero Turncoat.

It didn't quite work, the ban. There were still illicit screenings, some right under his nose in Old Delhi, but he turned his blind eye to them for the moment.

For the moment he had to contend with his grief. Word

282

had come from Kottagode of his mother's death. Rangamma was no more; she'd gone to the place, or space, where his father, the postman was, and now there was nobody between Hero and the sky. I understood his passion, his peculiar predicament. He more than anybody needed that supervening presence, that protective ozone layer of maternal grace of which the adipose tissue of the fat and fair Rangamma was but the outward and tangible token. Not all the new flab of a Nero could solace him against the emptiness that that excision left.

He made a lightning trip to Kottagode to perform her funeral rites and returning decreed a month's national mourning. During that month the Ministry of Laughter was silenced and Didi carried, dharmadramas apart, only mother films, with which, to my good fortune, the nation was so richly endowed.

The cult of Ma was so well received throughout the motherland he was a little taken aback when the following month his sequel flopped: the cult of Pa, the postman. The framed oleographs of the pink-lipped khaki-capped postman lasted a week on government office walls beside the Father of the Nation and then, outclassed, came down and were stored away in spite of Didi's warnings. He blamed me, Director of Didi, but in his very own Diwani-Aam the order was ignored, so much so that he collared the peon responsible and threatened to have him thrown from the ramparts as in old Shah Jehan's dispensation.

Shah Jehan was not the only Mughal spectre he raised. Aurangzeb, Shah Jehan's grasping son, last and gloomiest of the great Mughal emperors, furnished a model too. One day I was walking in the Life-Giving Garden, hoping for a glimpse of UD, or even a breath of that old cologne, when I heard her singing that same song of farewell from some hidden terrace. I listened motionless and still (motionless *and* still, Plumbum?), hardly breathing at all. Suddenly the voice was cut off and I heard her husband's

283

in its place, raised in remonstration. Shortly after, he appeared looking thunderous.

'Is this any time for singing?' he demanded, striding past. He stopped in his tracks and turned to me. 'What are you doing here?'

I spread my hands. 'Strolling, saab.'

'What's wrong with the Drum House garden? The trouble with this country is that no one works. They're either strolling or singing – or strolling *and* singing. I want you to start a campaign against this sort of wastage of time. A nation of strollers and singers!'

'Saab, Alamgir tried it too.'

'Alamgir?'

'Aurangzeb.'

'And what happened?'

'The musicians of Delhi staged a mass funeral for music. They carried her bier through Chandni Chowk chanting: *Music is dead.*'

'Good. Let's see what happens.'

So I went ahead with the proclamation that evening and sure enough the next day we watched the procession go by, starting from the Nav Bharat bandshop and snaking up to Chandni Chowk and back, instruments reversed.

He took it badly, flying into a rage. Lately he lost his temper easily – the bullet lodged in his brain, some said. I wondered if it wasn't the result of a career made out of playing with every emotion at short order. At any rate he was easily appeased.

I plucked a red rose for him. He held it to his nose – buried his nose in it – and closing his eye, breathed deeply. He seemed to totter where he stood. Then he recovered and smiled.

'Remember that morning by the river, Doggy? Was it you?'

284

It was vague enough to build a memory around, and I glowed as I must have that ideal morning.

But that evening it was a blistering rage again because of some ghosting of his image on the screen. He'd grown superstitious and took this doppelganger for an omen.

I was not the only one to suffer his rages. Almost everybody, except perhaps GJ, had his turn. Even the people, that cherished abstraction of his innocence, could catch the new flak. The day after his *Hung Parliament* threat (there'd been some absenteeism among the remaining members) he turned his invective on the masses. Suddenly the MPs were saints and their constituents were to blame. He put on an epic wig. 'We will preserve the institutions while abolishing the people,' he ranted, and I knew a widow had only to offer him a marigold and he would abolish the institutions instead. Why, the next day it was the MPs in trouble again. This time they were required to touch his feet before he was appeased. And that night I saw Alley Billi slope by with a sign under his arm which I watched him put up at the Drum House gate. It advised simple prostration in the Diwan-i-Aam.

Bootlicking was not the prerogative of MPs alone. Of late I'd noticed quite a few new faces in the fort. The corpulent Trotter from Lucknow was only one of them, and he at least had a job to do. Now there appeared a hairy crew of tantriks, shamans, swamis, medicine-men, witch-doctors and fake healers, each one intent on massaging Hero's legs and filling his ears with dodgy wisdom. It seemed at last he'd acquired the chamchas he never had as a star.

Hero Beslabbered.

His speech became mystical and quirky. Quarky too, Heisenberg rushing in where Newton feared to tread. Things no longer mattered – *matter* no longer mattered – they showed a tendency to matter. Good physics maybe, but bad politics, the uncertainty principle hoping to plug

285

the credibility gap (or the foodgrain gap) with nothing more substantial than a notion. Down there in Chandni Chowk it was the wretched zone of middle dimensions; and all the way from Kashmir to Kanyakumari the ground was solid underfoot. We slogged it together on that padayatra. The flagstones of the Red Fort rang under his heel now.

'Doggy?'

'Saab?'

'Doggy?'

'Here, saab.' I moved a step nearer.

'Are you Doggy?'

I went right up to him and he pinched me.

'You are Doggy, I hope?'

'I am, saab.'

'How lucky to be so sure, Doggy! Now myself I only think I am. I think therefore I am. No, no. I think therefore I *tend* to be, Doggy. No, no. I *tend* to think therefore I tend to be, Doggy. No, no. Not Doggy. Doggyish illusion.'

'The padayatra was real,' I said.

'The padayatra?' he interrogated the past. 'Oh yes!' A pause. 'You know, Doggy – *so*-called Doggy – you should make a Didiserial out of that. It was our Long March. Take fifty-two weeks – more if you want. It's our modern epic.'

I jumped at it. I would play myself; no one else could. But who would play him, the Hero?

'Ask Nero!' he said, and went off into shrieks of laughter.

And so I might have but we didn't have fifty-two weeks left us. We didn't have twenty-two.

He started keeping odd hours. Late at night I'd see him bent over his desk in the Royal Tower while the trains rumbled by on the track below his window, *dhak-dhak, tak-tak*. He was writing his memoirs. Or he'd pace for hours in the little walled garden he'd laid out under his tower,

286

watched by the moony cow he kept tethered there for milk. Or again I'd find him bent over the billiard table at 3.00 a.m., playing a solitary game of skittles. And there he might fall asleep, his shaven head a billiard ball at rest upon the green baize while the Black Cat commandos prowled about the floodlit Drum House lawns below.

Or again he might do something so bizarre I had to follow him at the grave risk of being discovered and torn apart by the populace.

One night, not late, he pleaded fatigue and excused himself from dinner. We ate together – the baleful Francis waiting – in their residence, Shah Jehan's Khas Mahal, beside the Diwan-i-Khas. UD looked up listlessly from her plate and then lowered her eyes again. The main course was a greenish mutton dhansak, if I remember, but it might as well have been kryptonite for her. When he'd gone I resisted the temptation to stay and draw UD out. I said I must go and see all was well with Didi.

I slipped out towards Nero's Rang Mahal or Coloured Palace, formerly the harem. He seemed to have gone that way. Through a gap in a curtain I saw Nero flirting with Alley Billi. So Hero wasn't there. I circled round and worked my way back through the shadows to his study. He was not there either. I doubled back to their curtained private quarters (Shah Jehan had few doors) passing on the way a Muslim woman draped in a burqa. The bed-chamber was empty.

Then I thought it odd that a woman in a burqa should be around at all, much less walking alone at night. Haq would not let his wives go roaming, surely. And yet there she was disappearing down the Khas Mahal steps, covered from head to foot in a black parachute.

But that gate was never used! I thought. In the old days it had been a short-order entrance for Shah Jehan and his bosom friends, but now it was blocked off. Apparently not wholly, for the woman did not come back up. I went

287

down after her. At the bottom I peeped through a sort of placket-hole in the stone and found I was a few handholds up from the ground outside.

And there, heading for the Delhi Gate, was the woman. I recognized the walk instantly. She was met by an officer who fell into step beside her, walking not with the authority of a husband (or at least a Field Marshal) but with a certain diffidence.

I ran back up the steps and cut across to the Delhi Gate on the inside. I got there in time to see the officer escort the woman through the security ring to the edge of Subhash Road. From there they made their way to Daryaganj, the shopping centre beyond the grand mosque.

Well, well.

The next time I was ready for them. I got a pass – even ministers had to – and hung about on Subhash Road. The officer and his lady appeared; I followed. They crossed the road by the wide overbridge which nobody used. When they came down the steps on the other side the officer was in civvies. They hurried along the pavement, the woman following now – and being followed. Outside the Eros cinema they stopped. The man bought tickets; they went in.

As open as that! My ban on cinemas was flouted not a kilometre from the Red Fort. I didn't know whether to be annoyed or pleased. It seemed Hero's edicts were null out here; his sway extended no further than that armoured cordon.

I bought my ticket. It was a new movie, *Vardi Aur Khadi* (The Robber Barons), with a couple of young twits. So movies were not only being seen, they were being made! I sat a few rows behind them and watched alternately the movie and my master – for it was he – but could make no sense of either. He sat there stolid and still (and motionless) under his burqa; the Chief of Staff fidgeted. At the end they filed out with the rest (they were sitting in the
288

cheap seats.) When they passed my row I bent to tie a shoelace and the burqa brushed against my cheek. And as it did I heard a sob come soughing down the fabric. Hero was weeping!

I ate a whole tandoori chicken (the menu said *full* chicken) in a dark corner of the garden restaurant next door and went back to the fort to bed.

The dark moons under Hero's eyes began to show under my gogs, even on his black skin. But he shaved punctiliously, the whole head (not trusting the barber's razor), and dressed with care. He even ordered an engraver to do his profile for a set of postage stamps and was so pleased with the result that he decided that every stamp in the country should carry that head. On consideration there was no reason, he felt, why the nation's currency should not carry it too. A set of stamp proofs appeared from the government stationer, but I wondered if the Daryaganj post office knew about them. I never did see the new coinage, though I believe the stamps got around, if sometimes stuck on, by wags and revolutionists, upside down.

But the portrait that pleased him most was the one on velvet by the corpulent Trotter. It showed Hero and UD in the Lucknow style of royalty but with a touch of science fiction. They might have been visitors from another galaxy, errant comets come our way trailing clouds of milky vapour. The texture lent itself to fuzz, and the artist brushed on light with glee. I still recall that streaming filmi-garish picture, those brazen aliens smiling stardust with all too human swank. My master's tunic bared (after Lakhnavi court fashion) his left breast; UD showed a leg, in Californian gold, where the cosmic wind had blown aside her weeds. Behind them, studded with jewels and flashing lights, was either the Peacock Throne or a flying saucer shaped like India. It was as if a once and future

Shah Jehan and his consort were beaming India from the sixteenth century into the twenty-first.

'He deserves a decoration,' Hero said, nodding his approval.

'Padma Bhushan, sir?' said Mishra, taking out a note pad.

'It's better than that. It's worth a Padma Shri. What is his name?'

'Eugene Trotter,' Mishra said.

'*Eugene*. What's his Indian name?'

'Just Eugene Trotter, sir.'

'OK. Padma Bhushan.'

The outlandish Trotter was put down for the award, and made in addition curator of the fort museum, thus becoming my unwelcome neighbour.

But my master's euphoria didn't last. He had the picture hung in his private sitting-room, above Didi, by the old inlaid Marble scales of justice with their medieval suns and moons, and would sit there in moody contemplation of the universe whence he came. It was a window, that gilded rectangle of velvet, a window on immensity where the scale of things, of success and failure, was different; or indifferent. Often when I came upon him there he seemed to me possessed of an infinite dejection which threatened to engulf the room and, like some predatory black hole, swallow itself up. His merest gesture conveyed an eternity of despair; the fall of a hand – those long fingers wilting like blasted lotus-petals – was a statement eloquent and pathetic.

One day I coughed and entered, as was my wont (Pb), and as he looked up at me – I saw him silhouetted against the royal balcony – I thought: *Superstar*. Then: no, that was not the word I wanted, nor *megastar*, not *dogstar*, certainly not *red dwarf*, but yes, something from modern astronomy, like *quasar* or *neutron star*. And then it gelled: *supernova*! It was only afterwards, looking it up in an encyclopaedia, that I realized what a supernova was: it was the flare of a star already dead.

'So, Doggy,' he said, dipping his hand in the Stream of Paradise, the water channel which bisected the sitting-room. It was dry, but in Shah Jehan's time it had run tinkling all night, feeding baths and fountains. 'I'm told they have my obituary ready. Your newspapers.'

That evening I issued my ban on all newspapers. What was the freedom of the press beside his happiness?

But he wasn't happy. In fact later that week a spy – an alley cat? – brought him a leftist newspaper with a scathing editorial and a post-ban date as proof. It was a red rag to a bull and he flew into one of his rages, the chief butt, I was pleased to see, being the unfortunate Billi himself. He was not pacified until GJ saw the editor down a manhole.

He had one last irritant after that: the hump. It was an old burden, but now it grew to mammoth proportions, a mountain or megalith on his back weighing him down with its topplings and slidings and – lately – its seismic urgings.

'It's like a volcano, Doggy,' he confessed in torment.

It rumbled, it shifted, it burned, it smoked, it threatened to explode, he said. It did more: it put him in mind of a successor, a son and heir. Just as the removal of the fat and fair Rangamma left an emptiness above him, now the burden of his hump pressed home a lack beneath. The lack was metaphysical; physically there was, if anything, a lengthening in the loins, and he began to snort and bellow and look about him for satisfaction.

UD, he saw, had failed him. There must be someone else. Nero, in the Rang Mahal, tittered and said she couldn't help him there, but she proved herself a ready procuress.

And before long the house next to the Khas Mahal began to fill up with nubile maids who did nothing in

291

particular by day and took turns in Hero's bed by night. Or rather, he came to them, in deference to UD's wishes. The Coloured Palace reverted to its old function as harem and the air around it grew soft with musk and rich emollients. The hump caused faintings in earnest now, and retchings, but also scandalized gasps and giggles and lascivious snickering which the Ministry of Laughter could readily explain.

Then suddenly the voices flicked off, another *son-et-lumière* conjuring, and the women vanished leaving a barren silence in their wake. The Coloured Palace seemed preternaturally quiet, and I did a round of it to find out why. I came on Hero sitting there, his face buried in his hands.

'I have been foolish, Doggy.'

I preserved the ambient silence, expecting moral anguish.

'I have been very foolish. Any of those girls could have finished me off. We must be very careful of who we bring in.'

They brought in Flora Fountain, after careful vetting. But he found faults in her which she hadn't noticed herself and though he kept her on he had nothing more to do with her.

'Her teeth are too sharp, Doggy,' he complained, and I suffered a twinge for him.

His paranoia picked holes in every new offering from each of the Union's states, Calcuttan beauties, Punjabi behns, Ghati maidens, Kizhanaduvian virgins, his various and tender seigniorage, but he was resolved to get himself an heir. He got the Ministry of Truth to write him his *Visited By God in a Dream* speech. God had told him he must produce a successor, he said, looking the Didicamera straight in the eye. We carried it live with a single rehearsal, and I recall interrupting a commercial in which the soyabean model was telling us how they'd packed *more* coffee into the new granules than into the same quantity of old instant powder. Quantum physics had reached there too.

I noticed UD – when she emerged from her seclusion – looking haggard, the Pappan fat (puppy fat it was not) put on through years of oily Northern cooking – can that explain Northy obnoxiousness? – shed in a matter of weeks. She took long walks along the fortress wall, the Black Cats prowling in her wake, stopping when she stopped, ducking out of sight when she turned. At night she paced the Royal Terrace, looking out across the moonlit river, but always careful to use two sets of inconvenient steps to avoid the Coloured Palace.

STAR *camera looks down upon her silvery wraith one moonlit night from its perch on top of the Diwan-i-Aam. It pans the royal half-mile from north to south, starting with the Royal Tower where a single light means Hero is in his study. Gently it traverses the dry watercourse of the Stream of Paradise, from the pitted marble cascade at the tower sluice along a grassed embankment and past a tiny pavilion to the royal baths. The stream emerges from the baths and runs in a marble channel along the Royal Terrace towards the Diwan-i-Khas where once stood the peacock throne. Through the hall it runs, then out again under the moon where UD paces, then once more under marble: the Khas Mahal or royal residence. One last time it emerges into the night to flow along that strip of terrace that UD carefully avoids, for now it runs into the hated Rang Mahal or Coloured Palace before ending in a garden well.* STAR *camera may, in order to imprint the layout of the principal buildings on the viewer's memory, turn around at the museum that ends the half-mile (I may be shown addressing the selfsame moon from my window) and do the pan in reverse: museum, Rang Mahal, Khas Mahal, Diwan-i-Khas, baths, pavilion, Royal Tower.*

Hero was not blind to his wife's distress but was driven by compulsions beyond his control. He turned away from

293

the surrogate idea and began to talk about marriage – *re*marriage.

Perhaps Vindhya sitting alone in her presidential palace, could be persuaded? The fancy took him: it would be a grand alliance, PM and President locked in a marital embrace. What more potent merger? GJ dissuaded him, arguing security, protocol and caste, but might not have succeeded had Hero himself not lost interest. For out of the blue, out of the remote past, light years ago it seemed, there appeared before his inner eye, another frail blossom of a girl, a jasmine bud dropped before a stone lingam.

He had remembered Indu.

He sent for her at once. And, so that he should have apparent and sufficient cause for fetching her, he decided on the Democracy Dance.

True, he was already thinking along the lines of a monarchy – his line clearly mattered to him – but it would be a constitutional monarchy, and therefore democratic. Parliament would remain, not necessarily forever pent in the Red Fort, but he would be king. The Indian people were not averse to kingship and people got the king they merited. So the Democracy Dance would not be a complete charade (though there would be props such as gaily painted party coffers for disposable black money and ballot boxes for soiled napkins.) It would, however, be a kind of dumb charade, for there could be no music.

It was fixed for the 24th of July. The rains had failed for the second year in a row so it didn't matter that the venue was outdoors, the stage the Royal Terrace, overlooking the Yamuna river. In fact there wasn't much left of the river – a string of murky pools in the distance – but at night, in the moonlight, it glittered plausibly. The other way, to the west, the nightsky of Delhi was radiant with marriage lights and fireworks, but by day the drought showed in the faces of the common people.

Like his people – more than they perhaps – Hero longed

for open spaces and green fields, but now the very grass around the fort looked like sackcloth. It must have been hard, even for someone who had known so narrow a space as the barrel of a gun.

He wasn't idle though. He'd been borrowing heavily to bail us out: our foreign debt was terrifying to contemplate so I for one was glad he kept its computations to himself. He was forever dreaming up new channels for aid to flow in: the Development Organization for South Asia and the Industrial Development League of India were savoury results of his taste for acronyms.

With the monsoon in abeyance, he established a Ministry of Rains whose first act was to import a supercomputer for advancing the weather and guiding the air-force cloud-seeders. There was the ritual tussle over whether the Centre should get it or the weather office in Pune. Predictably Delhi won, but then the two top weathermen could not work out a precedence schedule so the thing lay idle until Hero took it away from them and had it stored in a godown in the Red Fort.

Hero Arbiter.

There in the cellar one day, after I'd looked for him high and low, I came upon Pedro doing a hunt-and-peck tapdance on the keyboard while the XENO-G1/g0-5 chortled contentedly. *Pedro, Pedro, Pedro,* he was singing as he tapped (a new *Totanama?* I wondered) and a screed of computerunes poured intemperately from the machine. He'd got it going himself. But when Hero found it was operational he had it transferred to the throne room in the Diwan-i-Khas.

Meanwhile the Ministry of Truth spun new slogans for our ramparts – BUILDING THE NATION FROM SCRATCH was one that spoke directly to the ragpickers who thronged the encroaching rubbish heaps – and the Ministry of Laughter served up on the Chicago loudspeakers, every

295

quarter hour, a joke complete with canned laughter. My Didi ran old sitcoms and, on his special request, an Abbott and Costello festival.

'Do you know, Doggy,' he said, 'next year I feel we should shift the capital.'

'The capital, saab.'

'Yes. And the throne.'

'The throne, saab?'

He looked at me as if I were mad, so I said: 'Where to, saab?' though I guessed.

'I've been thinking, for several reasons it would be best to move it to Kanyakumari.'

I could see his mind working: from down there we would command the Indian Ocean, then the world. But also I felt he was missing his Deep South, the balm of coconut and cardamom and pepper on the wind. And those potent, smelly, sticky little finger-bananas – on the tree. Plus no doubt he would feel more secure there.

Lately his paranoia had made him a hermit even within the confines of the Red Fort. He slept in a different room every night, sometimes waking up to change beds after a bad dream. I brought him a red rose from the Life-Giving Garden, but he shrank back from it as if it were a firebrand. I realized he could not even bring himself to *say* red.

'White roses only, Doggy. How many times am I to tell you: white roses?'

He had never told me. Hibiscus, yes, I knew he didn't like the red. He marched me to the garden.

'Doggy, Doggy, white roses only. White only. Only white. White. Do you hear me?'

He took me by the scruff of the neck to a white rosebush.

'This sort of rose, Doggy. A white rose. See? White, white, white. What sort of rose is this, Doggy? It is a white rose. This, Doggy, is a white rose. It is white,

Doggy, white. Notice its whiteness. So white, simply white. There is no mistaking its whiteness. This white rose is not yellow, for instance. Doggy, it is white. Nor is it that, that, other colour. It is white. Just white. A white rose. Consider its whiteness, Doggy. It is pure white, purely white, exclusive in its whiteness, nothing but a white rose. It shares this quality with no other colour of rose. It is no other kind of rose. It is this kind. A white rose. Is it a black rose, Doggy? No, it is not. It is by no stretch of the imagination a black rose. It is white. It's whiteness shines clearly and unmistakably. How could you mistake the other kind – the not-white – for it? How could anybody fail to grasp its whiteness? It is not a blackish white or a yellowish white; it is not even a whitish white – it is a plain and simple white. A white rose. Tell me, Doggy. If a man held a gun to your head and told you this white rose was pink would you agree? If he offered you gold would that change its whiteness? If the sun failed us tomorrow, Doggy, would that make it a black rose? No, Doggy, oh no. Oooh no. Not all the gold, the pink, the black in this world can shake the whiteness of this rose. Because it is white. How white is this rose, Doggy! Let us celebrate its whiteness. Let us not be false to its whititude. O white, white, white, amid a sea of colours, Doggy! Conceive for a moment (Doggy) the integrity of this white rose. What a struggle it has been for this rose to resist the temptations of colour! How steadfastly it has rejected non-whiteness. Its whiteness pleases me, Doggy. This white rose's. It is the white rose of my dreams, Doggy. Pluck a white rose for me now, Doggy. Yes, this is the white rose I would like you to give me. Hand me the white rose. How clever of you, Doggy! A white rose! White! Remember, Doggy, in future: white, white, white, white, white.'

'Saab.'

He left me standing there and stalked off down the

powdered brick lane. I wondered that he could bear to tread on red. Then he turned sharply and came back, making to whisper in my ear. The porches of my ear stood open to the sky.

'Only, white, roses, Doggy,' he said wanly. And he wandered off to his private walled garden. It was rehearsed, I saw. He was still an actor first. He even looked like Othello in Act II.

The next day he decided to whitewash the Red Fort. I didn't interfere; I had my plate full. Already his watchdog (I saw to it the Black Cats kept their distance), I now became his food-taster.

'Doggy, would you say this sambar was, you know, all right?'

And I'd try a spoonful while he watched me with intent eyes.

I kept my own eyes open too. I saw that Francis, whom he trusted – why, I still can't imagine – had no fishy visitors in the kitchen; it was in my interest too. I picked the rice, had the cow milked in front of me. I liaised with his security chief, I turned away callers, I threw out the fake healers, I screened (my job as minister) his immediate bodyguard.

After all, my own blood flowed in those veins; it was my transfusion that saved him. If he died, part of me died.

So you can imagine the turn it gave me when I saw his list of invitations to the Democracy Dance. Almost everyone with the remotest grudge against him was included, among, of course, many others. Running my eye down the list, I felt my eyebrows climb higher and higher. I could only suppose he wanted to enact some bizarre rite of appeasement before his enemies. It was as if he dared them to be there. And they were, every one of them, on that fateful night. And one of them shot him dead.

Judge for yourself, gentle cinematurg.

At the top of the list was Nero herself, ex-Number 1 Villain, now minister and intermittent lover. But did that mean ex-enemy? Or did there still smoulder in that only gently undulating chest some few surviving embers of a hatred unconsumed – and unconsummated? She had been forgiven, and villains, even ex-villains, do not take kindly to forgiveness. Besides, there was that scene at Nandita's gate and all of those filmi beatings unavenged, including one off camera. But most galling of all there was the failure on that last set: she'd not, he'd not, been able to kill Hero at point-blank range.

Next on the list was the Number 2 Villain, Captain Memo, once unsuccessful rival for Indu's hand in the circus of their youth. Assorted filmi thrashings there too and the added humiliation of the once-removed: secondary thrashings, second-best replies, a second-hand Hero Honda motorcycle between his ageing legs.

Next Nandita, rejected lover, almost wife, doting doyenne. And now she'd lost Nero to him too. I would need policewomen to frisk her.

Flora Fountain, cabaret artiste and rejected surrogate would be there, in no mood for love. She had me worried too, for her weapons could not be taken off her: I could hear her already – she lived in the fort now – gnashing her too-sharp teeth with a hell-hath-no-fury vengeance.

Golgappa, rotund and orotund, gossip columnist, was next. Once grievously bashed and exposed at Hero's instance for maligning Nandita; his very wife had left him high and dry. He rolled up.

Guppy Agarwal was there, publicist-turned-soap manufacturer, embittered tycoon. A multi-millionaire, he'd still not forgotten the money he'd lost on *Kanyakumari* when Hero scrapped it on UD's whim. Hero could surely not have forgotten – though Guppy might have – the anonymous death threat in the mail, Guppy's handiwork.

Producer Chaman Lal lost crores too, on *Neta Harish-chandra*, when Hero suppressed it, and again when it was finally released – after he'd sold the rights. He'd made crores more, but never lost sight of his losses. He was there.

Hansraj Gupta, seasoned politician and instant bridge-builder, yet loser of the seat of Nandi to an upstart Southy. He'd lost his deposit too, and wandered in the political wilderness ever since, making social-worker noises. He had a score to settle.

The Three Stooges brought themselves along, Alok Dubey, Chandan Prasad and Jagdish Singh – or was it Jagdish Dubey and Chandan Prasad and – but no matter: they were there with the dogeared memories of portfolios 3a, 3b, 3c, and their khadi caps.

And of course GJ himself, Signor Kautilya, Shri Machia-velli, would-be President, would-be PM, would-be king, king-maker at all events, play-maker, minister of man-holes, poolside philosopher, jailee, encounter-manager, eggtarian.

There were besides sundry chubby boys who'd almost made it big on the Bombay screen and who didn't fancy the transition to Delhi and Didi; grudges aplenty there.

And there may (or may not) have been a mad particle physicist who wished to verify certain interpenetration experiments, for example: if all matter was reducible to a cosmic dance of atoms, might not a bullet pass through an excited human being without causing any damage to the viscera?

STAR camera may pick out the suspects among the arriving guests, for the most part truckling MPs and ministers, celebrity cricketers, and chubby boys, fatcats and Didistars. Nero will wear her bell outfit since none of the other guests have seen it yet: she has gold high heels, her gold lamé handbag, and little else under her gold cape. But she is late. Captain Memo is early.

*He wears his Startrek suit which everybody has seen; a new
accessory is the boxer's skipping rope which he holds like
maracas, like those hopping fancymen in* The Night of the
Iguana. *Nandita, still thirty-nine and graceful, wears pancake
makeup and an evergreen sari. Flora Fountain wears pink
fluorescent tights and ten thousand tiny spinning mirrors.
Golgappa wears a crisp bubbly polyester shirt with a golden
deep-fried look, and pepper-water brown slacks. Producer
Chaman Lal is all sharkskin and silver buttons. Guppy Agarwal
has his threadbare safari suit and the politicians have their
synthetic khadi.*

They surged onto the lawns, gabbling the way guests
will until they are led to meat and drink. The first surprise
I had laid on (I was master of ceremonies) was that they
had to pay for their fare: only the dance was free. This
alone may have opened old wounds among certain guests
(Guppy for one) but I wished to remind all comers that
ours was an austerity regime. So there was a bar up
against the old tourist kiosk and a kabab stall where for
ten rupees you could get a skewer kabab (cheese for
vegetarians) rolled up in half a round of diaphanous
handkerchief bread. That was all. Enough to make Golgappa murderous.

The cunning reader will have struck off Golgappa and
Guppy from the list of suspects; the hypercunning will
have reduced the list to two. Neither must jump the gun.

Hero, for once, was late. Whether he was waiting for
his Indu to appear out of the blue or trying to coax UD to
show her face, I don't know. I was busy with the microphone. Besides, Didi was doing a live coverage of the
dance and I had to keep running over to make sure the
picture was right. There were troupes of dancers from
most states and there were those among them who
needed restraining if everyone was to get a chance.

I've said he proscribed music, but as MC I was able to

301

persuade him that a drum was not music but rhythm. Nothing so empty and innocent as a drum – any number of drums, in fact – and he agreed. So the Dancers for Democracy brought their drums along, smooth-shanked Naga tribesmen from Kohima, hairy Bhangra leapers from Punjab, Kathakali demons from Cochin, Kathak spinners from Lucknow (their ankle-bells were OK too) and so on from the many regions of our rich and restless land. And finally, when it was the guests' turn to join in the dancing, all the drums would speak in unison. A drum spoke; every other instrument sang: that was argument that swayed him.

The Goans, fairly low down on the list, were on stage with their congas but the PM had still not made his appearance. I kept the camera clear of his empty seat – two empty seats – and went for drifting shots of the guests between numbers. He'd sent word that the dance was to start on time. But it was clear from the behaviour of the guests that the occasion was incomplete: they spent more time peering over their shoulders at the Khas Mahal, as if he might any moment appear, than they did watching the spectacle unfold before them. Eventually I avoided the audience altogether and zoomed in for the relief shots on details of illuminated architecture which might elevate the common man watching Didi, praying all the while for Hero to appear before Shah Jehan's artisans' wizardry should begin to pall.

And then he did.

I'd never seen him entirely in black before. Always there was some intervening zone of white perhaps, a hint of relieving colour, if no more than a point of gold flashing from a button. But now he was in black from head to foot. The very buttons down the front of his sherwani were black – with a satin finish, to absorb light, not reflect it – and in his buttonhole he'd stuck a black rose. The churidars encasing his legs, his socks, his curl-toed suede jodhpuris, were of that same lucivorous black. The head itself, always shaven and oiled to a gloss, now wore a bloom on the former sheen, the faintest velvet growth of a midnight shadow, shadow on shadow. He was a walking black hole to which we would, the entire company, guests, dancers, drummers, Didicamera and all, be irresistibly drawn by some stupendous gravity; we would be sucked into that blackness and never seen again. Or so I felt.

And then, just as my gaze stuck and he began to reel me in, the line snagged on a glint and broke. There was something indefinably wrong with that face. I looked up from the monitor to scan the original and, yes, it was wrong too.

For the rest of the evening I could not take my eyes off him. He'd set me a puzzle and I was one clue short.

By now the guests were on the Royal Terrace among the drums, dancing or not according to their capacity or temperament, but milling about, trying to get near him as he pretended interest in the nation's drums, testing each, big and small, of skin, of wood, of clay, of tin, for its democratic note. He smiled faintly, correctly at each approaching guest, shook no hands but gave his formal namaste, and moved on. UD had refused to join him, and his restless eye, I could tell, was sifting the crowd for the one object that would give him peace.

But Indu was a long way off wherever she was; wherever she was she wasn't in the Red Fort.

He threw himself into his quest again, attacking every drum, no less possessed than the drummers. Did he hope to pick up with his ears what the eye refused to see? To catch a certain footfall that wasn't there? The interrupted drummer would surrender his stick or simply stand back, honoured, and let Hero have a go. Hero brought his ear down to the drum and tapped or banged until he heard whatever it was he wanted to. Satisfied, he moved on and the drummer picked up the beat.

DHAAM! DHAAM! DHAAM!

The throbbing filled the fort like a heartbeat amplified,

and it never stopped. I'd heard of tabla masters who played all night till the callouses fell off their hands; now I expected to see it happen. The drummers became their drums; when their sticks broke they tossed them away and used their bare hands. The very sky vibrated: we were in the drum.

DHAAM! DHAAM! DHA-*RAAM!*

When he was satisfied that Indu wasn't coming he drifted off towards the royal baths. Drawn by his gravity the guests followed, Nero at the forefront.

DHAMAK! DHAMAK! DHA-RAAM!

The drumming continued, the pace quickened. The noise was stunning. Decibel for decibel I had not heard its like before. Ten Concorde jets might have done it, without the rhythm. It was so loud we were back in a kind of silence. We were delirious, we were deaf, shouting obscenities, endearments, blood in our eyes, gorged with sound, ready to tear one another apart and kiss the fragments.

He led us on, a Pied Piper from some anti-universe, all in black and pipeless. He led us through the baths, and there were inevitably those who fell in, dragging others in after them, splashing like pigs in rut, squealing with no apparent sound.

Then he turned on his heel and recrossed the stage, moving faster now as he headed back across the terrace to the Diwan-i-Khas. The main body of his followers pushed after him. In the scramble I noticed Francis the cook slip into the crowd of chasers. His movements were cat-like, his eyes murderous. I ducked in a few heads behind and we were swept together into the throne room.

Here in Shah Jehan's time the peacock throne had stood. Under the present emperor it had become part cave temple, with offshoots from the central cavern, and part surreal computer den, the walls hung with printouts of the national debt. Our import bill had grown so astronomically even Hero needed help. On the marble throne platform stood the XENO-G1/g0-5, its lights flashing, the tape rolling back and forth. I saw Flora Fountain leap onto it and do a little cabaret number for us which set the khadiwalas scrambling over one another to get at her. I knew I must keep a beagle eye on Francis, who was looking about him with a waiter's frosty arrogance, but then the particle physicist (the man with the goatee, anyway) got in the way. When I refused to dance with him he turned to Nandita. Over by the computer Captain Memo was doing a Captain Kirk mime, punching buttons at random before progressing to karate chops and fly-kicks. There were muted explosions down the line in one of the lesser computers. I tore off a fresh printout, the last from the XENO. It said: *the monsoon will be late this year*. I chucked it aside, lifting my eyes to the arch where Shah Jehan's artisans had carved and inlaid in agate: *If there be a paradise on earth.* I swung around to the opposite wall to read the rest, but then the ceiling began to spin. Pande-monium raged around me and I could see Hansraj Gupta, longtime legislator, begin to feel at home. The XENO was now spouting flames which spread along the aerial print-out stairways and sent a tongue curling around Golgap-pa's deep-fried polyester shirt. The ex-gossip columnist fell howling noiselessly and I ran to save him but the guests surged over him in pursuit of Hero.

All except Nero, who seemed to dither inexplicably by the flames.

Nero Fiddler.

I saw my master nip down off the terrace plinth so the crowd should miss UD's private chamber, but they saw him leap back up again on the other side and barged straight through the Khas Mahal.

UD! I ran – no, I flew – to the royal balcony where I knew she would take cover, but she was gone. I peered over the edge. Was that a human shape on the grass below? Or had he already had her bricked into the fortress wall? I began to sob hysterically.

Then I saw Nero streak past towards the Rang Mahal. She'd lost her cape and I saw her legs were painted gold. She had her gold lamé handbag clutched in one hand and was running, like a man, her heels gone too.

I gave chase, aimless hysterical chase, like a mad dog.

We'd gained on the other pursuers. Unlike them, we were on home ground. But so was Hero.

I'd recognized Nero's lamé bag from that night at the gate on Chanakya Road. It held the small handgun she'd pointed at me.

She flashed through the hall of mirrors – and a thousand gold legs flashed across the ceiling – hardly touching the ground. But then, just as she entered the main hall of the Coloured Palace, another leg, a black leg, shot out and tripped her. She fell hard on the marble and the bag went skidding across the floor. Hard on her heels, I leapt into the air clear of her and landed just beyond, in the dry bed of the Stream of Paradise.

And then the lights went out.

The drums throbbed for a bit, then petered out. The enfolding silence was like a hundred sonic booms. In the Diwan-i-Khas there was an actual explosion. That would be the XENO, which controlled not only the national debt and the monsoon but the power phases for the fort. From the total darkness on every side I felt it might have fused the whole of India.

Not *total* total darkness; there were stars up above, outside. But inside there might have been a dozen Black Cats in the Coloured Palace and I, Zero, blind philosopher, was ignorant of them.

Besides, I was interested in the bag.

It was advantage-Hero now. He could not have been less visible in the barrel of the circus gun. Did I hear him breathing there, steadying himself for the big one, one last trajectory, this time without a net, without the

306

ground, without any unyielding surface to catch him when he fell, spinning, falling, falling without end?

The room was full of bodies now, silently moving. The other guests had caught up. There'd been orgies in here once. Outside a Black Cat fired a sharp warning burst from his stengun. The bodies froze, then began their sweaty movements again. I heard a snap, like a handbag opening, then a louder shot.

THAAIN!

It began to rain, big fat monsoon drops.

EXIT

Brothers and Sisters I'm afraid there has been a coup. Please, no panic. I mean a *coup de théâtre*. I, Zero, have ousted the tyrant author. Now I am master of ceremonies in earnest. There will be, alas, no tea and cakes in the Rex Cafe and Stores, no chatter about cinema and society.

Rest assured the army is loyal. Just how loyal I must now relate.

I believe there was a plan afoot, under the previous regime, to leave the story up in the air. To have us grovelling, groping in the dark, the air heavy with meaning. The shot in the dark, the rule of the gun and so on. I did not like it. I don't like open endings, loose ends, symbols. Nor will I be pensioned off to the retirement valley. So I offer my own resolutions.

I concede we were all in it together, all culpable, but not equally. I agree we get the government we deserve, but some are more deserving. Let me sift out the weevils.

Nero escaped hanging. The fingerprints on the gun didn't tally. I understand she is now a lecturer in film

311

studies at Pune where her lectures are well attended. They would be sold out if there were not a barrier at the Film Institute gate to keep out thieves and idlers and assorted villains. She does not hold with the Lacanians.

Captain Memo turned his back on filmdom forever after that night. He sold his Hero Honda for a one-way ticket to London. There he returned to boxing but was debarred from the ring for punching a judge. Driven by the old intensities, he turned to writing, but found his gloves would not come off. He has learnt to type with them on.

Golgappa died, needing no cremation. He was remembered in *Talkie-Talkie*, but not the *Tatler*. One or two chubby boys suffered burns, though not serious burns. Not disfiguring burns at any rate, for they were back on the TV epic circuit before long, reconciled to the small screen. Yes, TV, not Didi.

So. Back to the edible oils for the chubby boys (and the soyabean girl), back to the cyclotron for the (?) particle physicist. A five-star hotel snapped up Francis.

Nandita and Flora Fountain found happiness together in Bombay. Chaman Lal, producer again, was a regular visitor at their Bandra home where he too read *War and Peace*. Guppy Agarwal lost more money but he bought himself a new safari suit, at a sale.

Who would have thought Alok Singh, whilom 3c, would become PM! 3a and 3b fell out and he was the compromise candidate. His speeches are written, if that is the word, by one *A.B.* His wife is a nervous wreck but she'll get used to the idea of being First Lady, will go on foreign tours and spending sprees and leave the post in tears.

GJ is a social worker, until the next election. He backed Alok Singh; he keeps him there. But the worm can turn, so he is looking for fresh bait.

But you are wondering about UD.

And you would like to be sure about Hero.

Yes, Hero died; instantly, I would think. But UD was not the shape on the grass I thought I saw from the royal balcony.

Long before the guests violated her chamber in their tantric fury, UD had left the Khas Mahal by the south entrance, on the other side from the Diwan-i-Khas and the terrace where the Democracy Drummers were drumming. The headache she pleaded was real; the drumming made it worse. Instead of going down the steps as she usually did to avoid the Coloured Palace, she crossed straight to it and stepped in. There was a light on in there, in Nero's room. She went in. Nero was there, painting her legs.

It was the first time they'd met since moving into the fort though they were neighbours. There must have been some initial awkwardness. After all, the last time they'd met, at the house on Chanakya Avenue, UD was happily married and Nero a guest. Now it was different. I don't know what they talked about, but talk they did. There were notes to compare, no doubt, because just before I kissed her goodbye, UD let fall, having got a second opinion, a cryptic judgement on her spouse.

'The flesh was willing,' she said, 'but the bone was weak.'

So much for the hump.

When the paint was dry, Nero slipped into her gold bell cloak and the two parted as friends, Nero hurrying off to the dance, UD making her way to the cool underground rooms below the Coloured Palace. Here Shah Jehan's ladies retired in summer, cooled by the Stream of Paradise flowing above, by the dark deep earth all round, by the fresh air that poured through the fretted sandstone screens set in the vents at ground level. During Hero's harem phase, these rooms had been opened up and aired and reappointed. Here, in comparative quiet, UD found a bed and fell asleep.

She didn't wake until the corybants began their chase. The explosion, the gunfire overhead would have told their tale. Then the silence would have drawn her out into the dark night.

It wasn't dark for long after that single shot. I saw several torches coming and going in the garden. Somewhere off towards the Drum House a generator came to life.

At the time I'd no idea UD was right below us. I made a lightning dash to my rooms by the museum and was making my way back to the Khas Mahal when I bumped into her.

'What's happening?' she said.

I threw my arms around her, in tears again. 'He's dead,' I said.

She took it calmly. We continued on our way to their palace. I went to his room and put on the burqa. There was also a bush shirt hanging there which I took. Then I went into her room where she gave me her shoes. I needed that extra inch. It was then that she let drop that line about him. She'd been chatting with Nero, she said. I squeezed her hand. Then I lifted the window of my burqa and kissed her goodbye. She kissed me back and dropped the veil.

I turned away but she called me back. She took off her platinum ring and gave it to me. Her fingers were so frail it slipped off easily. It had a fabulous stone set in it, a ruby, Shiraz-red even by lamplight.

'Don't be sentimental about it,' she said.

I went in search of the loyal army. Field Marshal Haq, Chief of Staff, was in the devastated Diwan-i-Khas, scene of so many kitchen cabinet meetings. He was on the phone, frantic. There was a torch lying on the desk before him which he hastily turned on me as I appeared in the door.

I gestured *come* with one finger, and brought the finger

314

to my lips. He put the phone down and came after me like a lamb.

We went down the Khas Mahal steps and out through the slit. Then we walked side by side along the wall to the Delhi Gate where the security ring parted for us. We walked in silence along Netaji Subhash Road to the Daryaganj overbridge. Once when he tried to speak I shushed him. Up there on the deserted bridge he shed his stars and stripes and put on the bush shirt. We descended on the other side and came to the Eros. He bought tickets and we went in.

The movie was almost over. The hero was in a motor-boat kicking up water. We sat for a moment, then I stood up again and gestured *stay*. He sat there loyally. I wanted to pat his head and say: *Good dog*. I walked back up the aisle to the ladies' cloak room. There I threw off the burqa. I was about to abandon it when the door opened and a woman walked in. I bunched up the burqa and began to polish the mirror with it. I'd seen that done in some foreign movie. The woman entered the stall and I slipped out into the night.

I felt in my pocket the way one does coming out from a movie. There was a bundle of feathers there, but it said nothing. I drew out Pedro like a gun. He was still warm. I felt pain and self-reproach for having forgotten him. When had he died? When the shot sounded, or earlier? Earlier, probably, in that infernal din. The drumming would have burst his ear-drums.

I walked south along the other side of the street from the Eros saying my goodbyes. At Delhi Gate (the old city gate, not the fort gate) there was a large pipal tree just outside the city wall, the sort that birds of every kind – pigeons and parrots mostly – value for its figs. I climbed a short way up the ropy trunk and placed him in the wide smooth hollow where the tree forked. There was no time

315

for grave-digging. *Ficus religiosa* would take care of him. A martyr to democracy, or democracy's drums.

Then I caught a bus, a train, a plane, many planes.

Far from court, far from care.

But now I must cover my tracks. You can buy a passport – any passport – in Kathmandu. (Did I take that route?) I boarded the plane singing, like every patriotic émigré, 'Sare Jahan Se Achha.' There's no place like home. I believe the poet Iqbal wrote that before he'd seen the world.

Here in Vancouver (let us suppose) I will sometimes pause at an intersection till the red hand has replaced the flashing green man – that green man whose stride always seems to me criminally evangelical – and drift off to that last night in Old Delhi. My fellow pedestrians will flow around me, checking their annoyance or satisfying it with a sidelong look, but in fact I'm no longer there. I'm walking along Netaji Subhash Road with a dead parrot in my pocket. The shot heard around the world is ringing in my ears, and the democracy drums are throbbing.

But one must come back. There are little jobs to attend to, the lawn to mow. I have found a bakery on 4th which makes bagels that are not unlike my fruit buns. I have a lover.

I keep in touch, though. Kiran Ahuja, Old Fogey, writes to a post office box. She's in Dehra Dun these days, has left the Ahuja. She has got over her bitterness; she can even bring herself to look in a mirror and like what she sees. They are having municipal elections in the valley. She tells me the poor will take the free liquor, the blankets, the transistor radios the other fellow gives away at election time – and then vote for their man. So the democracy dance is not in vain.

She also tells me UD is fat again and going into politics, as His wife.

I'm happy to say I put in that capital H quite deliberately. It didn't catch me unawares. I distrust capitals, though I seem to keep the capital I. I look forward to the day when we will need no heroes. When every man will find pleasure (and a little pain) in his job – when every man will *have* a job. Hero must have had his dreams too before he gave up, or in. Dejection, despair, are private hells, harmless enough until they overtake the group. Sometimes I am visited by a sadness that I shall not live to see our second moment in history – that I was not born back then, when we were something, or forward then, when we will be something again. Not a power, or a force, but simply a people who do things right, who have faith in themselves. At other times I wish I were Japanese. But I have not forgotten that strange video we produced the night Nero called. In my dreams I'm searching for the button that will speed us forward.

Until then our grocers will mix stones in their dal and we will wonder why our leaders are corrupt.

It's dinner time.

I hope its plain that Zero is not nothing; if anything, Hero is nothing – if such a thing exists. These are elementary findings of the new physics. The problem, as always in the zone of middle dimensions, is the problem of Nero.

I must feed the cat. I must neuter the cat. Or should I? God's problems.

I have a note which says *Post script*, this script. I will. But I strongly advise that *STAR* not be completed, or if completed never shown. (The cheque however may be sent to a Monaco account.) I shall sign the script *DOG*, which you can read forwards or backwards or any way you like, the Zero is always in the middle.

Bedtime.

There's a horse chestnut midden just outside my basement door. The neighbour rakes the fallen chestnuts and

317

leaves them there to rot. It's springy underfoot and it has a starchy fertile reek. When I want to conjure memories, deep dogsnout memories, I go there. UD in red. Him in black, with sequins. The sweeperess on Madame Cama Road: Madame Laxmi, will you rake these chestnut leaves? Occasionally they're false, secondary memories, his memories. Did the virus go so deep? Because I'm sure I have a vision of Indu as she was: a frail little girl balancing on top of a human pyramid – holding onto nothing, dreaming of contentment, a little happiness, a chance to prove herself, a little praise, a good crowd, safety from harm.

I remember the shock it gave me to see her hero, and mine, on the TV monitor that last night. How I looked up, did a double-take at the original. What was wrong with that face? What was missing? What was different? It took me all evening to work out that teaser. But when I did, my mind was made up. What was missing were my dark gogs.

He was wearing Nero's smuggled Ray-Bans.

And they let him down at the last minute, the last moment. Because in the dark of the Coloured Palace my old gogs, scratched and worn, would not have reflected the starlight. Nero's did.

So when I found the lamé bag, and in it Nero's gun, I had simply to aim between the two reflected stars – the same star – and fire.

Hero Undone.

He's mourned now. In our land of superabundant life we love the dead more than the living. But let the dust settle, and he'll be the villain.

Then I can go home.

But then I would be a hero.

A Selected List of Titles Available from Minerva

While every effort is made to keep prices low, it is sometimes necessary to increase prices at short notice. Mandarin Paperbacks reserves the right to show new retail prices on covers which may differ from those previously advertised in the text or elsewhere.

The prices shown below were correct at the time of going to press.

Fiction

☐ 7493 9026 3	**I Pass Like Night**	Jonathan Ames	£3.99	BX
☐ 7493 9006 9	**The Tidewater Tales**	John Bath	£4.99	BX
☐ 7493 9004 2	**A Casual Brutality**	Neil Blessondath	£4.50	BX
☐ 7493 9028 2	**Interior**	Justin Cartwright	£3.99	BC
☐ 7493 9002 6	**No Telephone to Heaven**	Michelle Cliff	£3.99	BX
☐ 7493 9028 X	**Not Not While the Giro**	James Kelman	£4.50	BX
☐ 7493 9011 5	**Parable of the Blind**	Gert Hofmann	£3.99	BC
☐ 7493 9010 7	**The Inventor**	Jakov Lind	£3.99	BC
☐ 7493 9003 4	**Fall of the Imam**	Nawal El Saadewi	£3.99	BC

Non-Fiction

☐ 7493 9012 3	**Days in the Life**	Jonathon Green	£4.99	BC
☐ 7493 9019 0	**In Search of J D Salinger**	Ian Hamilton	£4.99	BX
☐ 7493 9023 9	**Stealing from a Deep Place**	Brian Hall	£3.99	BX
☐ 7493 9005 0	**The Orton Diaries**	John Lahr	£5.99	BC
☐ 7493 9014 X	**Nora**	Brenda Maddox	£6.99	BC

All these books are available at your bookshop or newsagent, or can be ordered direct from the publisher. Just tick the titles you want and fill in the form below. Available in:
BX: British Commonwealth excluding Canada
BC: British Commonwealth including Canada

Mandarin Paperbacks, Cash Sales Department, PO Box 11, Falmouth, Cornwall TR10 9EN.

Please send cheque or postal order, no currency, for purchase price quoted and allow the following for postage and packing:

UK	80p for the first book, 20p for each additional book ordered to a maximum charge of £2.00.
BFPO	80p for the first book, 20p for each additional book.
Overseas including Eire	£1.50 for the first book, £1.00 for the second and 30p for each additional book thereafter.

NAME (Block letters) ....

ADDRESS ....

....

....